S0-AXE-580

Jasper's Beanstalk

Nick Butterworth and Mick Inkpen

Aladdin Paperbacks

On Monday
Jasper found
a bean.

On Tuesday he planted it.

On Wednesday he watered it.

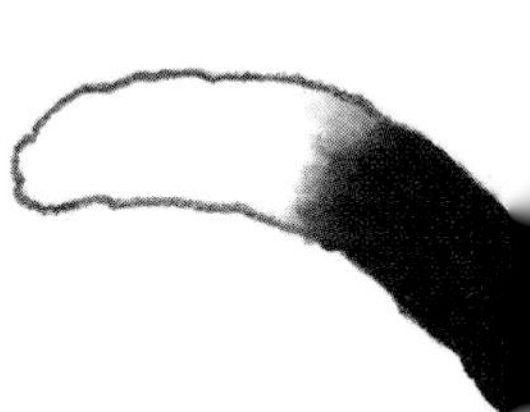

On Thursday
he dug and raked
and sprayed and
hoed it.

On Friday night he picke

p all the slugs and snails.

On Saturday
he even mowed it!

On Sunday
Jasper waited
and waited
and waited...

When Monday came around again he dug it up.

"'That bean
will never make
a beanstalk,"
said Jasper.

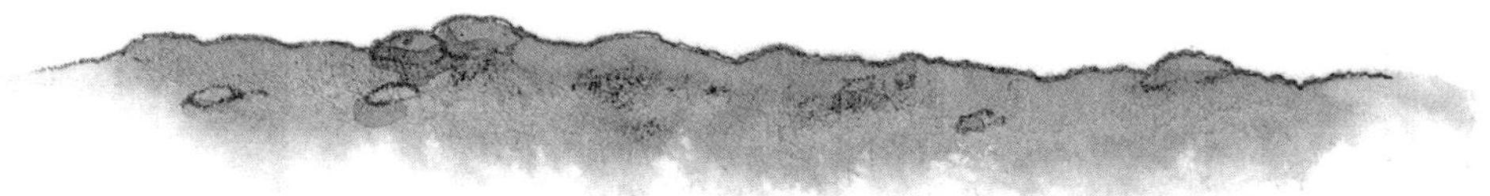

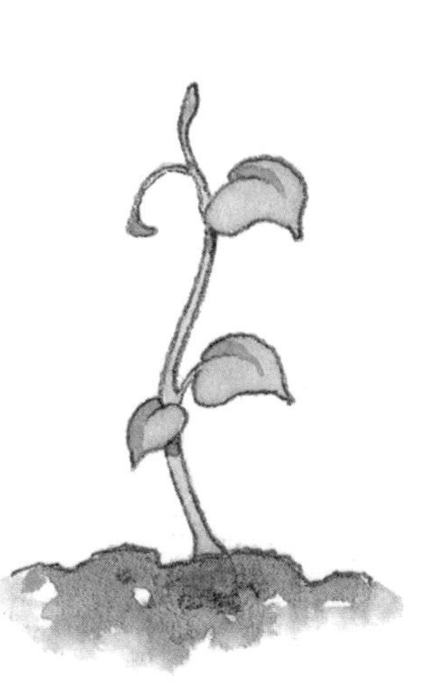

But a long long

long time later . . .

It did!

(It was on a Thursday, I think.)

Now Jasper is looking for giants!

First Aladdin Paperbacks edition June 1997

10 9 8 7 6 5 4 3 2 1

The Library of Congress has cataloged the hardcover edition as follows:
Butterworth, Nick. Jasper's beanstalk / by Nick Butterworth and Mick Inkpen. — 1st American ed. p. cm. Summary: Jasper hopes to grow a beanstalk, but becomes discouraged when the bean he plants doesn't grow after a week. ISBN 0-02-716231-1 [1. Beans—Fiction. 2. Cats—Fiction.] I. Inkpen, Mick. II. Title. PZ7.B98225Jas 1993 [E]—dc20 92-14886 ISBN 0-689-81540-9 (Aladdin pbk.)

Stonekeep™: The Official Strategy Guide

Rick Barba

Prima Publishing

Project Editor: Michael van Mantgem

Important:

Prima Publishing, Inc., has made every effort to determine that the information contained in this book is accurate. However, the publisher makes no warranty, either express or implied, as to the accuracy, effectiveness, or completeness of the material in this book; nor does the publisher assume liability for damages, either incidental or consequential, that may result from using the information in this book. The publisher cannot provide information regarding game play, hints and strategies, or problems with hardware or software. Questions should be directed to the support numbers provided by the game and device manufacturers in their documentation. Some game tricks require precise timing and may require repeated attempts before the desired result is achieved.

ISBN: 1-55958-733-4
Library of Congress Catalog Card Number: 94-69566
Printed in the United States of America

95 96 97 98 BB 10 9 8 7 6 5 4 3 2 1

Table of Contents

Foreword

Stonekeep began as a vision. A vision of what the future of computer role-playing games would look like. After many years, our vision bas become reality.

I'm glad that you have decided to play *Stonekeep*. We started out trying to recreate the feeling of actually walking around a dungeon, as real as we could make it, and then we took off from there. To do so, we had to create many new tools that have never been used in our industry before. We had the ultimate responsibility of making an all-new game world and engine that would please the discriminating player.

I've been involved in the *Stonekeep* project long before it was known as *Stonekeep*, and I've had the chance to oversee almost all phases of the development cycle. From the very concept to the last days of Quality Assurance, *Stonekeep* has taken a life of its own. A long but exciting road to travel.

There are some people at Interplay who deserve acknowledgment for their travel down the same long road: Brian Fargo, Todd Camasta, Jim Gardner, Spencer Kipe, Ron Nesler, Chris Taylor, Leonard Boyarsky, Kevin Beardslee, Phil Britt, Kevin Bass, and Michael Bernstein.

The entire development team has put many hours, and their hearts, into Stonekeep holding true to the motto, "Never ever let quality slip."

We hope we have succeeded in conveying our vision to you. In the end, your opinion is the one that matters.

Thank you,

Michael Quarles
Producer
Stonekeep

Acknowledgments

A lot of people helped make it possible to complete this massive project in a (more or less) timely manner. First and foremost, I'd like to thank the good people at Interplay for their thorough attention to matters of this book. Many, many thanks to Chris Taylor, Stonekeep's lead designer, for being accessible beyond the call of duty. How noble is Chris? Answer: He sat with me in his office for three straight morning-to-midnight days, playing the game from start to finish *without cheating* to verify the accuracy of our walkthrough. Clearly, there's not a Throg bone in his body. The guy's a saint.

Thanks also to Michael Quarles, Stonekeep's producer and lead visionary, for sharing precious time and beta software with me in the midst of his own monumental last-minute crunch. Michael put his soul into *Stonekeep* for five long years, and his uncompromising sense of quality glows from the final product. Finally, this project owes much to Marti Cadanasso, Interplay's licensing coordinator and resident energy source, for being a most prompt, gracious, and good-humored (read: *fun*) liaison to Interplay and the *Stonekeep* design team.

As usual, Prima's crack editorial crew supported me with poise and precision in every phase of the process. Special thanks to project editor and fellow Iowa grad Mike van Mantgem, for making the editorial process a collaboration of friends. This book owes much of its polish and accuracy to our excellent copy editor, Sam Mills. Thanks to Shawn Morningstar for her functional yet elegant book design. And thanks again to Roger Stewart and Hartley Lesser for putting me on the project, *keeping* me on the project (for two years), and hoisting my spirits during those long stretches when *Stonekeep* seemed (to those of us on the outside, anyway) like one of those shadow-skeletons from Level 11—ever-lurking, visible, yet incorporeal.

Rick Barba
October 31, 1995
Boulder, CO

How to Use this Book

Roleplayers are a diverse breed. Some play for the uncompromising win, considering it a fundamental breach of personal integrity to "cheat" by consulting a strategy guide. There are others who play hard and don't mind occasional help. Their alternative is aimless hours of repeating the same errors over and over, and a downward-slide into insanity.

And then there's the rest of us. We play for fun, for entertainment. We play for the story. We just want to see what happens next. We *love* strategy guides. We cheat like bandits, and we feel good about it.

Stonekeep: The Official Strategy Guide tries to honor these differences. Designed to offer multiple layers of help to *Stonekeep* seekers, this book includes everything from the most general combat strategies, to detailed maps and a step-by-step, hold-your-hand walkthrough. Chances are you'll need *some* level of help *somewhere* in this game. After all, *Stonekeep* is truly massive and complicated. Five years in the making, it finally hit the shelves in November of 1995 accompanied by great critical acclaim—and, soon thereafter, a howling chorus of players clamoring for help with that two-headed guy on Level 4. If you're among that chorus, read on. Here's what you'll find:

Part 1: The Stonekeep Universe offers an in-depth look at the game's rich background story and setting. Much of that story is revealed in the game, and in *Thera Awakening*, the *Stonekeep* novella. By contrast, *this* book's overview of the *Stonekeep* culture, history, and mythology comes directly from the "*Stonekeep* Designer's Handbook," Interplay's impressive 300-page tome that catalogs and defines all things *Stonekeep.*

Part 2: General Strategies features general health and combat tips; the *Stonekeep* Bestiary, a catalog of the main monsters and other creatures; and an Item Inventory, listing most objects and their uses in the game. For true *Stonekeep* aficionados, Part 2 includes an inside look at the game's combat system—we're talking *equations* here, man. Math. Scary stuff. The section concludes with a handy guide to *Stonekeep*'s magick system. Check out the rune-by-rune rundown of all the spells in the game. You'll learn the details of each spell—its effects, its Mana cost, how it is affected by meta runes, and so on.

Part 3: Level Solutions is probably why you bought this book. Here you'll find an efficient, step-by-step walkthrough that leads you from the "Entrance of Stonekeep" to a most thrilling and satisfying conclusion in the "Tower of the Shadowking." Part 3 also includes detailed maps for each of Stonekeep's 12 levels. Each map's number system corresponds with the numbered steps in the walkthrough, so cross-referencing is easy. By the way, these maps and their map keys provide an excellent "soft" guide to the game. If you don't want to be spoon-fed all the answers simply consult the maps to find a more general level of guidance.

Part I
The Stonekeep Universe

From the Designer's Handbook

Stonekeep didn't just rise from the ground—it rose from the fertile imaginations and feverish toil of Interplay's design team. For close to five years, the designers documented their vision of the *Stonekeep* universe in a massive, ever-expanding handbook. They filled this "design bible" with background on and guidelines for the characters, races, histories, mythologies, and technologies (or lack thereof) that form the basis of the *Stonekeep* story.

We took some of the more informative material from these rough notes and wrangled it into a concise historical overview. The following material comes *directly* from the final draft of the "Stonekeep Design Handbook." We merely reorganized passages, did some copy editing, and added passages from the Stonekeep novella, *Thera Awakening*, by Steve Jackson and David Pulver.

History of *Stonekeep*

Stonekeep is set on an Earth reconfigured by a fantastic alternate history. We're familiar with the legends of two powerful island nations, Atlantis and Ys, that once ruled the Earth and were destroyed by a massive earthquake. In *Stonekeep*'s timeline, however, powerful magick quelled the great cataclysm. Instead of disappearing beneath thunderous tidal waves, Atlantis and Ys flourished for many centuries.

Ys, located off the coast of France, boasted an established civilization far older than that of Atlantis. But during much of its early history it was a warrior culture, fighting off seafaring invaders from Gaul and the isles of Britain. Atlantean society, formed on a continent farther to the south off the shoulder of Africa, rose from a simple agrarian culture and evolved with remarkable speed into a high civilization. Both of these empires sought expansion, exploring the planet and establishing vassal states and colonies.

Eventually, Atlantis and Ys came into conflict over the very resource that had saved both from natural disaster. In both cultures, life revolved around the use of magick. Magick (as all roleplaying gamers know) consumes a substance known as Mana. The great spells cast with ever-greater frequency by the Lord Sorcerers of Atlantis and the Dark Warlocks of Ys were consuming much of Earth's available Mana.

When the seers predicted an end to magick—well, it caused quite a sensation. Atlantis and Ys each called for the other to limit the use of spells, and each continued to use magick at an increased rate.

Wars were fought, and many lives lost, but neither Atlantis nor Ys could gain a clear advantage. The two sides fought for many, many years. Eventually, the Dark Warlocks cast a spell intended to destroy Atlantis completely. The ritual took years, and many sacrifices, to complete. When the final casting was made, Ys unleashed something far larger than anticipated.

As it is written in *Thera Awakening*:

> Long centuries ago, magick had been the driving force behind human society—and human warfare. Two rival cabals, the Lord Sorcerers of Atlantis and the Dark Warlocks of Ys, had warred with spells as well as steel. The final struggle had been an exchange of ever-more-deadly sorceries. The final spell had been cast by the Dark Warlocks. It went out of control, and the result was the Devastation: the end of the world.
>
> Almost.
>
> Continents burned, oceans boiled, and both warring nations sank beneath the waves. Even the gods had not escaped unscathed. Neither the Dark Warlocks nor the Lord Sorcerers survived—nor had most of the rest of humanity.

Few survived the violence of the Devastation, a magickal spell so strong that the air itself burned for days. When the fires receded, the world was charred, a smoky remnant. All works of civilization, destroyed. The Devastation extinguished 90 percent of Earth's life.

After the Devastation, the races of the world struggled to rise up from barbarism. Mutants, spawned by wild magick, plagued the countrysides. In response, many human clans joined together to form "keeps." Dwarves, first among the races to recover, often came into the keeps and worked in harmony with humankind.

It took the survivors nearly a millenium to claw their way back to a semblance of civilization:

> The scattered survivors had taken centuries to rebuild human civilization, even with the help of the subterranean Dwarves. Other races were hit even harder—if the green-skinned Throgs and their smaller cousins, the Shargas, had been civilized before the Devastation, they were no longer. And none of the legendary Elves and few of the magick-using Faeries had been seen since the skies burned.
>
> Since then, magick had been rightly feared. Among the humans and Dwarves of Stonekeep, only a few elder Magickians retained any knowledge of the old ways. Their rune magicks were a closely guarded secret, passed to trusted disciples, to be used only for the safety of the Keep itself.

This is where the story of *Stonekeep* begins. The world is slowly returning to life, and intelligent culture once again is gaining a foothold in human affairs.

Mythology: The Gods

In *Thera Awakening*, the Dwarf Orvig quizzes his human foster son Rathe on the legends of the gods—which, as Rathe points out, "every child knows":

> "What do you know of the Gods?" Orvig asked.
>
> "Only what you taught me, what everyone knows," Rathe answered, surprised. "That beings called Light and Darkness created the universe. They were the Eldest Gods. When they created Earth, they gave birth to the Younger Gods, men, Dwarves, everyone. Then they went away."
>
> "Correct," Orvig said. "But what of the Younger Gods?"
>
> "There are ten," Rathe said impatiently. "One for each of the heavenly spheres. Khull-khuum, who is the sun. Helion, the nearest to its fires. Aquila, the evening star. Thera, that is the Earth. Azrael, who is the red planet. Marif, the world of many moons. Safrinni, the ringed planet. And Yoth-soggoth and Kor-soggoth, the unseen pair. . . ."

During the Devastation, the Youngest Gods were trapped by one of their own—Khull-khuum, also known as the Shadowking.

> "Where are the gods now?" Orvig countered.
>
> "The Devastation happened," Rathe said. "There was a war among the gods, echoing the war of men. Khull-khuum, the Shadowking, betrayed his brothers and sisters. Some fought, or tried to escape, but they weren't strong enough, and the Shadowking trapped their essences in mystic orbs. Only the goddess Thera did not waste her energy trying to flee or battle him. Instead, she worked her own magick to change his spell. So when they were trapped, the orbs that held them flew from Khull-khuum's grip, and escaped into the heavens. . . ."

As Rathe's story suggests, the gods are represented by the bodies of the solar system:

Khull-khuum	***Sun***
Helion	***Mercury***
Aquila	***Venus***
Thera	***Earth***
Azrael	***Mars***
Marif	***Jupiter***
Afri	***Saturn***
Safrinni	***Uranus***
Yoth-soggoth	***Neptune***
Kor-soggoth	***Pluto***

Most of the Youngest Gods attempted to fight the magick of the Shadowking, but they were unprepared and disorganized, and broke ranks, trying to escape Khull-khuum's wrath. As Rathe recounts, only Thera did not flee. She worked to change the spell, and kept the orbs containing the trapped gods out of the clutches of the Shadowking.

Most humans understand this as a fight amongst the gods. Dwarves and other races have similar theologies. To the Throgs, for example, Khull-khuum is known as Throggi. The Youngest Gods are still worshipped by some. More often then not, they are used in a past tense. "When the gods return" is a common oath.

The Races

If you've played any of the game, you know that diversity is more than just a catchword in *Stonekeep*. Humans, Shargas, Dwarves, Throgs, Faeries, Trolls, Elves, and plenty of mutant creatures (alive and "undead") populate the realm. Here's a quick look at how the *Stonekeep* design team envisioned the races inhabiting the post-Devastation countryside.

Humans

The humans of *Stonekeep* descended from the citizens of Atlantis and her colonies. Much of the species died off during the Devastation. Now humans are concentrated around the Mediterranean Sea, sequestered in large fortified keeps. Stonekeep was one of these centers of humanity—before Khull-khuum pulled the structure into his subterranean realm.

The human species of *Stonekeep* is much like contemporary humanity, with few physical differences. Perhaps a little shorter of stature due to environment and diet, humans of "keep culture" toil under a much shorter life expectancy. A 20-year-old male like Drake is considered fully mature, despite his years of monastic seclusion.

Dwarves

Whether these workers of stone developed the traits of their hardy culture before, after, or during the Devastation is unknown. Much of their history has been lost.

Thera Awakening describes the Dwarf–human relationship:

> Since the Devastation—the great magical disaster that had nearly ended civilization—men and Dwarves had lived together, as partners. But they also lived apart. While humans dwelt in the upper levels of the great keeps, the Dwarves delved far below. The Dwarves were crafters and farmers, partners of mankind, growing the succulent mushrooms and forging the hard steel that Stonekeep needed, in exchange for the lumber and fresh food harvested by men. But they rarely ventured out into the light.

To say that *all* Dwarves live underground and work stone for metal would falsely stereotype them. But a great many do. Dwarves are often master traders—they were among the first races to reach out after the Devastation.

Organized into Clans, Dwarves usually dwell in large extended families. Each Clan is a nation unto itself, but all Clans meet regularly to decide their future actions. (Examples of Clan names: Chak'ra, Chuk'ta, Ruk'sa, Klax'va.) All Dwarves feel kinship for one another, but the Clan is the dominant social grouping.

Dwarves have roughly the same lifespan as humans, and have large families. They are the most numerous race. As a rule, Dwarves are more goal-oriented than humans.

Throgs

Large, green-skinned, and of nasty temperament, Throgs are a harsh, warrior race ruled by Shamans. Their technology is based on stone, wood, bronze, and some iron. Because they abhor the sun, they live underground or in dark forests. They worship their own god, Throggi.

However, Throgs are not always antagonistic. If you read *Thera Awakening*, you may recall that rebel Throgs joined with the human Rathe and his Dwarf compatriots to overthrow the evil Throg Shaman, Gotha Karn, and his copper-helmed minions.

Shargas

Small, green-skinned Throg relatives. Many Shargas are weak and pitiful. Some consider them the dirtiest race of all. Yet Sharga soldiers can be quite skilled in combat. Not nearly as intelligent as their Throggish cousins, Shargas tend to be more cunning. While a Throg would never surrender, a Sharga might give up, even if he held the advantage. They can be master grovelers.

Faeries

For centuries, these evanescent creatures seemed to exist only in humankind's legends and tales. Faeries can assume four different forms—male, female, Faerie-glow (a small, glowing glob of light that floats in the air), and Troll. Faeries are pranksters, a trait aggravated by their magick-using talents. The Devastation nearly wiped them out; only the Elves were hit harder.

Elves

None have been seen since the Devastation, when Khull-khuum methodically destroyed their cities. Elves are said to be tall, long-haired, and fair. Before the Devastation, they were natural magick-users.

Magick & Technology

Magick

Before the Devastation, magick was a social given, used to some extent in all cultures much as we use technology today. Transportation, communication, medicine, cold beer and more were all magick-based. Magick use took many forms, from item-based spells to great rituals to simple cantrips everyone used.

The Lord Sorcerers of Atlantis and the Dark Warlocks of Ys formed the magick-using elite. All races had their magickians, but humans excelled at the practice. No Throggish Shaman could match a Dark Warlock, let alone a Lord Sorcerer. Only direct intervention of the Eldest Gods was more powerful than the combined might of the cabals of Atlantis and Ys, and the Elders disappeared from this plane long ago. Thus was the power of magick.

Since the Devastation, humans only use Rune Magick, and that rarely. Not only was much knowledge lost and Mana levels greatly reduced, but magick must now be feared. In *Thera Awakening*, Rathe asks Orvig about runes inscribed in blood on the underside of the Whispering Death:

"Runes are the heart of magick," said Orvig slowly. "That much I know. There are other kinds of sorcery—rituals and such, or Elf magick—but they were lost in the Devastation. Rune magick is made by scribing the rune you want to use on the rune-item, like a staff or a wand, or even a sword. It stores the energy that powers the spell. But the nature of the spell is in the lines of the rune. . . . Each race has its own runes."

"Who else uses magickal runes?"

"The savage Throgs have their shamans," Orvig said, "although their small cousins, the Shargas, have no such art. And the tiny Faeries use runes as well, though neither man nor Dwarf from Stonekeep has seen their kind in many a year. And your own race, of course. Aye, human runes are mighty."

Technology

As *Stonekeep* opens, human technology still has not reached its pre-Devastation level. Some technology has been rediscovered, new technologies have been invented (mostly in areas magick once controlled). But by pre-Devastation standards, it is all quite primitive.

Stonekeep technology is comparable to that of our 14th and 15th centuries, with some exceptions. Human and Dwarvish mathematics and some other sciences are fairly advanced. Telescopes are common among humans. Most humans and nearly all Dwarves are literate. Humans keep libraries of parchment books, and Dwarves have invented a "printing press" that embosses thin sheets of iron and steel.

Overall, Dwarves seem to be more technologically advanced than the other races; they are familiar with explosives, certain types of machinery, and other technical items. Steel-making is a guarded Dwarven secret; Dwarven plate armor and weapons are known for their craftsmanship.

Throgs and Shargas are the least accomplished of the keep-era technology users. The Faeries, of course, do not use technology.

The Story of *Stonekeep*

As depicted in the game's introductory movie, a mysterious stranger spirits the young Drake from the fortified city of Stonekeep during Khull-khuum's blistering attack. Drake watches in horror as his boyhood home sinks beneath the earth's shattered crust. All therein perish.

Khull-khuum long ago captured his brothers and sisters, and trapped them in orbs of power with a mighty spell. His sister Thera, however, was able to alter the spell at the last moment so the orbs were lost to him. Khull-khuum has sought these orbs for 10 centuries.

The hooded stranger delivers Drake's unconscious body to the steps of Guilander Mount, home to a sect of warrior-monks, then disappears. The monks adopt Drake as one of their own, and train him in their ascetic ways.

As the game begins, it is 10 years later. Drake has returned to Stonekeep's former site. While camped at the edge of the chasm—all that remains of Stonekeep—Drake receives a visitation from the goddess Thera. She uses the few powers she retains to separate Drake's soul from his body, sending his life-force into the bowels of the earth. His quest: find all nine orbs and return them to the spell's casting point, the Truth Beyond the Shadow—a monument accessible only through the Tower of the Shadowking.

Along the way, Drake will be joined by Dwarves, Faeries, Elves, and even the mysterious Wahooka (*aka* "the King of Goblins") himself. If Drake and his companions can defeat the Shadowking and learn the secret of the orbs, our young hero will see Stonekeep rise from the earth . . . and take his rightful place as king.

The Characters of *Stonekeep*

Here are some of the characters Drake encounters as the tale unfolds. These descriptions are taken from the Designer's Handbook to best illustrate how *Stonekeep*'s creators originally saw the game's personalities.

Drake

Drake is the hero of the story, and the player's alter ego in the game. A young man, he was trained for many years in a monastery, so he is still fairly new to the world. He is competent in the use of some weapons, most notably the sword and spear. He has no knowledge of magick at the start of the game. He is curious, but cautious.

Khull-khuum

The Shadowking. Slightly insane. He firmly believes in what he is doing, thinking it's for the best—for *everybody*. An immortal god, Khull-khuum has sought the lost orbs for a thousand years, give or take a decade. This would give anybody a couple of quirks. The firstborn of Light and Darkness, Khull-khuum caused the Devastation in a mad plan to "protect" his brothers and sisters.

Farli Mallestone

Farli is your typical Dwarf: single-minded, doubting at first, but a solid friend when it counts. Dwarves are organized into Clans, and are fiercely protective of their Clan and its members. Farli left his Clanhall to search for his older brother, Dombur, one of a missing expedition. Unfortunately, Farli left without his Clan elder's permission. Dwarven law forbids this.

Farli is young for a Dwarf, and he feels that his youth is a liability. He is, however, determined to succeed—in this case, to find his brother.

Farli does not like Throgs and Shargas, but is not necessarily set on wiping them from the face of the earth. Because of the tales he has heard, he also does not like Wahooka. Farli is secretly fascinated with Faeries and Elves, as he had never seen them before leaving his Clanhall.

Farli's voice is always tinged with excitement, especially when he sees something for the first time. It is subtle, as his Dwarf instincts do not allow overt displays of excitement. He is especially observant when it comes to stonework and geological constructs. He usually spots trick walls, closed pits, and so on.

Karzak Hardstone

Karzak is extreme, even for a Dwarf. While of the Chak'ra Clan, the same as Farli, Karzak believes Throgs and Shargas should be wiped from the earth—in a violent and bloody way, if possible. "Never talk, never bargain, just swing yer ax. That's what gets 'em going." (Think of Sean Connery's character from *The Untouchables*, only worse.) He isn't suicidal, though. "Remember, lads, our job is to make the *other guy* die for his 'sophy. And if some dog does take me down, I'll be the most expensive piece of meat he EVER bought."

Karzak does not like new things; little surprises tend to set him off. He was extremely unhappy about being captured by a Throg trap, and is still a little touchy about that. If there's one thing he hates more than a Throg, it's . . . cuteness. A trip through the Faerie realm would be most hard on his constitution.

Dombur Mallestone

Dombur is Farli's older, absent-minded brother. Dombur is the Dwarf equivalent of a scientist, always interested in something—in *everything*, actually. Throgs, Shargas, humans, whatever. Dombur wants to *know* things—things that just don't seem very important to anybody except Dombur.

Dombur was captured by Throgs while on a mission to procure rare minerals for an experiment, but he didn't really notice. He can be a fountain of wisdom, yet at any given moment he may know nothing except the mating habits of the giant wasp, for example. When Dombur discusses anything he isn't interested in, he is distracted. When he discusses something he *is* interested in, he is *extremely* distracted.

Skuz

A Sharga. He joins with Drake to save his own skin. Deep down, Skuz is a nice guy. A wimpy nice guy.

Heh. Heh-heh.

Skuz likez people, cuz Skuz knowz dat people kan kick hiz butt.

Skuz is friendly. With everybody and everything. He has a very simple goal—survival. The underworld is no place for a wimpy Sharga, is it? All those Throgs after you to work, work, work, with occasional suicidal assaults on Dwarven fortresses. Monsters everywhere. And a dragon to feed. Not a nice place for a wimpy Sharga, not at all.

Skuz is the typical Sharga except that Skuz is *smart*. So smart that Skuz could be the Sharga leader if he wanted, except you can get dead as a Sharga leader. Very dead. Skuz doesn't like that.

Skuz always refers to himself in the third person, as do all Shargas. "Please don't hurt Skuz. Skuz be friend with you." Skuz always approaches larger people (that is, just about everybody) in a fawning, subservient manner.

Enigma

Last of the Elvish race. Once, the Elven minority was a dominant power in the world. Allied with neither of the human superpowers, Atlantis and Ys, Elves stood apart and studied greater things than warfare and politics.

This eventually cost them, for when Khull-khuum cast the counter-spell that triggered the Devastation, he knew that only Elves had the power to stop him. He concentrated the destruction on Elvish cities and towers. Enigma was in the Faerie Realm with his love, Lady Iaenni, when the Shadowking channeled the power of the Devastation into his Elvish homeland; he returned to find destruction, death, Elf genocide. He has spent the last thousand years searching for Elven survivors, with no success.

Enigma is exactly that—an enigma. He does not like to talk, and when he does, it is briefly, quietly, and to the point. Yet there are grim undertones to his calm demeanor. "Anger" does not begin to describe his feelings toward the Shadowking. He still cares for Iaenni, the Faerie Queen, but knows he will never be happy at her side. Thus, he searches the world for something, or someone, who will help him quench his thirst for revenge.

Throgs, Shargas, and other henchmen of the Shadowking mean little to him. Enigma stays in the shadows and avoids obstructions—but when he must fight, he kills cleanly and quickly. And with little satisfaction.

Sparkle

A Faerie, Sparkle is a child. A tiny, floating, inquisitive child. On caffeine. Very, very good caffeine. Always talking, always chattering away. Annoying, sometimes. Really, *really* annoying.

Wahooka

The great prankster. He has his own agenda when it comes to the orbs. A mysterious personality, he will help Drake. Wahooka is also known as the King of Goblins. Related to both Faerie and Throg/Sharga families, he is ancient and powerful. While not evil, neither is he by any means "good" or "righteous."

The Dwarves know of Wahooka, since he has tormented them more than any other race. Wahooka takes particular delight in insulting Dwarves. The Dwarves, on the other hand, wish him a long and painful death, preferably one of Dwarvish devising.

Faeries treat him as a lost child. He probably was born of a Faerie female and a strong Throg Shaman, but he could be stronger and more powerful than even the gods. He is at least as old as the Devastation. Faerie blood and Shaman training give him a strong magickal power. He will not deal with Faeries in any manner, however.

Wahooka's powers include teleportation, dimensional tampering (his cloak holds far more then it should), clairsentience, precognition (in a very limited manner), telekinesis, invisibility. He is capable of far more.

He is also extremely greedy. Treasure, especially bright gems and magick, are powerful bargaining chips. Wahooka will try to trick any out of their gems and magick, but often as not gets a little "stupid" when it comes to acquiring such items. His greed is a primary motivation for his dealings with Drake. He wants the orbs because they are both rare and magickal. However, Thera's magick has made finding them extremely difficult. He is willing to let Drake do most of the work, and then perhaps steal the orbs away in the end.

Wahooka speaks in an insulting and patronizing manner (Yoda crossed with Scrooge with a dash of Gollum): "Bah! You dirty naked apes, you haven't a clue as to what is going on!" or "What!? You do not recognize the Great Wahooka!? You didn't get out of that monastary much, did you?"

Wahooka is very strong, extremely intelligent, and quite acrobatic. He is both impulsive and deliberate. He can spend years devising a plan, longer carrying it out, and then blow it in an instant.

Although he enjoys playing elaborate practical jokes on the "lower" lifeforms, Wahooka hates it when a joke is played on him. He likes to project his voice and startle people.

Wahooka keeps informed about what happens in Stonekeep, in addition to whatever happens in the world, and knows much about the altercation between the gods. He isn't above bartering this information for goodies.

He avoids combat unless absolutely necessary. He is immortal—if he doesn't need it right now he can wait, like a vulture, for obstacles to simply pass away.

Part II
General Strategies

Hints, Tips, and an Inside Look at Stonekeep's Game Systems

Part of the beauty of *Stonekeep* is its "split personality." You don't have to be a rocket scientist to play the game. You can hack and blast, sling spells and explore, meet fabulous creatures, and forget about statistics and numbers and tables and such. The simple, intuitive interface lets you immerse yourself in roleplaying fun without the calculator or slide rule.

On the other hand, the complexity of, say, the *Stonekeep* hit-zone-radius (HZR)equation can keep even hardcore, caffeine-crazed number-crunchers delighted for hours. Surely, no *Stonekeep* strategy guide would be complete without the obligatory combat equations and tables.

So this part of the book has a little something for everyone. First, we'll open with some general strategy tips for better health and combat. (Be sure to check out that "Mana Source Heal Routine" tip.) Next comes a "bestiary"—a list of *Stonekeep* monsters, with some tips on how to fight each one. After that, we'll review all the important game items—potions, roots, and so on—and examine the effects of each. Finally, we'll take a quick look at *Stonekeep*'s three primary game systems: the Journal stats, the combat system, and the magick system.

General Strategy Tips

This section is for those who don't particulary care about hit-point calculations, but still want some help. You'll find a lot of good stuff here, most of it courtesy of the *Stonekeep* design and testing team. Some tips are general, some very specific. Some refer to combat, some to magick, some to health.

Mana Source Heal Routine

When you find your first Mana Circle (at 41 on Map 2: "Lower Ruins of Stonekeep"), you also find a runewand and a Curing rune nearby. This golden trio is your ticket to 100 percent vitality for the rest of the game. Whenever you find a new Mana "outlet"

(usually a Mana Circle, though there are several other Mana sources in the game), remember this routine:

- Recharge your runecasters.
- Put a runecaster inscribed with a healing rune in Drake's hand.
- Heal each member of your party to 100 percent vitality.
- *Recharge again!*

To expedite this routine, keep a Curing or Healing rune inscribed on at least one of your runecasters at all times.

Do the Mana Dance. *Max out your Magick rating to five stars at the very first Mana Circle on Level 2. Blast walls, recharge, blast, recharge, blast, on and on and on.*

Max Out Your Magick Skill at the First Mana Circle

As I said above, the first Mana Circle in the game (see step 41 in Level 2) has a runewand and two rune scrolls nearby. Do not leave the room without a Magick skill of five stars! It will take a while, but it's worth it—and it's kind of fun, too.

Here's what to do:

- Inscribe the Firebolt rune on the runewand.
- Inscribe the Power × 2 meta rune (if you have it) right over the Firebolt rune on the runewand.
- Blast away at everything in sight—walls, floors, chairs, tables. Don't leave the room; stay close to the Mana Circle.
- When your runewand's Mana runs out, just recharge in the Mana Circle and blast away again.
- Continue until you achieve a five-star Magick rating.

Why is this such a good thing? When you achieve a Magick skill rating of five stars, you reduce your Mana cost by 2 Mana points per spell. That *really* adds up after a few good spell-slinging battles.

By the way, when you're blasting those walls, remember that the Journal icon flashes in the upper left corner of the screen whenever you increase a skill rating. You don't need to keep opening your Journal to check the Magick rating; it's a waste of time. Just keep blasting away, and watch for the book flash. And smile, dammit. This is *fun.*

Instant Mana Access

Once you get both the Circle and Homing runes, you can cast a Circle spell to place a magick blue circle near a Mana Circle (or some other unlimited Mana source). Later, whenever your Mana runs low, simply cast the Homing rune to teleport to the magick circle. Then go to the Mana Circle to recharge, heal, and recharge again. Step back into the blue magick circle and cast Homing again. Zap! You're back where you started the process.

Keep Mobile

Stonekeep is a classic combat game. And classic combat games love to slaughter lead-footed contestants. Don't be a statue, man. Move forward, back. Spin. Keep moving. Time your movements to your weapon's attack. If your weapon is heavy and has a delay, use that to your advantage. Back away between strikes, then swoop forward as the ax or hammer falls.

Match Weapons to Monsters

How do you do that? Sorry, humanities majors. You have to check the tables in the Appendices. Really, it's pretty painless, even though numbers *are* involved.

In the "Monster Combat Stats" table, pay particular attention to the numbers in the "Strong" and "Weak" armor columns to see what category of damage (Cut, Crush, or Pierce) most hurts a given monster. The lower the number, the weaker his armor. Then check the Weapon Stats table to find a weapon that is particularly wicked in the monster's weak category.

A quick example: You're getting charbroiled by a nasty fire elemental on Level 12. You check his Monster Combat Stats. His armor gives him 100 points of protection from both crushing and piercing damage—but only 15 points of cutting protection. Aha!

Now you review the weapons in your inventory, then check the Weapon Stats, searching for a good cutting weapon. Hey, look at that shadow-sword—not only is the damage range a hefty 50–100 points per hit, but 100 percent of its damage is in the cutting category.

Die sparking, elemental scum!

Be Incredibly Selfish

This may seem obvious, but I'll say it anyway: As Drake goes, so goes the alternate universe. Yes, your NPCs (non-player characters) are nice, loyal folks. But Drake's the *man*, if you know what I mean. Always upgrade Drake first. Give him the best weapons, the best armor. Remember, NPCs don't die!

Let me belabor the point here. Chris Taylor, *Stonekeep*'s lead designer, even suggests that you "use your NPCs as living shields." When fighting gnarly beasts, spin to maneuver opponents to one side or the other. Thus, your NPCs take the brunt of the damage.

Hog the Glory

Here's a sneaky suggestion, one in the same vein as the previous tip. Let Drake do all of the fighting (and get all of the kills) against most opponents. This way, you build up the crucial skills and stats that you need later against more fearsome foes.

Drake's Dwarven Flock. *Looks like Drake is surrounded by pudgy birds, doesn't it? Give the Dwarves two shields apiece, and Drake gets all the kills . . . and the experience he needs.*

How do you ace out your NPCs? Easy. Give them two shields. It's despicable, I know. But they look kind of cool, like mutant birds or something. All they can do is fend off attacks and watch while you rack up monster kills, adding notch after notch to your glory belt.

Build Agility Before Strength

Don't get me wrong. Strength is *good.* In fact, in the long run, Strength is probably more important than Agility in *Stonekeep.* But there are far more strength-boost items in the game than agility builders. I suggest that you use fists and daggers a lot in the early levels—remember, light weapons build agility, heavy weapons build strength.

Be a Vandal

There's a lot of neat stuff to break in *Stonekeep.* Tables, chairs, beds, barrels, bone piles, rubble—*smash it all!* Each blow you strike increases your familiarity and skill with your current weapon. You also build either your Strength or Agility rating (depending on the weight of the weapon). Not a bad payoff for giving in to your basest instincts.

When In Doubt, Turn Sideways

Stonekeep is a dangerous place. Booby-trapped walls spew arrows and fireballs. Boulders try to mow you down. It's not pretty. But here's a good tip: When something ugly suddenly roars down the corridor, don't try to run. Just say *Olé!* and turn sideways. Most of the time, the thing passes by harmlessly.

Why does this work? Drake actually stands on the *back edge* of any square he occupies. When turned sideways, Drake is practically leaning back on the wall, leaving plenty of room for large objects to roll past. Remember this technique when campfires block your path, too. Walk right into the fire's square (but not *through* it), turn sideways twice, then back away on the other side. Not a singe.

Open-Door Policy

This one's so good, it's almost a cheat tip. Stonekeep monsters cannot step through doorways. Thus, if you open a door and find a Throg thug waiting, don't wade into him. Nail him through the doorway with missile weapons—rocks, darts, axes or daggers, crossbows. Or blast him with a ranged magick attack—firebolts, icebolts, or spheres, for example. The poor Throg has no choice but to stand there and take it. He can't hit back. It isn't fair. *Awww, too bad.*

Sitting Duck. *Stonekeep monsters won't go through doorways. Must be some threshhold phobia. Poor guys. Blast them with missile weapons.*

Be Ant Food

Well, not really. But almost. This is another Chris Taylor tip. Leave a worker ant alive on Level 1. After you find the chain-mail armor on Level 2, return to the ant. Equip Drake with two shields. Provoke the ant with a punch—don't kill it!—then let the angry thing gnaw away at Drake for awhile. Go away. Have a sandwich, maybe a cream soda. Don't worry about Drake; the ant can't harm him. Meanwhile, Drake is training without pain. His shield skill is going up. Life is beautiful sometimes.

"Tape Your Mouse Button" Locations

There are a few places in *Stonekeep* where you can walk away from the game while building stats and skills. At these locations, plant Drake in front of the object, put a

weapon in each hand, tape down both mouse buttons—he alternates attacking with his left and right hands—then go work on that master's thesis you've been putting off for the last 22 years.

When you return, Drake's stats and skills will look *much* different.

No Guts, No Glorystone. Plant yourself in front of the Glorystone on Level 7, put a weapon in each hand, tape down both mouse buttons (the weapons alternate blows, left and right), and go do something productive. When you return, check your stats and skills.

Try this cheat tip at the following places:

- In front of the ant hole at 40 on Map 1.1. Fifty giant ants crawl out of the nest, one at a time, *begging* to be squished. (Don't go away for too long, though.)
- The wasp nests in Level 4: "Sharga Mines"—but only if you have enough armor. (Wasps inflict a maximum damage of 22 points, all in the cut category.)
- The two frozen guys you find on Level 9: "Ice Caverns." You can't hurt them, but you can sure pad your stats. (Remember that the intense cold is taking its toll on your party, bit by bit.)
- The best place of all: The glorious Glorystone on Level 7: "Dwarven Fortress." Beat on it for days, weeks. Build up every weapon in your arsenal.

A *Stonekeep* Bestiary

You meet (and fight) a lot of creatures in your quest to free the gods from Khull-khuum. Here's a list of the denizens of *Stonekeep*. I've included some combat tips for each. You should note also that "special effects" spells have different effects on different monsters. Special effects spells are rune magicks that actually alter the target's behavior—Scare runes, for example—as opposed to simple attack spells (such as the Firebolt rune) that elicit the same response as a weapon strike.

Why the different effects? *Stonekeep*'s design team included about half a dozen different "monster scripters" with the power to customize the behavior of individual monster types. So, although a Shrink spell shrinks most creatures, it actually *enlarges* a Faerie glow. And while your Scare rune sends most Throgs running, it has no effect on a Throg leader. *Nothing* scares a Throg leader. They've seen it all, apparently.

The primary special effects runes are Scare, Shrink, Stoptrack, and Tornado. You can also "freeze" a target with your Icebolt rune, and "stun" a target with your Energybolt rune. (In each case, the target stops moving for a few seconds, which gives you quite a tactical combat advantage.) In this bestiary, I've noted any unusual reactions to spells by each creature.

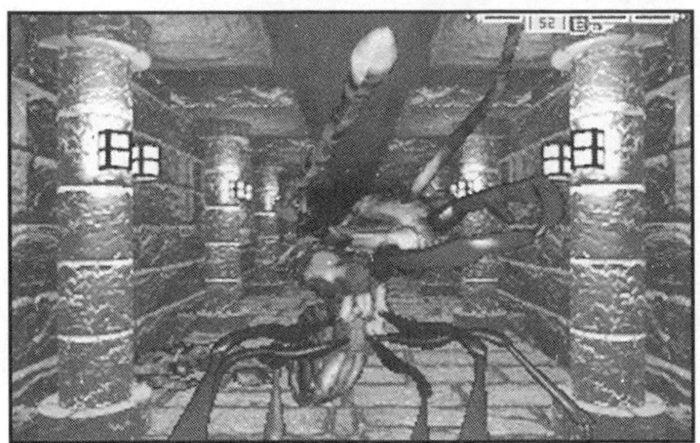

Ant

Two kinds—wimpy, and less wimpy. Worker ants don't even *fight* unless you attack them first, then they go down with a punch or two. Warrior ants are more belligerent, but two or three jabs with a good piercing weapon reduces them to a quivering pile of ant parts.

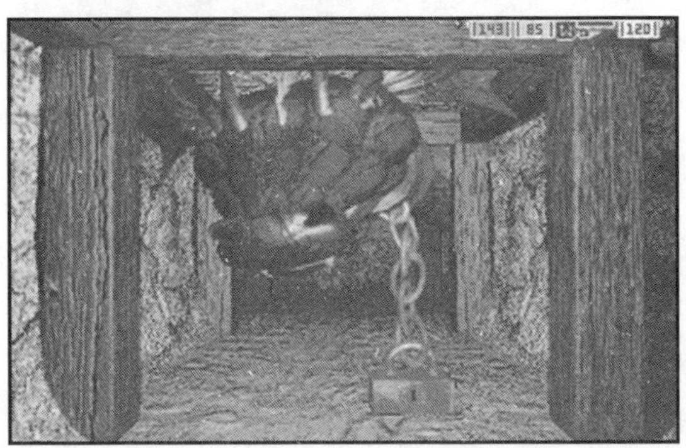

Dragon

Meet the fabulous Vermatrix Goldenhide. She is invulnerable to your puny weapons and runes. Indeed, your attacks merely anger her. Vex her enough, you end up a charcoal briquet. The dragon is immune to all magickal spells.

Dwarf

Dwarves are natural allies of humans, so don't be a fool and attack—they fight back with great skill. Fire does not harm a Dwarf, but a good piercing weapon will. Target his face or other extremeties. (Note that there *is* a band of "dark Dwarves" in Stonekeep, so Dwarf combat is likely.)

Special effects: If you use a Shrink rune on a Dwarf, he gets *really* small. You cannot stun Dwarves with energybolts.

The Ettin

He may act like a big goof, but he can afford to—he's the Ettin. Being that, he is invincible. Too bad he guards something you desperately need. The Ettin is immune to all magickal spells.

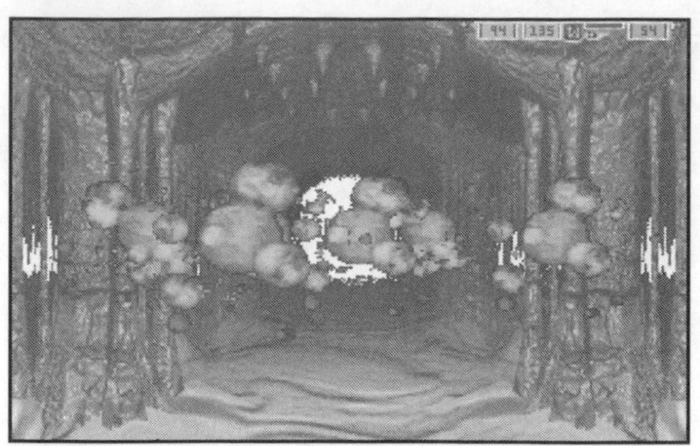

Faerie (Male, Female)

Neither type will attack you. This is good, because Faeries are indestructible. If you attack one, it simply reverts to "glow-form" and zips away. Faeries are immune to all magickal spells, except one. If you cast a Shrink spell on a Faerie glow, it grows to immense proportions. (This is typical Faerie humor.)

Fairie Queen

Iaenni is beautiful, wise, and smart enough to appear only during non-interactive sequences. Thus, you cannot attack or cast spells at her (though I know many of you will try).

Fire Elemental

These flaming creatures are quite deadly, but an enhanced Shield rune protects your party from their powerful firebolts. As you might imagine, they are impervious to fire attacks. Use cutting weapons—in particular, a shadow-ax or shadow-sword—to chop elementals to ashes.

Special effects: Fire elementals are immune to all special effects spells.

Floating Skull

Two types—regular (seen here) and the shadow-skull variant. These grinning geeks blast you with crushing energybolts. Regular skulls have *very* strong cut armor, but are susceptible to piercing damage (which seems odd, since they're boneheads, but there you are). Crushing weapons work almost as well. Shadow-skulls have much better overall armor, but suffer double-damage from pure magickal attacks—energybolts, for example.

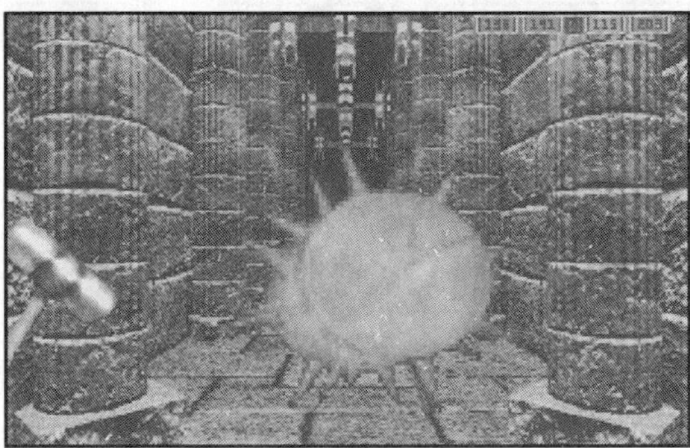

Floating Spiker

Three kinds—regular, tough, and scary-big. Fortunately, there's only one scary-big spiker in the game, but it's almost invulnerable, so you have to trap it or run screaming. Use piercing weapons on the regular guys. A couple of thrusts from your Dagger of Penetration will pop a spiker into an exploding fireball.

Special effects: You can destroy spikers by casting a Power × 2 Spoilspell at them.

Fungus (Exploding)

I *really* hate these guys. Fungi spit spores that cause up to 40 points of damage. You can avoid or run past them, but it's best to slash them up and gain experience. Use a cutting weapon. (Fungal crush armor is an impressive 30, but their cut armor is only 8.)

Special effects: You can freeze *and* shrink this annoying fungus, if you so desire.

Ice Queen

She may *look* like an aerobics babe, but don't be fooled. She's by far *Stonekeep*'s most intelligent super-opponent. The Queen is invulnerable until you use Coldfire (found on Level 9) against her. Then she reverts to sneaky guerrilla tactics—running, hiding, sniping at you with her wicked icebolts. Use Circleward runes to corner her, then blast her with magickal fire attacks—enhanced firebolts work nicely. After all, you want to melt her heart. Literally.

Special effects: Don't hurl icebolts at this woman—they actually heal her wounds!

Ice Sharga

This polar variant of the species is much friendlier and much tougher than his warm-weather cousin, the green-skinned Sharga. (See "Sharga.") If you get a perverse urge to attack one, know that Ice Shargas suffer 2.5 times the normal amount of damage from fire spells. Piercing weapons are effective against them, as well.

Ice Witch

These spiky little iceballs are minions of the Ice Queen. Like their queen, they attack with icebolts and are particularly vulnerable to fire attacks. If ice witches get in close, pierce them with daggers or spears.

Special effects: Ice witches are afraid of fire spells, but are immune to the Tornado rune.

Khull-khuum, the Shadowking

This is the head honcho. You can try to fight him, but check his stats first: 1500 hit points, skill of 25—off the charts. Each of his blows causes 50–150 points of damage. He's immune to special effects spells, and he's nearly invulnerable to magick attack spells. His armor is mighty, very mighty. To defeat him, try a shadow-weapon. Hit and run . . . and good luck, chump.

Shadow-Skeleton

Two kinds—regular and "lesser." These incorporeal phantoms deal out painful piercing damage, and suffer only half-damage from magick attacks. If you pass through any shadow-skeleton, it can poison you. It is a good to keep your distance, so try enhanced Firebolt or Sphere runes against them. For close combat, cutting weapons (such as swords or axes) work far better than any other type.

Special effects: As with regular skeletons, you can destroy these shadow variants with a Power × 2 Spoilspell.

Sharga

These green fellows come in several strengths and varieties, but you can't really tell which is which. Some are quite tough, and some are "smart"—when they sustain a certain amount of damage, smart Shargas consume the heal substances they carry. Overall, Shargas suffer double-damage from fire-attack spells. Piercing weapons hurt them most, crush weapons least. Aim for the face and legs.

Skeleton

Two kinds—big and "lesser." The big skeleton is *very* tough. He can absorb 250 points of damage, while dealing out cutting blows worth 60 damage points per hit. His magick resistance is high, and his pierce armor is formidable. The lesser version is about the same, only—well, *less.* Best to hammer these bony beasts, though a good sword can work, too. If you want to keep your distance and try magick attacks, blast them with an enhanced Sphere rune.

Special effects: Skeletons, as you might expect, are immune to Scare spells. What could scare a skeleton? However, because a skeleton is an undead creature who is, in effect, a walking magick spell, you can destroy it with a Power × 2 Spoilspell.

Slime

This green malevolent goop whacks you with crushing blows from its pseudopods. Slimes can split into two creatures (each with lower stats than the original "mother" slime); they can also shlurp back together. Fire attacks deal them double-damage or worse, so toss a lot of oil bombs and blast away with firebolts. Also note: Slime armor provides four times more crush protection than cut protection. In hand-to-pod combat, use a sword or ax.

Special effects: If you cast a Tornado spell on a slime, it merely splits in two and suffers no damage. Slimes are afraid of fire spells; if you blast a slime with fire, it slides away and cowers in a corner.

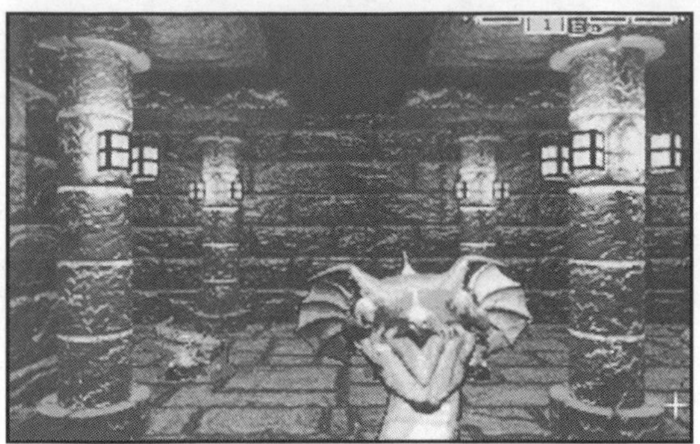

Snake

These venomous serpents come in dungeon and water varieties. Each kind inflicts not only painful bite wounds, but also toxic, vitality-sapping venom. Fire attacks are effective, particularly against water snakes. In tight combat, any type of weapon is fine. Snake armor fends off Cut, Crush, and Pierce damage almost equally.

Special effects: All snakes are immune to Tornado spells, and water snakes cannot be frozen or shrunk.

Tentacle Thing

This horrific beast is *Stonekeep*'s toughest, goriest, most brutal monster. The Thing's body is bad enough, with all those relentlessly churning teeth. But each of its three tentacles has its own "life," too. (Check the "Monster Combat Stats" table.) The combined attack strength of all four Thing parts is truly awesome.

Keep your distance, shrink him, then use ranged attacks (power-enhanced firebolts work best). If your Mana runs out, throw axes, daggers, darts. Pick off the tentacles first, if you can. If the beast does get in close, forget your crush weapons. Pierce him with a Dagger of Penetration, and for God's sake, *keep moving!*

Special effects: Tentacle Things are immune to Tornado and Stoptrack spells.

Throg

As with Shargas, there are several types of Throgs. All are fairly tough, and all are vulnerable to cutting or piercing weapons. (Magick attacks work, too, but when you raise a runecaster, Throgs recognize it and crouch behind their shields or retreat around the nearest corner.) Throgs are tall, leaving plenty of weak-armored lower body areas to target. Aim for the legs.

Special effects: Certain Throg leaders are immune to Scare spells.

Throg Shaman

Similar to Throg guards, but they can cast powerful Throg attack spells. When you get in close, Shamans beat on you with their Throg runecasters. Gorda Karn, the Shaman leader on Level 5, is immune to Scare spells.

Troll

These gnarled, evil cousins of Faeries are invisible until you obtain a certain object in the Faerie realm. Trolls are immune to fire attacks, and fond of teleporting behind you during battle. Use a good cutting weapon and aim for Troll faces and hands, where their armor is weak. Look for five items in the Faerie realm that provide magickal protection from Troll attacks. And watch out for the Terrible Troll! He's bigger and meaner than the other six trolls in Troll Country.

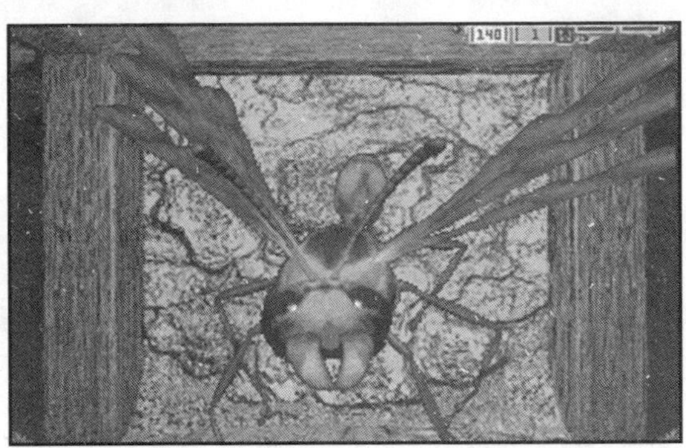

Wasp

Wasps come in two varieties—the regular wasp and the purple Faerie wasp. Regular wasps live in nests of 100 on dungeon ceilings. They are harmless (and quite curious) unless attacked. Then they swarm from the nest, eight at a time. Although wasps are vulnerable to piercing weapons, they're very active and hard to hit.

Faerie wasps are tougher and deadlier than regular wasps. They're also loners. In fact, you'll find only three in the Faerie realm. However, all three attack you on sight with magickal energybolt blasts. Magick attacks are only 50 percent effective against Faerie wasps. But when you get in close, a good piercing weapon will do the job—*if* you can hit the frenetic creature.

Special effects: If you freeze or stun wasps, they fall to the ground for a few seconds, making them easy targets. Wasps are immune to Tornado spells, however.

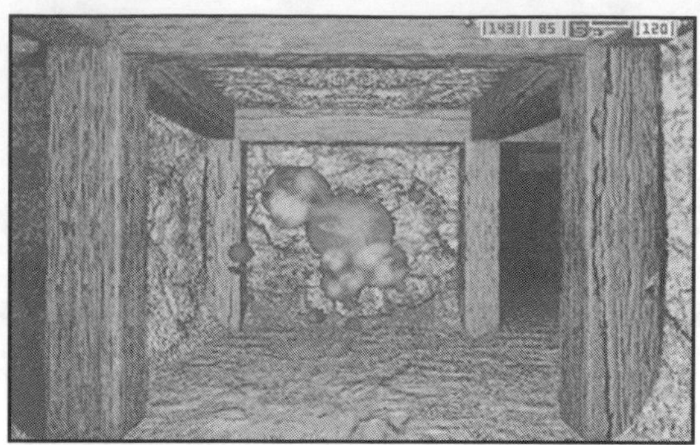

Will-o'-the-wisp

These blue, sparkling entities wander the southern passages of the Faerie Realm. They resemble Faeries in glow-form, but have a much lower sentience level. Once they find you, 'wisps hover in your face. If attacked, they turn bright red and lash out with electrical bolts. Knock them into glittering dust with a few blows from any good weapon. Note, however, that 'wisps are immune to *all* magickal attacks.

Zombie

This ancient undead evil terrorizes the Dwarven Fortress on Level 7. With a whopping 600 hit points, Mr. Zombie is an extremely tough opponent to destroy. Magickal fire attacks can be effective, but other types of magick inflict only 25 percent of their normal damage. His crush armor is quite high, but cutting or piercing weapons can find their mark.

Stonekeep Item List

Hundreds of objects lay scattered about *Stonekeep*'s dungeons and corridors. Some are valuable, some not. Here's a list of most items that have some effect on the game. I note what each item is called in your Journal, and describe its effect when ingested or used.

Potions

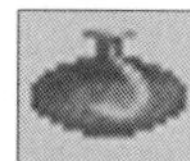

Small Heal Potion (Blue)

"A healthy potion." Raises vitality 10–15 points.

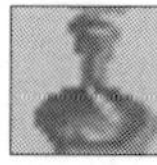

Regular Heal Potion (Blue)

"A healthy potion." Raises vitality 15–30 points.

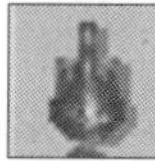

Super Heal Potion (Blue)

"Small vial." Raises vitality 30–60 points.

Life Restore Potion (Brown)

"Bubbling blue potion." Raises lowest stat (Health, Strength, or Agility) by one star.

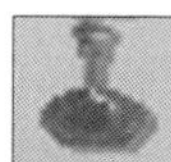

Strength Gain Potion (Dark Green)

"Decanter with a green brew." Raises Strength rating (if less than 7) by one star for five minutes.

Agility Gain Potion (Light Green)

“Light green potion.” Raises Agility rating (if less than 7) by one star for five minutes.

Cure Potion (Brown with Green Streaks)

“Smelly Throggish brew.” Cures afflictions such as poison or weakness.

Throg Strong Juice

“Throg-holding-a-boulder vial. It reeks!” Boosts Strength rating to its maximum of 10 stars for one minute. (If you drink a second vial of Throg Strong juice during that minute, you receive a permanent one-star increase in your Strength rating.)

Roots

Weak Heal Root

“A good smelling root.” Raises vitality 3–10 points.

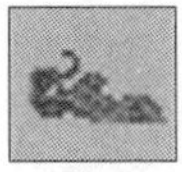

Regular Heal Root.

“A good smelling root.” Raises vitality 5–15 points.

Super Heal Root

“A really good smelling root.” Raises vitality 10–30 points.

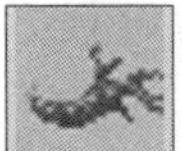

Poison Root

“This root smells musty.” Poisons the eater, causing gradual loss of vitality points until cured. (Also creates resistance to specific poison in Throg Temple.)

Mushrooms

Green Mushroom

“A green mushroom.” Cures afflictions such as poison or weakness.

Red Mushroom

“A red mushroom.” Adds a one-star bonus to all stats (Health, Strength, and Agility) for two minutes.

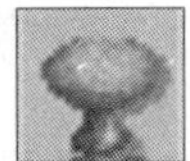

Spotted Mushroom

“A spotted mushroom.” Reduces Strength and Agility ratings by one star for two minutes.

Flowers and Plants

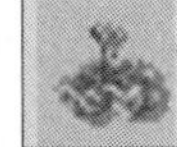

Primrose

“Primrose.” Use for passage to the Faerie level and to the Unseen Court of the Faerie Queen. Also buys performance of “The Song of Wahooka” from Faerie Players on Level 8.

Gladiola

“Gladiola.” Edible, but nothing happens. Also buys performance of “I’d Rather Be a Dwarf” from Faerie Players on Level 8.

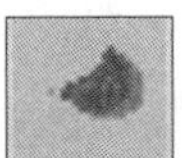

Foxglove

“Foxglove.” Edible, but nothing happens. Also buys performance of “Why the Shadowking Is Like He Is” from Faerie Players on Level 8.

St. John's Wort

"St. John's Wort." Restores full vitality, cures poison. Also buys performance of "The Curse of Lament" from Faerie Players on Level 8.

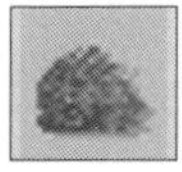

Wild Thyme

"Wild Thyme." Edible, but nothing happens. An ingredient of Snort's Brew.

Four-Leaf Clover.

"A four-leaf clover." Makes Trolls visible.

Brownie Moss.

"Sticky moss." Raises Drake's vitality 2–20 points; raises vitality of Enigma, Skuz, or Sparkle 5–50 points. Has no effect on Dwarves or Wahooka. Also an ingredient of Snort's Brew.

Daisy Chain.

"A daisy chain." Trade with Sweetie the Faerie for important item.

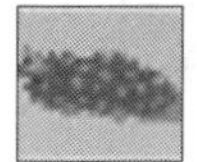

Rowanberries

"Rowanberries." Induce drunken-ness.

Rings

Luckstone Ring

Provides 20 percent resistance to Troll attacks. Also, 1 percent of your attacks target perfect hit zone radius (see the following section, "The *Stonekeep* Combat System")

Magick Armor Ring

Adds 1 point apiece to wearer's Armor ratings for Cut, Crush, Pierce.

Magick Deflection Ring

Adds two stars to the wearer's Health rating (for magick resistance only—stars don't appear in Journal).

Ring of Ducking

Increases Health rating by one star (for magick resistance only—stars don't appear in Journal). Adds a total of 9 points to Defense ratings (+3 Crush, +3 Cut, +3 Pierce,). Also gives you a 1 percent chance of suffering no damage each time you're hit.

Ring of Poison Resistance

Increases Health rating by four stars (for poison resistance only—stars don't appear in Journal).

Faerie Items

Book (The Last Tome of the Elves)

"A book." Trade with Winkle the Faerie for useful item.

Book (Giggle's Poem Book)

"A book." Trade with Giggle the Faerie for important item.

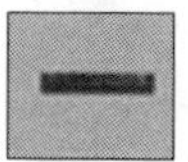

Charcoal Stick

"A stick of charcoal." Trade with Chuckle the Faerie for important item.

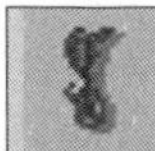

Decanter (Empty)

"Empty decanter." Ingredient for Snort's Brew.

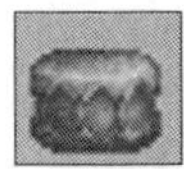

Drum

"A Faerie drum." Trade with Winkle the Faerie for useful item.

Faerie Cake

"Some Faerie cake." Raises Drake's vitality 5–25 points; raises vitality of Enigma, Skuz, or Sparkle 10–25 points. Has no effect on Dwarves or Wahooka.

Faerie Pants

"Rough green pants." Provides wearer with 20 percent resistance to Troll attacks.

Faerie Shirt

"This shirt is inside out." Provides wearer with 20 percent resistance to Troll attacks.

Fiddle

"A fiddle." Trade with Binkle the Faerie for important item.

Fine Faerie Cake

"Fine Faerie cake." Raises Drake's vitality 10–40 points; raises vitality of Enigma, Skuz, or Sparkle 20–50 points. Has no effect on Dwarves or Wahooka. Trade with Surly the Faerie for important item.

Horseshoe Medallion

"A medallion shaped like a horseshoe." Provides 20 percent protection from Troll attacks.

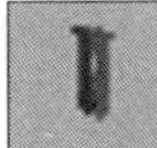

Iron Spike

"A spike made from iron." When placed in the ground, it creates a barrier Trolls cannot cross.

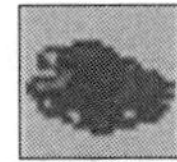

Jester's Cap

"A jester's cap." Provides wearer with 20 percent resistance to Troll attacks.

Parchment

"A piece of parchment." Trade with Chuckle the Faerie for important item.

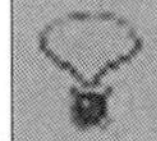

Pendant of Iaenni

"A magickal pendant." Use to pass the Guardian Skeleton on Level 9.

Portrait of Iaenni

"A portrait." Trade with Faerie Queen for information.

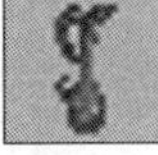

Snort's Brew

"Decanter with a red brew." Induces drunkenness. Trade with Chuckle the Faerie for important item.

Miscellaneous Items

Bucket

"A bucket." Use to draw water from wells.

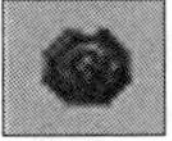

Coin.

"A gold coin." Use these to buy wares from Geldor Armorsmith.

Coin Bag

"Bag to hold coins." If I say more, I'll be arrested for felony stating of the obvious.

Coldfire

"Magickal fire. It is cold to the touch." Use to counteract Ice Queen's invincibility.

Cylinder

"A cylinder." Use with cylinder switches on Level 2.

Dark Mirror Shard

"A piece of dark mirrored glass." Use on Drake to see door to Tower of Shadowking.

Dowel

"A wooden dowel." Use to disarm spell trap, unlock secret door on Level 5.

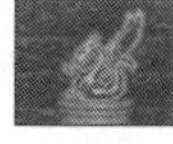

Dragon Statuette

"A marble statue." Use to open gate to the Underlands.

Dwarven Meal

"Ahh. . . Smells like a home-cooked meal." Raises Vitality 1–50 points.

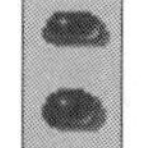

Gems

"A (red, blue, green) gem." Trade with Wahooka and Mad Throg Shaman for clues.

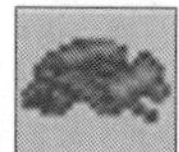

Gorza's Scroll

"A piece of parchment." Return to Gorza the Ice Sharga to get useful items.

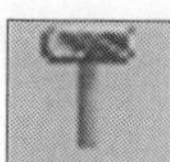

Ice Hammer

"This hammer is made of ice." Use to enter the Ice Queen's lair.

Key Ring

"A key ring." Holds all keys found in game.

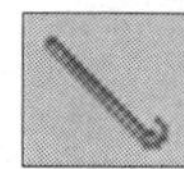

Metal Bar

No description in Journal. Dropped by dark Dwarf. Farli uses it to open secret door on Level 12.

Odd Dropping

"A pile of. . . Why did I pick this up?" Reduces Strength and Health ratings by one star for five minutes when ingested by any party member except Skuz (who displays no effect whatsoever).

Silver Ankh

"Powerful magicks course through this ankh." Necessary for final silver ritual. Also activates teleports on Level 12.

Silver Circle

"Powerful magicks course through this circle." Necessary for final silver ritual. Also activates teleports on Level 12.

Silver Crescent

"Powerful magicks course through this crescent." Necessary for final silver ritual. Also activates teleports on Level 12.

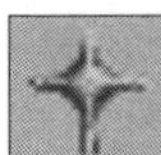

Silver Cross

"Powerful magicks course through this cross." Necessary for final silver ritual. Also triggers teleports on Level 12.

Skull

"A skull." Use as throwing weapon. Trade with Wahooka on Level 3. Also buys performance of "Troll Hint" from Faerie Players on Level 8.

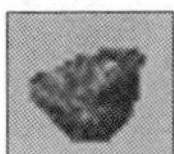

Stone

"A stone." Use as throwing weapon, or in stoneshooter. Also buys performance of "Ice Wars" from Faerie Players on Level 8.

Stone Bag

"Bag to hold throwing stones." Need I say more?

Stoneshooter Pieces (3)

"A piece to a strange device." Give to Dombur on Level 7 to get stoneshooter.

Throg Food

"Bad smelling Throg food." Reduces Strength rating by one star for five minutes.

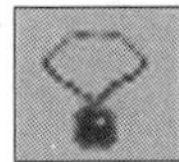

Throg Pendant

"A Throg pendant." Use to open main door to Temple of Throggi in Level 5.

Throg Shaman Feathers

"Feathers." Protects party from Throg magick glyph damage.

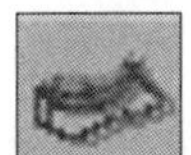

Wineskin

"A wineskin." Holds up to five draughts of healing potion from Fountain of Thera. (Each draught raises vitality 15–30 points.)

Yang Symbol

"A mystic symbol." Opens secret door when combined with Yin symbol.

Yin Symbol

"A mystic symbol." Opens secret door when combined with Yang symbol.

A Quick Look at the *Stonekeep* Journal

The Stonekeep Journal is a powerful tool—it's easy to use, and *very* cool. Use it to record information, review important clues, check your character statistics, inscribe runes on runecasters, and inspect the items you've acquired.

Remember, this is a strategy guide, not a manual. If you've read the *Stonekeep* manual, you know how to use the Journal. You know about all those statistics and skills. Most of it is self-explanatory, anyway. But the game documentation doesn't address a couple of Journal quirks. Let's clear that up.

NPC Character Descriptions: What Do They Mean?

The first few pages of the Journal always list information for Drake. His statistics are easy to understand—the more stars he has (under Health, Strength, Ax, Sword, whatever), the better his rating. Easy enough. But what about those narrative passages describing the companions who join Drake along the way? What the heck does "slightly robust" mean? How does "very strong" differ from "notably strong"?

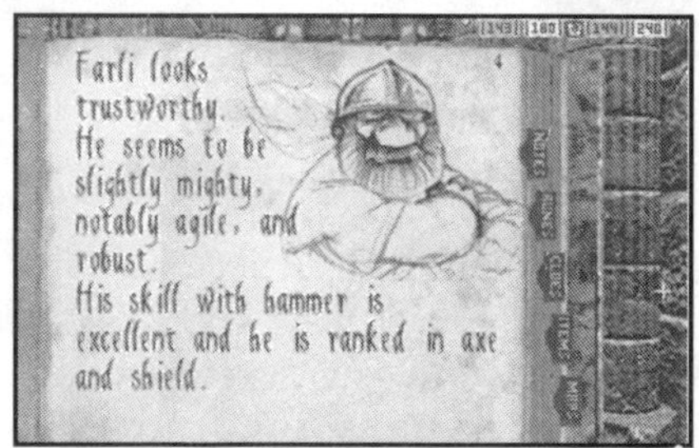

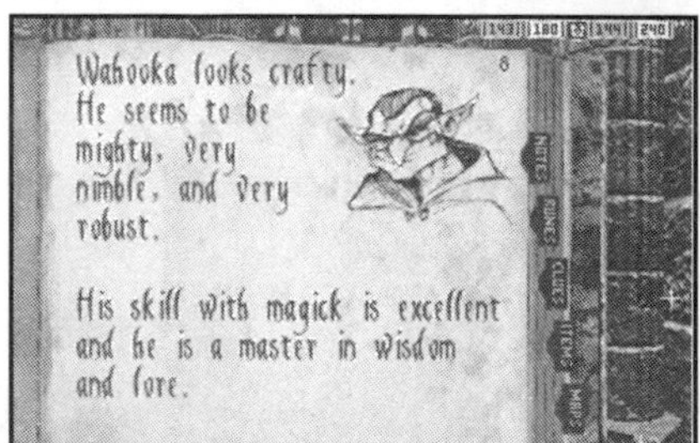

Crack the Code. Drake's stats are easy enough to interpret, but how do you translate all that verbiage describing NPCs like Farli and Wahooka?

First, let's quickly review the categories. The Strength rating measures raw physical strength. The Agility rating measures raw dexterity and speed. Health measures overall constitution—how vital you are, how resistant to poison and magick. In Drake's statistics, these three ratings can range from one to 10 stars.

Drake's Statistics. Remember that for every two stars of Strength or Agility, you gain another star of Health. Each new star of Health adds 20 more points to your Vitality Meter's maximum number.

Guess what? These same three categories apply to Drake's companions, with the same one-to-10 rating range. But the ratings are indicated by descriptive phrases rather than numbers. The following table shows exactly how the phrases in the NPC statistics sentence translate to numbers:

NPC Statistics Table

Rating	*Strength*	*Agility*	*Health*
1	very frail	very clumsy	very fragile
2	frail	clumsy	fragile
3	slightly frail	slightly clumsy	slightly fragile
4	slightly strong	slightly agile	slightly healthy
5	strong	agile	healthy
6	very strong	very agile	very healthy
7	notably strong	notably agile	notably healthy
8	slightly mighty	slightly nimble	slightly robust
9	mighty	nimble	robust
10	very mighty	very nimble	very robust

Note When you get to Level 8: "Faerie Realm," you'll find that Sparkle the Faerie is different. She cannot be "read" as easily by Drake, and gets a different description.

Now let's take a look at the skill ratings of the NPCs. A quick review: Skill is a primary factor in the *Stonekeep* combat equations determining the accuracy of a blow. Skill ratings represent how well a character has trained with certain categories of weapons. All swords fall into the Sword skill category, all axes in the Axe skill category, and so on.

Here's a quick look at the skill categories:

Axe:	●●	Hammer:	●
Brawl:	●●	Magick:	●●●●●
Dagger:	●●●●●	Polearm:	●●
Shield:	●	Sword:	●●●●●
Missile:	●●	Stealth:	●●●●●

Skill Categories

Note that Brawl refers to fistfighting; Missile refers to combat with all ranged weapons, including archery items; the Magick skill influences how fast you can use runes, and how much Mana you spend to cast them; the Polearm category includes spears, quarterstaffs, and the like; and the Stealth skill, as you might expect, determines how quietly the character moves.

On Drake's page, the skill level in each category of weapon is represented by stars, ranging from none to five. But NPCs have a sentence describing one primary skill (usually a weapon), then two secondary skills. Again, these descriptive terms correspond to the same zero-to-five-star ratings Drake's page uses.

Here's how:

NPC Primary Skill

Rating	*NPC Equivalent*
0	untrained
1	poor
2	fair
3	good
4	great
5	excellent

NPC Secondary Skills (Add both skills together)

Rating	*NPC Equivalent*
0–1	untrained
2–3	unskilled
4–5	skilled
6–9	ranked
10	a master

Note that NPCs are limited to the skills listed in their skill sentence—thus, they can use only the weapon types in the sentence. You can equip Farli with a hammer, axe, or shield, but you can't give him any other kind of weapon.

Wahooka, Enigma, and Sparkle have some unique categories. You can't give them any weapons, and their secondary "skills" don't quite relate to actual game skills. (If you're wondering what it means to be a master in "wisdom" like Wahooka or ranked in "Tea Party" like Sparkle—forget it, it means nothing, game-wise.)

NPC Skills

NPC	*Primary Skills*	*Secondary Skills*
Farli Mallestone	hammer	axe, shield
Karzak Hardstone	axe	hammer, shield
Dombur Mallestone	dagger	axe, shield
Skuz	dagger	sword, pole arm
Enigma	archery	magick, lore
Wahooka	magick	wisdom, lore
Sparkle	magick	Faeriness, Tea Party

The *Stonekeep* Combat System

Conflict is central to any story. And raw physical conflict—*i.e.*, combat—is the heart of *Stonekeep*. You fight a *lot*. Each time you strike something with a weapon, *Stonekeep*'s complex combat system determines where the weapon hits and how much damage it does.

In *Stonekeep*, you have gross control over where your weapon lands. Drake's character statistics determine the fine control. This is represented by a *hit zone radius* (HZR). The HZR is a circle around the pixel point where you clicked to attack. The actual "hot point" (where your weapon lands) can be any pixel in the circle, chosen randomly by the computer. As you improve and get better stats for Drake, this circle shrinks. When the circle shrinks, your weapon hits closer to your target pixel.

As it is written in the *Stonekeep* design bible, "Consider this the Grand Unified Theory of Stonekeep Combat."

Weapon Statistics

Individual weapons are tracked separately by the *Stonekeep* combat system. All weapons differ from one another—even one sword from another sword. The more you use a particular weapon, the more familiar you get with it. The more familiar you are with the weapon, the *better* you get with it.

Makes sense, doesn't it?

Remember, we're not talking about weapon *types*, although *Stonekeep* tracks that, too. No, we're talking about your familiarity with an *individual* weapon—the Dwarven sword you got from Farli on Level 2, or that stone hammer you took from the statue of Throggi on Level 5.

Familiarity with weapons is not something that *you* can track in the game, but don't worry—*Stonekeep* knows. A Familiarity rating for each weapon ranges from 0 to 5. Even individual shields have a Familiarity rating in the game.

Weapon Skill/Familiarity Counters

Each Weapon Skill and Weapon Familiarity has a counter. This count increases by 1 point each time you successfully "use" a weapon, shield, or runecaster. What constitutes successful use? For a weapon, it's a hit that does damage. For a shield, any blocked blow. For a runecaster, you get a point anytime you cast a spell.

When you reach the magick number (see the following table), the Skill or Familiarity rating increases by one increment and the counter resets to zero. As you can see from the table, Familiarities increase at a faster pace then Skills.

Note that changing weapons does not change the Familiarity or Skill counters for the previous weapon.

Level	*Familiarity*	*Skill*
1	2	20
2	4	50
3	10	110
4	24	225
5	52	500

Remember, hits do not accumulate from level to level. The counter resets to zero each time you reach a new Skill or Familiarity rating.

Weapon Damage: Cut, Crush, Pierce

If you've glanced at Drake's offense/defense stats page (always page 3 in your Journal), you may be wondering about those odd categories—Cut, Crush, and Pierce. Most weapons in *Stonekeep*, whether yours or your opponent's, deal out "complex damage" divided into those three sub-types.

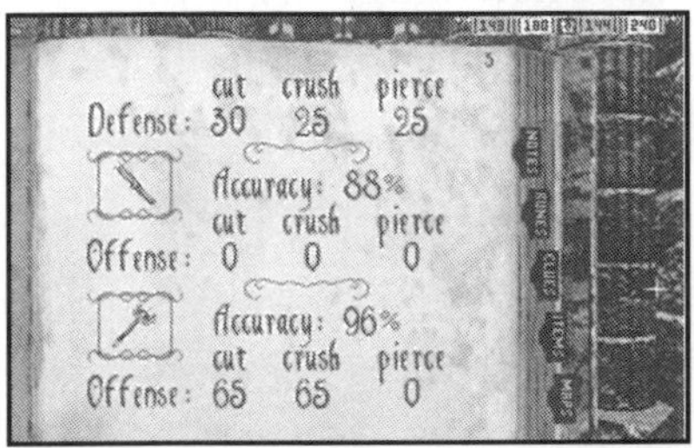

Drake's Weapon Page. Turn here to check the effectiveness of Drake's current weapon(s), shield, and armor. The top line represents your armor protection, the middle line your left-hand item (in this case, a runecaster), and the bottom line your right-hand item (here, an axe).

The damage types are self-explanatory. *Stonekeep* weapons and monsters inflict (after all the combat equations are calculated) a gross amount of hit-point damage. The amount of overall damage is then divided among Cut, Crush, and Pierce damage categories according to the weapon's or monster's damage distribution percentages.

Yes, I see your eyes glazing over. Let me just add one more thing: You can find these damage distribution percentages in the Weapon Stats and Monster Combat Stats tables at the back of the book, in appendices A and B.

Combat Equations

Now let's get down to the nitty gritty. Believe me, this will be *far* more information than the average person wants to know. But this is a strategy guide, right? Get out your calculator, man. *Let's crunch numbers.*

In the following equations, round all numbers to the closest integer value after calculation is complete. When you see "Random," it means a random value between 0 and 1.

Weapon Delay Equation

Here's the equation for the actual delay between blows for any weapon. Note that the "Drunk Level" in the equation refers to the four states of inebriation possible from drinking Snort's Brew or eating rowanberries on Level 8: "Faerie Realm."

```
# Frames (at 12 frames per second) =
(Weapon Delay - Character Agility) +
(Weapon Weight - Character Strength) +
(Drunk Level × 4)
```

The values for Weapon Delay and Weapon Weight come from the Weapon Stats table in Appendix B.

If the weapon-user (Drake or NPC companion) is enchanted by a Quickness spell, multiply # Frames by .75; if it's a Power × 2 Quickness spell, multiply # Frames by .5; and if it's a Power × 3 Quickness spell, then # Frames = 0. In other words, the only delay is in the number of frames for the weapon attack itself—there's no further delay between blows.

Hit Zone Radius

The hit zone radius (HZR) is used to determine where each blow actually lands. This equation calculates a radius around the point that you target with your aiming cross hairs. Then *Stonekeep* directs the blow to a random spot within that radius. Obviously, the smaller the HZR, the more accurate the blow. The HZR range is 1 to 26.

Here's the equation:

```
HZR = 12 - Skill Modifier + Agility Modifier + Weapon Quality Modifier + Weapon Weight Modifier + Vitality Modifier
```

OK, you might want to know what some of these modifiers mean. Pay attention now. *You will be tested later.*

Skill Modifier. Here's how the Skill Modifier is calculated:

```
Skill Modifier = 2 × Effective Skill
```

What's the "Effective Skill," you ask? OK, let me check my notes. Ah, yes, the Effective Skill is equal to the lesser of the Weapon Skill value (as found in your Journal) or Weapon Familiarity value (as found nowhere that *you* can find it).

I'm really glad I could answer your question.

Donuts will be served later.

Agility Modifier. In the HZR equation, "Agility Modifier" refers to a value that corresponds to the current Agility rating of the character using the weapon. But that Agility rating is not simply the one you see in your Journal. Actually, we're talking about an *adjusted* Agility rating. Adjusted by what? Adjusted by factors such as armor weight and weapon weight.

Here's how the Agility Modifier value is calculated:

Adjusted Agility	*Agility Modifier*
1	+1
2–3	0
4–5	-1
6–7	-2
8–9	-3
10	-4

Vitality Modifier. If the weapon-user's vitality (hit points) is 25 percent of capacity or less, then the modifier is -5. Otherwise, the modifier is zero.

Weapon Weight Modifier. This modifier can't be any less than zero. The equation is as follows:

```
Weapon Weight Modifier = Weapon Weight - Character Strength
```

Weapon Quality Modifier. You can find each weapon's Weapon Quality rating in the Weapon Stats table in Appendix B. Here's how the rating translates into a modifier value:

Quality	*Modifier*
Excellent	-2
Good	-1
Normal	0
Poor	1
Bad	2

Strength Hit-Point Bonus

Most weapons get a hit-point bonus from your Strength rating. Aside from runecasters, of course, only two weapons—the Sharga crossbow and the stoneshooter—get no Strength boost.

The following table lists the bonus damage for each Strength rating:

If Strength Rating is:	***Then bonus damage added to Damage Equation is:***
1	1
2	3
3	5
4	8
5	11
6	15
7	19
8	23
9	27
10	32

Note that you don't automatically get the full bonus added to the hit points of your attack. The number is factored into a very complex set of damage equations, none of which you will find in this book. But in general, the stronger you are, the more damage you inflict with your weapons.

Poison Resistance Test

When a character is poisoned, *Stonekeep* generates a number between one and 10. If that number is equal to or less than the poison strength value after it is subtracted from the character's Health rating, then the player resists the poison and is not affected. Some items (such as the Ring of Poison Resistance) can alter a character's health for purposes of resisting poison only.

Experience

The three statistics (Strength, Agility and Health) start at 1, and slowly increase as you use your weapons and complete tasks set within the story.

Every successful strike with a weapon adds to either the Strength or Agility counter, depending on the weight of the weapon and the rated Strength of the character. If the weight of the weapon is equal to or greater then the character's Strength rating, then increase the Strength counter. Otherwise, increase the Agility counter.

When either counter reaches the square of double the next level, the stat is increased by one and the counter resets. If a stat is raised by other means than combat, the counter does not reset. When a stat is raised, the book icon flashes in the corner.

So the equation is:

$$[\ 2 \bullet (\text{ stat level } +1\ )\ ]^2$$

If you hate equations, as many of us do, here's a simple table that shows you how many solid, damage-causing hits you need to ascend to higher stat levels. Remember, once you reach that next level, the counter resets to zero.

Agility, Strength Gain Table

Stat Level	*# Hits Needed*
1	—
2	16
3	36
4	64
5	100
6	144
7	196
8	256
9	324
10	400

Health ratings increase in a somewhat different manner. Your Health rating increases by one star for every two stars you gain of Strength or Agility. Every Health point gained adds 20 points to your maximum vitality (hit-point) level.

NPC companions gain experience at the same rate, but because they will only use weapons they're skilled with, and they are considered completely familiar with their weapons, the combat system need only track three skills apiece.

Monster Attacks

When monsters attack, they do not have a hit zone radius. They either hit or miss, depending on their skill, modified by the character's Agility (the chance to dodge to the side). Every time a monster makes a physical attack, it has a chance to hit as follows:

Monster Chance to Hit = 80% + (10% × Monster Skill) - (10% × Modified Agility)

(min. 20%, max. 100%)

```
Modified Agility = Characters
Agility + Armor Agility Modifier
```

The combat system generates a random number between one and 100; if the random number is lower then the Monster Chance to Hit value, then the monster hits its target with the attack. The system then calculates shield (if any) and damage results. If the monster misses, then its target takes no damage.

The *Stonekeep* Magick System

Magick, of course, is an essential part of *Stonekeep*. Without it, you won't get far. This guide assumes that you've read the *Stonekeep* manual and mastered the art of inscribing runes and casting spells. (For a quick walkthrough of the process, see step 41 in Level 2: "Lower Ruins of Stonekeep.") Instead, this section focuses on how each spell works.

Do You Believe In Magic? You'd better, or you're dungeon meat in Stonekeep. Casting spells is easy, but consult this section for information on individual spells.

Before we get to the spells themselves, we'll take a look at a few general magick tips, then review the five "meta runes" that can modify spells.

Some Quick Magick Tips

It won't take you long to get the hang of rune magick in *Stonekeep*, particularly if you keep in mind the following guidelines.

Watch That Knob

Keep an eye on the glowing knob at the top of the runecaster. As the caster uses up Mana, the knob's glow progressively dims. This gives you a way to estimate quickly how much Mana you have left. Also note: If a runecaster does not have enough Mana to cast the active rune, the spell fails and that runecaster expends 1 point of Mana (if it has any left, of course).

The Greater Spell Cancels the Lesser

Spells do not "stack." Only one spell of a particular type can be active on a target. If you cast a spell on a target while another spell of the same type is active on that target, the greater spell (in terms of duration or intensity) takes precedence, canceling out the lesser spell.

Magick Skill Rating Affects Accuracy and Mana Cost

Remember that your Magick skill rating affects the accuracy of targeted missile spells (such as firebolts or icebolts). It can also affect your Mana cost for casting spells. If you have a Magick skill of four stars, then each rune costs one less Mana point to cast. If your Magick skill is five stars, then you get a discount of 2 Mana points per spell. Your Mana cost will never go below 1 Mana point, however.

Meta Runes

The five runes listed in the following table cannot be cast by themselves. They are spell modifiers—that is, they enhance the effects of other runes. Meta runes are inscribed on the runecaster directly over the rune you wish to enhance.

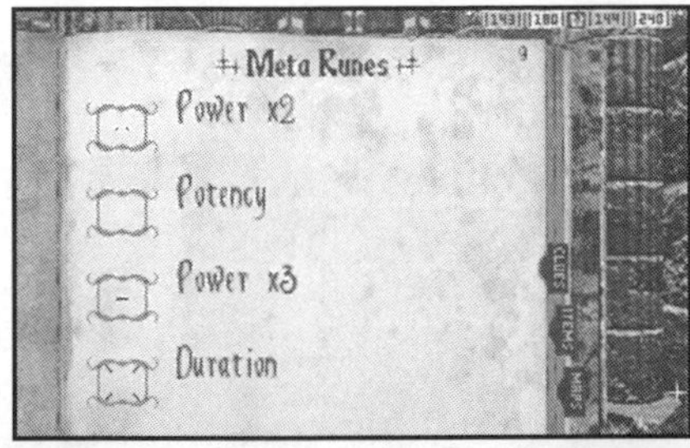

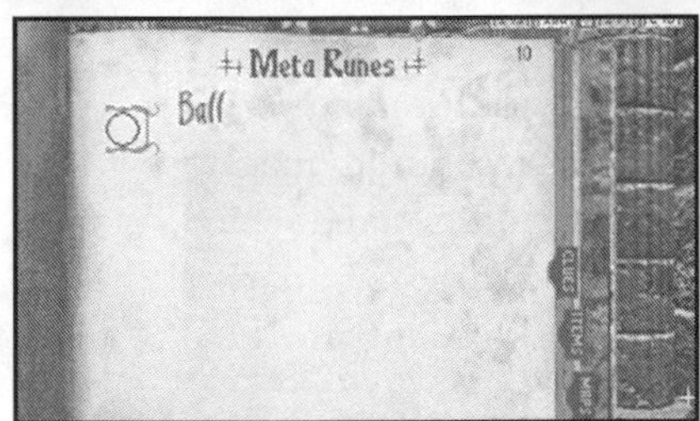

Rune Bargain. Meta runes are easily worth the extra Mana it costs to enhance spells with them.

Remember that meta runes increase the Mana cost of the spell by a multiplier (listed under "Cost" in the following table). For example, an Icebolt rune normally inflicts 20 points of damage and costs 4 Mana points. If you enhance it with a Power × 2 meta rune, it can inflict 40 points of damage. But now it costs 6 Mana points—the regular Icebolt cost of 4 Mana points times the Power × 2 cost multiplier, which is 1.5.

Meta Runes

Name	*Cost*	*General Effect*
Ball	× 1.5	Increases area or number of targets affected
Power × 2	× 1.5	Roughly doubles effect of spell
Power × 3	× 2.0	Greatly increases effect of spell
Duration	× 1.25	Makes spell last longer
Potency	× 1.5	Reduces target's magick resistance by 50%

You can use more than one meta rune to enhance a particular spell. To determine the Mana cost of multiple meta runes, add up all the cost modifiers. Then multiply the base Mana cost of the rune times the sum modifier, and round up. The maximum modifier cost would be × 6.25 (Ball, Power × 3, Duration and Potency).

Rune Descriptions

The following section details the effects of all magickal runes in *Stonekeep.* Note that an asterisk (*) by a spell means that it must overcome the magickal resistance rating of the target.

Armor

Mana cost: 4

General Description: When cast at a party member in the mystic mirror, this rune adds 10 points of armor factor for 10 minutes. During this time, the target's armor glows.

Ball:	Affects the entire party.
Power × 2:	Adds 2× points of armor factor.
Power × 3:	Adds 3× points of armor factor, and the target is immune to non-magick weapons.
Duration:	Effect lasts 20 minutes.
Potency:	No additional effect.

Circle

Mana Cost: 20

General Description: This rune creates a magickal blue circle on the ground in front of your party. (If there is no square available, or it is not empty, this rune will not work.) Only one circle can exist at a time. If a new circle is cast, the old circle is removed. When you cast a Homing spell (see "Homing") at any other location in Stonekeep (except the hall of the Shadowking), the entire party automatically returns to this blue circle.

Ball:	No additional effect.
Power × 2:	No additional effect.
Power × 3:	No additional effect.
Duration:	No additional effect.
Potency:	No additional effect.

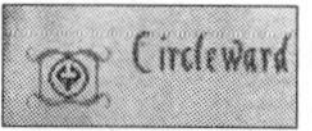

Circleward

Mana Cost: 5

General Description: This spell creates a magickal trap in the form of a circle on the ground. (The target square must be clear.) Any creature, including members of your party, who walks over this circle will set off an explosion causing 40 points of fire damage. An item thrown into the square can also set off the Circleward, removing it.

Ball:	No additional effect.
Power × 2:	The explosion causes 80 points of damage.
Power × 3:	The explosion causes 150 points of damage. The explosion is larger.
Duration:	No additional effect.
Potency:	No additional effect.

Curing

Mana Cost: 2

General Description: This rune restores vitality points to the target, not to exceed the target's maximum vitality. It will not heal afflictions (such as poison or weakness). Each casting of this spell heals 15 points of vitality.

Ball:	The spell affects all targets in the square, or the entire party in the mystic mirror.
Power × 2:	The spell heals 30 points of damage.
Power × 3:	The spell heals 50 points of damage.
Duration:	No additional effect.
Potency:	No additional effect.

Duck

Mana Cost: 1

General Description: This spell makes a "quack" sound.

Ball:	One additional quack.
Power × 2:	One additional quack.
Power × 3:	Two additional quacks.
Duration:	One additional quack.
Potency:	No additional effect.

Energybolt*

Mana Cost: 4

General Description: When you cast this rune, a bolt of raw magickal energy flies out to strike the target. The target suffers 40 points of magickal damage and loses 10 percent of its strength for one minute. If the target has magick resistance, it takes only 5 points of damage and loses no strength.

Ball:	Multiple bolts fly out, striking all creatures in the target square and inflicting 40 points of damage on each.
Power × 2:	The damage is 80 points. Strength loss is 25 percent. If target resists, the damage is 5 points with no strength loss.
Power × 3:	The damage is 120 points, strength loss is 50 percent and the creature has a 25 percent chance of being stunned for

	four to eight seconds. If the target resists, it won't be stunned, and the damage is 5 points with no strength loss.
Duration:	If the target is stunned, it will be stunned for 10–20 seconds.
Potency:	The target's magickal resistance is reduced by 50 percent.

Featherfall

Mana Cost: 4

General Description: When cast on Drake in the mystic mirror, the entire party floats slowly down pits, taking no damage from the fall itself. This spell lasts five minutes.

Ball:	No additional effect.
Power × 2:	No additional effect.
Power × 3:	No additional effect.
Duration:	The spell lasts 20 minutes.
Potency:	No additional effect.

Firebolt*

Mana Cost: 1

General Description: A bolt of fire shoots from the rune caster, striking the target in a small explosion. The spell does 25 points of damage.

Ball:	A single bolt still flies out, but the explosion is much larger—hitting every creature in the targeted square with 25 points of damage.
Power × 2:	The bolt is larger, with multiple impacts, and the damage to the target is doubled to 50 points.
Power × 3:	Damage inflicted on the target creature is 75 points, and damage to all other creatures in the square is 10–25 points. The bolt is larger still, with multiple explosions on impact.
Duration:	No additional effect.
Potency:	The target's magick resistance is halved.

Flame*

Mana Cost: 4

General Description: A column of flame explodes in front of the party, damaging every target in the square just ahead. The Flame rune inflicts 50 points of damage on all targets that fail a magick resistance test.

Ball:	The spell attacks one additional square, but all targets take half damage—or nothing at all, if they pass their magick resistance test.
Power × 2:	The spell inflicts 90 points of damage.
Power × 3:	The spell inflicts 130 points of damage. If there is another square behind the target square, then any target in that square will suffer some damage, too.
Duration:	No additional effect.
Potency:	The target's magick resistance test is halved.

Healing

Mana Cost: 5

General Description: This spell restores 40 points of vitality to the target, and also heals any of the target's afflictions (poison, weakness).

Ball:	The spell affects all creatures in the targeted square, or all party members in the mystic mirror.
Power × 2:	Heals target 80 points.
Power × 3:	Heals target 200 points.
Duration:	No additional effect.
Potency:	No additional effect.

Homing

Mana Cost: 2

General Description: This spell transports your party back to a previously cast magick circle (see Circle above). If no such circle exists, the spell automatically fails. If your party is standing within the current magick circle when this spell is cast, you return to the location where you cast the last Homing spell.

Ball:	No additional effect.
Power × 2:	No additional effect.
Power × 3:	No additional effect.
Duration:	No additional effect.
Potency:	No additional effect.

Icebolt*

Mana Cost: 4

General Description: A bolt of ice flies out and strikes the target, inflicting 20 points of damage.

Ball:	Multiple bolts fly out, striking all targets in the target square, doing 1–20 points of damage to each.
Power × 2:	Damage to the target is 40 points, and there is a 10 percent chance that the target will be frozen (can't move) for five seconds. Frozen targets can be unfrozen with the use of Warming or Firebolt runes.
Power × 3:	Damage is 80 points, and there is a 50 percent chance that the target will be frozen for five seconds. Frozen targets can be unfrozen with the use of Warming or Firebolt runes.
Duration:	Increases frozen duration to 15 seconds.
Potency:	Halves the target's magick resistance.

Invisibility

Mana Cost: 5

General Description: This spell renders your entire party invisible for three minutes. If you move quietly with this rune cast on you, most monsters ignore you.

Ball:	No additional effect.
Power × 2:	No additional effect.
Power × 3:	No additional effect.
Duration:	Duration is 10 minutes.
Potency:	No additional effect.

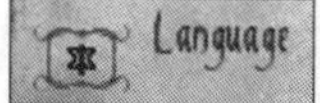

Language

Mana Cost: 2

General Description: When you cast this spell on Drake, he can read and understand other languages. The effect lasts 10 minutes.

Ball:	No additional effect.
Power × 2:	No additional effect.
Power × 3:	No additional effect.
Duration:	Duration is 30 minutes.
Potency:	No additional effect.

Quickness

Mana Cost: 10

General Description: Cast this spell on Drake to reduce the delay between his weapon strikes by 25 percent for one minute. Unfortunately, it also increases the hit zone radius (HZR) by 25 percent, reducing the accuracy of your blows. (For more on the HZR, see the foregoing section, "The *Stonekeep* Combat System."

Ball:	The entire party attacks faster by 25 percent.
Power × 2:	Reduces weapon delay by 50 percent, but widens the HZR by the same percentage.
Power × 3:	No delay between weapon attacks, but the HZR is now twice its normal size.
Duration:	The duration is two minutes.
Potency:	No additional effect.

Scare*

Mana Cost: 3

General Description: If the target fails a magick resistance test, it flees in panic for 30 seconds, or until you attack it again.

Ball:	Affects all creatures in the target square.
Power × 2:	No additional effect.
Power × 3:	No additional effect.
Duration:	The target flees for one minute.
Potency:	The target's magick resistance is halved.

Shield

Mana Cost: 4

General Description: This spell makes Drake or a party member immune to non-magickal ranged attacks. The duration is five minutes.

Ball:	Affects the entire party.
Power × 2:	The target is immune to non-magickal attacks, and suffers only 50 percent damage from magickal ranged attacks.
Power × 3:	The target is immune to all ranged attacks, magickal or non-magickal.
Duration:	The duration is 10 minutes.
Potency:	No additional effect.

Shrink

Mana Cost: 4

General Description: The target is shrunk to 75 percent of its normal size. This may also reduce the target's remaining health and attack strength for the 30-second duration of the spell. The spell has no affect on Drake or the traveling party. Some monsters (such as the dragon, the Ettin, and the Shadowking) are completely resistant to this spell.

Ball:	Affects all creatures in the target square.
Power × 2:	Shrinks target to 75 percent of normal. May also slow target.
Power × 3:	Shrinks target to 25 percent of normal. May also slow target.
Duration:	The duration increases to one minute.
Potency:	The target's magick resistance is halved.

Silence

Mana Cost: 2

General Description: This spell reduces by 50 percent the amount of noise the target makes. The effect lasts five minutes. Note that the Silence rune works on most background objects.

Ball:	Affects entire party.
Power × 2:	Reduces noise by 75 percent.
Power × 3:	Reduces noise by 100 percent.
Duration:	The spell effect lasts 20 minutes.
Potency:	No additional effects.

Slow*

Mana Cost: 2

General Description: If the target fails a magick resistance test, they slow to half their normal walking speed for 30 seconds. Note: This spell cannot be used on any party member. (Stoptrack has priority over Slow.)

Ball:	Affects all creatures in the target square.
Power × 2:	Also slows the target's weapon attack speed.
Power × 3:	The target cannot walk, and its weapon attack speed is slower.
Duration:	The spell's effect lasts one minute.
Potency:	The target's magick resistance is halved.

Sphere

Mana Cost: 4

General Description: Material spheres launch from the runecaster, striking the target. Each sphere inflicts 8 points of crushing damage, regardless of meta rune enhancements. The target's armor becomes only 10 percent effective against spheres. Each cast of the Sphere rune launches three spheres, one after another.

Ball:	Launches the three spheres of a single cast all at once. If there are nine spheres in the cast (as with a Power × 2 modifier), they launch in three flights of three spheres apiece.

Power × 2:	The spell launches a total of nine spheres.
Power x3:	The spell launches a total of 27 spheres.
Duration:	No additional effect.
Potency:	No additional effect.

Spoilspell

Mana Cost: 6

General Description: When you cast a Spoilspell at a party member, his magick resistance (which is his Health rating, but against magick only) increases by two stars for one minute. Spoilspells also destroy some other magickal effects. A Spoilspell cancels any currently active spell that has a duration (such as Armor, Invisibility, Quickness, Scare, Shield, Shrink, Silence, Slow, Language, Stoptrack, Strength, or Warming).

Ball:	Targets the entire party.
Power × 2:	Increases magick resistance by four stars.
Power × 3:	Increases magick resistance by six stars.
Duration:	The spell's effect lasts three minutes.
Potency:	No additional effect.

Stoptrack*

Mana Cost: 3

General Description: If the target fails a magick resistance test, it cannot move from its current square for 30 seconds. Note, however, that the target can still attack, cast spells, and defend itself. (Stoptrack has priority over Slow.)

Ball:	Targets all creatures in the target square.
Power × 2:	No additional effect.
Power × 3:	No additional effect.
Duration:	The spell's effect lasts one minute.
Potency:	The target's magick resistance is halved.

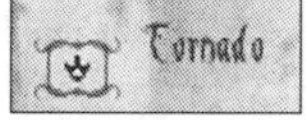

Strength

Mana Cost: 4

General Description: The target's Strength rating is increased by one star (to a maximum of 10 stars) for 30 seconds.

Ball:	Targets all creatures in the target square, or the entire party in the mystic mirror.
Power × 2:	Increases strength by two stars.
Power × 3:	Increases strength by four stars.
Duration:	The spell's effect lasts one minute.
Potency:	No additional effect.

Tornado*

Mana Cost: 5

General Description: A whirlwind swirls around the target. The target spins, ends up facing a random direction, and suffers 25 points of electrical damage. If the target passes a magick resistance test, it suffers only 5 points of damage and will not spin.

Ball:	Targets all creatures in the target square.
Power × 2:	The target spins and suffers 50 points of damage, or 8 points of damage (and no spin) if it passes a magick resistance test.
Power × 3:	The target spins and suffers 100 points of damage, or only 10 points of damage (but with spin) if it passes a magick resistance test.
Duration:	No additional effect.
Potency:	Halves the magick resistance of the target.

Vampyre*

Mana Cost: 5

General Description: When you cast this rune, a blackness attacks the target, causing 10 points of damage. Meanwhile, Drake is healed, up to a maximum of 5 vitality points. If the target passes a magick

resistance test, however, then Drake suffers 10 points of damage, and the target heals, up to maximum of 5 vitality points.

Ball:	Affects all creatures in the target square, but the damage and healing is calculated on a case-by-case basis. For example, Drake could drain two targets, but lose health to a third target.
Power × 2:	The damage is 20, vitality restored is 10.
Power × 3:	The damage is 40, health restored is 15.
Duration:	No additional effect.
Potency:	Halves the target's magickal resistance.

Warming

Mana Cost: 2

General Description: If you cast this spell at a frozen target, the target unfreezes. If you cast Warming at other targets, they are immune to general cold for five minutes. During this time, the spell also halves damage the target suffers from cold attacks.

Ball:	Affects the entire party when cast in the mystic mirror, or unfreezes all targets in the target square.
Power × 2:	The target suffers only 25 percent damage from cold attacks.
Power × 3:	The target is immune to cold damage.
Duration:	The spell's effect lasts 15 minutes.
Potency:	No additional effect.

The Runecasters

Runes are swell, but they're pretty worthless without runecasters. There are five runecasters in the game, and some have special powers:

Runecaster	*Rune Slots*	*Mana Capacity*	*Special Powers*
Runewand	2	25	None
Runescepter	3	40	None
Throg caster	4	40	Throggish runes cost 2 Mana less
Elfwand	5	60	Lowers magick resistance by 10%
Silver runestaff	6	120	Lowers magick resistance by 20%

Orbs and Their Magick

Khull-khuum has imprisoned his nine brothers and sisters, the Youngest Gods, in magick orbs. Your job, as hero-in-training, is to collect these orbs. Each god has great magick, and so each infuses his orb with great magickal power. Guess what? You can harness this power.

In most cases, each orb has both a "passive" power and an "active" power.

Passive power is magick that kicks in the moment you grab the orb. You don't have to *do* anything. Place the orb in your inventory, and this passive power is always in effect. Active power is orb magick that must be "cast." You either click the orb on Drake (in the mystic mirror) or place it on the ground to activate the power within the orb.

Here is a list of the nine orbs with their passive and active powers:

Helion (Mercury)

Passive power: When this orb is in inventory, your party takes no more damage from the intense cold of the Ice Caverns on Level 9, nor from ice-based spells or effects.

Active power: Helion's Orb is also known as the Orb of Warming. When you place it on the ground, it glows red and casts a Ball-enhanced Power × 3 Warming rune. (The Ball meta rune spreads the spell's warming effect throughout the grid square, which includes your party.)

Aquila (Venus)

Passive power: This orb has no passive effect in your inventory.

Active power: Aquila's Orb is also known as the Orb of Healing. If you open the mystic mirror and click the orb on any party member, the entire party is fully healed—all afflictions are cured, and full vitality is restored. The orb works only twice per map level.

Thera (Earth)

This orb has no passive or active powers.

Azrael (Mars)

Passive power: When you place this orb in your inventory, you gain one star in Weapon Skill for any weapon currently in Drake's hands; also, the weapon's delay time is halved (to a minimum of 1).

Active power: If you open the mystic mirror and click this orb on Drake, you cast the equivalent of a Power × 3 Quickness rune on the entire party. This not only decreases the delay between your weapon thrusts, but also increases weapon accuracy by narrowing the hit zone radius. (See Hit Zone Radius in the foregoing section, "The *Stonekeep* Combat System.") The effect lasts 10 minutes, but you can do it only twice per map.

Marif (Jupiter)

Passive power: Marif's Orb is also known as the Orb of Strength. When you place it in your inventory scroll, it increases your Strength rating by two stars. Once you have Marif's Orb, enemies can no longer afflict you with weakness, nor can they cast a Stoptrack rune on you.

Active power: If you open the mystic mirror and click this orb on any member of your party, that character's Strength rating increases to its maximum of 10 stars for 10 minutes. Buffed! You can do this only twice per map, however.

Afri (Saturn)

Passive power: This orb has no passive power.

Active power: When you place this orb on the ground in front of you, it casts a magickal proximity map into the air. The map is an 11-by-11-square area with your current location in the center square; it reveals all corridors and monsters within that area.

Safrinni (Uranus)

Passive power: This orb functions as a perpetual Featherfall rune. When you place it in your inventory, your party is "lightened" and takes no more damage from falls into pits.

Active power: Safrinni's Orb is also known as the Orb of Levitation. If you stand at the bottom of a pit (with a hole in the ceiling above) and click this orb on Drake, the entire party rises to the top of the pit for a few seconds.

Yoth-soggoth (Neptune)

Passive power: With this orb in your inventory, the casting cost for all rune magick is halved, down to one rune. (You cannot halve a single Mana point.)

Active power: Click this orb on Drake in the mystic mirror to fully recharge all of your runecasters. You can use this power twice per map area.

Kor-soggoth (Pluto)

This orb has no active or passive game effect. It's only a plot element in the story, providing magick defense for your endgame confrontation with Khull-khuum.

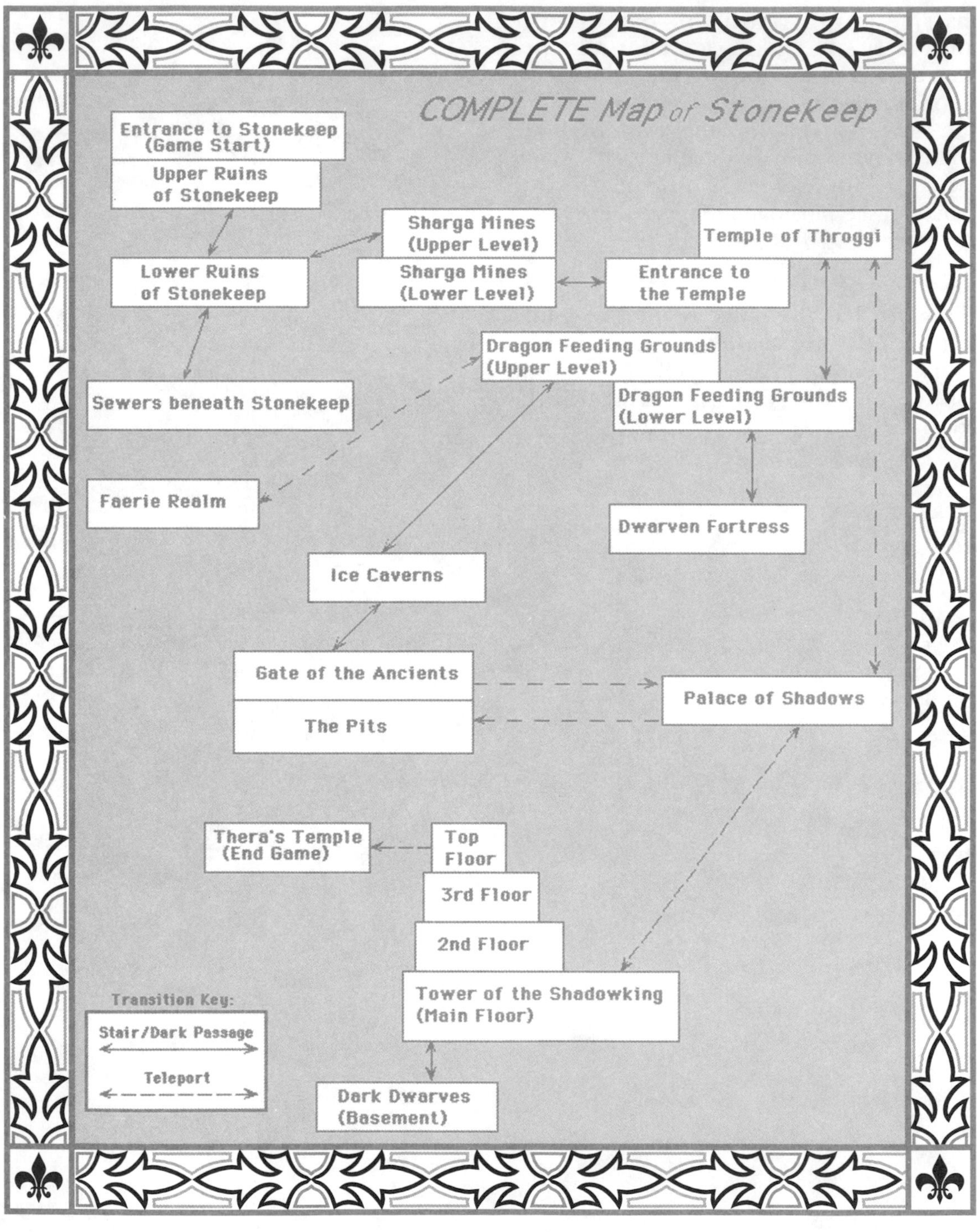
COMPLETE Map of Stonekeep
Entrance to Stonekeep (Game Start)
Upper Ruins of Stonekeep
Lower Ruins of Stonekeep
Sewers beneath Stonekeep
Sharga Mines (Upper Level)
Sharga Mines (Lower Level)
Temple of Throggi
Entrance to the Temple
Dragon Feeding Grounds (Upper Level)
Dragon Feeding Grounds (Lower Level)
Faerie Realm
Dwarven Fortress
Ice Caverns
Gate of the Ancients
The Pits
Palace of Shadows
Thera's Temple (End Game)
Top Floor
3rd Floor
2nd Floor
Tower of the Shadowking (Main Floor)
Dark Dwarves (Basement)
Transition Key:
Stair/Dark Passage
Teleport

Part III

The Walkthrough/ Level Solutions

Level 1

Upper Ruins of Stonekeep

This first level of *Stonekeep* includes two map areas: the Entrance (Map 1.1) and the Upper Ruins (Map 1.2). The following solution path leads you back and forth between the two areas. Along the way, you must fend off roving warrior ants and Sharga guards.

Puzzles and combat are straightforward. You won't need many tips or hints here. The designers want you to get comfortable with the game's interface as you find your bearings in this strange underground world.

Key to Maps 1.1 & 1.2

1. Start (Thera), rubble (root)
2. Chest (scroll, dagger, potion, roots), leather breastplate
3. Passage to Upper Ruins (pull handle)
4. Hidden brick (lever)
5. Hidden brick (dagger of penetration), oil bombs
6. Shadowking
7. Sharga (root, coin, brass key)
8. Barrels (wooden shield)
9. Barrels (ants, roots)
10. Barrel (roots)
11. Passage to Entrance
12. Alcove (roots)
13. Sharga, hidden brick (root), journal
14. Shargas (roots)
15. Hidden brick (root)
16. Hidden brick (lever to 17)
17. Potions, oil bomb
18. Campfire (firedaggers), Sharga, chest (potions)
19. Shargas (roots)
20. Barrels (Sharga, hammer)
21. Hidden brick (potion)
22. Sacks of grain, ants (bronze key)
23. Mess Hall
24. Shargas (roots, steel key, Orb of Afri), scroll
25. Hidden brick (lever to 26)
26. Oil bombs, chest (potions)
27. Sharga (roots)
28. Arrow trap (arrows)
29. Button (to 28), Shargas (roots), hidden brick (potion), scrolls
30. Locked door—use bronze key
31. Hidden brick (potion)
32. Rubble (root, coin)
33. Ants, arrows, quarterstaff
34. Forge, helm, axe, dagger, handle (activates forge)
35. Brick (root), chest (metal shield)—use steel key
36. Barrels (oil bombs)
37. Hidden brick (root)
38. Root
39. Passage to Entrance
40. Ant nest, barrel (roots), bronze key
41. Ants
42. Ants, hidden brick (switch to 43)
43. Chest (oil bombs)—use bronze key
44. Passage to Upper Ruins
45. Passage to Upper Ruins
46. Passage to Lower Ruins—use steel key
47. Rubble (broken sword)
48. Shargas (roots, brass key)
49. Rubble (arrow), hidden brick (root)
50. Root
51. Passage to Entrance
52. Shargas (roots)
53. Sharga (root), chest (oil bombs)—use brass key
54. Fountain of healing
55. Sharga
56. Hidden brick (root)
57. Stone bag
58. Leather leggings
59. Hidden brick (lever to 60)
60. Chest (potion, broadsword)
61. Root, rubble (root), ant
62. Passage to Lower Ruins

Map 1.1 Entrance to Stonekeep

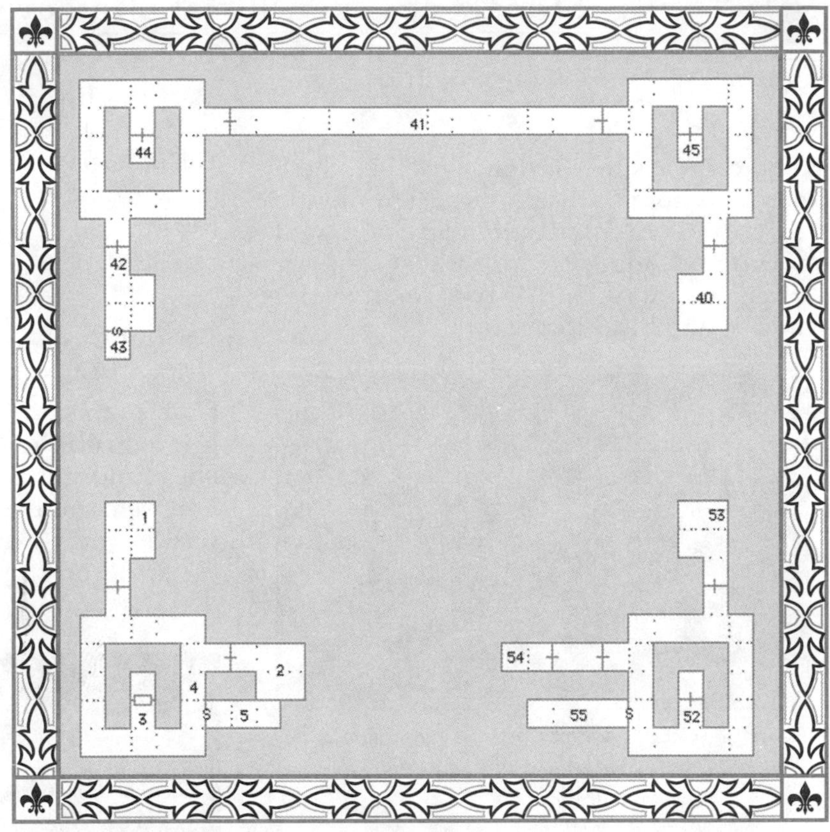

Map 1.2 Upper Ruins of Stonekeep

Door
Locked Door
Secret Door
BR = Brass Key Unlocks
BZ = Bronze Key Unlocks
ST = Steel Key Unlocks

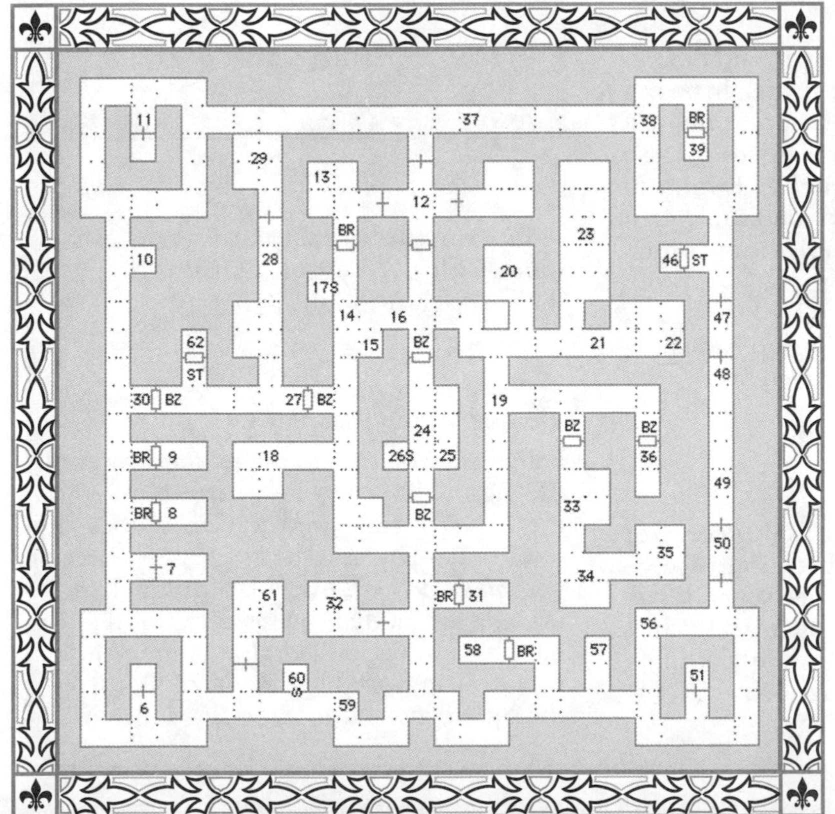

1. Start

Thera speaks to you, saying: "Take these artifacts to aid your quest. The mystic Mirror of Afri will aid your personal vision and Aquila's Scroll will store whatever you may find." You receive the mirror and inventory scroll.

Thera She Goes! The Earth Goddess leads you to the stairway. Don't follow her down the stairs until after you've explored the entire area.

You'll find a ***skull*** on the ground next to some ***bones***. Collect skulls as throwing objects. You can punch at bone piles just to see them disintegrate. This room also contains two piles of ***rubble***. Punch at them to reveal a ***stone*** and a ***heal root***. Exit the room through the only door, which leads into a corridor.

Tip Stones and skulls are everywhere. Gather them up. You never know when you might want to fling something heavy at someone annoying.

A single ***worker ant*** patrols this corridor in a counter-clockwise direction. A couple of good punches can destroy it, if you feel so inclined. However, worker ants won't bother you unless you attack them first, so you can simply ignore this one.

Take the first left and go east to the end of the hall. Read the plaque on the wall: *Guard Room.*

Go right and enter the first door on the left.

2. Guard Room

Grab the ***leather breastplate*** from the first pile of rubble on the right. Open the chest and get the ***scroll***, ***heal potion***, five ***heal roots***, and the ***simple dagger***. To read the scroll, open your inventory, then click the scroll on Drake in your mystic mirror.

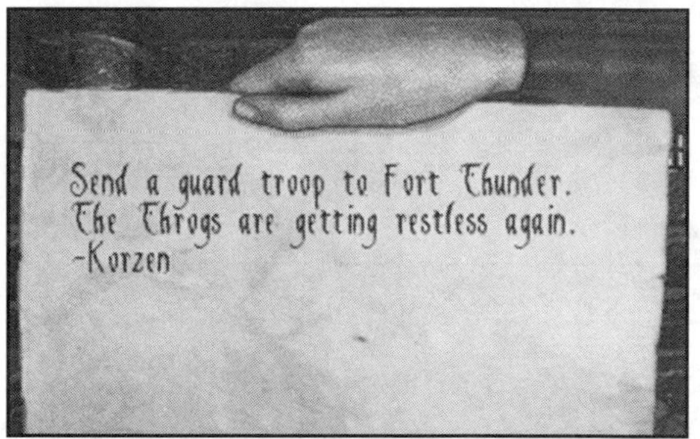

Korzen's Scroll.

Put on the breastplate. Arm either hand with the dagger. Exit the room. In the corridor, turn left.

3. Exit Door

Follow the corridor to the next doorway on the right. (Thera is hovering there.) Flip the ***handle*** on the west wall to unlock the door, but—pay attention, please—*don't go through the door yet!* Instead, push the handle back up again, then pull it back down. The handle you just pulled also triggers access to a very important ***secret lever***. Return to the square just south of the last doorway.

Not Just a Lock. Yes, this handle unlocks the stairwell entry door. But it also triggers access to a most handy weapon.

4. Secret Lever and Door

Find the ***hidden brick*** on the west wall and move it. Pull down the ***secret lever*** behind it to open a ***secret door*** on the east wall.

Caution If you go down the stairs to the Upper Ruins without pulling this secret lever, you lose access to the lever later! This lever also opens another secret door in another portion of the Entrance. (See 55, below.)

Trick Brick. Stonekeep abounds with hidden compartments behind bricks in its seemingly solid walls. This particular lever activates a secret door to a super-secret room.

5. "Yes!"

Go through the secret door you just opened. Grab the three ***oil bombs.*** Move the ***hidden brick*** on the north wall and take the ***Dagger of Penetration.*** You'll also find a ***stone*** in that ***rubble*** on the ground.

Return to the exit doorway at 3. Open the door and follow Thera downstairs.

Note The dagger is a *powerful* weapon. But, if you use it too much, you won't develop the stats and skills you need in later stages of the game.

6. The Shadowking

You automatically follow Thera to a meeting with the Shadowking, who quickly casts a spell to paralyze you. The following dialogue ensues:

Shadowking: Lost one, is this the best you can do? This mortal is not worth my time.

Thera: Khull-Khuum, do not gloat so soon. My champion will defeat you.

Shadowking: Your imprisonment is the start. You have escaped me once. You shall not escape me again. I have you now and I will find the rest. Now, back to your cell!

Thera's Orb appears floating beside him in midair.

Shadowking: You are foolish to put your trust into this one, Thera. I will show you that you should not believe in your foolish mortals. Begone!

The orb disappears.

Shadowking: Mortal, know that your soul is still your own by my whim. The tides of destiny will not save you at the appointed time. Know that we shall meet again. Tread lightly until then, for my wrath is legion.

After the Shadowking disappears, step into the corridor and turn right, then follow the corridor around and take the first left turn. (Remember, you can ignore the wandering ***worker ant***) Go to the first door in the hall; it's on the right-hand side.

7. Guard Room

A ***Sharga*** awaits you. Slay him, then take his ***sword***, ***heal root***, ***gold coin***, and ***brass key***. The root is a healing herb, and adds points to Drake's vitality meter if you have him consume it. Exit and go north to the next room.

Fun with Shargas. These green guys look and sound pathetic, but don't underestimate their hostility.

8. Barrel Shield

Use the brass key on the ***lock*** on the south wall. (Don't forget to return the key to inventory—you'll need it again.) Enter the room. Smash the barrels, then grab the ***small wooden shield***. Exit and go north to the next room.

Keys to Success. You can't get anywhere in Stonekeep without special door-unlocking devices (cleverly labeled "keys" by the designers).

9. Ants and Roots

This room is locked, too. Again, use the brass key in the lock. Enter the room. Prepare for combat: When you smash the left barrel, two ***warrior ants*** emerge from a hole in the wall. You'll find two ***heal roots*** in the barrel on the right. Exit the room.

The next door to the north is locked from the other side, so continue north to the alcove on the east wall.

10. Alcove

Break open the intact ***barrel*** to get three ***heal roots***. Continue north up the hall to the intersection. Beware: Two ***ants*** patrol here—one a harmless worker, the other a

belligerent warrior. Follow the corridor to the left. You'll see that it forms a 5-by-5 square around a central passage.

11. Jammed Door (Passage to Entrance)

This door won't budge from this side, but you can push it open later when you come down the stairs from the other side. For the record, it leads up to Stonekeep's northwest Entrance area, but you must reach that area another way.

Continue past the door until you reach the first passage on the left. Go 9E. (Beware: Three ***warrior ants*** patrol this passage.) Turn south and go through the door.

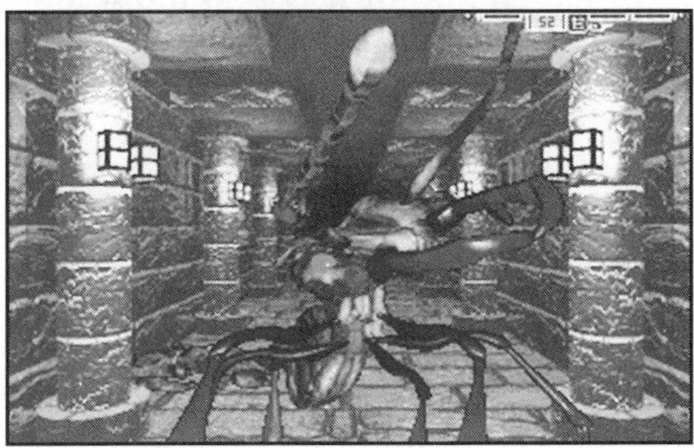

Ant! Warrior ants aren't shy, are they?

12. Central Alcove

This alcove features doors in all four directions. Grab the two ***heal roots*** from the floor. The south door is permanently locked from both sides. The east door leads to a room containing nothing of interest, except a ***skull***.

13. Guard Room

Behind the west door, however, a tough little ***Sharga*** waits. As soon as the player enters this room, the Sharga howls, "*Grrr!* This *my* home! Monster, you leave!" Then it attacks.

Once this Sharga sustains a certain amount of damage, it will flee to the north wall and try to move a ***hidden brick***. The secret compartment behind the brick contains a ***super heal root*** worth many vitality points.

Tip

Don't let the Sharga reach the super heal root! When the Sharga attacks, run *past* it to the hidden brick on the north wall, then turn and fight. This prevents the Sharga from retrieving the root.

Eyes On the Prize. Be sure to grab that book on the table. Your journal holds your maps, runes, notes, and keeps track of found items and your personal statistics.

This room contains a very important item—an enchanted ***journal***. Grab it from the table, then use the brass key from inventory to unlock the south door. Exit to the south.

14. Sharga Ambush

Get ready—stepping into this square provokes some serious combat. Squads of ***Shargas*** patrol this corridor. First, a group of three attacks.

Tip Hustle east four or five squares, then turn to face the Sharga squad. They'll stop. Now creep forward. One Sharga always precedes the others. You can nail this lead Sharga with a blow or two, then hop back to safety.

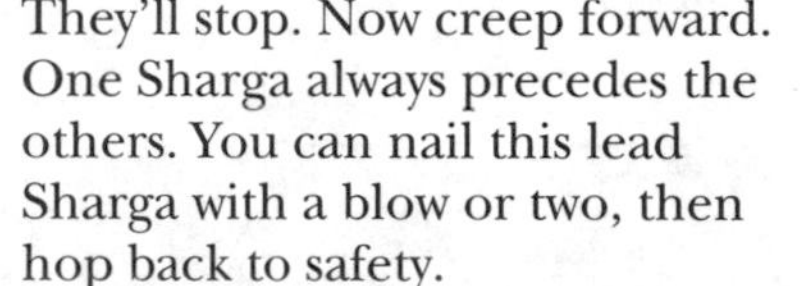

If you survive, remember to plunder their remains for ***heal roots***. Now return west to the corridor. Two more ***Shargas*** roam the hallway.

Tip If you retreat north to the door (the one leading to the journal room), you can separate the pair—one Sharga returns to its post. Dispatch the one who remains, then go after the one who fled.

After each battle remember to search the corpses for ***heal roots***.

15. Hidden Brick 1

Search the south wall here for a ***hidden brick***. Move it to get the ***heal root*** stashed behind it.

16. Hidden Brick 2

Just around the corner you'll find another ***hidden brick*** on the south wall. Behind it is a ***secret lever***. When you pull this lever you hear a grinding noise. Drake says: "That sounds like it came from right around the corner." Son of a gun—he's right! Go 2W, N, then turn to face west.

17. Secret Potion Room

Inside this secret room you'll find three ***potions***—a blue ***heal potion***, a light-green ***agility gain potion***, and a ***cure potion*** (called "smelly throggish brew" in your journal); and an ***oil bomb***. Continue south past the locked door on the right (you don't have a key for it yet) to the second right turn. You'll hear fire crackling; go west toward the campfire.

18. Sharga Camp

There's a ***campfire*** here. If you search it once, you'll take up to five points of fire damage and say: "Ow!" but you'll end up with a magickal ***firedagger***. Search the fire again ("Ow!") for a second ***firedagger***.

Tip If you've previously found any bottled potion, you can use it to put out the campfire and avoid fire damage. (The potion will be destroyed, however.)

If you walk over the campfire, you'll sustain some fire damage. But it's worth it: In the corner of the room you'll find a ***chest***, guarded by another ***Sharga***. Once

Fire Hurts. So it's frequently a good idea to extinguish a roaring campfire before walking through it. Potions work nicely.

you cross the fire, the guard attacks. Finish the battle and open the chest to get two bottles—an ***agility gain potion*** and a ***strength gain potion*** (called a "decanter with a green brew" in your journal).

Tip *Alternative Solution to 18:* Instead of grabbing the firedaggers right away, you could cross the fire first, kill the Sharga, remove the potion bottles from the chest and use one to put out the fire. This way you can grab the firedaggers, pass through the fire again, and leave the room without sustaining more fire damage. However, you'll lose the potion.

Exit the room. Turn right at the corridor. Go 3S, 6E, then head north.

19. Shargas

Two ***Shargas*** lurk in this hallway. After you dispatch and loot them for ***heal roots***, continue north to the end of the hall. Go east one square, then turn north and enter the Ale Room.

20. Ale Room

Against the north wall of this room you'll see four barrels. In them, from right to left, you'll find:

- Nothing.
- Nothing.
- A drunk (and harmless) ***Sharga.***
- A ***standard hammer*** (on the floor behind barrel).

Exit the Ale Room and go east into the Kitchen area.

21. Hidden Bonus

A ***hidden brick*** on the north wall hides a fat blue bottle of ***health potion.*** Continue east into the Kitchen.

22. Kitchen (Sacks of Grain)

This square contains two ***sacks of grain.*** As you approach them, Drake says, "Elizabeth served many home-cooked meals in this kitchen." If either sack is destroyed, two ***warrior ants*** attack from the hole in the east wall. When one dies, another emerges from the hole to take its place, up to a total of six ants. The last ant carries a ***bronze key.***

Tip The ants won't go past the end of the Kitchen entryway at 21. Hustle out of the Kitchen, then turn to face the ants. Leap in and out, picking them off one at a time.

23. Mess Hall

Nothing here but broken plates, tables, chairs, and a couple of skulls. Exit and head west.

Tip This next battle is very tough. If your vitality is critically low, you might want to check out step 54 next.

24. Sharga Leaders

The bronze key will unlock both doors to this room. In this walkthrough, you enter from the north. Two ***Sharga Leaders*** await you. *Save your game here!*

Tip Sharga leaders are *much* tougher than ordinary Shargas. They're virtually impervious to your standard Sharga-issue sword. You can go to the Armory at 36 to get ***oil bombs.*** Note: The Sharga Leaders do not leave this room.

If you approach them, the Shargas speak:

Sharga (Shax): *Grrr!* You not welcome here! Gr'thic stop you now.

Sharga (Gr'thic): *Grrr!* Gr'thic not want to stop monster. Gr'thic think Shax stop monster.

Shax: Gr'thic and Shax get the monster!

Drake: I don't think that we're going to be friends!

Tip "Smart" Shargas know that quick healing is the key to effective combat. These Shargas carry heal roots and potions and consume them at appropriate times to ensure their survival. Kill them quickly, or they leave little behind for *you.*

Each Sharga has two ***heal roots***, which they will use when they get low on health (below 50 percent). One of them holds the ***Orb of Afri***, the other a ***steel key***. When you pick up the orb, Drake says: "This is intriguing. It looks similar to the orb that Khull-Khuum used to trap Thera. I wonder if another of the lost gods is trapped in here? I should examine this orb closely."

Meet Shax and Gr'thic. Yeah, they're stupid, but they're tough. Very tough.

Tip  The Orb of Afri is the first of the nine receptacles you must retrieve in the game. Follow Drake's suggestion to "examine this orb closely" by putting it on the ground. When you do so, it casts a proximity map into the air. Use the map at any time to scan the immediate area and locate all living monsters!

Orb of Afri. Once you get the orb, put it on the ground and watch the show.

Take the ***scroll*** from the bookcase. It reads:

Councilmembers, the enchantment on the silver dragon statuette has been finished, as per your instructions. Passageway to the Dwarven Realms has been secured.

— *Mage Icarius*

Open the ***hidden brick*** on the west wall to get a ***super heal root.***

25. Hidden Brick

In the same room, move the ***hidden brick*** on the south wall and pull the ***lever***. A ***secret room*** is revealed to your right.

26. What a Chest!

Grab the three ***oil bombs*** on the floor of the secret room. Next, open the ***chest*** and grab the three ***bottles***—a ***heal potion***, an ***agility gain potion***, and a ***strength gain potion***. Exit through the room's north door and follow the corridor around to the left. Stop at the first door on the right.

27. Bronze Door

Use the bronze key to unlock the door, then enter. Slay the ***Sharga***, grab his ***heal roots*** (if any), and head north up the first corridor on the right. Grab the ***dagger*** along the way. Stop before you get to the dead Sharga lying on the floor!

28. Arrow Trap

The west wall harbors six ***arrow holes***. If the trap is set, you will trigger two **arrows** when you walk into this square.

Trip the mechanism by throwing an item (rock, skull, or the like) into the square. Remember to do this *three times* to trigger all three pairs of arrows. Now the trap is out of ammunition. You may proceed safely. (Remember to grab the arrows that land on the ground.)

Proceed north through the door.

Arrow Trap. That dead Sharga is a pretty good clue that something's amiss. Better let other dead guys pave the way—i.e., toss some skulls.

29. Captain's Quarters

A ***Sharga*** stands with its back to you. Don't be suckered. When you step forward to assault this apparently easy prey, two ***Shargas*** jump you from the left. After you fend them off, grab their ***heal roots.***

Move a ***hidden brick*** in the east wall to find a blue ***heal potion***. Take the three ***scrolls*** from the bookcase in the corner and read them.

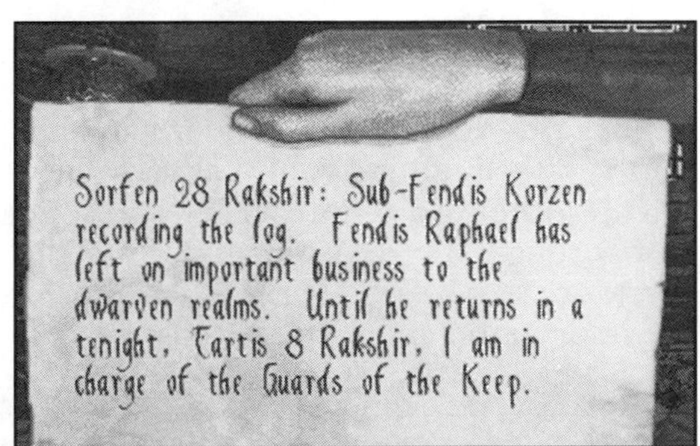

Sorfen 28 Rakshir: Sub-Fendis Korzen recording the log. Fendis Raphael has left on important business to the dwarven realms. Until he returns in a tenight, Eartis 8 Rakshir, I am in charge of the Guards of the Keep.

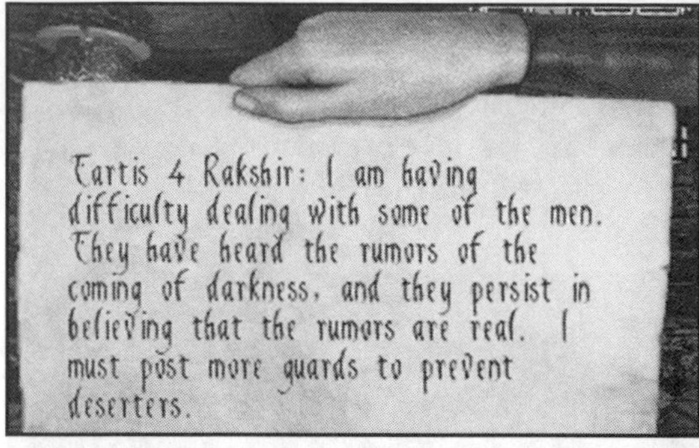

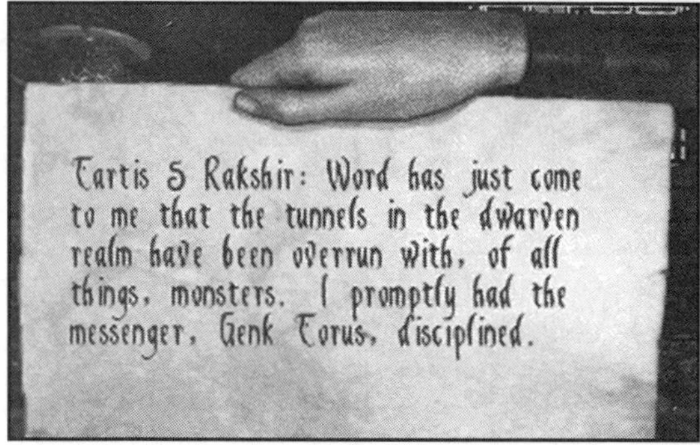

Captain's Scrolls

Push the ***button*** on the west wall, near the entrance, to deactivate the arrow trap back at 28. If you've already triggered and gathered all six arrows, never mind.

Exit the room. Go south to the wall and turn right. Head due west to the locked door.

30. Door for Later

Unlock this door with the bronze key, but don't go through it—you've already been on the other side. Spin around and go east through the doorway at 27 into the corridor. Now go 5S, 3E, 2S, then unlock the door to the east with the brass key.

31. Hidden Brick

There's nothing in the ***barrel*** here. But if you move a ***brick*** on the south wall, you reveal a hidden compartment containing a blue ***heal potion***. Exit and try the room across the hall.

32. Simple Treats

Punch at the rubble to find a ***heal root*** and a ***gold coin***. Exit to the corridor and go 3N, 3E, 5N, 3E, then turn south to face the door.

33. Armory

The bronze key opens this door. Hear those clicking footsteps on the other side? Enter and prepare to face lots of ***ants***—eight in all, though only a few are the warrior variety. This room is made up of three 2-by-2 areas. The first area contains a couple of ***arrows*** and a ***quarterstaff***. Here, Drake says, "This was the armory. I should scavenge what I can." On your way south to the next room, you'll find two more ***arrows***.

34. Forge Ahead

Keep on the lookout for more ants. Grab the ***helm*** near the forge. Punch the rubble next to the forge to uncover a sweet little ***throwing axe***. The ***handle*** on the east wall turns the forge *on* and *off*. Proceed east into the last 2-by-2 room. On the way, get another ***arrow*** and ***dagger*** on the floor.

35. Armory Chest

Open the ***hidden brick*** on the west wall and take the ***heal root.*** Use the steel key to open the ***chest.*** Take the ***small metal shield*** and use it to replace your wooden one. Now exit the Armory and go east to the last room in this area. On the way, note the wall sign: *Beware! Dangerous Materials.*

One for the Defense. Snatch the metal shield from this chest.

36. Armory Storeroom

Unlock the door with the bronze key and enter the room. Smash the ***barrels***—the first two contain nothing, but the third contains three "oil-filled containers" (better known as ***oil bombs***). Exit to the corridor.

Work your way back to the central alcove (12) and into the northernmost passage. Take two steps east down the long corridor, keeping a sharp eye out for patrolling ***ants.***

37. Root Canal

Check the north wall here for a ***hidden brick.*** Behind it, you'll find a ***heal root.***

38. Northeast Corner

Take the ***heal root*** from the floor, then turn left and continue around the northeast corner of the Upper Ruins.

39. Passage to Entrance NE

The first door on the right is locked; unlock it with a brass key. Climb the stairs to the northeast corner of Stonekeep's Entrance. Two roving ***warrior ants*** patrol this area. Knife them dead, then turn right and follow the corridor around to the first door on the left.

40. Ant Attack!

Enter the room and smash the ***barrel.*** A ***warrior ant*** quickly emerges to attack from a hole in the west wall. After you kill it, grab the two ***heal roots*** that were in the barrel you smashed. You can also nab the ***bronze key*** nearby. Be quick, though—a new ***warrior ant*** will come out of the hole after a couple of seconds. Kill it, if you want, but know that you've tapped an ant nest. (In fact, a total of 50 warrior ants dwell here!)

Tip Battle ants for a few minutes here. If you plant yourself in front of the ant hole and hack away, you can build strength and skill with various weapons. (Don't take too much damage. Keep an eye on your health points.)

41. Northwest Passage

After you exit the room, turn left and follow the corridor around to the next door on the left. This leads to a long, ant-filled passageway that runs to the northwest area of Stonekeep's Entrance. (Only one of the four ants is a ***warrior ant***;; the other three are harmless ***worker ants***.)

When you reach the end of the passage, go through the door to the intersection. Turn left. Follow the corridor. More ***ants*** patrol—two warriors and a worker. Continue to the first door.

42. Switch

A pair of ***warrior ants*** await you. Just inside the door, on the east wall, you'll find a ***hidden brick***. Move it and flip the ***switch*** behind. You'll hear a door slide open. Turn right and enter the secret room.

43. Secret Room

Use the bronze key to unlock the ***chest***. Retrieve the three ***oil bombs*** within. Exit the room.

Tip Oil bombs make lethal throwing weapons against ants and Shargas, but you're better off saving them. They're much more useful on Level 2.

44 and 45. Passages to Upper Ruins

Return to the Upper Ruins via stairway 44 or 45. Go to the north-east corner, then head south to the first door on the right.

46. Passage to Lower Ruins

Use the steel key to unlock this door. Don't take this stairway yet, though. It leads to the Lower Ruins, but you still have business to transact up here. Continue south down the corridor.

47. Chamber

Go through the door. In the small chamber between the two doors, punch the ***rubble*** to find a ***broken sword***. Continue south through the next door.

48. Key Shargas

Two ***Shargas*** guard the southern passage. Kill them and loot for ***heal roots*** (two apiece) and a ***brass key***. Continue south down the hall.

49. Hidden Arrow

An ***arrow*** lies buried in the ***rubble*** pile here. You'll also find a ***heal root*** behind a ***hidden brick*** on the west wall. Continue south through the door.

50. Heal Root

There's a nice, juicy ***heal root*** on the ground here. Again, continue south through the door. Beware of patrolling ***warrior ants.*** Turn left and follow the corridor around to the first door on the right.

51. Passage to Entrance SE

This door leads up to the southeastern area of Stonekeep's Entrance. Open it and climb the stairs.

52. Sharga Guards

Three ***Shargas*** attack, one at a time, when you exit the stairwell. Slay them and take any ***heal roots.*** Go east down the corridor and follow it around to the first door on the right.

53. Chest Bombs

A lone ***Sharga*** awaits you. Dispatch the little fellow, take his ***heal root***, then open the ***chest*** with the brass key and remove the two ***oil bombs.*** Exit the room, turn right, then follow the corridor to the next room.

54. Fountain of Thera

Here it is—through a pair of doors, a ***fountain of healing!*** Drink as much as you want—each gulp provides you vitality points, going only as far as your current upper limit. Exit and go south to the next room.

55. He's Giant, He's Green, But He Ain't Too Jolly!

Nor is this ***Sharga*** particularly tough. Just wade in and spill some green gore.

The Bigger They Are . . . This big guy went down awfully quick, didn't he?

Note You'll find that this secret room is permanently sealed shut if you didn't find and manipulate the secret lever back at 4.

Return to the stairwell at 52, descend the stairs, then step out into the corridor in the Upper Ruins. Go 2W, then north to the wall.

56. Hidden Root

Find the ***hidden brick*** in the north wall. Move it and take the ***heal root*** stashed behind. Retreat south, and turn right at the first hall.

57. Bag of Stones

A ***bag*** on the ground here contains three ***stones***. When you pick it up, Drake says, "This bag will hold my throwing stones rather well." Place the bag over the other stones you've stashed in inventory to automatically bag them all. Go back out to the corridor, then go 2W, 2N, then west to the door.

58. Biker Pants

Unlock the door with the brass key and enter the room. Take the ***leather leggings*** and put them on Drake. Exit the room, follow the short passage back to the main corridor, then turn right. Work your way west—the corridor zigzags back and forth for a dozen or so squares.

59. Hidden Switch

Move the ***hidden brick*** in the north wall. (A couple of ***worker ants*** may hang out and watch, but as usual, they won't bother you unless you attack first.) Pull the ***lever*** to open a secret room just up the hallway.

60. Secret Room

Enter and open the ***chest***. Grab the ***heal potion*** and the ***broadsword***, then exit. Continue west and enter the next room on the right.

61. Ant Hole

You'll find two ***heal roots*** in here—one on floor, another hidden in the ***rubble***. When you punch the rubble a couple of times, though, a ***warrior ant*** attacks from the hole in the wall. Exit to the corridor.

Time to leave this level behind. Go 2W, 3N, 3W, 8N, then through the door to the east. You should have unlocked this door earlier from the other side with a bronze key. (See 30.)

62. Passage to Lower Ruins

Unlock the first door on the left with your steel key. Descend the stairs to the Lower Ruins of Stonekeep.

Level 2

Lower Ruins of Stonekeep

This second level of Stonekeep includes just one map area—the Lower Ruins. Tougher, more competent Shargas dwell here, and you'll also face a pair of new enemies—snakes and slime. The puzzles and traps are slightly more complex, as well. In fact, one pair of devices can only be used with items that are found exclusively on the *next level.*

This level introduces your first companion. You'll have to liberate the fellow, but it isn't a difficult task. Once he joins your party, the NPC (that's "non-player character," for you novices) greatly increases your combat strength. (After all, two axes are better than one. . .)

Note The walkthrough sequence for Level 2 assumes you followed this book's walkthrough for Level 1. If that's the case, you, descended to the Lower Ruins from the stairway located at 62 on Map 1.2, Upper Ruins.

If you came down the other stairway (46 on Map 1.2), you can still use this walkthrough, though not in the sequence outlined here. The numbers on Map 2 refer to descriptions of each encounter numbered in the Level 2 walkthrough.

Key to Map 2

1. Start
2. Wahooka
3. Slime
4. Slime (gem), leather leggings, dart
5. Hidden brick (root)
6. Illusory wall, Sharga (roots, potion)
7. Shargas, rubble (darts)
8. Shargas (roots), hidden brick (gem), rubble (root)
9. Shargas
10. Hidden brick (potion)
11. Snakes, rubble (gem—triggers more snakes)
12. Slime, ivory key, grain sack (gem)
13. Farli Mallestone (Dwarven sword)
14. Barrels (potion)
15. Slime, barrels (axe, firedagger)
16. Illusory door, Shargas (potions), iron key
17. Fountain of healing
18. Cylinder switch
19. Cylinder switch, chest (leggings)
20. Sharga (roots)
21. Slimes, hidden brick (lever to 22)
22. Chest (gems, potions)
23. Slime
24. Snakes, wineskin, rubble (gem), potion
25. Hidden brick (rune scroll)
26. Gem
27. Sharga (roots)
28. Slimes, scroll
29. Scroll, chest (key ring, potion)
30. Wall button (seals 31)
31. Pit, hidden brick (lever to 32)
32. Pit ladder, exit button (at top)
33. Sharga (roots)
34. Wall button (to door across hall)
35. Slimes, root, chest (potions)
36. Slime, scroll, potions
37. Sharga, lock (to 38)—use ivory key
38. Secret corridor (use 37)

39A-D. Arrow traps (arrows)

40. Slimes, runewand, scrolls (two runes)
41. Mana Circle, chest (potions)
42. Shargas (roots, oil bomb)
43. Illusory wall
44. Shargas
45. Passage to Sewers
46. Sharga trap, chest (chain mail shirt, potions)
47. Snakes, root, rubble (snake hole)
48. Slime (gem), dart, rubble (gem)
49. Wahooka
50. Snake, root, dart, hidden brick (gem)
51. Passage to Upper Ruins
52. Wahooka
53. Passage to Sewers
54. Passage to Sewers
55. Locked door (only Farli can unlock)
56. Marble dais (opens 57)
57. Passage to Sharga Mines

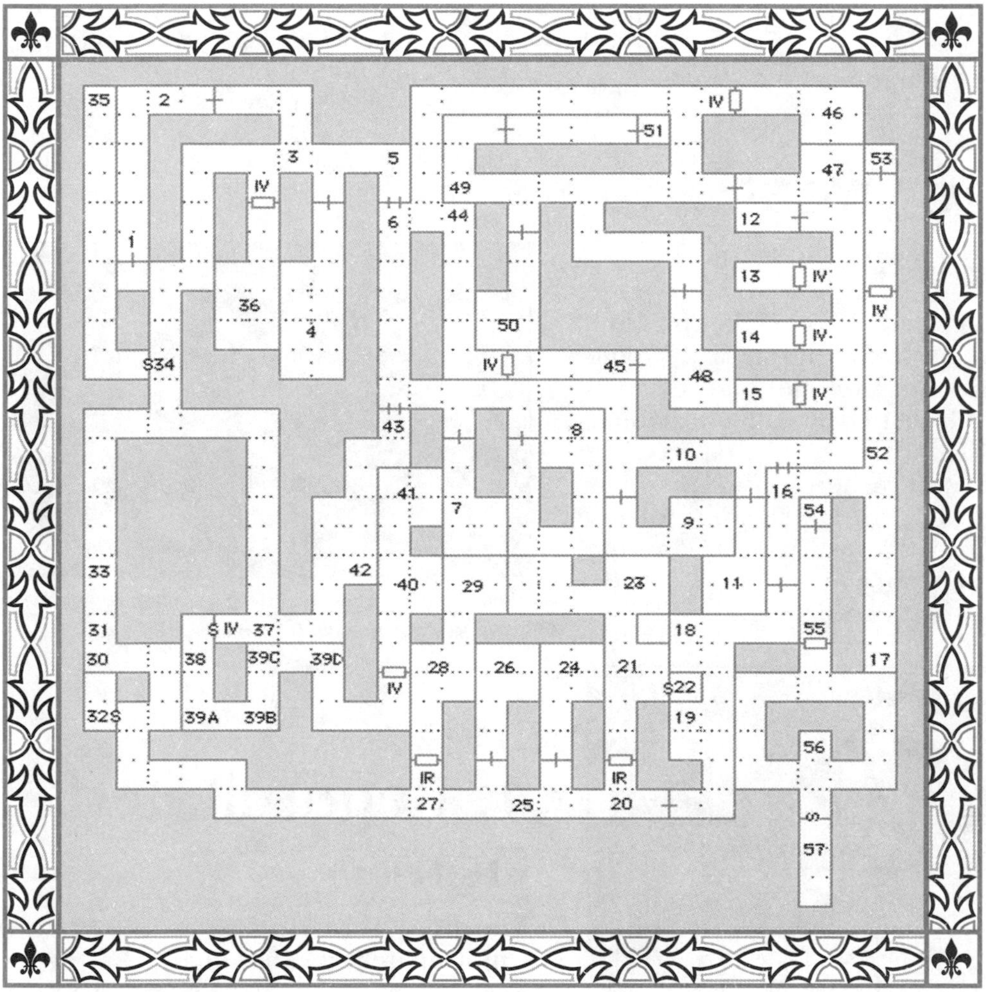

Map 2 Lower Ruins of Stonekeep

▯	Locked Door
┼	Door
$	Secret Door
ǂ	Illusionary Wall

IR = Iron Key Unlocks
IV = Ivory Key Unlocks

1. Start

This stairway comes down from the Upper Ruins (62 on Map 1.2, Upper Ruins). Go straight ahead to the end of the passage, then turn right.

2. The Great Wahooka

Meet Wahooka. If you keep your distance, he beckons you forward: "Come closer . . ., closer. I will not bite you." Go ahead—you have to deal with him sooner or later. Take note of his parting comment: "Return here with a precious offering and I will share some of my infinite knowledge with you." Continue through the doors to the next corner, turn right, and proceed south.

The Great Wahooka. Or, if you prefer, Wahooka the Great. Can you trust this guy?

3. Slime!

A ***slime*** patrols this corridor. If you get too close, it will attack; otherwise, it just slimes around, ignoring you.

Tip Slimes are fairly resistant to normal weaponry. Sharp weapons cause minimal damage, blunt weapons not much more. But a fire attack—oil bombs, firedaggers, magickal weapons or fire-related rune magick—increases the damage.

Turn east, then enter the first room on the right.

Slime. Or, if you prefer, slime! These overgrown Jell-O molds hate fire. Keep that in mind.

4. Regurgitated Gem

Another disgusting ***slime*** awaits you. Unfortunately, if it has ingested the ***green gem***, you must kill it. You'll also find a pair of ***leather leggings*** and a ***throwing dart*** in this room.

Take the green gem to Wahooka back at 2. The goofy little goblin teleports in and gestures greedily for loot. Don't waste time—give him the green gem right away. Wahooka only waits about 10 seconds before huffing off.

Caution If you attack Wahooka, he won't reappear for the rest of the level.

After you give him the precious item, Wahooka says: "Watch out for traps! The Shamans of the Throgs set many of them around here, hoping to stick a couple of Dwarves." Step back through the door, then go 3E, 2S, then 3E.

Tip Wahooka has only three clues for you. Give him *one gem* the first time, *two gems* the second time, and *three gems* the third time. After that, he'll just pocket any additional gems and stiff you on the clue.

5. Root Stash

The north wall here contains a ***hidden brick***. Move it to get a tasty and oh-so-expeditious ***super heal root***. Spin around and face the opposite wall.

6. Fake Wall

Run right into the bricks—it's an ***illusory wall***! You can pass right through it! A smart ***Sharga*** carrying two ***heal roots*** and a ***heal potion*** challenges you. After you terminate his pitiful existence, plunder whatever it leaves behind.

Go south to the wall, turn east, then enter the first door on your right.

7. Sharga Lounge

A pair of ***Sharga*** regulars (read: "stupid" Shargas) waits for you on the other side of the door. Two more ***Shargas*** lurk just around the corner to the left. Once victory is secured, punch through the ***rubble*** pile in the far corner for your reward—two ***throwing darts***. Exit and go into the next room to the east.

8. Sneak Attack

Follow the entry hall all the way around to the main part of the room. When you step into the northwest corner of this 2-by-2 area, three ***Shargas*** jump you from behind. Search their cowardly corpses for ***heal roots***. (They have one apiece.)

A ***hidden brick*** on the north wall conceals a ***red gem***, and you'll find another ***heal root*** in the rubble pile. Exit the room and continue around the corner to the east. Go through the door that lies ahead.

Tip Unless you're keen on combat, skip room 9 until later, when you have more health or more "help" (i.e., an NPC companion).

9. Waste of Time?

A couple of ***Shargas*** want to make your exploration unpleasant. They're not tough, but you won't find anything worthwhile stashed in this room. Exit into the corridor and go east a couple of steps.

10. Hidden Treasure

You'll find a fat ***heal potion*** concealed behind a ***hidden brick*** on the south wall here. Continue east to the next room on the right.

11. Hissing Treasure

Two snakes greet you. Their bite wounds hurt, but they also leave a lingering legacy—poisonous venom. Skewer them, then punch at the rubble pile in the room. Two more snakes emerge from a hidden hole. (In this room, snakes emerge in pairs with every five steps you take.) Fortunately, this combat is worth it—under the rubble lies a red gem.

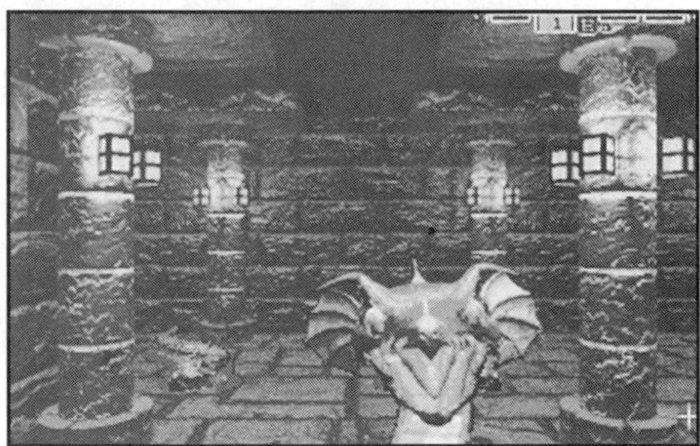

Snakes! Big ones, too!

Tip If you missed the dagger of penetration back on Level 1, and I sure hope you didn't, use an axe against snakes at close quarters. The accurate toss of a throwing axe considerably weakens an approaching snake.

Now you can return to Wahooka at 2 with the two gems. The quickest route back is via the illusory door at 6. When you give Wahooka one gem, he says, "*More!* You must give me *more!*" Fortunately, you have more. Give him another gem, and he'll give you the second clue: "Search the sewers below for the key to the Underlands."

Return to the corridor outside the room where you just fought the snakes (11). Continue east to the corner, then turn north; a series of four rooms leads west off the corridor. The first three are locked. The fourth, despite appearances, is unlocked.

12. Grain Room

Slime awaits you. Slay it and it drops an ***ivory key***. This key unlocks the other rooms off the hallway outside. Also, the ***sack of grain*** on the left holds a ***green gem***. Go to the next room to the south.

13. Farli (the NPC)

You hear pacing sounds as you approach this room. Unlock the door with the ivory key. Inside is ***Farli Mallestone*** (the NPC). He steps out of the room, and the following conversation ensues:

Farli: Greetings, human. I am Farli Mallestone of the Chak'ra clan.

Drake: Well met, Farli. I am Drake. How were you locked in this room?

Farli: I was exploring these ruins against the wishes of my elders, looking for my brother Dombur and his party, lost a season ago. Have you seen him?

Drake: Alas, I have not.

Farli: I will find him. During my search, I was looking in this room when I was hit from behind. Before I could recover, the door was locked. I heard Throggish voices in the distance.

Drake: Throggish?

Farli: Throgs are underground dwellers of a dark nature, along with their brethren the Shargas, mortal enemies of my clan. I have split many a Throg skull with my axe. It is their way to hit a noble warrior from behind.

Drake: If they are around, we should journey together for safety.

Farli: Aye, that is wise. You have saved my life. As my people say, I have debt to pay and paid it shall be!

Farli Mallestone, NPC. He may be a Dwarf, but he's hell with a weapon. He's loyal, too.

Farli now joins the party, armed with ***chain mail shirt and skirt***, a ***helm*** and a ***Dwarven axe***. He'll offer you a fine weapon: "Take this sword. It is of good Dwarven steel and will serve you with honor!" Take the ***Dwarven sword*** that Farli tosses on the ground. Go south to the next room.

Tip Farli's chain mail armor is better than yours. Trade him.

14. Storeroom

Unlock the door with the ivory key. Inside are some ***barrels***. Smash the ***barrels*** to find a ***stone*** and a ***heal potion***. Exit and continue south to the next room.

15. Slimy Storeroom

Again, open the locked door to this storeroom with the ivory key. A ***slime*** guards this room. In ***barrels***, you'll find a ***throwing axe*** and a ***firedagger***. Exit the room into the corridor. Go 2S, 2W, then turn to face the south wall.

16. Sharga Meat, Anyone?

Yes, another ***illusory door***. When you pass through it, three very ill-tempered ***Shargas*** descend upon you. (These, too, are "smart" Shargas, as are several others on this level.) With stout Farli at your side, you should dispatch this trio efficiently and snatch all the ***heal potions*** they drop. Don't drink them yet! Put them in inventory (you'll see why in a minute), and note—one of the Shargas has dropped an ***iron key***.

Say, do you hear running water?

17. Fountain of Thera

From the illusory door, head due east, then turn right at the corner and proceed south until . . . isn't it beautiful? Drink up, drink deep, drink as much as you can. Drink until vitality points are maxed out for both Farli and Drake.

Now go back to the illusory door (at 16), but don't go through it; instead, turn south. Follow the corridor south, and go through *that* door. Continue along the corridor to an odd-looking mechanism on the wall.

Fountain of Thera. Fill your belly with the pink stuff until your health points max out.

18. Cylinder Switch

The mechanism is a ***cylinder switch***. The bottom cylinder is missing, the top cylinder is depressed—it's stuck in the top position. You can change the setting using a cylinder, but where will you find a cylinder? *Answer:* Not on this level. Skip this puzzle for now and move on. (If you're impatient for the solution, glance ahead to Level 3: Sewers Beneath Stonekeep, 19 and 22.)

Cylinder Switch North. This cylinder switch controls mechanisms deep in the Stonekeep sewers. But you can't change the setting without a control cylinder. When you find one, use it in the empty bottom slot.

19. Cylinder Switch

Just around the corner to the south you'll find another ***cylinder switch***—missing the *top* cylinder. The switch is stuck in the bottom position. As with the switch at 18, you must find a cylinder to change the setting. For now, plunder the ***chest*** just to the south for ***chain mail leggings***. Then follow the corridor around the corner to the south, and go through the door.

Cylinder Switch South. This cylinder switch controls drainage in the Stonekeep sewers, but again, you have no control cylinder to use in the empty slot.

20. Sharga Guard

A smart ***Sharga*** guards the first door on your right. Vanquish him and loot the corpse for ***heal roots***. Unlock the door using the iron key.

21. Triple Room

This room is divided into three 2-by-2 areas. Fend off a ***slime*** attack or two, then move into the first area and locate the ***hidden brick*** on the north wall. Pull the ***secret lever*** concealed behind it to reveal a ***secret room*** behind the east wall.

22. Gem Horde

The only thing here is a ***chest***—but man, *what* a chest! Inside, you'll find two ***blue gems***, a ***green gem***, a ***red gem***, and two ***heal potions***. Now move north into the next 2-by-2 area.

23. Second 2-by-2

A third ***slime*** patrols the other two areas of the room. You won't find much in the either area of the room. Exit to the corridor and go west to the next room.

24. Sssssss!

Hear that? Big clue. This room is crawling with ***snakes***. Fortunately, most of them are small, easily dispatched with a single blow. Watch out, though, for the big mama. After the battle grab the ***heal potion*** in the corner. That ***wineskin*** on the floor makes a good health elixir container. You'll find a ***red gem*** buried in the rubble pile, as well.

Exit and go west one square.

Tip Kill the small snakes first! (Best way: Toss ***oil bombs*** through the open door.) They are easier to kill, but inflict the same damage as the big snake.

25. Hidden Brick Bonus × 2

A ***hidden brick*** on the north wall conceals a ***rune scroll*** that reads:

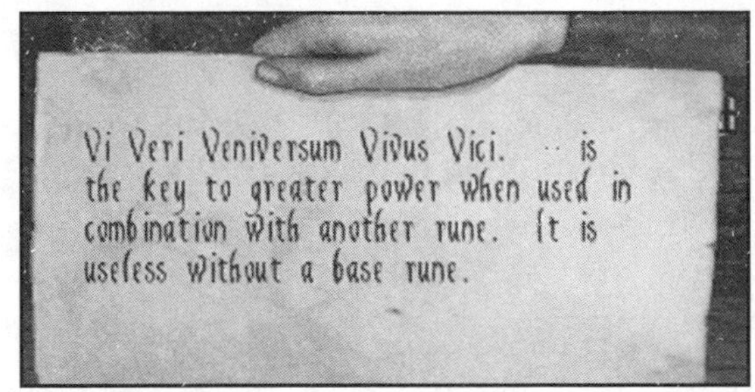

Power × 2 Rune Scroll

This Meta Rune doubles the power of any rune it's paired with. We'll call it the "power × 2" rune. As you read the scroll, the rune is inscribed in your journal, in the Runes section. Remember, runes aren't worth much without a runecaster.

Tip At this point, you might want to head back to the Fountain of Thera. Fill the wineskin with five bracing draughts of heal potion and return to the next room.

Enter the next room to the west.

26. Green Gem

The only thing here is a ***green gem***. Look carefully—it's hidden in a far corner behind some broken furniture. (You now have plenty of gems for a return trip to Wahooka, but just hang on to them for a while.) Exit and go to the next room to the west.

27. Sharga Valenzuela

Be careful. An annoying (and smart) little ***Sharga*** lurks by the door, ready to pitch stuff at you. Make him pay dearly, and grab his remaining ***heal roots***. Use the iron key to unlock the door.

28. Key Message

Another *slime* patrol. Kill them, then grab the *scroll* from the floor just ahead. It reads:

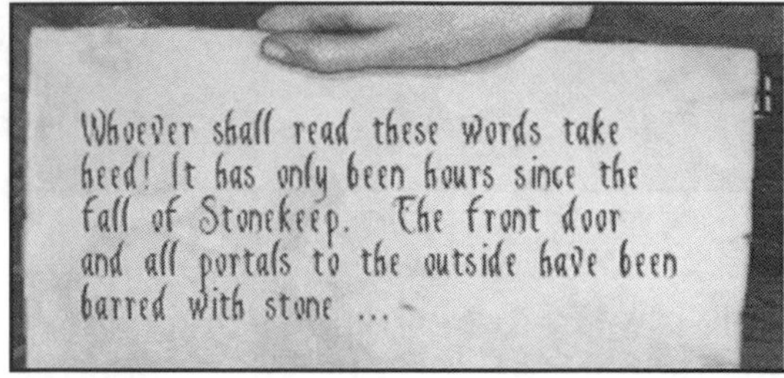

Scroll, Part 1

Proceed to the northern area of the room. Watch for a second *Slime*.

29. The Other Half

The *scroll* you find here completes the message. It reads:

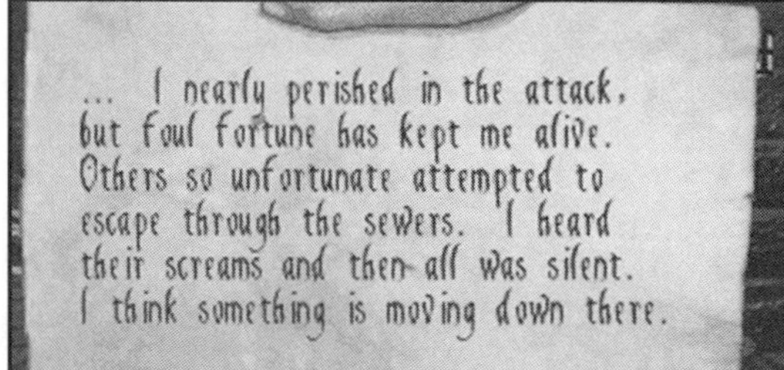

Scroll, Part 2

A *chest* in the back corner of the room contains a ***heal potion*** and a ***key ring***, a useful item. Put all of your keys on this ring, if you wish. Exit the room and follow the corridor west. Keep an eye peeled for a roving *slime*. The corridor twists and turns until you come to a large, open *pit*.

30. Pit Sealant

Turn and press the *button* on the south wall. This seals the pit behind you.

Note If you want to close the pit from its north side, toss a dart at the wall button.

31. Pit to Level 3: Sewers

If you're one of those rocketeers who flies down hallways like a maniac, though, you might end up at the bottom of the pit. If so, all is not lost. This ***pit*** leads to the sewers beneath Stonekeep—but don't get too excited. It's an *extremely* limited sewer area, and you take about 15 points of damage in the fall. When you hit bottom, examine the north wall. A ***hidden brick*** there conceals a ***secret lever***. Pull it to reveal a secret passage to the ***pit ladder***.

32. Pit Ladder

Climb the ladder. At the top, you'll find a ***button*** on the west wall. Press it, and another ***secret door*** opens directly behind you. After you step through, the wall seals shut behind you. Go around the corner to the left. You're now on the south side of the pit. Press the ***button*** on the south wall (as in 30) to seal the pit. Now proceed north.

33. Tough Sharga

Stepping into this square triggers a frontal assault. A smart and *very* tough ***Sharga*** pelts you with stones, then rushes in to finish the job with swordplay. Keep moving while you fight! Again, check for ***heal roots*** near the corpse after you prevail.

Continue north to the end of the corridor; turn right. Go 2E, then 2N.

34. Wall Button

Find the ***button*** here on the east wall. Get ready: Pushing it opens a ***secret door*** directly behind you that may unleash a vicious ***slime*** assault on your backside. Dispose of the amoeboid menace, then enter the secret room.

Tip Close-quarter combat with slime can be deadly. If you don't have the dagger of penetration, you'd best blast slime from a distance. In this case, push the wall button, quickly grab a fire weapon (oil bomb, firedagger, or the like) from inventory, then turn left and hustle to the end of the hall. Spin around quickly to face the gooey beast—it's probably tracking you.

35. Secret Room

More ***slimes*** patrol this room. Dispose of it, then head north (pick up the ***heal root*** on the way). Help yourself to the contents of the ***chest*** at the room's far northern end—two fat ***heal potions*** and a ***strength gain potion***. Exit to the corridor and turn left.

You now have quite a load of gems for Wahooka. Work your way north to square 2 and offer him his treasure. When you give three gems to Wahooka, you receive this clue: "To succeed in your quest, you must find *all* of the orbs." This is the last bit of information you can bribe out of the trickster on this level.

Turn around, go back through the door, then go 2E, 2S, turn right and go to the first door.

36. Scroll Clue

Unlock the door with the ivory key. Whack the ***slime*** wiggling around this room, take the ***heal potions*** then find the ***scroll*** on the floor and read it. It says:

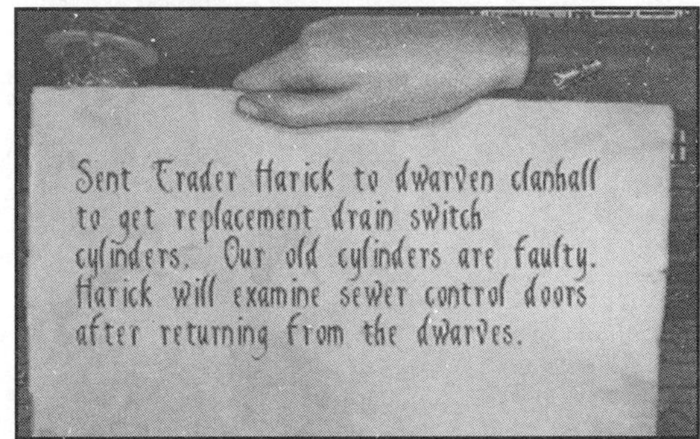

Cylinder Clue Scroll

Open the ***hidden brick*** in the center of the west wall. Take the ***blue gem***.

Exit the room, go left around the corner, then head back south past the wall button square (34) to the next intersection. Turn left, go 3E, then turn south and prepare for battle.

37. Key Lock

A single ***Sharga*** blocks your path. Unblock it with your weapon, then go to that ***lock*** on the wall, dead ahead. Use your ivory key on it, and a ***hidden door*** opens to your immediate right.

38. Secret Corridor

Enter and read the sign on the west wall: *Mage's* Study—*Do Not Enter!* Follow the corridor to the first ***flagstone*** on the floor.

Red-flag that Flagstone! If you feel like taking three arrows, step on it. Otherwise, toss a skull or rock twice before you proceed.

39A-39D. More Arrow Traps!

The flagstone is a pressure plate that triggers an arrow booby trap. Out of sight, on the east wall, are six ***arrow holes***, each loaded with a single ***arrow***.

To trigger each arrow trap safely, stop at the square before each pressure plate and place a skull or rock on it. The first three arrows fire and bounce harmlessly off the wall to the right. (Add them to your inventory.) Now pick up the skull and place it on the pressure plate again to trigger a second flight of three arrows. Repeat this process at each of the four pressure plates. By the end, you'll have quite a fat quiver of arrows in your inventory!

After you get past all four arrow traps, use the ivory key to unlock the door at the end of the twisting hall.

40. Mage's Study

A couple of ***slimes*** impede your progress here. Be sure to finish them off—one of them may hide a very important item in its gelatinous innards: a ***runewand***. You'll find three scrolls on a shelf in the first 2-by-2 area of this room. The first scroll reads:

With the addition of the Mana Circle to my studies, I can proceed with my experiments into the source of magickal energies. How do these Circles recharge Mana? Must research.

The second scroll reads:

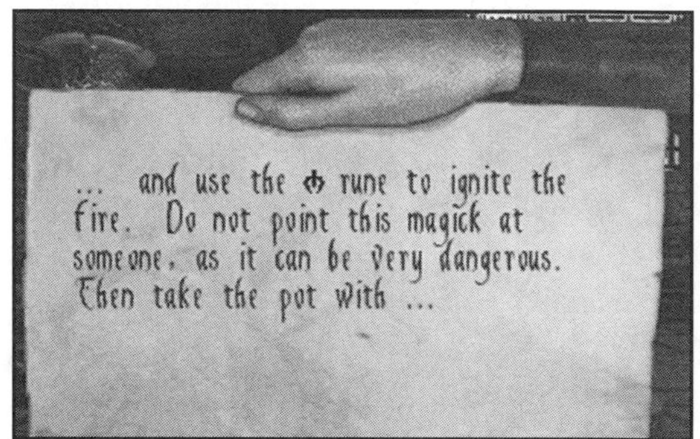

... and use the ♦ rune to ignite the fire. Do not point this magick at someone, as it can be very dangerous. Then take the pot with ...

Firebolt Rune Scroll

The third gives you a ***curing rune***. It reads:

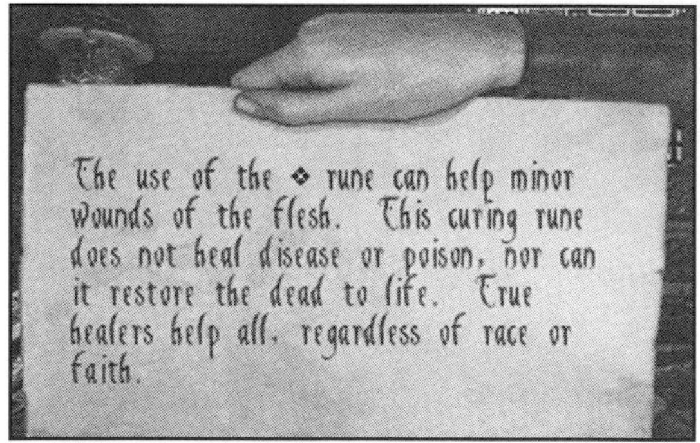

The use of the ♦ rune can help minor wounds of the flesh. This curing rune does not heal disease or poison, nor can it restore the dead to life. True healers help all, regardless of race or faith.

Curing Rune Scroll

After you read the rune scrolls, the runes appear in your journal in the Runes section. Continue north to the other 2-by-2 area of the room.

41. Mana Circle

An unlocked ***chest*** in one corner holds a ***heal potion***, a ***strength gain potion***, an ***agility gain potion***, and a ***scroll*** that reads: *Send Orson payment for the Mana Circle.* In the opposite corner you'll discover the ***Mana Circle*** referred to in the scroll back at 40. Time to fire up that runewand.

To inscribe runes onto the runewand:

1. Put the runewand in Drake's right hand.
2. Open your journal to the Runes section.
3. Move the quill–cursor over a rune. See how the cursor sparkles?
4. With the cursor still sparkling over the rune, click the right mouse button to bring up the runewand. (The runewand will rise up next to the journal.) Note how the rune flashes on the journal page.
5. Move the quill–cursor over one of the empty square notches on the runewand.
6. Click either mouse button to inscribe the rune onto the runewand.

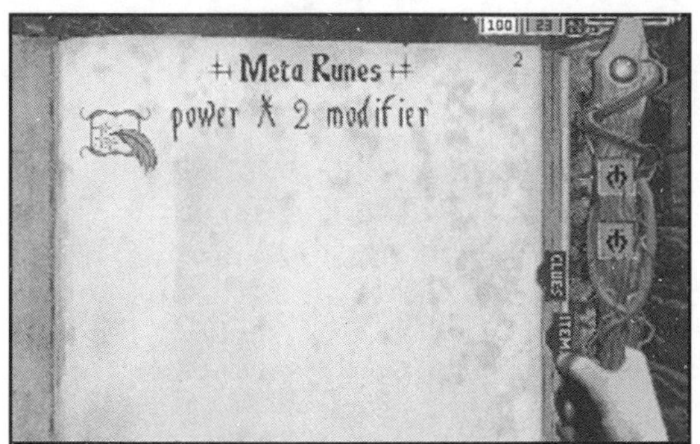

Rune Magick. Inscribe runes onto your runewand to put magick at your fingertips.

To use the power × 2 modifier rune:

Repeat the foregoing procedure to inscribe the power × 2 rune on any rune you've inscribed on the runewand.

To use the runewand:

1. Face your target and click the right mouse button to raise the runewand.
2. Left-click on the rune you want to activate. (It will flash.)
3. Use the cross-hair cursor to aim at the target, then right-click to cast the magick.

To recharge any runecaster:

Simply step into any Mana Circle. The screen will flash, indicating the runecaster now has a maximum charge.

Tip First, use the Cure rune to heal your party. Then practice magick here for a long, long time. Blast the walls with fire bolts, recharge in the Mana Circle, and repeat until you have a five-star rating in magick.

Go back past the arrow traps through the secret door. Go straight ahead to the wall, then turn left and prepare for a tough battle.

42. Two Tough Shargas

As you round the corner of this passage, two very tough—and smart—***Shargas*** (bearing ***heal roots*** and an ***oil bomb***) jump out from behind the wall and attack. It's a brutal attack, too, seemingly not worth the risk. There's nothing of interest but a looted, empty ***chest***. But lo and behold. . . .

43. Fake Wall

. . . the far northern end of the room is another ***illusory wall.*** Step through and continue north.

44. Sharga Squad

At the end of the corridor you'll find the other illusory wall (6), but don't pass through. Instead, turn east and take one step. This triggers a double ***Sharga*** attack from around the corner ahead. Fortunately, these two guys aren't particularly tough.

Tip If things get hairy during your battles in this area, remember: Shargas can't follow you through illusory doors.

45. Passage to Sewers

If you take another step east, then head south, you come to a locked door. Use the ivory key to open it. Ahead lies a stairway to the sewers beneath Stonekeep (Level 3). Don't descend just yet. You still haven't explored the northeast area of these Lower Ruins.

Go back to the square just east of 6. Go north, then east to the locked door straight ahead.

46. Watch Your Back!

Unlock the door with the ivory key. A lone ***Sharga*** waits to attack. However, instead of a maniacal, headlong rush to combat, this guy retreats to the back wall . . . and waits. Why? Take a few steps toward him and you'll find out—it's a trap! Two more ***Shargas*** jump you from the right.

Fortunately, you now have the capable weapon of Farli Mallestone by your side. A ***chest*** in the corner contains a ***chain mail shirt*** and two ***heal potions***. Exit to the corridor, then enter the next room to the south.

47. Snake Hole

Two hissing ***snakes*** await the honor of your presence. After your *tête-á-tête*, pick up the ***heal root*** in the corner. If you punch at the ***rubble*** in front of the ***hole*** on the north wall, two more ***snakes*** slither out to attack. If you take ten more steps in this room, two more ***snakes*** appear. And that's not all, folks! Every five steps you take in the room draws another pair out of the hole up to a total of 24 snakes.

When the carnage is over, exit the room and head west. Take the first left turn, follow this corridor to the next door, and open it.

48. Gem × 2

A shlurping ***slime*** skulks on the other side of the door. The onerous thing hunkers over a ***green gem***. Kill it to get the gem and take a ***throwing dart*** from the floor. You'll find a ***red gem*** hidden in a rubble pile here, too. Exit, turn left, and follow the corridor to the intersection. Go west until Wahooka appears.

49. Wahooka Again!

Ah, the King of the Goblins again, greedily gesturing for gems. If he's already given you three clues, simply ignore him and turn left. If not, give him the required number of gems.

Note If you're not following this walkthrough and you still don't have enough gems, mark this spot for later. When you have enough gems for another clue, you'll find Wahooka here *and* at location 2.

Go into the room on the south wall ahead.

50. Snake Room

A single ***snake*** greets you. In the room lie a ***heal root*** and a ***throwing dart***. Behind the ***hidden brick*** on the northern wall you'll find another ***green gem***. Exit the room. If you want, you can turn left and follow the corridor around the corner to the next door.

51. Passage to Upper Ruins

Through a pair of doors you'll find the other stairway leading to the Upper Ruins. (It takes you to 46 on Map 1.2, Upper Ruins.) You probably don't want to go back upstairs at this point, but here it is, just in case.

This is a good time to return to the fountain of healing (at 17) and drink up. Don't forget to fill the wineskin, as well.

Now turn around and head due north until you hear the mellifluous voice of the great Wahooka.

52. Wahooka Again

If Farli is with you—and obviously, if you've been following this walkthrough, Farli *is* with you—the conversation will go something like this:

Wahooka: Bah! Well, you are getting *closer* to your destiny. Come closer still and let us talk.

Continue north.

Wahooka: Beyond this door are the sewers of Stonekeep.
Drake: Is it dangerous?
Wahooka: Bah! What should it matter to you? You are already dead!
Drake: What if this door is locked?
Wahooka: Then this clue is for free: The remains of the tusk shall unbar your way.

Unlock the door with the ivory key.

53. Passage to the Sewers

Behind the door ahead a stairway leads to the Sewers beneath Stonekeep (Level 3). OK, you've earned it. Go for it, man.

Note Turn ahead to the next section, Level 3: Sewers Beneath Stonekeep. You must complete that level before you can return here to complete the following steps in the Lower Ruins.

54. Passage to Sewers

If you need anything back in the Sewers (God forbid), just go back through these doors. From here, head due south.

55. Locked Door

Only Farli can open this locked door. If Farli is with you, he says: "Before I was captured, I found the key to this door." He searches his clothing and exclaims, "Ah! Here it is." Once he unlocks the door, it remains unlocked. Proceed around the corridor.

56. Marble Dais

A ***marble dais*** sits in an alcove on the north wall here. Got anything else marble on you? Right, the marble statue. Put it on the dais and turn to the south.

Good Dais. Put your dragon where it counts, mate.

57. The Gate to the Underlands

Behind the south wall is a darkened passageway. This passage leads to Level 4, Sharga Mines. Well? What are you waiting for?

Level 3

Sewers Beneath Stonekeep

The third level of Stonekeep includes one map area—the Sewers that run beneath the keep. Water snakes, slime (two varieties: normal and tough), and Shargas (normal and smart) predominate here, but be prepared for one truly creepy encounter. As the scroll said: "I heard their screams and then all was silent. I think something is moving down there."

As Wahooka has hinted, your goal now is to gain access to the mysterious "Underlands." Remember the goblin's second clue? *Search the sewers below for the key to the Underlands.* To do this, you'll have to go back and forth a few times between these Sewers and the Lower Ruins of Stonekeep (Level 2).

Note

Again, the sequence of this walkthrough assumes you followed the path outlined in this book for the previous level, descending to the Sewers from the Lower Ruins via the stairway located at 53 on Map 2, Lower Ruins. If you came down via the other stairway (at 44 on Map 2), you can still use this walkthrough, though not in the outlined sequence. Instead, use the numbers on Map 3 to refer to the numbered encounters in this section's walkthrough.

Key to Map 3

1. Start
2–6. Snakes
7. Floodgate
8. Skull
9. Root
10. Snakes
11–13. Snakes
14. Dart bag, darts
15. Snake generator (drain)
16. Snake/slime boundary
17. Skulls, hammer
18. Slime
19. Cylinder
20. Mana Circle
21. Helm, slime
22. Skull
23. Turn marker
24. Floodgate
25. Sharga (roots, skull)
26. Shargas (roots)
27. Cylinder
28–29. Shargas
30. Secret passage
31. Chest (rune scroll, oil bombs, firedagger)—use triangle key
32. Shargas (roots, potion)
33. Sharga (roots)
34. Wahooka (triangle key)
35. Passage to Lower Ruins
36. Green mushrooms
37. Skull
38. The Thing
39. Secret Passage (to Lower Ruins)

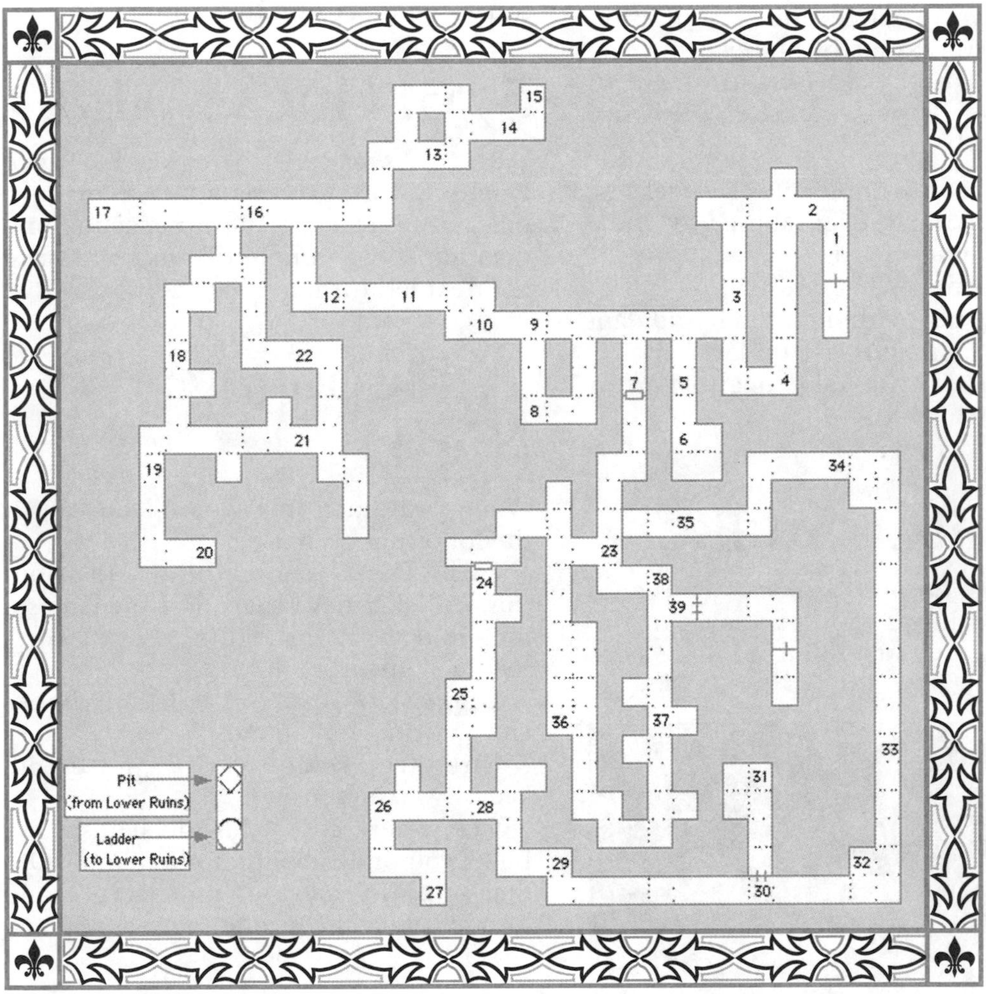

Pit (from Lower Ruins)

Ladder (to Lower Ruins)

Map 3 Sewers Beneath Stonekeep

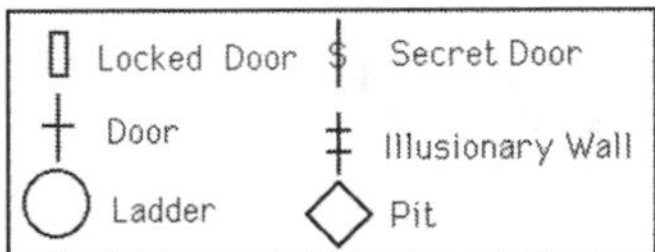

1. Start

These stairs lead down from the Lower Ruins. (The top of the stairs is at 53 on Map 2, Lower Ruins of Stonekeep.) The first time Drake and Farli descend to the sewers, they have the following conversation:

Farli: These are the sewers of Stonekeep. It is said that the dwellers above used these caverns as a water source.

Drake: Hmm. What else?

Farli: My people built a drain and dam system to maintain the water level.

Drake: That knowledge might come in useful. Watch your step.

2. Water Snake

Before long, up pops a ***snake***. Get used to this. These large reptiles swarm in the waters of the Sewers. Kill it, go three steps west, then head south.

Snake Soup. Water snakes abound in the sewers. Fortunately, Farli wields a weapon.

3, 4. More Snakes

Hello! Isn't it fun the way ***snakes*** just leap up to greet you? Thank goodness for Farli. He's pretty good with the scaly bastards, isn't he? Continue taking left turns. If it feels like you're going in circles, well, you are. But turn right after you get back to 3. Go forward a couple of squares and take another left.

5, 6. Guess What?

Yeah . . . ***snakes***. Do you see a pattern emerging? After you slaughter these guys, head back north to the intersection and turn left. Go a couple of squares west to the next left turn.

7. Floodgate North

When you reach this square, you trigger the following exchange:

Farli: There is something odd about this wall! I believe there is a mechanism for sliding it to the right . . . but I don't see the controls here.

Drake: How can you tell that? Looks like a normal wall to me.

Farli: Keen Dwarven senses, my friend, keen Dwarven senses.

Gee, where could this mechanism be? I'll let you think about it for a minute. OK, time's up. Go back to the intersection and turn left. Take the next left turn as well.

8. Skull

Do you feel like ***snake*** food yet? Hang on, it's just begun. A ***skull*** lies on the floor here.

9. Heal Root

Look for a ***heal root*** under the water in this square. (To find it, move the cursor around until it changes to the "pickup" hand.) Move forward.

10. What's That?

Oh, it's a ***snake***. Watch it playfully loop up to you, fangs first. Gore it. More ***snakes*** slither up on you here—they keep coming, in fact. Hey, here comes one. Slice it. Dice it. Move ahead. One may even slip up behind you. Man, this is fun.

11, 12, 13. You Won't Believe What's Here, Man

Are you ready for this? ***Snakes!*** Singles, pairs, you name it. See, what you've hit here is Snake Alley. In fact, there's actually a "snake generator" nearby.

Tip If your vitality gets dangerously low—and it probably will—revisit Thera's Fountain back at 17 on Level 2.

14. Dart Bag

Wow, a ***dart bag***. I guess slogging through zillions of snakes was really worth it. Nearby you'll also find a couple of ***darts***.

15. Snake Generator

Here it is. Nothing's happening now, but when you get more than three squares away—and the number of snakes in the sewers is fewer than 25—a brand new snake slithers through the unseen drain here every minute and immediately moves out into the sewer corridors.

Note If you manage to drain the water from this level later, the snake generator slows to half this rate.

16. Invisible Boundary

Here's one of those juicy insider tips that only a strategy guide written with the full cooperation of the *Stonekeep* game designers can tell you. This square marks the east/west boundary between snake territory (east) and slime territory (west). If you're sick of snakes—and no doubt you *are* by now—you can relax a bit once you cross this line.

17. Skull and Bones

Search the water here to find some ***skulls***. They have no magickal powers, but give you a certain amount of leverage when dealing with Wahooka later. (Of course, if you've been gathering ***skulls*** all along, you probably have enough to last a couple of lifetimes.) You also find a ***hammer***, if you look hard enough.

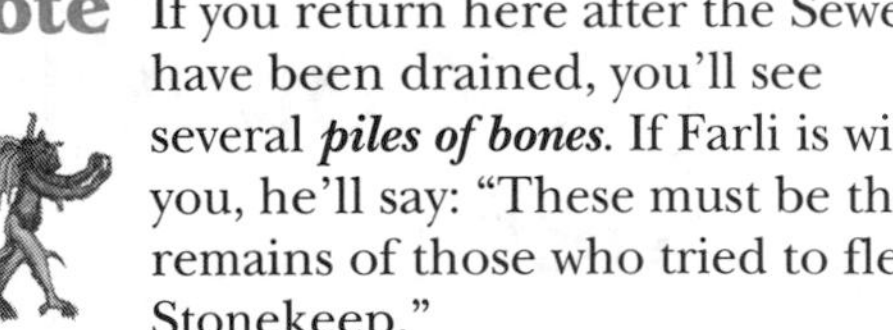

Note If you return here after the Sewers have been drained, you'll see several ***piles of bones***. If Farli is with you, he'll say: "These must be the remains of those who tried to flee Stonekeep."

At the dead end, turn around and go 5E, 2S, then turn right and start working your way along the corridor.

18. Change of Pace

Prepare for another attack here. It's a ***slime*** this time, however—watch for the approaching bubbles. After you fight off the blob, continue south to the intersection, then follow the cavern to the right (west).

Bubbling Death. It's an approaching slime, looking for organic material to ingest.

19. The Control Cylinder

Here's where your luck changes a bit. You'll find a ***cylinder*** in the water here. (You can't miss it—if Drake steps over it, he howls: "Ow! My foot!") What good is a cylinder, you ask? Remember those odd cylinder switches back up in the Lower Ruins . . . ?

Note If you came down from the Lower Ruins to the Sewers via the other stairway (35 on Map 3, Sewers Beneath Stonekeep), this may be the *second* cylinder you find.

Ah, but you haven't exhausted your good luck yet. Follow this corridor south and east to its dead end.

20. Recharge!

Did you notice the screen flash as you stepped into this square? You can't see it yet, but you just stepped into another ***Mana Circle*** for a full recharge of your runewand. (If you don't *have* the runewand yet, or if it is already fully charged, you won't see the flash.) Use the Cure rune on your entire party then recharge again.

Now it's time to give that cylinder switch a try. But let's take a different route back. Retrace your steps back around the two corners, then head east.

21. One Wet Helm

Grab the old ***helm*** along this path. Keep an eye out for the bubbles of a submerged ***slime*** nearby.

22. Skull Souvenir

Another ***skull*** lies submerged here. Maybe it once wore the helm you just found. Work your way back to the start—the stairs at 1 leading up to the Lower Ruins.

Tip Prepare to meet many ***snakes*** along the way. The snake generator at 15 has been working nonstop since you left it. The worst area is that same 2-by-2 section (around 10) where you met so many snakes before.

Once you get back to the Start (at 1), here's what to do:

1. Head back upstairs to either of the Cylinder switches (located at 18 and 19 on Map 2, Lower Ruins).
2. Use the cylinder on the switch.
3. Depress the newly-placed cylinder to change its setting.

Tip Before you return to the Sewers, be sure to drink from the Fountain of Thera (at 17 on Map 2, Lower Ruins). And for Thera's sake, fill up that wineskin while you're at it!

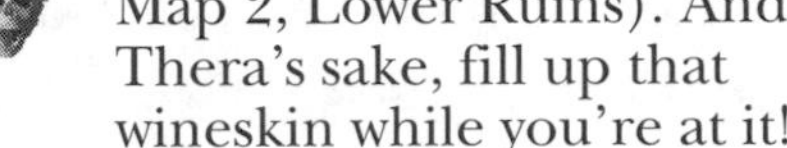

You've now opened two Sewer floodgates—the one at 7 that you've seen, and another at 24 that you haven't seen yet. Return to 7, wade through the now-open passage, then work your way south.

23. Turn Marker

Important: Turn west here! Go 2W, N, 2W, S, W, then head south.

24. Floodgate South

Here's the other floodgate you opened when you used the cylinder in the Floodgate switch.

25. Captain Graz

In this square is a single strong ***Sharga***, named Graz. Graz is tough—in fact, he's the leader of all Shargas on this level. Graz has twice the strength of a regular Sharga; he also has three ***heal roots*** and a ***skull***.

Graz. OK, so he sounds like a strangulated Muppet. Don't let that fool you. Graz has twice the strength of a regular Sharga.

If Farli is in the party, Graz says: "Masters told Graz that you be here! Die, stuntie!" Then he attacks. If Farli is *not* in the party, Graz says: "Masters told Graz that you be here! Die, humie!" Then he attacks you.

Continue south to the intersection. Keep primed for combat. See that Sharga guard down the east passage? Chances are he won't see you yet; if he remains passive, don't disturb him. Instead, turn west.

26. Twin Shargas

A pair of ***Sharga*** guards attacks here, one at a time. These two are smart Shargas; they carry two ***heal roots*** apiece, and use them if hurt. After you kill them, be sure to feel around in the water for any they might drop. Continue down the passage.

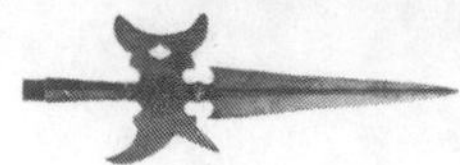

27. The Other Cylinder

Here's what the smart Shargas were protecting so fiercely—another ***cylinder***.

Note If you're not following this walkthrough, and you came down from the Lower Ruins to the sewers via the other stairway at 35, this will be the *first* cylinder you find. If that's the case (and gee, I hope it isn't, because I worked so darned *hard* on this walkthrough), you need to go back up to the Lower Ruins and use this cylinder on the Floodgate switch (see 18 on Map 2, Lower Ruins).

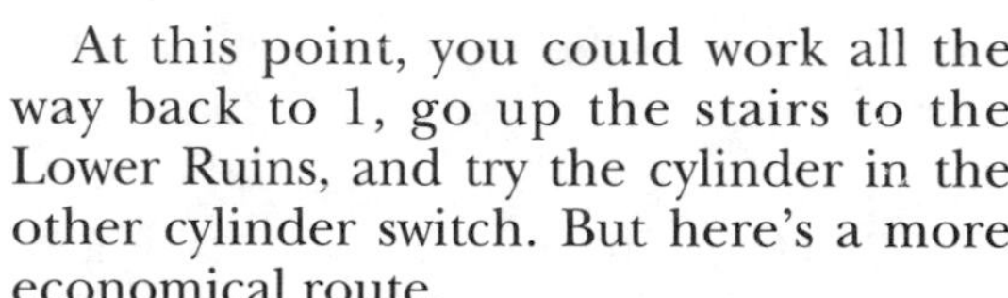

At this point, you could work all the way back to 1, go up the stairs to the Lower Ruins, and try the cylinder in the other cylinder switch. But here's a more economical route.

28, 29. Twin Twins

A pair of ***Shargas*** waits at each of these two locations.

Note The Sharga pair at 28 are designed to "reinforce" those at 29, but not vice-versa. Thus, if you came down from the Lower Ruins via those darned *other* stairs (at 35), you encounter the Shargas at 29 first. When this happens, the pair at 28 rush to reinforce the two already fighting you. (Imagine battling four Shargas at once!) But of course, in *this* walkthrough, you encounter the 28 pair first—the 29 pair won't reinforce them, but instead wait for you to finish the first battle and approach.

30. Secret Passage

Hear that wind? That signals a ***secret passage*** to the north. Squeeze through.

31. Hidden by Waters

If you haven't drained the sewers yet, you'll find only three ***heal roots*** here. Hidden underwater, however, is a locked chest in the corner of the alcove. Even if you could see it, none of your keys could open it. Exit the room and continue west.

32. Ambush!

Two smart, tough ***Shargas*** wait for you here. One of them has two ***heal roots***, the other has one ***heal root*** and one ***heal potion***. Be ready for a fierce battle.

33. Reinforcement

Here's a backup ***Sharga***. Again, he's tough and smart. If you mow him down fast enough, feast on his two ***heal roots***.

34. Dead Heads?

If no monster is around when you enter this square, Wahooka appears and engages you in the following dialogue:

Wahooka: Ahhh! Greetings again, mortal.

Drake: What do you want this time, Wahooka?

Wahooka: Once again, I grant thee the key to your future in return for a small favor. Bring me the heads of three men long dead.

If Farli is with the party, he says: "Do it yourself, gobbo!" (If Farli is *not* in the party, Drake says: "Can't you do it yourself?")

Wahooka: Bah! Not in this miserable wet corner of hell! (He disappears.)

If you go back south, past 33, then return to this square with three ***skulls*** in your inventory, Wahooka reappears—again, if there is no monster around. He says, "Give them to me! Give them now!" If you give Wahooka three skulls, he responds: "Ah! Finally. Here you go." He gives you a ***triangle key*** and disappears.

There He Goes Again. Wahooka's exits are always interesting, aren't they? If you give him three skulls, he'll give a triangle key in return.

Note Don't attack Wahooka during this exchange! If you do, he'll disappear and say: "Bah! It is your fortune that you throw away, human." Wahooka won't return on this level if attacked, nor after you get the triangle key.

OK, without further ado, let's drain this godforsaken place. Continue west down the passageway.

35. Stairs to Lower Ruins

Go up these stairs to the Lower Ruins, then do the following:

1. Go to the unused Cylinder switch (at 18 or 19 on Map 2, Lower Ruins).
2. Put the cylinder in the cylinder switch.
3. Push in the newly placed cylinder to change its setting.

Tip Again, before you return to the Sewers, be sure to stop and splash around in the Fountain of Thera (see Map 2, Lower Ruins, 17) for awhile.

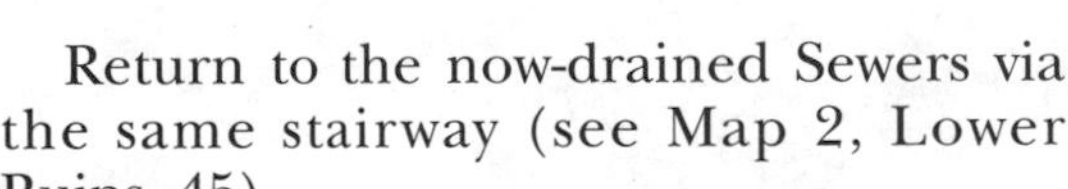

Return to the now-drained Sewers via the same stairway (see Map 2, Lower Ruins, 45).

Note **About Draining the Sewers:** When you drain the Sewers, a few changes occur. Of course, now you can see objects previously hidden beneath the surface of the water. You can see various ***drains*** and ***pools of water*** as well. Sewer creatures are also affected. Slimes and water snakes can no longer launch surprise attacks from beneath the surface of the water.

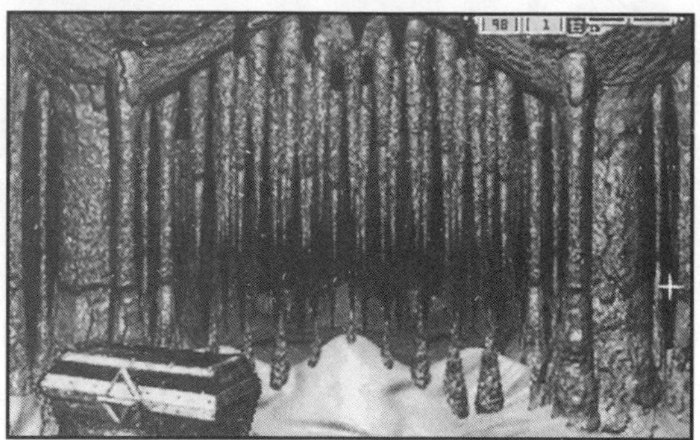

Triangle Chest. It won't open . . . and what's with that odd triangular latch?

Work your way back through that secret passage at 30. A locked chest, as mentioned in 31, sits in the secret room. Note the odd, triangular pattern on the latch. Hey, didn't Wahooka just give you a triangle key? Use it to unlock the chest, which contains a ***firedagger***, a couple of ***oil bombs***, and a ***rune scroll***. It reads:

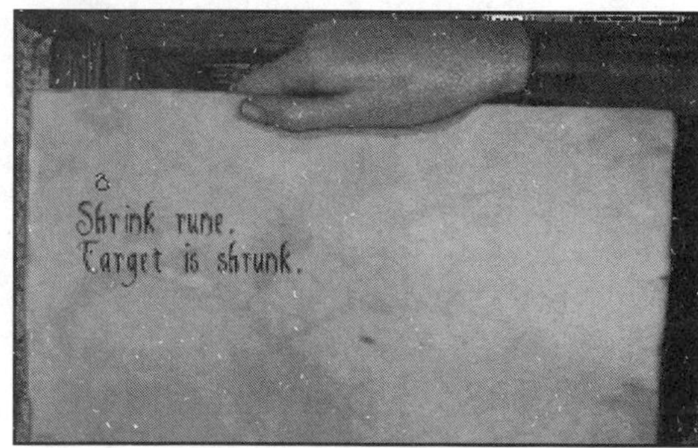

Shrink Rune Scroll

Tip After you drain the Sewers, it's a good idea to re-examine places you've already visited, checking to see if you missed anything under the water. (You probably did.) This is also a good time to return to the Mana Circle at 20 to recharge your runewand.

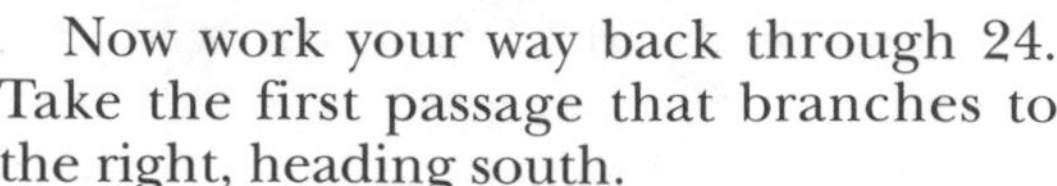

Now work your way back through 24. Take the first passage that branches to the right, heading south.

36 Poison Cure

Grab the pair of ***green mushrooms*** rooted here. Then continue south.

37. Skull

You'll find a ***skull*** here, if you're interested.

38. The THING!

Good Lord, there it is. Each of those three ***tentacles*** has a life of its own—each has slightly more hit points than a strong Sharga, so this Thing is a very, very difficult opponent to defeat in straight-up combat.

Tip Infighting with the Thing is near-suicide. Those big bloody teeth will get you—and if *you* don't go down, Farli probably will. My advice: Fire up that runewand and zap the creature with the Shrink rune you found in the chest at 31. That cuts the Thing down to size, though it's still quite deadly. Keep your distance, and blast it with Power × 2 firebolts from your runewand.

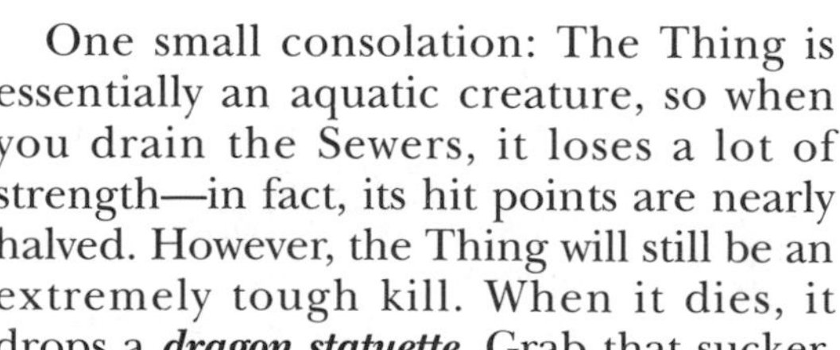

One small consolation: The Thing is essentially an aquatic creature, so when you drain the Sewers, it loses a lot of strength—in fact, its hit points are nearly halved. However, the Thing will still be an extremely tough kill. When it dies, it drops a ***dragon statuette***. Grab that sucker.

Remember the Mage Icarius scroll you found in the Upper Ruins? It spoke of an enchanted dragon statuette, then said: *Passageway to the Dwarven Realms has been secured.* Could this be the very one? If so, how is it used? Fear not, you'll find out soon enough.

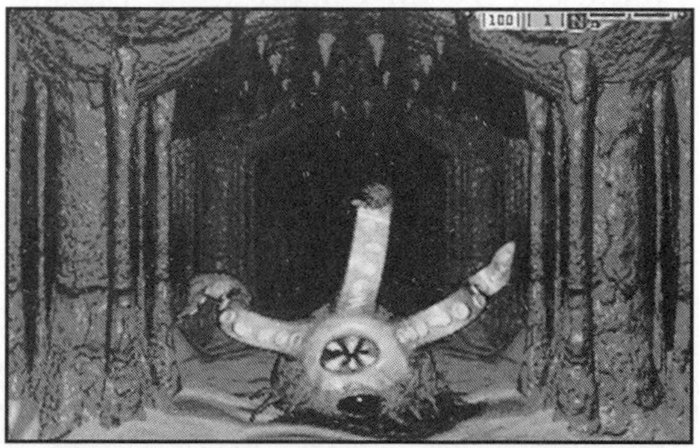

The Thing. Cute, isn't it? Each tentacle has a life of its own, and the body is powerful and relentless. Keep your distance, if you can.

39. Secret Passage

When you reach this square, you'll hear a low whistling sound coming from the east wall. This is another ***secret passage***. Go through the opening and follow the corridor until you enter the stairwell leading back up to the previously inaccessible southeast area of the Lower Ruins.

Now turn back to step 54 in the walkthrough of Level 2: Lower Ruins of Stonekeep.

Level 4

Sharga Mines

The two map areas of Stonekeep's fourth level represent the upper and lower levels of the Sharga Mines. In this walkthrough, steps 1 through 44 occur primarily in the Upper Mines, found on Map 4.1. Steps 45 through 79 describe events in the Lower Mines, found on Map 4.2.

Prepare to battle scores of Shargas, a few snakes and slimes, and a strange spitting fungus. Another potential companion awaits rescue so he can join your party. This level also features another powerful super-foe—and the first interesting plot twist of the game.

One final bit of advice: *Don't leave the Sharga Mines without the Orb of Afri!*

Key to Maps 4.1 & 4.2

1. Passage to Lower Ruins
2. Wasps
3. Shargas, rubble (rune scroll), chest (oil bombs, roots)
4. Sharga (roots), root, chest (roots)

5A-B. Toadstools (trigger Sharga attacks)
6A. Mana Circle, rune scroll
6B. Shargas

7. Cave-in
8. Shargas
9. Cave-in
10. Slime
11. Mushrooms, root
12. Shargas (mushrooms)
13. Chest (money bag, coins)
14. Shargas (crossbows, bolts)
15. Exploding fungus
16. Wasps
17. Exploding fungus
18. Button (opens door), Sharga
19. Door to cellblock area
20. Cell (Karzak Hardstone)
21. Cells
22. Sharga, cave-in
23. Exploding fungi, cave-ins
24. Sharga
25. Shargas
26. Plate mail, plate leggings, helm, axe, chest (skull key, gems, pick, root)
27. Exploding fungus
28. Ladder to pit bottom (see 32)—runescepter, rune scrolls
29. Sharga (goes to 31)
30. Bone pile (rune scroll)
31. Sharga (from 29), pit switch
32. Pit
33. Pit switch
34. Shargas, chest (quiver, arrows)
35. Crossbow sniper trap (bolt)
36. Barrel (conceals button to 37)
37. Sniper hideout (crossbow, quiver, bolts, roots)—open at 36
38. Ettin's pit (roots)
39. Ettin
40. Chest (gems, Throg gate key, Aquila's Orb)
41. Exploding fungus
42. Cave-in
43. Roots, pick, carcass (gem)
44. Passage to Lower Mines
45. Sharga (crossbow, quiver, bolts)
46. Sharga
47. Snake
48. Portcullis, switch
49. Exploding fungus, roots, mushrooms
50. Toadstool, Shargas
51. Chest (roots, coins, oil bomb)
52. Exploding fungi
53. Bone pile (mushrooms)
54. Sharga
55. Shargas
56. Wall crack
57. Bone pile (mushrooms)
58. Snake
59. Cave-in, snake
60. Ballista bolt
61. Cave-in, snake
62. Grug the Sharga
63. Snake
64. Skrag the Sharga
65. Barrel (conceals button)
66. Chest (gem, rune scroll, skull, broken sword)
67. Wall button
68. Meat, coins, roots
69. Sharga (dagger)
70. Giant Sharga (coins, gems), barrels (mushrooms)
71. Intersection
72. Slime
73. Cave-in, slimes (root)
74. Slimes
75. Toadstool
76. Sharga
77. Root
78. Locked door
79. The Throg gate—use Throg gate key (from 40)

Map 4.1 Sharga Mines, Upper Level

Map 4.2 Sharga Mines, Lower Level

Locked Door
Ladder
Door
Secret Door
Pit

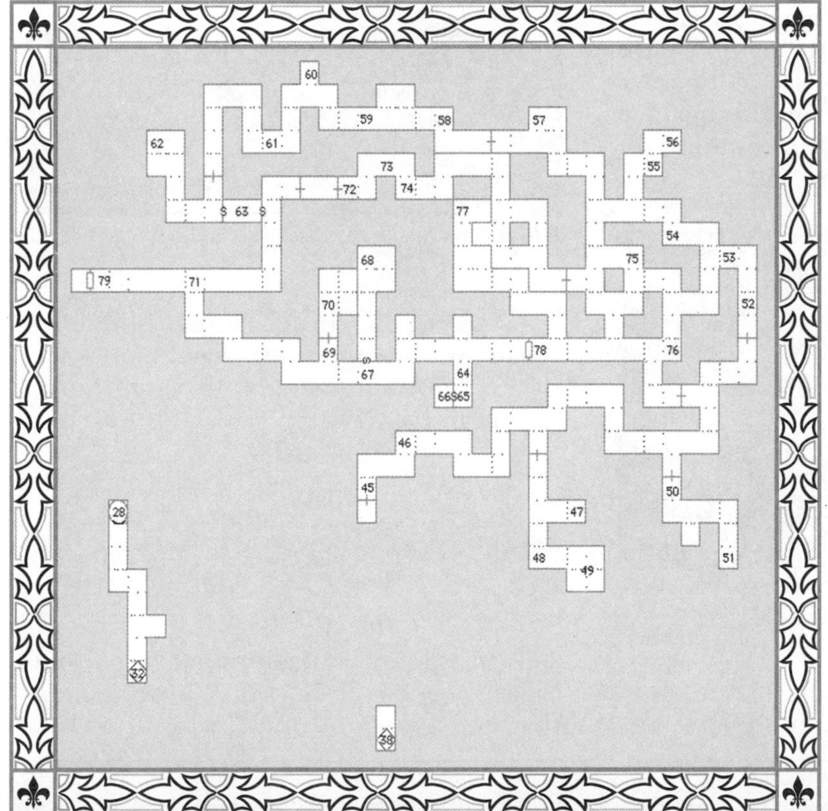

1. Just Past the Gate

Enter the Sharga Mines from the dark tunnel on the south wall leading down from the Lower Ruins. (As usual, you can move freely between these two levels.) The first time you enter the mines, Drake speaks with Farli:

Drake: Where are we now?

Farli: I know not. Records of the clan show nothing here.

Drake: By Thera! Any ideas?

Farli: Only one.

Drake: Yes?

Farli: My people did not carve this mine out of the earth.

Head west toward that hovering ***wasp***.

2. Wasp Nest

A swarm of 100 giant ***wasps*** nests on the ceiling here. Don't attack the sentinel wasp hovering beneath the nest; it won't bother you. (Just ignore its unnerving, in-your-face inspection.) If you *do* attack the wasp, eight more wasps angrily seek revenge.

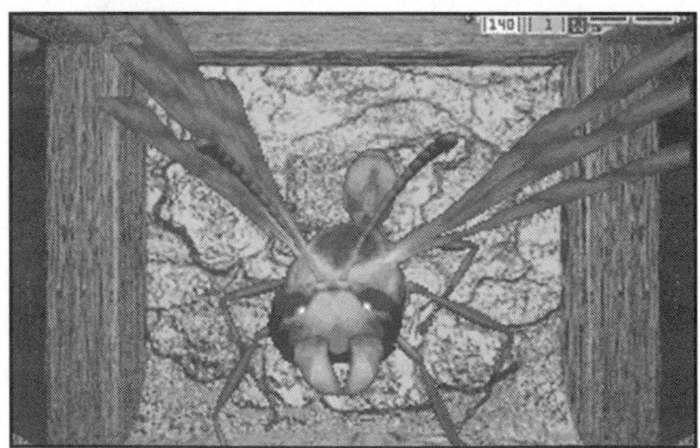

Wasp Inspection. Do you pass muster? Yes, if you remain passive. Ignore the inquisitive wasp and move on.

If you trigger a wasp attack, run away. You can't eliminate all the wasps—for every kill, the nest generates a new attacking wasp, to a maximum of eight. However, escape is easy. These wasps fly no more then two squares away from their nest.

Go north from the wasp nest, following the corridor around to the intersection. Turn right and proceed warily.

3. Sharga Ambush

Stop at this square. Two very tough ***Shargas*** launch a crazed assault around the corner of this 2-by-2 room. If killed, they leave behind two ***stones*** each. The ***rubble*** pile hides a very important ***rune scroll.***

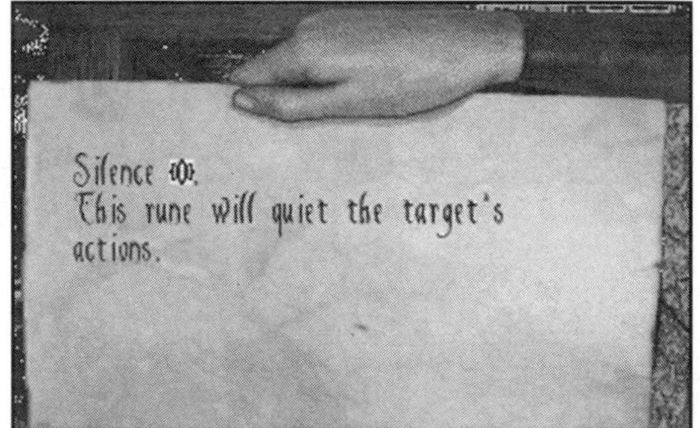

Silence Rune Scroll

A ***chest*** in the corner contains three ***oil bombs*** and two ***super heal roots***. Exit down the corridor and take the first right turn, heading west.

4. Sharga's Good Side

This Sharga may attack immediately, but there is a chance he won't hear you. In that case, you find him facing the wall.

He won't turn until you attack, giving you a heck of a tactical advantage. After he goes down, grab the two ***super heal roots*** he drops.

You find two more ***super heal roots*** in the ***chest*** that sits in the corner of the room, and one ***heal root*** on the ground next to it. Exit and head south.

5A & 5B. Alarming Toadstools

What a charming little fungus. When you step into any square adjacent to this ***toadstool***, it produces a loud warning sound—loud enough, unfortunately, to alert Sharga guards in the vicinity. The toadstool shrieks as long as you (or any other creature) are in or adjacent to its square. The noise ceases immediately after you move two or more squares away from the toadstool.

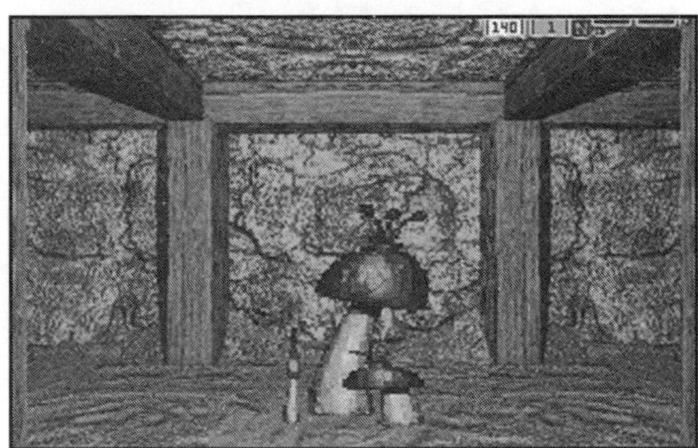

Don't Be Alarmed. Toadstools won't bite. Of course, monsters alerted by the annoying screech might chew you up. Quiet the fungi with your blade, or use a Silence rune.

Toadstools do not impede your movement through their square. You can destroy them, but not easily. A toadstool can take at least 50 hit points of damage before expiring.

The toadstool at 5A alerts a hidden Sharga duo, who then approach from around the corner to the west.

Tip Fire weapons inflict extra damage on a toadstool. If you kill the toadstools before they sound an alarm, the hidden Shargas never appear.

6A. Mana Circle

From 5A, go two steps south and press the ***button*** on the west wall. A door opens behind you. Enter and recharge in the ***Mana Circle***. Pick up the rune scroll and read it.

Featherfall Rune Scroll.

From the toadstool at 5B, follow the passageway as it zig-zags north and west. The toad stool at 5B alerts another hidden Sharga duo that attack from the north.

6B. Two Tough Shargas

Two grizzled ***Sharga*** veterans want to ambush unsuspecting hero-types like yourself. After you show them the egregious error of their ways, move on to the north.

7. Ceiling Zero

After you pass this square, the ***ceiling*** caves in behind you. It's not as bad as it looks—15 blows with a normal weapon, 10 blows

with a Sharga mining pick, or a mere five blows with a Dwarven mining pick get you through the debris. Better yet, try a couple of Power × 2 firebolt blasts.

Blocked Shaft. The ceiling's on the floor. Simply hack through the cave-in with any weapon. Picks work best, naturally.

In this case, however, you don't really need to bash your way through the cave-in. Continue north, and simply follow the zig-zagging passageway. Grab the ***dart*** along the way.

8. Two More Shargas

Another pair of ***Shargas*** lurks around this corner. Vivisect the sneaky vermin, then move on south. At the first intersection, follow the path to the right.

9. Heads Up!

When you pass through this square, another ***cave-in*** collapses behind you. Don't excavate yet. Turn south to face more pressing concerns.

10. Death by Gelatin

This is no ordinary ***slime*** blocking your path. This is a tough mother slime. After you smash it into a green jelly stain, move into the 2-by-2 room.

11. More Fungus Among Us

Grab that ***red mushroom*** patch in one corner and the ***heal root*** in the other corner. Now go back to the cave-in at 9 and hack your way out. Go north to the corner, then head east. Follow the corridor around to the ***wooden door***. Go through the door.

12. Will Shargas Never Cease?

Apparently not. ***Shargas***, like diamonds, are forever. Three more of the scruffy fellows hide as usual around a corner. Slay them and take their ***red mushrooms***.

Continue down the passageway. Don't miss the lone ***crossbow bolt*** on the way.

13. Money Bag

Open the ***chest*** and remove the ***money bag***. Open inventory and click the bag on your collected coins. Two more ***coins*** are in the chest as well. Continue west.

14. Crossbow Shargas

Some interesting tactical combat looms ahead. Two ***Shargas*** with crossbows are platooned with a tough ***Sharga*** for support. The two bowmen open fire immediately. When you approach, they may turn and run, leaving the tough guy to cover their tails. When the crossbows run out of bolts, the two bowmen resort to swordplay again, and your hands are full.

Crossbows at 40 Paces. Three surly Shargas, two armed with crossbows, block your passage west.

After the fun, continue down the mineshaft.

15. What the Hell Is It?

It's an ***exploding fungus***, that's what! This odd greenish-blue plant spits deadly ***spores*** at you, but a blow or two puts a swift end to the nuisance.

Spore Spitter. This odd subterranean fungus is deadly, but fairly easy to kill.

16. More Wasps

Another ***wasp nest*** hangs from the ceiling, home to 100 more ***wasps***. Again, leave it alone! Simply pass by and continue north.

17. Another Spitter

Hunkering behind that big boulder in the corner is another ***exploding fungus***.

18. Locked Door

Push the ***button*** on the west wall to unlock this door. Go through and lay waste to the ***Sharga*** guard who waits on the other side. Did he say something about a prisoner?

19. Door to Cellblock

Behind the door dead ahead to the north is a passage to the lower level of the Sharga

Mines. Skip it for now and head west through the other door. Turn south down the passage, then take the first right turn.

20. Karzak Hardstone

The ***Dwarf*** trapped in the ***holding cell*** is Karzak Hardstone. Here's a handy translation of the Dwarf-speak you hear:

Farli: *Chad'ra chu ka?!* (Who are you?)
Karzak: *Katja chu nee ka Chak'ra Karzak Ta'chak.* (This stonechild is honorable Karzak Hardstone.)
Farli: Drake, we must free him! *Karzak, nee ko Farli mat'chak o Drake.* (Karzak, we are Farli and Drake.)
Drake: Aye.

Karzak the Magnificent. This noble Dwarf might make a good companion—if you can free him.

You cannot free Karzak without a key, so move on south down the corridor.

21. More Cells

If you continue west, you'll find two more ***holding cells***. The first one is empty. The second one is less empty, but barely so. Better keep moving south down the corridor. Karzak needs a key.

22. Sharga & Cave-In

A gritty ***Sharga*** prison guard waits for you here. Dispatch the fellow and continue south. Bust through the ***cave-in***. Keep going, for Karzak's sake.

23. Two Spitters, Two Rock Piles

Two ***exploding fungi*** want to mess up your armor. Hack them apart, smiling. Behind them lies another huge pile of debris, marking yet another ***cave-in***. Hack through that, too. Keep going. Don't stop. Oh no! Another ***cave-in*** behind the first one! Getting tired? Ignore the fatigue, spurn the pain. Hack away.

24. The Lone Sharga

This ***Sharga*** works alone, so you've got him outnumbered (unless you lost Farli). Take him down a notch, then get ready for a battle royal just around the corner.

25. Treasury Guard

This ***Sharga*** troop guards a treasure-laden room behind them. All three Shargas are tough, but they won't advance or pursue—apparently, they're under strict orders not to abandon this post. (However, they will throw stuff at you.) It's fairly easy to hop forward, strike a blow, then hop back without taking much damage, or toss oil bombs to your heart's content.

26. Spoils of War

Strewn on the ground is a wealth of warrior booty—***upper Dwarf plate mail***, some ***Dwarven plate leggings***, a ***Dwarven helm***, and a ***Dwarven axe***, for starters. The ***chest*** in the corner holds a ***skull key***, a ***red gem***, a ***green gem***, a sturdy ***Dwarf pick***, and a ***heal root***.

First Rate Plate. Look at all that gorgeous Dwarven handiwork. Time to give Farli a full armor upgrade.

Now head back north to Karzak's cell at 20 and set the Dwarf free, using the skull key on the cage. Karzak steps forward:

Drake: Death awaits us. We are searching for Farli's brother, Dombur. He was taken prisoner by the Throgs.

Karzak: Then we must hurry to the Throggite Temple before he is sacrificed to their dark god.

Farli: Then this is no time for idle chatter.

Karzak: Aye.

Tip Karzak is in bad shape, due to his harsh imprisonment at the hands of Sharga thugs. Note his health rating of only 4 points. Better feed him some heal substances immediately. Just as important, *arm* the fellow! Give him the Dwarven axe.

Party Time. What a threesome. Now find the Cowardly Lion, and it's off to Oz!

Return southward to the square just east of the Sharga guard you fought at 24. Go south to the intersection. Turn right and go through the door.

From the doorway, go west a square, turn right, then go N, 2W, N, then turn left.

27. Another Annoying Spitter

As you approach this ***exploding fungus***, Farli axes it out of existence. (If he doesn't, do it yourself.) Turn right and go to the ladder.

28. Passage to Lower Mines

This ***ladder*** leads to the lower level of the Sharga Mines. Go down here now—it will save you unnecessary pain later, as you'll see.

Ladder Down. Go down into the pit the easy way, retrieve the powerful runescepter, and inscribe your favorite runes.

At the ladder's bottom, follow the short corridor to the end. A powerful ***runescepter*** lies near a pile of bones. (Note that it has a Mana charge of 40.) You'll also find two ***rune scrolls*** on the ground near the scepter.

Note If you're following this walkthrough, you already have the Curing rune. But the message on *this* Curing rune scroll describes the rune on the scroll with no words. It "Only reads things"—a Language rune! Use this rune to translate unreadable markings found elsewhere in Stonekeep.

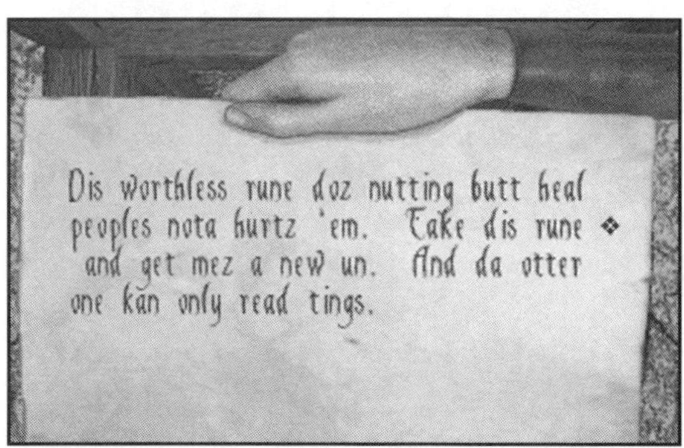

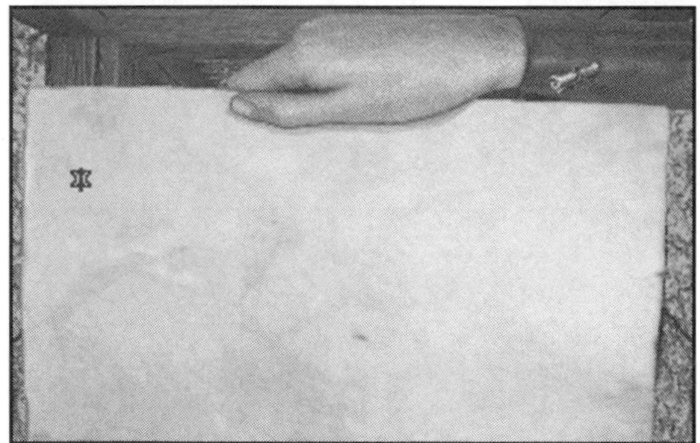

Rune Scrolls from The Pit

Return to the ladder and climb back to the upper level of the Sharga Mines.

29. Sharga Decoy

When you reach this square and turn west, you see a ***Sharga***, who quickly slinks away in a most suspicious manner. Follow him around the corner, *but around the next left turn!* Instead, go straight south.

Stop at the square just before the big ***boulder*** and turn left, facing east.

30. Make No Bones

Instead, break bones. Hidden in that ***bone pile*** is a ***rune scroll***. It reads: *Firebolt rune. Ranged fire attack.* You should already have the Firebolt Rune inscribed in your journal, but if not, congratulations, you've just found a darned useful attack rune. Continue around the corner.

31. Pit Switch 1

That skulking ***Sharga*** decoy now stands with his back to you, and there's a ***handle*** on the wall next to him. Don't be noble—slash him to pieces from behind. (Actually, he'll spin quite quickly to face you, and he's pretty tough.)

Don't pull the handle on the wall! It activates a hidden pit just up ahead at 32.

32. Avoid a Pit-iful Experience

Sure, the floor *looks* solid here. But if you had walked over it while the tricky Sharga was still alive, he would have opened a ***pit trap*** by pulling the handle at 31. You'd then hurtle down to a very uncomfortable landing, with each party member taking about 15 points worth of damage.

Note  *If You Fall Into the Pit:* The bottom of the pit is in the lower Sharga Mines—the same spot where you found the runescepter and scrolls (see 28). To escape, simply follow the short corridor north to the ladder, which leads back up to 28.

33. Pit Switch 2

This ***handle*** on the wall also opens and closes the pit. Unless you just feel like fooling around, you don't need to use it.

Go back through the wooden door and continue east down the long passageway to the next door. Watch out for ***exploding fungi*** halfway down the hall.

Step through the door, and turn right.

Tip Revisit the Mana Circle at 6A for a recharge.

Head south, and battle the pair of ***Shargas***.

34. Armor Chest

Open the chest and take the ***quiver*** and two ***arrows***. Go back east, then north to the toadstool patch at 5A. From there, go 2W, 2N, 2E, 2N, 3E, 4S, then turn left and follow the passage around the turns. On the way, punch out bone piles to get a ***dart*** and a ***coin***. Stop just before you reach the ***crossbow bolt*** on the ground.

35. Bolts From . . . Where?

Hear that muffled giggle? Note the ***arrow holes*** on the north wall just up ahead. You've seen arrow traps before in Stonekeep, but this is a *living* one—a ***Sharga*** sniper, armed with a ***crossbow*** and 15 bolts, sniveling behind a ***secret wall***.

Every time you step into the "trigger square" adjacent to the arrow holes, the sniper fires a crossbow bolt, damaging a random party member. If you race across the trigger square, however, the fired bolt will miss you and fall to the floor. But there's no way to lure the coward out.

Tip  Race back and forth 15 times to expend the sniper's ammunition, then gather up the bolts.

36. Barrel Button

Race past the sniper and smash the ***barrel*** here to reveal a ***wall button***. Push the button to open the ***secret room*** back at 6. Now go back and make the little chucklehead pay.

37. Romp in the Sniper's Nest

Be careful. If you didn't trick the Sharga sniper into exhausting his supply of bolts (see the *Tip* above) he will open fire with his crossbow the moment you enter the secret room. But if you strike one good blow with your weapon, you'll reduce him to a pathetic, groveling pile of Sharga . . . whatever.

Now you face a moral decision. Spare the helpless fellow? No way, man. You need his ***crossbow***, ***quiver***, and any remaining ***bolts***. Bury your blade. Exult in your barbarity. Loot! Pillage! Hey—he's only a Sharga.

Sniveling Sniper. This slain Sharga drops useful items—a handy crossbow, complete with a quiver of bolts. Unfortunately, he also drops—well, I'll let you find out for yourself.

Continue west down the corridor, and go through the wooden door.

38. The Ettin's Trap

This is a covered ***pit trap***, like the one back at 35. If you step onto this square, your party falls in, and each member suffers 1-30 points of damage. You can avoid this calamity, however. Just move ahead to step 39.

Then again, perhaps you like to fall shrieking into dank black hellholes. If so, read the following section.

Note *If You Fall in the Ettin's Pit:* If the Ettin is alive, and this is the first time you've fallen into the pit, the Ettin is summoned. Step back, then step forward into the square directly below the pit opening. The Ettin pushes his boulder into the pit.

You have a brief moment to press the back arrow and get out from under the falling boulder. If you don't hop back, all of your party members take 100 points of damage—probably enough to kill them all. If you *do* hop back in time, grab the two ***heal roots*** in the

pit, and use the fallen boulder as a ladder to climb out of the pit. If you stumble into the pit again, you'll only take about five points of damage from the fall.

39. Edfilduhr the Ettin

Note Before you enter the Ettin's room, be sure you have the Silence rune (from 3) and a runecaster full of Mana.

Welcome to the cave of the monstrous two-headed ***Ettin***. If you sneak in quietly—without smashing bone piles, etc.—the big oaf will be sound asleep when you arrive. However, about anything you do will awaken him. And if you do, you're dead meat—the Ettin is invincible!

So here's what you do:

1. Step into the north-east corner, then turn right to face the barrels.
2. Use the Silence rune on the middle barrel.
3. Break the nearest barrel.
4. Step forward to the chest.

Gettin' the Ettin. Seems Edfilduhr would just as soon bludgeon himself as bludgeon you. Remember, you can't kill him and he can't kill himself . . . but he will kill you if you are foolish enough to wake him.

40. Ettin's Treasure

Loot his chest for some significant treasure: two ***green gems***, a ***red gem***, a ***blue gem***, and the important ***Throg gate key*** (called "a throggish key" in your journal).

But best of all, in the chest lies ***Aquila's Orb***, the second of the nine receptacles of the gods.

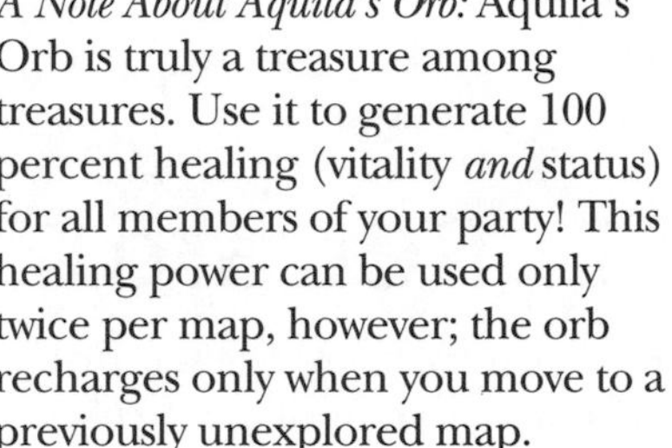

Note *A Note About Aquila's Orb:* Aquila's Orb is truly a treasure among treasures. Use it to generate 100 percent healing (vitality *and* status) for all members of your party! This healing power can be used only twice per map, however; the orb recharges only when you move to a previously unexplored map.

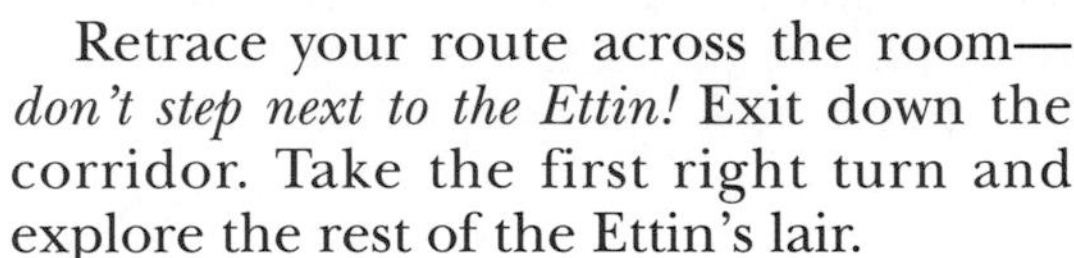

Retrace your route across the room—*don't step next to the Ettin!* Exit down the corridor. Take the first right turn and explore the rest of the Ettin's lair.

41. Exploding Fungus

Slash the ***exploding fungus*** and move on.

42. Cave-in

The ceiling collapses behind you in a ***cave-in*** when you step out of this square. Just hack through with a few swift blows.

43. Dead End

Scoop up two ***heal roots*** and the shoddy Sharga ***mining pick***. You'll also find a ***green gem*** buried in that ***carcass*** on the floor.

44. Passage to Lower Mines

Now work your way back to the northern tip of the map. Use this stairway to climb down to the lower level of the Sharga Mines.

Note Most of the following walkthrough steps (from 45 to 79) refer to events that take place on Map 4.2, Sharga Mines (Lower Level).

45. Rude Welcome

As you step out of the stairway, a foolish (but tough) ***Sharga***, armed with a ***crossbow*** and a ***quiver*** of four ***bolts***, attacks your party. After he expires, gently relieve him of his weaponry. Continue down the hall.

46. Waiting . . .

This ***Sharga*** is less tough. Dispatch him quickly and move on down the mineshaft to the first door on your right.

47. Guardian Snake

Hear that hissing? It's a ***snake***, believe it or not. Nail the circling reptile here, in this alcove. If you don't, and go past, it will slither up behind you for a sneak attack.

48. Portcullis Switch

Seems impassable, doesn't it? The ***portcullis*** is quite sturdy and unbreakable. To open it, you must pull that ***handle*** down—the one on the back wall. But of course you can't reach it. So throw something at it.

Tip Best bet: Get a good rock in your hand, center it on the wall handle, then move the rock to the very top of the screen. Click to throw.

Portcullis. Throw stuff at that switch in there. Rocks, bottles . . . whatever works.

49. Mushroom Patch

Once you get past that ***exploding fungus*** in the entry, gather up three ***heal roots***, a ***spotted mushroom***, three bunches of ***red mushrooms***, and two ***green mushrooms***.

Note Come back again later! Five minutes after you pick the mushrooms, a new crop grows in. (The new crop is a random assortment.)

Exit the room through the door and continue down the mineshaft to the east. Go through the next door on the right.

50. Shut Up!

Another ***toadstool*** alarm goes off when you enter this room. Sauté the damn thing, then step forward and brace yourself. First, three very tough ***Shargas***, alerted by the toadstool, launch a frontal assault. An even tougher ***Sharga*** follows up with a wicked counterstrike.

51. Reward

Here's the payoff. A ***chest*** holds two ***super heal roots***, a pair of ***gold coins***, and an ***oil bomb***. Exit the room into the corridor, then go 2E, 3N, 2E, and north through the door.

52. They're Ruining Your Suit

Two more ***exploding fungi*** hurl at you. Aggressively trim their hedges and move on around the corner.

53. Surprise

Punch through the ***bone pile*** here to uncover a batch of ***red mushrooms***. At the intersection, turn right.

54. Sharga Patrol, Part 1

Several Shargas roam this area. First, a lone ***Sharga*** sentry takes a whack at you. After the battle, continue down the corridor. Take the passage that branches north.

55. Sharga Patrol, Part 2

Two more ***Sharga*** regulars may wander up to you and make a feeble attempt to stand between you and your destiny. After you crush them in body and spirit, proceed to the end of the alcove.

56. Peeping at Throgs

Look through the ***crack in the wall***. An arrogant ***Throg*** brutalizes a poor ***Sharga***. This chilling sight prompts the following conversation:

Farli: That Throg will beat him to death. And he does not fight back.

Drake: The Shargas are nothing but slaves.

Farli: Aye, and my people hate slavery more then Shargas.

Drake: So it would seem.

Farli: If only the green ones would fight back . . .

And so the plot thickens. Retreat from the alcove, go west to the intersection, then turn right and follow the mine shaft.

Crack User. Put your eyeball to this crack in the wall. Do you see now why Shargas are such a testy bunch?

57. Bone Fungi

Another batch of ***red mushrooms*** lies buried in a ***bone pile***. Pick them and move on.

58. Serpentine

Here comes another slithering ***snake*** attack. It's nice to have companions at a time like this.

59. Cave-In and Snake

Bust through the ***cave-in*** debris, then fight off another venomous ***snake***. Continue west down the passage.

60. What Bolt Did You Say?

Along the way, grab the large ***ballista bolt*** lying next to the dead snake in this alcove. What is it, you ask? Hey, do I look like Mr. Science? (Actually, it's a spear-type weapon.

61. Another Cave-In and Snake

Another ***snake*** lies in wait behind the debris of another ***cave-in***. Continue down the passage to the door. Go through the door and follow the shaft to the cowering ***Sharga***.

62. Grug the Sharga

Meet ***Grug***, groveler nonpareil. Unlike your usual Sharga, Grug is not hostile. Sensing this, neither Farli nor Karzak attack the pathetic creature. As your party approaches, Grug says, "Oh, masters, donna hurt Grug. Pleaz!"

Groveling Grug. Don't hurt this fellow. Give him a hand, and he'll "show you home."

Note I beg you to remember that all written dialogue in this walkthrough, including the phonetic spelling of Sharga dialect, is lifted directly from *Stonekeep* design documents and scripts.

With Grug, you get two chances to prove what a barbarian you are—or aren't. If you don't strike him down immediately after his plea for mercy (and killing Grug doesn't take more than a single blow, because he's badly hurt), Farli says, "Lo, this one is too small to slaughter. I will leave his fate up to you, Drake." This gives you a second moment of choice. If you do *not* slaughter the small one within a couple of seconds, the following conversation unfolds:

Drake: Relax, little one, we come in peace.

Grug: Watta 'bout the stuntie? ("Stuntie" is slang for Dwarf.)

Farli: I've seen too much slavery in my day, greenie. You'll not visit your god by my hand.

Drake: What are you doing here?

Grug: Scaly-one hurt Grug. Grug no go home now.

Drake: Show us this "scaly-one," Grug.

Grug: Yah! Follow Grug, masters. Masters kill scaly-one. Grug show you home.

Grug leaves. Follow him. If you lose sight of him, don't worry. He'll stop at each turn, waiting for your lumbering party to catch up.

63. Scaly One

Grug leads you to a secret door here. When the door opens, step past Grug and slay the "scaly-one"—a giant ***snake***. Grug sits back until the snake is dead, then leads you "home" as promised—all the way to the headquarters of the Sharga Freedom League!

Caution As you follow Grug, you pass scary-looking Shargas marching down passages. Repress that conditioned impulse to gore them—they're all Throg-hating freedom fighters who are more or less on your side!

64. SFL Rebel Leader

Grug leads you to ***Skrag***, the Sharga Freedom League (SFL) leader, who stands in this alcove opposite the crackling ***campfire***. Skrag is a Sharga shaman—he *looks* no different than regular Shargas, but he can cast spells.

If the SFL is hostile—that is, if you foolishly attacked an SFL sharga along the way—then Skrag will attack you. If the SFL is *not* hostile, then Skrag talks to you. The first time you meet, the conversation goes like this:

Skrag: Hiyaz, I'z Skrag. Youz are Drake.

Drake: Yes. How did you know?

Skrag: Skrag throw barabari leavez onna fire. See youz come. Youz gotta destiny az bigga dis mine.

Drake: Can you help us?

Farli: Do you know about my brother?

Skrag: You must pass beyond dat gate, and enter da Temple of our enemies. Der you will findz your help and kin. (laughs)

Drake: Where is the gate to the Throg Temple?

Skrag: Go west, young Drake. West beyond the hidden doorway. Da giant can unlock yer way. Youz need some mana, doncha?

He then casts a spell that recharges all of your runecasters.

When your first conversation with Skrag is done, he says, "Now, go. Take da battle to da enemiez. And remember Skrag. It will help youz."

65. Secret Button

Go past Skrag into the alcove and bash the ***barrel***. Behind it is a secret ***button***. Push it to open a ***secret room*** behind you.

66. SFL Treasure

Enter the secret room and open the ***chest***. Apparently, the League is more than happy to share its assets with you, now that you are an ally. Some of these "assets" are kind of odd—a ***skull*** and a ***broken sword***, for example. Other assets are more valuable. Take the ***green gem*** and the ***rune scroll***.

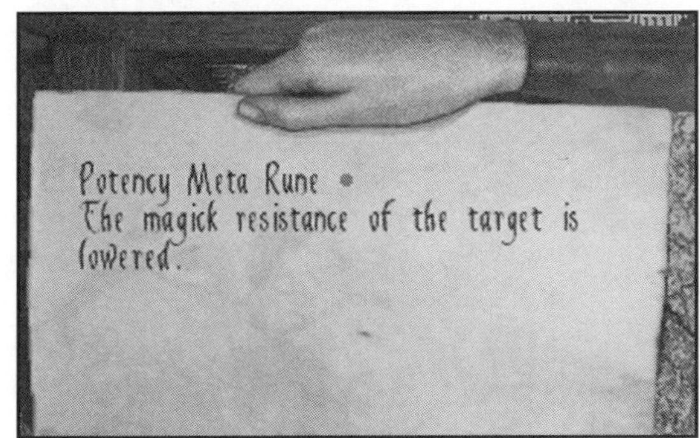

Potency Rune Scroll

Exit the shaman's alcove and head west to explore some of the areas you hurried past while following Grug. (Fight the urge to slay any Shargas you see on the way.)

67. Wall Button

Push the ***button*** on the south wall. A ***secret room*** opens behind you.

68. Meat 'n' Money

Four ***Shargas*** stand guard in this room, but don't attack them. Grab the hunk of ***meat*** (called "bad smelling Throg food" in your journal), four ***coins***, and three ***heal roots***. Exit and continue west to the next room.

69. Shrimp Sharga

Meet the Mickey Rooney of the SFL. If you approach him, this ***small Sharga*** says, "Ha, youz don wanna open dis door." Open the door—you'll catch a glimpse of a very big Sharga—and the little squirt says, "Ha ha, toldcha so!"

Mutt and Jeff. This odd pair must be pretty unpopular in the SFL. No one seems to care if you kill them.

For fun, whack the little guy. His dying scream is one of the funniest moments in the game. Strangely, his death has no effect on the SFL rank and file. Step through the door.

70. Sharga Grande

The very big, very tough Sharga—Tiny, to his friends—is a tad upset about your treatment of his buddy. "Youz hurt Tinyz friend! Tiny hurtz you!" In fact, Tiny can put a big hurt on you. Avoid his blows if you can.

After you kill the big galoot, pick up what he drops: six ***coins***, a ***blue gem***, and a ***green gem***. Now search the ***barrels*** in his room. Two are empty, but the one in the corner holds some ***red mushrooms***. Exit and continue west.

71. Throg Gate Intersection

If you want, you can head west at this intersection; this route takes you to the ***Throg gate*** and passage to Level 5: *Entrance to the Throg Temple*. But that leaves unexplored territory here in the mines, and since all roleplayers are obsessive-compulsive types, your sleep patterns would be seriously disrupted by an overriding sense of anxiety. No, better to head east here, then north to the wooden door.

72. Slimy Door

Listen for the telltale sound of some fairly tough ***slimes***. Then burst through both doors, weapons flashing.

73. Cave-in

More ***slime*** waits on the other side of that ***cave-in*** debris. Do the obvious—the only good slime is a dead slime—then head east.

74. You Guessed It

Yep, still more ***slimes***, one after another, some quite tough. It's kind of fun to blast these guys with firebolts from a runecaster, but you be the judge. Continue east, slinging fire at slimes all the way, then work your way south until you reach the next wooden door.

75. Toadstool

Slice up this ***toadstool***, just for fun. Continue exploring.

76. Sharga Tory

This ***Sharga*** hasn't joined the SFL rebellion, so your Sharga-bashing days aren't over yet. *Have a nice day!* Head west, then north up to 77.

77. Heal Root

The only item here is a single ***heal root*** on the floor. Exit the room and head west to the door.

78. Sharga Freedom League, East Entrance

This door is locked. The first time you try to open it, a muffled voice sounds from behind the door:

Sharga Rebel: (muffled) Whats da password?

Drake: What?

Sharga Rebel: You needa password to enter da SFL.

Farli: (grunts)

Drake: I don't know the password.

Sharga Rebel: Den go away!

The second time you try to open the door:

Sharga Rebel: Wats da password?

Drake: What's the SFL?

Sharga Rebel: Da Sharga Freedom League, stupie! Now go away!

The response you get the third time you try the door (and every time after) depends on whether or not you saw the "crack-in-the-wall" scene at 56. If you *didn't:*

Sharga Rebel: Wats da password?

Drake: I don't know the password.

Sharga Rebel: Den go away!

If you saw the "crack-in-the-wall" animation at 56, your third attempt to open the door prompts this dialogue:

Sharga Rebel: Wats da password?

Drake: I don't know it.

Sharga Rebel: Den . . .

Drake: (interrupting) . . . but before you tell me to go away, I want you to know that I hate Throgs, too.

Sharga Rebel: Really? Dats da password.

Drake: I am looking to . . . what?

At this point, a ***Sharga*** opens the door, and you can enter the area. Every time you return to this door and the Sharga sentry asks for the password, Drake replies, "I hate Throgs, too"—and the sentry lets you in.

Caution Again, if you attack this Sharga (or *any* Sharga in the SFL), all of the SFL becomes hostile, and on subsequent returns the sentry won't ask for a password or open the door. However, if you manage to kill *all* the Shargas in the SFL—an aggressive tactic, but feasible—the door is permanently unlocked.

Now work your way northwest to the intersection at 71, then turn left.

79. The Throg Gate

You've come to the ***Throg gate***. You need the ***Throg gate key*** to open it. If you haven't yet removed the ***Throg gate key*** from the Ettin's chest (40), Wahooka's voice echoes through the cavern, saying, "Bah, you fool! The Ettin has the key!"

Level 5

Temple of Throggi

The fifth level of Stonekeep includes two map areas, the Entrance to the Throg Temple (Map 5.1), and the Temple of Throggi itself (Map 5.2). New enemies—Throgs and Throg Shamans—tax your combat skills, as do some old foes.

Magick becomes increasingly important as you move deeper into Stonekeep. Rune scrolls abound, and various shamans engage you in spell-slinging duels. Be sure to mark all areas (such as Mana Circles) where you can recharge your magickal runecasters.

Key to Maps 5.1 & 5.2

1. Passage to Sharga Mines
2. Exploding fungi
3. Wahooka
4. Poison root, heal root
5. Dead Dwarf, gem, axe, magick ring, scroll
6. Gem
7. Poison roots
8. Arrow trap maze (begin)
9. Arrow trap maze (midpoint)
10. Rubble (helm)
11. Refuse
12. Ants
13. Exploding fungi, button, secret door
14. Mana Circle
15. Refuse
16. Strength vial
17. Skeleton (broadsword, helm, quiver)
18. Trap trigger (to 19)
19. Arrow trap (triggered at 18), carcass (blue gem), heal root
20. Throgs, barrel (roots)
21. Stairway to Temple of Throggi
22. Stairway to Temple Entrance
23. Throg
24. Throg
25. Throg
26. Throgs, chest (roots), root
27. Trash pit
28. Tentacle Things
29. Rune scroll
30. Root
31. Ladder
32. Tough Throg (dowel)
33. Rune trap, gem, roots, rune scroll
34. Barrels (dowel, roots), handle (unlocks 35)
35. Locked door (unlock at 34), recharge orb
36. Throg Shaman
37. Bucket
38. Barrels (Throg food)
39. Barrels (Throg food)
40. Well
41. Campfire (ring)
42. Tough Throgs
43. Throg bodyguard
44. Throg bodyguard
45. Throg Shaman (dagger), rubble (rune scroll)
46. Throg Shaman leader (pendant—opens 48, runecaster), heal root, rune scroll
47. Throg leader (if alerted)
48. Temple door (see 46)
49. Throgs
50. Handles (unlock 51, 52, 53)
51. Dead Dwarf
52. Dombur Mallestone
53. Button (opens secret door)
54. Button (opens secret door)
55. Button (opens secret door)
56. Tough Throg
57. Throggi statue (Orb of Azrael, poison orb, magick weapons)
58. Tough Throgs
59. Tough Throgs
60. Throg leader (before alert)
61. Root
62. Coin
63. Barrels (axe, sword, dagger, short bow)
64. Roots, rubble (gem)
65. Chest (coins, roots, rune scrolls)
66. Throgs
67. Handle (unlocks 68)
68. Door (unlock at 67)
69. Trash pits
70. Throg, strength vial
71. Hole (use dowel to open 72)
72. Handle (closes pits at 69)
73. Throg Shaman
74. Throg (coins, key), root
75. Portcullis (use Orb of Azrael)
76. Super Secret Room (teleport from Map 11)
77. Passage to Dragon Feeding Grounds

Map 5.1 Entrance to the Throg Temple

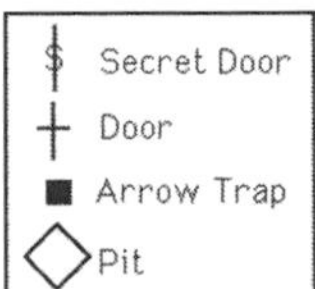

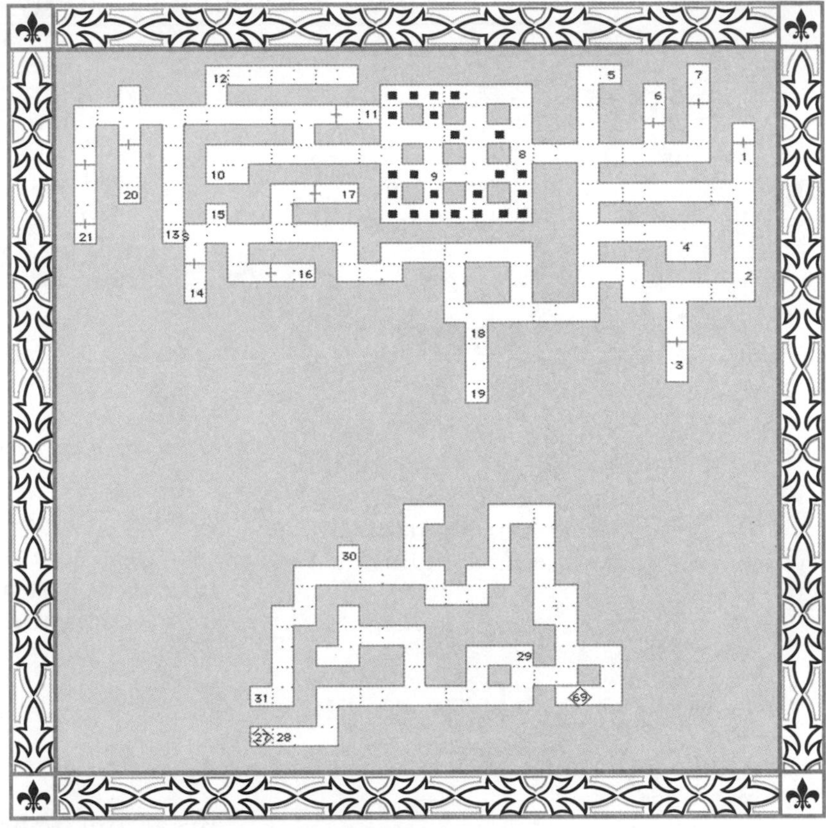

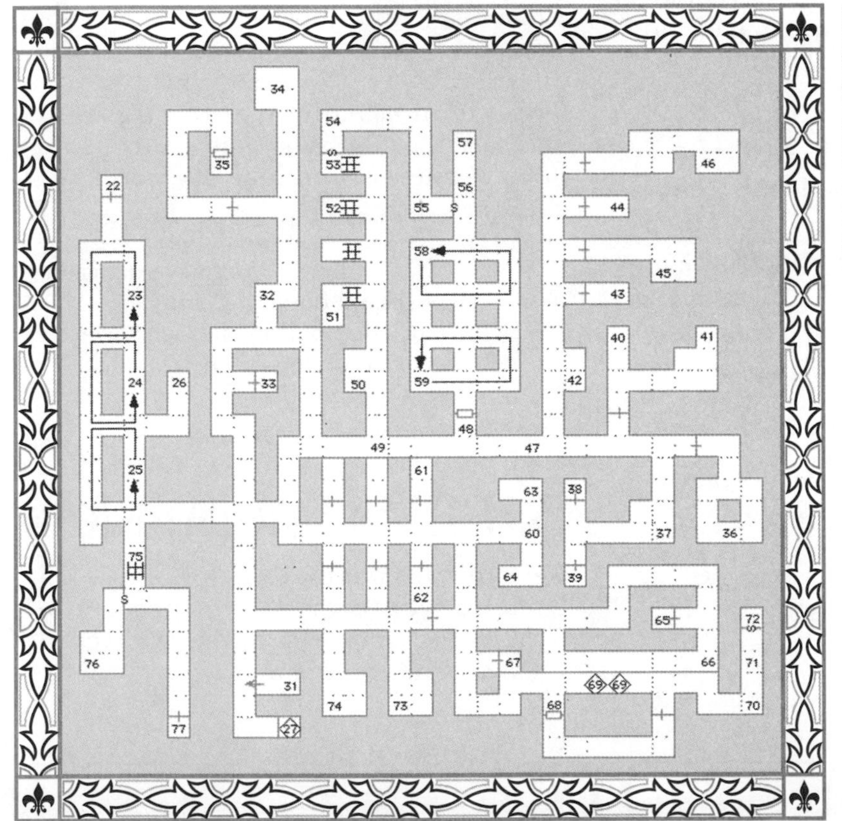

Map 5.2 Temple of Throggi

1. Start

These stairs lead down from the Throg gate in the lower level of the Sharga Mines (at 79 on Map 4.2). From here, head due south.

2. More Spores Afore

Know a good fungicide? Three of those blasted ***exploding fungi*** line the passage. Chop them up, continue around the corner, then take the first left turn. Go to the door.

3. Wahooka Redux

Step inside. Your good buddy Wahooka appears and says: "Greetings again, lost one. Have I mentioned that in the days of old, heroes would bring gifts to their elders in return for their ancient wisdom? Have you a gift for me, hmm?"

Drake's respectful response: "Greetings, O he of the long wind."

Here's how to play the Wahooka Game:

1. Give Wahooka any item (except an orb). The finicky goblin refuses it and says: "Hmmm, very nice. But not what I was looking for. Bring out your next gift!"
2. Offer him another item (again, except an orb). He'll refuse again, saying, "Bah! Not that!"
3. Now offer Wahooka *any weapon or armor item.* His response? "Ahh! Yes, yes, this is it. Well—it was nice seeing you again."

At this point, Drake says, "Don't you have something for me?"

Wahooka responds, "Bah! Oh well, yes, I suppose I do. A word of warning, human, keep an eye out for the god of this temple." And away he goes.

Note If you try to give Wahooka an orb, he'll refuse it, saying, "No, no! Not that! That is very special, human, very special."

Grab the ***heal root*** on the floor, then exit the room to the corridor and turn left. Go down the passage to the intersection, then head north to the next room on the right.

4. Storeroom

Break open the grain sacks to find a ***poison root***. (Your journal says, "This root smells musty.") A ***heal root*** lies in the opposite corner. Exit and head north. Skip the next hallway to the right—it leads back to the start, and contains no items of interest. Continue due north.

Tip Go ahead, eat the poison root. You'll suffer 5–8 points of damage, but you'll build immunity to a particular poison later in the game. (For more detail, see 57 in this section.)

5. RIP Stonebuilder

Behind two ***barrels*** lies the body of a Dwarf adventurer. If you break the barrels and step forward, the Dwarves in your party recognize him:

Farli: I knew him. Dunton Stonebuilder. He was a stout friend of my brother.

Karzak: Dunton, you will be avenged. I so swear.

Pick up Dunton's items—a ***blue gem***, a ***battle axe***, a ***magickal armor ring***, and two ***scrolls***, including one with a last message from good Dunton. It reads:

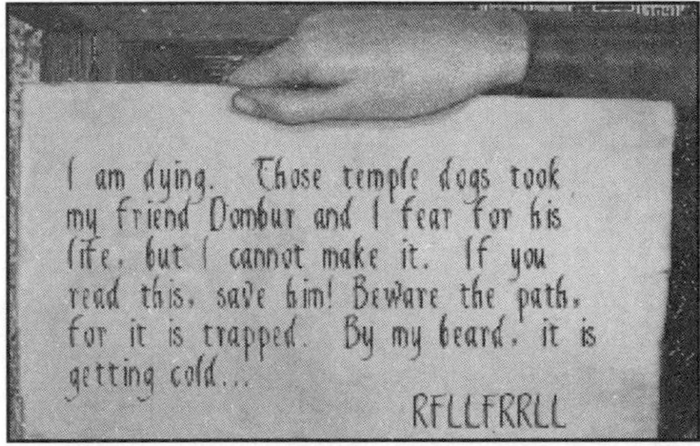

I am dying. Those temple dogs took my friend Dombur and I fear for his life, but I cannot make it. If you read this, save him! Beware the path, for it is trapped. By my beard, it is getting cold...

RFLLFRRLL

The other scroll informs you that green mushrooms "cure poison and other ailments." Jot down the scroll sequence—*RFLLFRRLL*. Then put the ring on Drake's hand in the mystic mirror. It increases Drake's armor (defense) rating by a total of 3 points—1 point each for *cut, crush,* and *pierce.*

Exit and go to the next room to the east.

6. Another Storeroom

All the barrels in this room are empty. Grab the ***blue gem*** from the floor, then exit and go east to the next room.

7. And Yet Another Storeroom

Bash the ***barrels*** to find three more ***poison roots***. Feed these to your other party members; again, they may suffer slow damage from the slow-acting poison, but they also build some immunity to a particular poison later in the game. Exit the room and head west.

8. Brink of Maze

You stand on the brink of a square maze bristling with ***arrow traps.***

9. Trapped Floor Maze

The simple code at the bottom of Dunton's scroll (RFLLFRRLL) leads you safely through the maze. If you haven't figured it out yet, here's the correct path: *Go right three squares, left two squares, left four squares, right two squares, then right two squares, two squares left, one square left, then one square right* to emerge from the trap area. Once you're out, continue due west.

Caution If you deviate from the correct path, you set off the arrow traps. Each trap shoots one arrow. Each arrow does about 15-30 points of piercing damage to the party member it hits.

10. Dombur's Helm

Search the ***rubble*** in the corner for the ***Dwarven helm***. When you pick it up, Farli says, "That is my brother's helm." Exit the room to the passage leading north. Then turn right.

11. Stinkpit!

Outside the door to this room, click on the sign on the north wall. If you use the Language rune on Drake, he reads it: "Stinkpit." Otherwise, Farli sniffs something unpleasant, and says, "I think it is a garderobe." Inside is lots of putrid, disgusting ***refuse*** and one ***super heal root*** in the back.

Garbage In, Garbage Out. Didn't your mom teach you to keep your hands off rancid, festering putrefaction?

Caution If you touch any of the garbage, you may suffer mild sickness, depending on the level of your poison resistance.

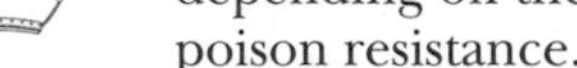

Exit the dump and head west. Take the first right turn.

12. Anty Maim!

Yes, this secluded alcove looks promising. But all you find here are three hostile ***warrior ants***. Exit the alcove and continue west a couple of steps, then take the first left turn.

13. Spit and Polish

Better yet, polish off the spitters. Three noxious ***exploding fungi*** try to spore you to death. Flatten them into salad, then push the ***button*** on the west wall to open a ***secret door*** behind you on the east wall. Go through the new opening, then take the first right turn.

14. Mana from Heaven

Enter the small room. Step into the green ***Mana Circle*** for a full recharge of your runecasters. Exit back to the corridor, turn right, and continue east.

Mana Circle. Step in, juice up, head out.

15. Pheeeew!

Just a step further up the hall is a very bad-smelling alcove, full of ***refuse***, rotting flesh, and other rejectamenta. If you touch any of this smelly stuff, there's a chance you'll become mildly poisoned. Better continue east past it. Take the next right turn up ahead.

16. Throg Vial

Behind the door ahead you'll find an odd ***vial***. Your journal calls it a "Throg-holding-a-boulder vial," and adds: "It reeks!" When you grap the object, Farli grunts with revulsion:

Farli: Aaargh. Now that is disgusting stuff. I would not be so quick to quaff that.

Drake: Can it really be *that* bad?

Farli: Yes. Once we reach our clanhall, I will be able to introduce you to a nice Dwarven stout brew.

Drake: Right. Well, enough of that then. But I think I'll be keeping this, just in case.

Drake's instinct here is correct. If you drink this vial, your Strength rating is increased to your 10-star maximum for one minute. If you drink *another* such Throg vial during that minute, a one-point Strength bonus will become permanent! Not a bad deal. Maybe you'd better keep it in inventory for now.

OK, ready for a new nemesis? Exit the room and return to the corridor. Continue east, then take that first passage to the left.

17. Mister Bone-jangles

Do you feel lucky? Get ready: Inside this room is the ***skeleton*** of a long-dead adventurer. This guy is very, very tough. He's also very possessive of something, mumbling "Treasure. . . mine. . . you, thief. . . the eye" when you enter the room.

After you defeat him—make that *if* you defeat him—grab his ***broadsword***, his unusual ***helm*** (which your journal calls "a helm from the far east"), and that ***quiver*** made especially for "magickal black arrows," whatever they are. Put on his helm—you'll see a nice increase in your defense rating.

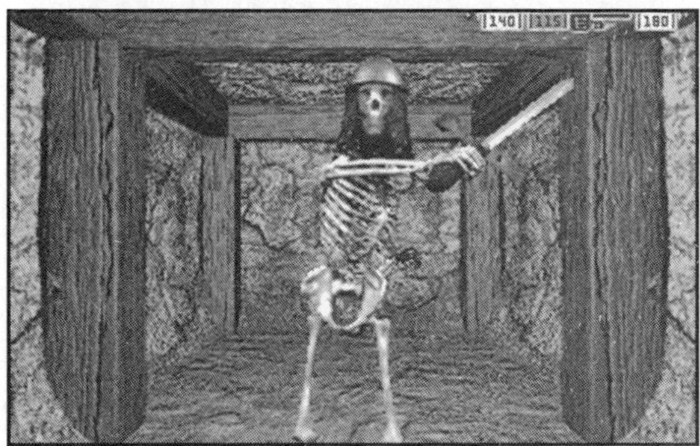

This Guy Wants to Pick a Bone With You. But your trusty Dagger of Penetration, so lethal in most fights, is pretty useless against a bunch of bones. Better hammer him—or better yet, blast him with rune magick.

Tip The bad news is, this skeletal opponent is as tough as they come. He's impervious to piercing weapons, such as your Dagger of Penetration. The good news is. . . hmm, let's see. Is there any? OK, he can't leave the room, making cowardly retreat easy. Also, know that five or six power-enhanced firebolts from a runecaster can take him down. Afterwards, recharge back at the Mana Circle at 14, then return and continue.

Exit the room, return to the corridor, and turn left. Work your way in an easterly direction down the passage. Take the first right turn. Follow the passage, then take the next right turn.

18. Arrow Trigger

See the pile of bones? What happened to that guy? If you take a step forward, you find out: Six ***arrows*** fly from an ***arrow trap*** at the end of the corridor. Grab those arrows, then head south and check out the trap.

19. Yo, Sapphire

Punch out the ***carcass***, Rocky-style, on the ground just under the arrow holes of the trap. Take the ***blue gem***, then grab the ***heal root*** in the corner.

You've gone as far east as you want to go—nothing else of interest lies there. Now work your way back west through the secret passage at 13. Go north to the intersection and turn left. Go west two steps, turn left, and go through the door.

20. Throg Throttling

Two huge ***Throgs*** are posted here. You can sneak in and blast them a few times from a distance before they turn and attack.

Throgs! They're big, cruel, ugly. And you thought Shargas were bad!

Break open the barrel in the room to get two ***super heal roots*** and a couple of meaty shanks of ***Throg food*** (you can eat the Throg food, but it isn't a particularly pleasant experience). Exit the room and follow the corridor to the left. Go through both doors.

21. Stairway to Throg Temple

This stairway connects the Temple Entrance area to the Temple of Throggi.

22. Stairway to Temple Entrance

This stairway leads back down to the entrance area of the temple.

23, 24, 25. Throg Patrols

A single ***Throg*** wanders each of these three areas, patrolling in a circular motion (see paths marked on map). Each guard stops occasionally. Each guard carries a ***throgsword*** and a ***shield*** (made of "worked leather"). The Throg at 23 carries a ***gold coin***, and the Throg at 25 carries two ***gold coins***.

Tip It is possible (and perhaps *advisable* if your vitality is low) to sneak past all of the Throgs posted at 23, 24, and 25 by slipping quickly down the western-most corridor. But if one Throg guard sees you, he alerts his fellow guards.

26. Throg Reinforcements

Two ***Throgs*** lay in hiding here. When you enter this alcove, you see a ***chest.*** As you approach it the Throgs jump you from behind. Kill them, then open the chest and loot its juicy contents—two ***super heal roots.*** Don't forget to snatch the ***heal root*** next to the chest.

Exit the alcove and head south. You'll see a ***portcullis*** (interlaced spears) ahead. You cannot pass through this barrier yet. Take the first left, heading east. Turn right at the first intersection and head south to the end of the passage. Turn left and approach the door.

27. Trash Pit

The ***sign*** on the south wall, written in Throggish, reads: *Beware of The Things!* If you use the Language rune, Drake can read it. If not, Farli simply says, "Something is below."

Caution A rune scroll lies in the trash pits below. However, you should already have it, and you must fight three *very* powerful creatures to get it. If your vitality is low or your runecasters are not fully charged, I recommend you skip this step for now and jump ahead to 32.

Cast a Featherfall rune ("Lesser Aerial Magick") on each of your party members. Open the door and leap in.

28. Trash Pit Monsters

Two tri-tentacled ***Things*** attack immediately. This is the same type of beastly hard creature you battled in the Sewers beneath Stonekeep back in Level 3. One was bad enough, but here are two—and that's not all! If you manage to slay them, a third ***Thing*** awaits you around the corner just ahead.

Bad Things Aplenty. Did you learn your lesson in the sewers? Blast them with firebolts before they get close!

Tip Forget fighting these guys at close quarters. You want to hit them from a distance with firebolts (enhanced with power modifiers, if you have them). Begin firing the moment the creatures lurch around the corner.

29. The Magick That Floats

If you manage to survive the Thing attack, explore the trash pits. Don't touch any of the ***refuse***, or you'll get sick. Most of the alcoves are treasureless dead ends. Keep moving until you find this ***rune scroll*** on the floor:

Featherfall Rune Scroll

30. Have a Bite

Grab the ***super heal root*** from the floor in this alcove, then scoop up the ***green mushroom*** just to the west.

31. Ladder Up

Take the ***ladder*** to the top, then step forward through the one-way passage—when you turn around, you face a solid, impassable wall. (The only way back down to the trash pits is through the hole at 27.) Work your way north past the intersection, then past the door (at 33) on the right. Continue around the corner.

32. Throg With Dowel

A ***tough Throg*** lurks just around the corner to the north. End his miserable existence, then take the small ***wooden dowel*** he drops. Now go back to the door you just passed.

33. Spell Trap

The door's unlocked. But if you step directly into this room, you get hit with multiple Throg spells. Before you enter, turn to face the north wall. Find the small ***hole*** in the lower right corner of the wall, then insert the wooden dowel in the hole. This disables the Tornado spell.

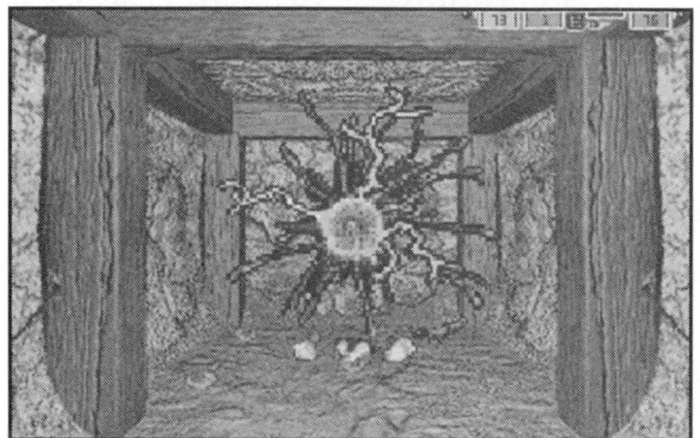

Throg Spell. Put the wooden dowel in the north wall before you enter the room, or you'll take this blast to the chops.

Now enter the room. Pick up the ***blue gem***, the three ***super heal roots***, and the ***rune scroll***. Open the scroll:

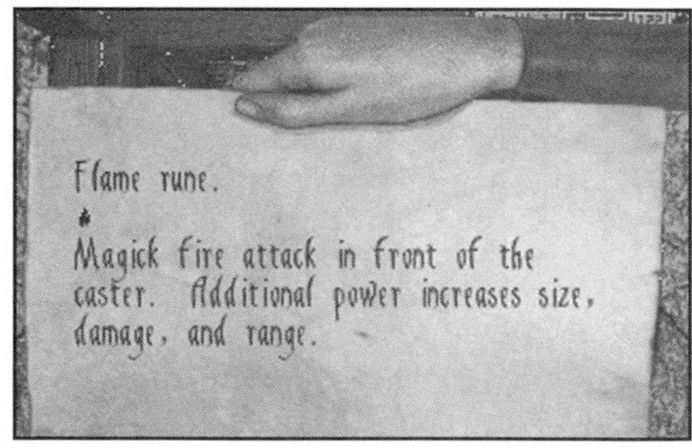

Flame Rune Scroll

Exit the room, turn right and go to the dead Throg you left at 32. Continue north into the room full of barrels.

34. Roll Out the Barrels

Break open the ***barrels*** to find another ***wooden dowel*** and four delectable ***heal roots***. Pull the ***handle*** on the wall to unlock the door at 35. Go south, then take the first righ turn and go through the wooden door. Follow the corridor around to the next door.

35. Orb Juice

You unlocked this door by pulling the wall handle back at 34. . . didn't you? (If not, go do it now.) Open the door. Wow, what the hell is that?

Power Lips. Don't touch that orb! Instead, touch it with your runecasters for a full recharge.

Whatever it is, don't touch it. You'll get *such* a shock (ten points worth, in fact). Instead, click each of your rune-casters on the glowing white ***orb***. This fully recharges them. Heal your party and recharge again.

Now exit the room and work your way back south to the dead Throg at 32. At the corridor, turn left. Go 2E, 5S, then head due east a long way, until you reach the wooden door.

36. Mad Throg Hermit

Enter the room. A somewhat loopy ***Throg Shaman*** paces back and forth. He's peaceful, unless attacked. If you step up to him, he says, "My pretty little stone. Where is my stone? My little pretty stone. I lost my little pretty stone."

Padded Room Candidate. This guy lost his pretty little stone. Replace it with a sapphire.

If you give him one of your blue gems, he says, "Aw, there is my pretty stone. My little stone. I saw you in the passage, I did. Played by Throggi himself, and nobody knew. No one, no one knew. But I did. Imprisoned, not I, not I. Heh. Oh, my pretty stone is home. Single stone return home."

If you give him *another* sapphire, the Hermit sounds almost sane, and says, "Thank you, thank you, nothing like this has happened since I enchanted the green orb with poison. Heh-heh."

Exit his room and take the first left.

Note

The mad Shaman defends himself if attacked. Such a tactic is barely worth it. After battle, all you find is a ***broken runecaster***.

37. Throg Kitchen

Ahead, you see a crackling ***campfire***. Some wretched ***Throg food***, a couple of ***barrels***, and a ***bucket*** lie scattered around the fire. Grab the bucket and continue down the corridor. You reach an intersection that branches north and south to two small rooms.

38. Butcher Stores

In the northern room, two ***barrels*** hold more of that bad-smelling ***Throg food***.

39. Meat Matter

In the southern room, two more ***barrels*** hold still more sickening shanks of ***Throg food***. Let's get out of here, shall we? Exit the kitchen area back to the corridor, head west a couple of steps, then go through the door on the right.

40. Well, Now!

It's a ***well***. Put your bucket (the one from 37) on the well-hook, then turn the crank on top to lower the bucket. Turn the crank again to raise the bucket, which is now full of water. Take the full bucket to the eastern section of the room.

Fire Ring. Use the bucket to draw water from the well, then douse the campfire in the next alcove. Grab the magickal ring from the ashes.

41. Give Me a Ring

Click the bucket of water on the ledge of the ***campfire*** to douse the fire, then take the ***magickal armor ring***. (You can get the ring *without* dousing the fire, but you'll sustain fire damage.) Put the ring on any party member. (Remember, it increases its wearer's Armor rating by a total of 3 points—1 point each for *cut*, *crush*, and *pierce*.) Exit the room to the corridor, take three steps west, then turn right.

42. Purely Throggish

Two ***tough Throgs*** wait in ambush here. Lay waste the fools, then move on north to the next room.

Note Throgs recognize runecasters. If you hold one up, they run away.

43 & 44. The Shaman's Bodyguards

A single ***Throg bodyguard*** inhabits each of these two rooms. Get them one at a time, then go to room 45.

Note Entering either of the other two rooms in this area (45 or 46) alerts the Throg bodyguards at 43 and 44, and they wait for you in the hallway.

45. Sub-Shaman

This ***Throg Shaman*** hides just around the corner of his room. Turn the corner and get in his face *fast*—if you wait too long, he can hurl deadly spells with his runecaster. He also carries what your journal describes as "a wicked ***Throg dagger***." Grab it when he falls. Then punch through the ***rubble*** pile, find the ***rune scroll***, and open it:

Note When you attack this Shaman, you send an alert to the Throg Guard leader posted at 60. This powerful Throg then moves to position 47 and waits for you to exit the Shaman's area.

Shield Rune Scroll. Exit the room into the corridor. Go north to the last room, and enter.

46. Honcho Shaman

This ***Throg Shaman*** is the high priest of the Throg Temple. When you round the corner and face him, he says, "Well, you have come to the heart of my temple, where none but the Throg may go. By Throggi, I am Gorda Karn and I will see you die for that!"

Drake casually replies, "You have little chance of that."

Gorda's Gold. If you want, you can sling spells from a distance—but Gorda Karn's an experienced Shaman. Better to get in close, hand to hand.

Tip As with the previous Shaman, the best tactic here is to engage in close-quarters combat. This prevents Gorda Karn from casting magick spells at your party.

When killed, Karn drops a ***Throg pendant*** and a ***Throg runecaster*** with a full Mana charge of 40. This runecaster serves two functions: Use it as a runecaster (click the mouse button corresponding to Drake's "equipped" hand) or as a staff (click the mouse button corresponding to Drake's "empty" hand).

Search the room for the ***super heal root*** in the corner, and the ***rune scroll*** on the rubble pile. Open the scroll to inscribe it in your journal:

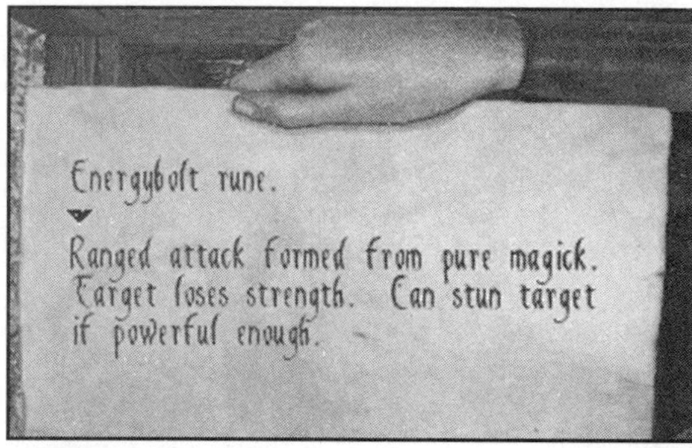

Energybolt Rune Scroll.

Exit Gorda Karn's rooms, then go south. Stop just before you reach the intersection—someone waits just around the corner to the right!

47. Throg-lodyte

Here's the powerful ***Throg leader*** on this level. Originally posted at 60, he was alerted by your entrance into the Sub-Shaman's quarters at 45, then hurried here to investigate. Now he waits patiently for you to turn the corner and attack. Do it, then continue west.

Big Dog Throg. The leader of the Temple Guard waits just around the corner. See him?

48. Temple Door

This door leads to the Temple itself. Normally it is locked, but you can open it two ways. If you have the Throg pendant from Gorda Karn at 46, the door unlocks for you, or you can force it open with brute strength if your Strength rating is maxed out at 10 stars. This, you may recall, is what happens for a minute when you drink the Throg strong juice.

A more efficient path into the Temple lies to the west. Continue west to the next corridor on the right.

Ugly Throg Gargoyle. Redundant phrase, isn't it? To open this door, you need a shot of Throg strong juice—or a Throg pendant.

49. What Sneaky Guys

Here's an interesting experience. Two towering ***Throg*** guards make a run at you, then suddenly stop. After some unsettling eye contact, they turn and leave! Unfortunately, they don't go far. In fact, they're waiting just around that corner up ahead. (Geez, what a clever ploy.)

50. Four Switches

Decimate the Throg jail guards, if you haven't done so already. The four ***handles*** on the wall activate four ***portcullis*** gates just off the corridor to the north. Behind each portcullis is a jail cell. Pull the handles down to open the cells.

51. Throg Victim

In this first cell, you find a ***dead Dwarf*** prisoner on the floor. Farli says, "Another of the folk these Throgs must answer for." If Karzak is in your party, he adds, "Aye, and they'll answer to my steel, they will!"

Exit and continue north.

52. Dombur Mallestone

The second cell is empty, but the third one holds ***Dombur Mallestone***, brother of your Dwarf compatriot Farli. If the portcullis is *not* open yet, you hear the following conversation:

Farli: Dombur! Brother, are you alright?

Dombur: Why, Farli, how good to see you. You should not be out of the hall, what would the elders think?

Farli: Dombur! You haven't changed. Drake, we must open this 'cullis.

Drake: Right.

If the portcullis is open, then:

Farli: Dombur, we have come to free you!

Dombur: But these runes are so interesting. Could you come back later?

Karzak (if present): This is no time for talk. There are Throgs to kill.

Drake: You can come with us. We have found many mysteries so far.

Dombur: That's nice. Hmmm, yes, well. The Shaman has been gone for while, it seems.

(At this point, Dombur joins your party.)

Drake: (whispers to Farli) I hope we can find a healer for him.

Farli: Nay, he has always been thus.

Drake: Ah.

Now a Foursome. With Dombur at your side, you lead a veritable Dwarf brigade.

Dombur, like Karzak earlier, is a bit weak from the ordeal of his incarceration. Give him a weapon and feed him plenty of heal substances. Continue north to the fourth jail cell.

Note Farli's bespectacled brother is not nearly as strong nor as adept at combat as the average Dwarf. Dombur, as you might suspect, is a sort of Dwarf philosopher.

53. Passage North

This cell is empty, but examine that south wall. Push the hidden ***button*** there to open a ***secret passage*** behind you. Go on through the new passage.

54. Another Button

The ***button*** on the north wall here also opens and closes the secret passage into the cell at 53. Head east and follow the twisting, turning corridor to the dead end.

55. Yet Another Button

Push the ***button*** on the west wall to open the door directly behind you. You can see someone patrolling the hall on the other side, but he doesn't see you—yet.

56. Surely the Temple

You've discovered a secret route into the inner sanctum of the Temple. That single ***tough Throg*** guard paces north/south down the Temple's central passage. Wait until he passes heading left-to-right (south). Step into the hall, then turn south to face the guard.

Now the Throg attacks, and he's mean—after all, he's guarding the holiest shrine of the Temple. Worse, he's immediately reinforced by the pair of Throgs patroling at 58—a particularly brutal assault.

57. Shrine of Throggi

Go north to the four-armed statue of Throggi. Its eyes are ***orbs***, one green and the other red. *Don't take the green orb!* If you do, it cracks open and ***poison gas*** wafts out. Instead, take the red orb—it is the ***Orb of Azrael***, third of the nine receptacles of the gods that you must retrieve in *Stonekeep.*

Note  If you *do* grab the green orb, the poison-gas damage is less points if you ate the poisoned heal root back at 4.

Throggi. Avoid the evil green eye, and grab only one of Throggi's weapons.

Each of Throggi's arms holds a stone weapon—***longsword***, ***battle-ax***, ***hammer***, and ***spear***. If you take one, it breaks off and transforms into a real, magickal weapon. Choose wisely, and *don't be greedy*—you can take only one weapon.

Tip Take the stone spear and give it to Skuz. He uses it well.

Caution If you try to take a second weapon, all of the weapons disappear and Throggi wallops your party with his powerful stone arms. (Damage from a stone arm punch can be up to 80 points.)

Now turn and head south.

58 & 59. Guardians of Throggi

Two pairs of ***tough Throgs*** patrol the inner sanctum of the Temple, marching in a circular pattern. You can avoid them completely, if you want, by simply retracing your steps back through the cellblock area down to 49.

Tip If you decide to battle the Throg guards, you may lose a companion or two, and deplete the party's vitality to critically low levels. If this happens, use Aquila's Orb to revive fallen comrades and replenish the entire party's vitality ratings.

If you choose to fight the Temple guardians, exit through the south door after the battle. Step into the corridor, then go 8W, 4S, and turn left. Dead ahead are the Throg Barracks.

60. Throg Guard Leader (Maybe)

If you've already visited the Sub-Shaman's room at 45—and if you're following this walkthrough, you *have*—then you've already faced the Throg Guard leader at 47, and he's no longer here at 60. If not, be prepared for a very tough battle.

Time to start clearing out the Barracks on either side of the hallway.

61. Two Lousy Roots?

Slay the unhappy ***Throg*** confined to his quarters. Talk about your Spartan trappings. These Throgs apparently sleep on dirt piles, and have no personal possessions whatsoever. Grab the two ***heal roots*** and leave.

62. I'm Rich!

A ***gold coin***. Wow. Don't spend it all in one place. OK, so you don't find much of substance in the Barracks. Continue east, then turn left into the northern wing.

63. Throg Armory

Break open the ***barrels***. The first one contains three ***skulls*** and a ***throwing axe***. The second contains a ***longsword*** and a ***Throg dagger***. The third contains a ***short bow***. Exit the armory and go south to the other wing.

64. More Good Stuff

Take the two ***super heal roots*** in the corner, then punch through the ***rubble*** to get the ***blue gem***. Exit to the corridor, then take the first left turn. Go 4S, then go due east and follow the corridor around until you come to the door on your right.

65. Throg Treasure

Open the ***chest*** to get three ***gold coins***, a ***heal root***, and two ***rune scrolls***. Open each scroll—one contains a Throggish rune, the other a Mannish rune:

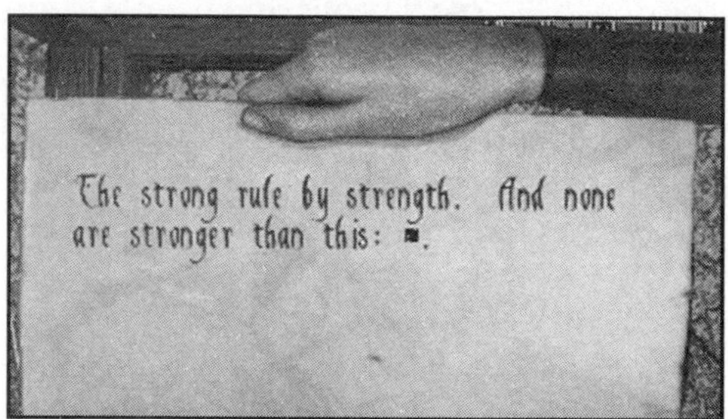

Strength Rune Scroll

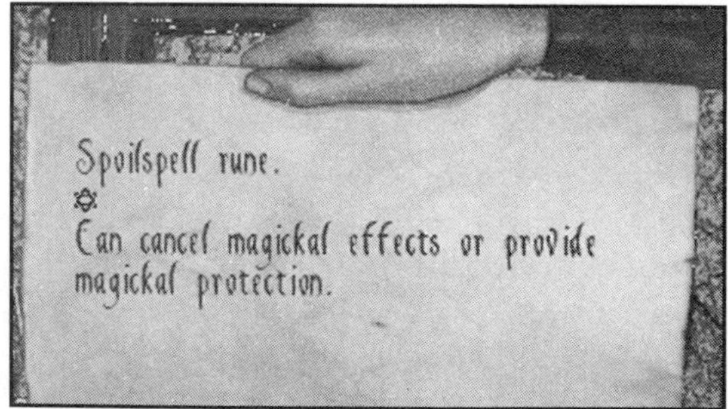

Spoilspell Rune Scroll

Exit the room, turn right, and head south. Be prepared for combat as you turn the corner up ahead.

66. Throg Patrol

Two ***Throgs*** hang around here, looking for a good fight. Give it to them, then continue west. Follow the corridor around to the intersection, then turn left. Go 4W, 2S, then go east through the door.

67. Lock Handle

The wall ***handle*** unlocks the door located at 68—but only for eight to 10 seconds! Pull the handle and hurry to the next door.

68. Locked Door

This door unlocks for eight to 10 seconds when you pull the handle at 67. If you make it in time, you can detour around the twin pits at 69. But here's a dilemma: After you pass through the door, it locks behind you.

Uh-oh. Are you trapped? Follow the corridor and see.

69. Trash Pit

If you fall into either of these traps, you end up in the trash pits. (To escape from the trash pits, go to the ladder at 31.) This is not a good thing. Instead, continue east around the turns.

Double Pits. You can't hop over them. So find the detour around them.

70. Throg Strong Juice

A ***Throg*** bearing two ***gold coins*** guards another vial of ***Throg strong juice*** (called "Throg-holding-a-boulder vial" in your journal). If you drink the contents of the vial, you become "super-strong"—your Strength rating maxes out at 10—for one glorious minute. When the juice wears off, you return to normal strength, but take 10 hit points of damage from the shock to your system.

One more thing. If you are already under the influence of another vial of Throg strong juice when you drink this one, your Strength rating permanently increases by 1.

Note The other vial of Throg strong juice was downstairs in the Temple Entrance area at 16. If you're following this walkthrough, you should have that vial in your inventory right now.

Up ahead to the north lies what appears to be a dead end. But take two steps forward, then turn right to face the east wall.

71. Secret Mechanism

See the small ***hole*** in the wall? Insert the ***wooden dowel***. This opens a sliding door to the north.

72. Secret Room

Pull down the ***handle*** on the north wall to close the pits at 69 for approximately 30 seconds. Hustle back across the closed pits, then follow the corridor past 68, then around to the next door on the left.

Go through the door, then take the first left turn.

73. Lesser Shaman

This ***Throg Shaman*** calls out in alarm: "By Throggi! Intruders in the Temple!" Hey, you're a little late, pal. Put this guy out of his misery and leave. You won't find anything of value here. Go into the next room to the west.

74. Thanks for the Warning

When you enter this room, the ***Throg*** says, "You go or you die!" If you are low on health, go. If not, make him gargle his words. He carries a couple of ***gold coins*** and a useless ***key***. Don't miss the ***heal root*** and the ***Throg dagger*** in the corner.

Exit to the corridor. Go 4W, 5N, 5W, then south to the ***portcullis***.

75. Orb-activated Gate

This portcullis will not open unless you have the Orb of Azrael (found at 57) in your inventory. If you have the Orb, the spears retract into floor and ceiling when you step up to the portcullis. Continue down the corridor.

76. Super Secret Room

You can only access this room via teleport from level 11. (See step 61 in Level 11: Palace of Shadows.)

77. Passage to the Dragon Feeding Grounds

Do you really want to visit a place with "feeding grounds" as part of its name? OK, gamer. Down the stairs.

Note

If you open the door before Dombur has been rescued, Farli says, "We cannot leave without my brother." Drake replies, "We must go back for him, then." The door closes and will not reopen until you rescue Dombur.

Level 6

Dragon Feeding Grounds

The sixth level of Stonekeep includes two map areas—the Feeding Grounds, Lower Level (Map 6.1), and the Feeding Grounds, Upper Level (Map 6.2). Here, you meet more Throgs, a few Sharga slaves, and the marvelous and terrifying Vermatrix Goldenhide, the dragon whose "feeding grounds" you explore.

Level 6 also serves as a transportation hub to three other levels—any travel to Levels 7, 8, and 9 begins here. In fact, to fully and successfully complete Level 6: Dragon Feeding Grounds, you must shuttle several times between this level and the Dwarven Fortress in Level 7.

Key to Maps 6.1 & 6.2

1. Passage to Throg Temple, Sharga
2. Shargas
3. Chest (rune scroll)
4. Boulder (triggered at 5), root
5. Trigger (for 4)
6. Toadstool alarm
7. Throg glyph (on door)
8. Throgs (roots)
9. Throg (guard key)
10. Chest (potions)
11. Wall button (opens door to 12)
12. Mana Circle
13. Snake, carcass (root)
14. Plate armor, dagger, helm
15. Shargas (roots), chest (component)
16. Sharga
17. Ants
18. Chest (component)
19. Green mushroom
20. Toadstool alarm

21 A-C. Exploding fungi

22. Green mushroom
23. Guardpost door—use guard key
24. Throgs (coins)
25. Passage to Feeding Grounds, Upper Level
26. Passage to Feeding Grounds, Lower Level
27. Chest (potions)
28. Dragon's tail
29. Exploding fungi
30. Cave-in, exploding fungus
31. Throg Shaman (feathers)
32. Dragon's rear leg, lock
33. Exploding fungi
34. Dragon's belly
35. Exploding fungi
36. Root
37. Dragon's front leg, lock

38, 39, 40. Faerie glows

41. Passage to Faerie Realm
42. Dragon's head
43. Cave-in
44. Mana Circle
45. Magick flint rock
46. Primrose patch
47. Shargas (mushrooms, pick)
48. Chest (key half, rune scroll)
49. Cave-in
50. Exploding fungus
51. Throg Shaman (feathers, rune scroll, key half), root, feathers
52. Arrow trap (arrows)—triggered at 53, wall button (disarms trap)
53. Trigger (for trap at 52)
54. Wall button (disarms trap at 52)
55. Barrel (roots)
56. Oil bombs
57. Throg (guard key)
58. Throg glyph (on door)
59. Wall button (disarms trigger at 60)
60. Arrow trap trigger (disarmed at 59)
61. Passage to Dwarven Fortress
62. Coins, gems, potion, chest (coins, gem, potion, rune scrolls)
63. Coin

64, 65. Exploding fungi

66. Pit
67. Root
68. Throg (coins, rune scroll), root
69. Stairs to Lower Level
70. Stairs to Upper Level
71. Exploding fungi, chest (rune scroll, component, potions)
72. Exploding fungus
73. Skuz the Sharga
74. Passage to the Ice Caverns
75. Throg Shaman (rune scroll)
76. Chest (mushrooms)
77. Mana Circle
78. Chest (coins, scroll)

Map 6.1 Dragon Feeding Grounds (Lower

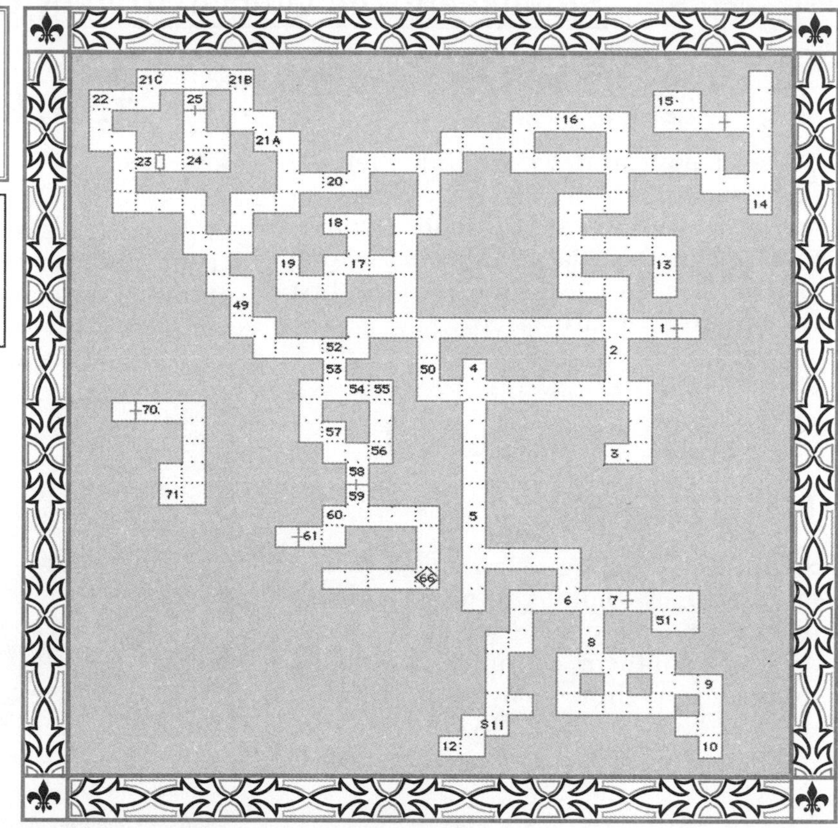

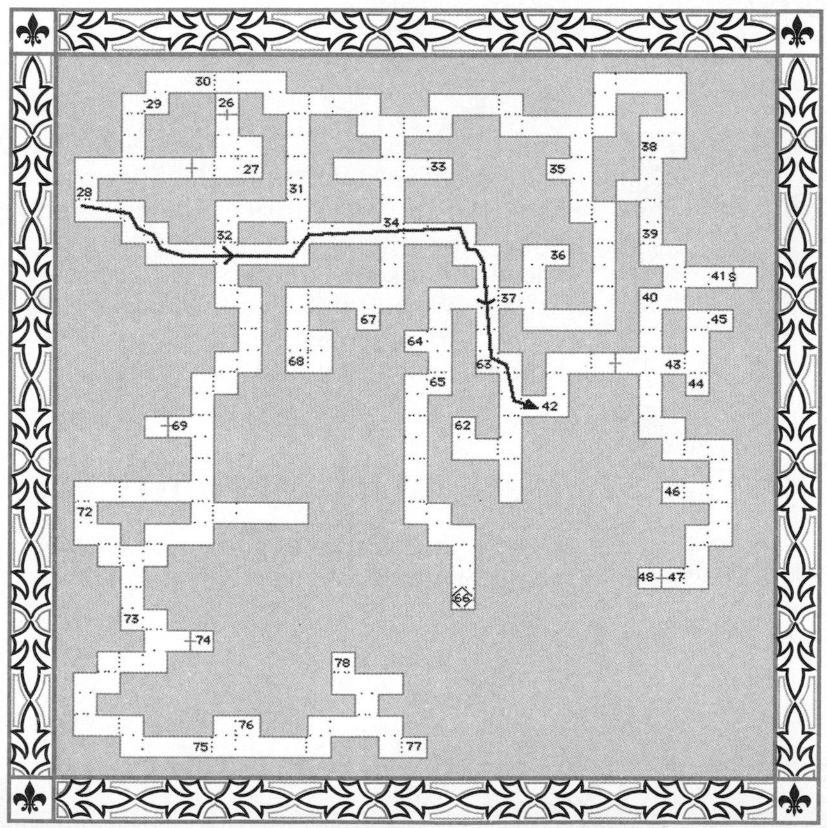

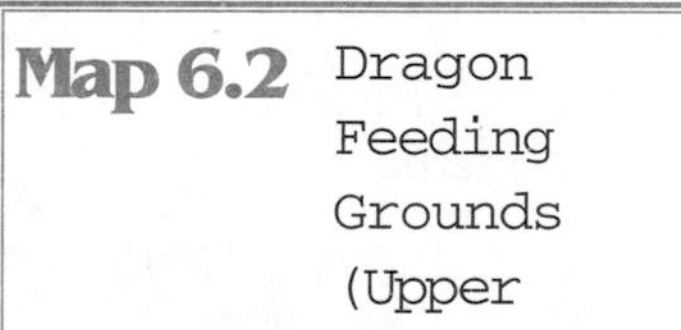

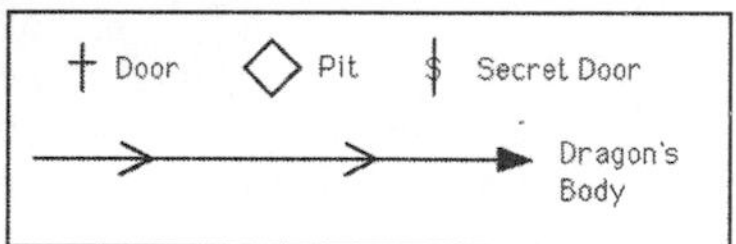

1. Start

These stairs lead down from the Temple of Throggi (at 77 on Map 5.2). When you arrive, Drake muses, "I wonder what we will find in this place." Answer: A lone ***Sharga***. Slay the pest, then take the first left turn. Go forward a step.

2. A Couple of Ingrates

Stepping here triggers an attack by two more ***Shargas***. Didn't you just try to free them from enslavement in the last level? After you kill them, continue south to the intersection, then turn left and follow the corridor.

3. Circle Rune

Open the ***chest*** and take this important ***rune scroll***.

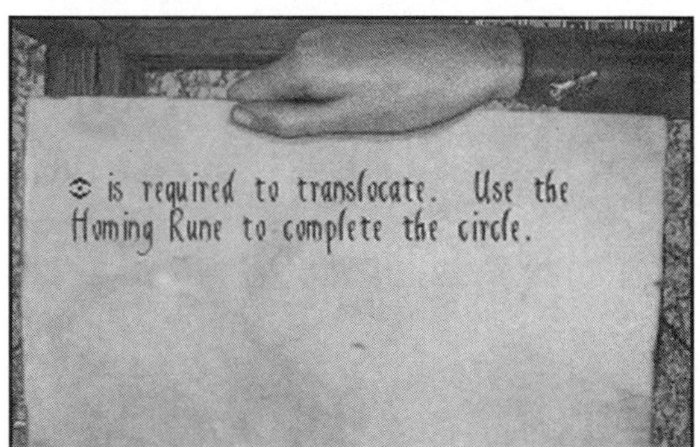

Circle Rune Scroll.

Retrace your steps back around the corridor, then head west.

4. Stonekeep Rocks!

In the first alcove on the right you find a large ***boulder***. It's big and heavy and ominous, and seems immovable. Grab the ***super heal root*** behind it, then turn to the south. Take exactly five steps.

Boulder. Big rock. Looks immovable. But all those smashed bone piles behind you suggest otherwise. Run south and hop into the first left corridor.

5. Boulder Trigger

A ***trigger*** here launches the boulder back at 4. (Didn't you notice the smashed bone piles along the corridor?) Hustle ahead and take that left turn just ahead—or face a gruesome death. Or you can simply turn sideways, facing east or west. Continue east, then turn the corner.

6. Loud Stoolie

Here's another screeching ***toadstool alarm***. Silence it, then head due east.

7. A Shocking Entrance

The first time your party approaches this strangely marked door, the following conversation ensues:

Dombur: That is *definitely* a Throggish magick glyph.
Farli: They must have some way of passing through it safely.
Drake: Some way of identifying themselves, perhaps.

Don't go through the door yet! If you do, that deadly ***Throg glyph*** inflicts up to 90 points of damage to each member of your party!

Tip To learn how to pass safely through a Throg glyph, see step 31 in this chapter.

Throg Glyph. Don't go through here if you don't have a certain Throg item yet. What item? Hint: It's red, and birds have many.

Take a step back from the door and head south.

8. Throg Guards

Two surly ***Throgs*** block the passage. After the battle, each drops a ***super heal root***. Step south to the intersection, then go 3E, S, 2E, turn south, and prepare for battle.

9. Throg Guardpost

A tough ***Throg*** rushes to the attack. When he dies, he drops his ***Throg guard key*** (called "a Throggish key" in your journal). Grab it, and head south past the ***campfire***.

10. Good for What Ails You

Open the ***chest*** and take the ***super heal potion***—the blue bottle called "a small vial" in your journal—and two ***heal potions***. Now head back to the toadstools at 6. Head west, and follow the corridor to the end.

11. Secret Passage

Push the ***button*** on the east wall to open a secret passageway behind you. Go through and on to the end of the short passage.

12. Magick Recharge

Step into the ***Mana Circle*** to recharge all runecasters. Exit the secret passage.

Now return to the spot where you first saw the boulder at 4. Go 6E, 5N, 2W, 2N, then head east down the passage.

13. Sssssnake!

Haven't seen a ***snake*** in a while, have you? Your Dwarves should help you make mincemeat of it quickly. Behind it, buried in a ***carcass***, is a single ***heal root***. Hardly worth it, but there you are.

Exit to the corridor, then turn right and continue north around the passageway. At the first intersection, turn right, and follow the corridor.

14. Knight Pancake

Note the remains of a poor ***dead explorer*** on the ground. Looks like that boulder put him in a tight spot. Too bad for him, but it's very, very good for you—he bequeaths you his ***plate breastplate*** and ***plate leggings***, which you should don immediately. He also dropped his ***dagger*** and ***helm***.

Turn and go north until you reach the door on the left-hand side.

Plate Armor. Fine-crafted body armor for the discriminating hero.

15. Sharga Heal Squad

Enter the room. Three tough ***Shargas*** lurk in the back corner. These are fine, upstanding examples of the "smart" variety of Sharga, carrying three ***super heal roots*** apiece.

Note

As you may recall, smart Shargas consume their roots when weakened in combat—if they have time. The faster you kill them, the more roots are left for you.

Open the ***chest*** in the corner. When you remove the ***component*** that your journal calls "a piece to a strange device," Drake says, "This looks like Dwarven manufacture." Dombur admits, "It looks familiar." What is it? Hmmm. Move on.

Exit the room to the corridor, turn right, and go 3S, 2W, N, 4W, 2N, then turn and prepare for combat.

16. Lone Sharga

A single tough ***Sharga*** waits for you here. Hammer him into green meat, then go west to the corner. From there, go S, 3W, S, W, 3S, W, 2S, then west into the room.

17. Hostile Ants

Two ***warrior ants*** patrol this room. Smash them into quivering ant parts. Go into the northern alcove.

18. Strange Device, Part B

Open the ***chest*** and take yet another ***component*** (called "a piece to a strange device") inside. If you already have the other piece (from the chest at 15), Drake says, "I've seen something like this before." Dombur adds, "So have I. . . but I can't quite place it."

Go back past the dead ants at 17 into the other alcove to the west.

19. Green Relief

Pluck the ***green mushroom*** here, then exit to the corridor. Go 2N, E, 3N, 3W, S, then one square west.

20. Screamer

Smash that annoying ***toadstool alarm***, then continue west to the intersection. Turn right and follow the passage.

21 A-C. More Spitters

Why are all the fungi so malevolent around here? Duck the spiky spores of all three of the ***exploding fungi*** in this passage, chop them to pieces, and continue.

22. Green Mushroom

Grab that poison-healing ***green mushroom***, then proceed down the passage until you reach the locked door on your left.

23. Guard Door

Unlock this door with the Throg guard key (from 9). Open the door. Yes, you've stumbled into another Throg guard post.

24. Throg Guard Post

Three very ***tough Throgs*** man this post—two just inside the door (as you can see), one more just around the corner. The third Throg carries a couple of ***coins***.

25. Passage to Feeding Grounds, Upper Level

These stairs lead to the second level of the Dragon Feeding Grounds. Climb on up.

26. Passage to Feeding Grounds, Lower Level

At the top of the stairs, you emerge into a small antechamber. Check out the ***chest*** in the corner.

27. First Aid

Open the ***chest*** and get three much-appreciated ***heal potions***. Exit through the door to the west. Continue west to the wall, then turn left and feast your eyes on an amazing sight.

28. Dragon's Tail

Yeah, that's one *big* tail there. Don't attack it, for God's sake. As you might imagine, there's a heck of a beast attached to this thing. In fact, the tail *itself* can be pretty deadly. But to fully understand this tail's behavior, you have to understand the way the whole dragon works.

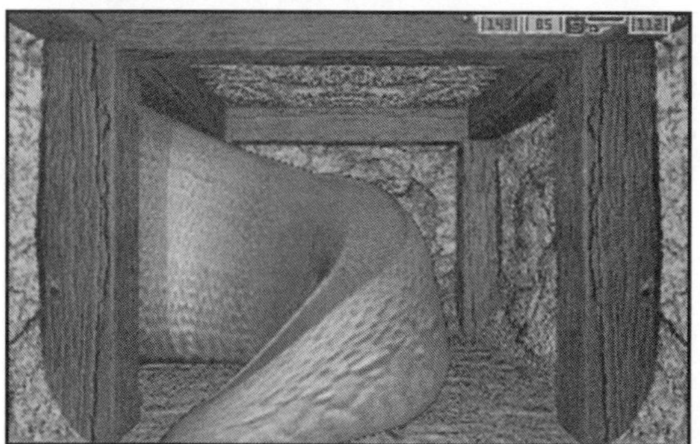

Whale of a Tail. And it packs a whale of a wallop. Don't hit this thing, or your party is in for a world of hurt.

Here's the scoop: The dragon's response to you depends on its anger level, which we'll cleverly label the Dragon Anger Level (DAL). The six distinct levels of dragon anger are:

0 asleep
1 awake but calm
2 slightly annoyed
3 unhappy
4 angry
5 homicidal

The dragon starts the game asleep—that is, with a DAL of 0. Any attack on the dragon's body (including the tail) increases the DAL by one for the first attack and one more for every two attacks after that. Striking at the dragon's head with a weapon increases the DAL by one for each attack. Every 30 minutes of real time reduces the DAL by one (to a minimum of 0).

But what about the tail? If the dragon is asleep, or is awake but isn't attacked, the tail waggles in a benign manner. If you make the foolish mistake of attacking the creature here, the tail lashes out when you approach, delivering 10–40 points of crush damage.

All you can do here is turn around, then head east to that first passage on the left.

29. More Spores

Two more of your favorite ***exploding fungi*** grace this section of hallway. Use your expertise in demolitions to level them, if you so choose.

30. Cave-In

Another ***cave-in***. Hey, here's a chance to get some real exercise. And for added fun, you'll find another ***exploding fungus*** just beyond the debris. From the fungus, go S, E, then head south.

31. Magick Act

A ***Throg Shaman*** casts an Energybolt rune at you, then suddenly disappears, leaving behind a few ***feathers***. Drake's response: "Where did he go?" Good question. Grab those feathers and keep going.

Tip Once you get Throg Shaman headdress feathers, your party no longer suffers damage from the Throg magick glyphs that guard certain doorways.

32. Dragon's Rear Legs

Take a good look at this rear leg of the dragon—a formidable ***dragon lock*** holds it in place. Again, don't even *think* of attacking the creature. The dragon is immune to damage—all you'll do is raise that DAL, a very bad mistake.

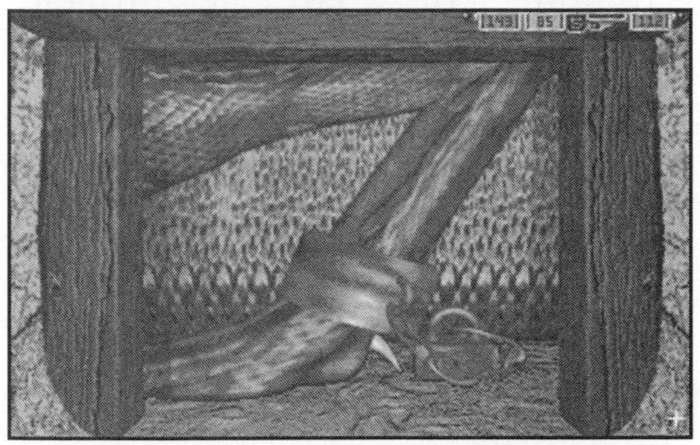

Leg Shackled. That's one heck of a drumstick. You wouldn't want to unlock something this big. . . or would you?

Again, return to the northern passage and turn right, heading east. Try the next passage leading south.

33. Exploding Fungi

You'll find two more ***exploding fungi*** in this small alcove. This area contains nothing of value, so just ignore them. (You can also ignore the ***chest*** in the opposite alcove; it's empty.)

34. Dragon's Midsection

Here's the ***belly*** of the beast, breathing rhythmically. It looks vulnerable—but it's not. Return north to the corridor, turn right, and continue working your way east again to the next passage that runs south.

35. I Hate These Things

Gosh, two more spore-spitting ***exploding fungi***. Make them pay for their exasperatingly bad manners—or ignore them—then continue south down the passage.

36. Root of Good

Grab the ***super heal root***, then go back south a couple of squares to that passage leading west.

37. Dragon's Foreleg

Looks a lot like the dragon's rear leg, doesn't it? Same heavy-duty ***dragon lock*** on the ankle there. OK, time to retreat north again. When you reach the northern corridor, turn right again and follow the passage.

38, 39, 40. Faerie Glows

At these locations, your party encounters a dazzling purple light that zips away when you approach. These ***Faerie Glows*** happen quickly. Enjoy them while they last. Follow them, if you can. They're leading you somewhere!

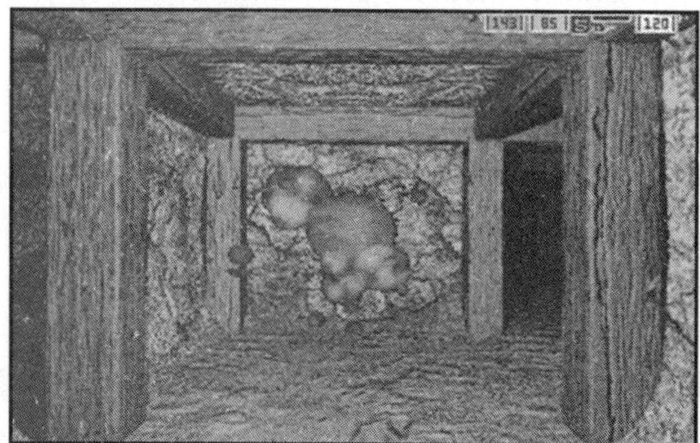

Follow That Glow. What's cute, purple, and playfully coy? Answer: A Faerie Glow. Where are they going, anyway?

41. Passage to . . . Where?

See how all the faerie glows dash into the same alcove and disappear? Note that for later, then continue south. Go through the first door on the right.

42. Dragon's Head

When you approach the head of the sleeping dragon—that is, when you step on the square adjacent to the dragon's head, and the DAL is 0—you automatically increase the DAL by one, waking up the dragon.

Vermatrix Goldenhide. Life Rule Number 1: Never anger dragons. Those teeth are the least of your worries.

Here are the conversations that can occur the first time your party reaches the dragon.

If the DAL = 0:

Dombur: Ah, what a magnificent sample. It has been many years since a scholar has had a chance to study. . .

Farli: (interrupts) *Shhh.* We don't want to wake it!

Dragon: (waking) *Ahhh!* What is this?! (Go to following "DAL 1 or 2" speech.)

If the DAL = 1 or 2:

Dragon: *Arrrr!* The smell of man is on you, intruder. What brings one of your kind here? You've come to view my chains, haven't you?

Drake: Ah, no, Lady Dragon. I have never seen such a wondrous beast as yourself.

Dragon: I am Vermatrix Goldenhide, leader of the Great Dragons. It is my bane to be chained like a common worm.

Drake: Can you not break free?

Dragon: Alas, these chains are bonded with magick.

Drake: Ah, well, I am Drake, Champion of Stonekeep, and these are my trusty companions. We will do what we can to free your bonds.

Dragon: You would have my thanks and reward if you did.

Drake: Who has chained you?

Dragon: Those cursed Throgs. On the command of Throggi, they said. Broke the key in half, before my eyes. Ran from this room, with my flames licking their backside. (laughs) Ahh, to be free. . .

Drake: Well, then, we will find one of their Shamans and ask a very *polite* question.

If the DAL = 3 or 4:

Dragon: What do you want?!

Drake: I'm just exploring here.

Dragon: I am the great Vermatrix Goldenhide! I am the leader of the Great Dragons! (beat) You are not an explorer! You have come to mock me and steal my treasure, haven't you?

Drake: No! I am looking for treasure. . .

Dragon: I knew it!

Drake:. . . but not *your* treasure.

Dragon: Prove it.

Drake: You are obviously in trouble. I will try to help you.

Dragon: The Throg Shamans were the ones to capture me. They will eat you alive. . . if I don't! (beat) They put me in this magick lock and broke the key into two halves. Find those pieces, fix the key and return to free me. For if I escape before you return, I will spend the rest of *your* life hunting you down!

If the DAL = 5

The dragon howls "Enough!" and begins to "breathe" on the party. You're toast.

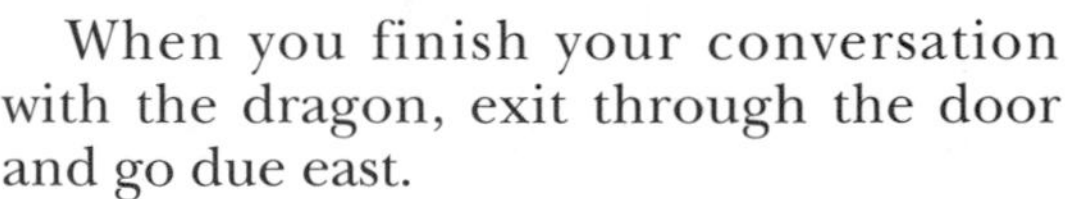

Tip Your first encounter with Vermatrix Goldenhide should make your next task clear: Find the two halves of the "dragon key" to unlock her chains.

When you finish your conversation with the dragon, exit through the door and go due east.

43. Look Out Behind

When you step through this square, a ***cave-in*** drops from the ceiling behind you.

44. Mana Circle

Look south—another wondrous ***Mana Circle!*** Recharge your runecasters, then head north to the odd-looking, crystal-shaped rock.

45. Magickal Flint Rock

This large rock is made of ***magickal flint***. You can't do anything with it yet. Mark its location—you'll be back. For now, return to the cave-in and hack your way out. In the corridor, turn left and head south. Enter the alcove on the right.

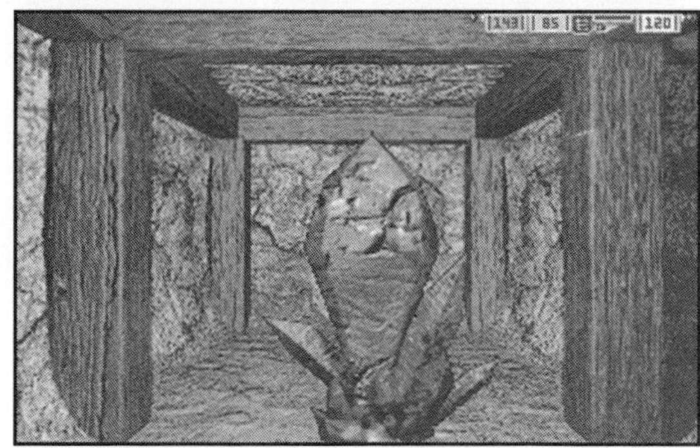

Get a Piece of the Rock. But how? You need a chisel or something.

46. Primrose Patch

Gather all seven yellow ***primroses*** growing in a patch on the floor. Step back into the corridor and continue south.

Tip Don't give these flowers away! You need them to gain access to the Faerie Realm, Level 8.

47. Mushroom Shargas

Two smart ***Shargas*** attack when you turn the corner here. Each carries two ***green mushrooms***, excellent poison antidotes. One also drops a ***Sharga mining pick***. Go west through the door.

48. A Key Moment

Open the ***chest***. Take out one half of the ***dragon key*** and the ***rune scroll***:

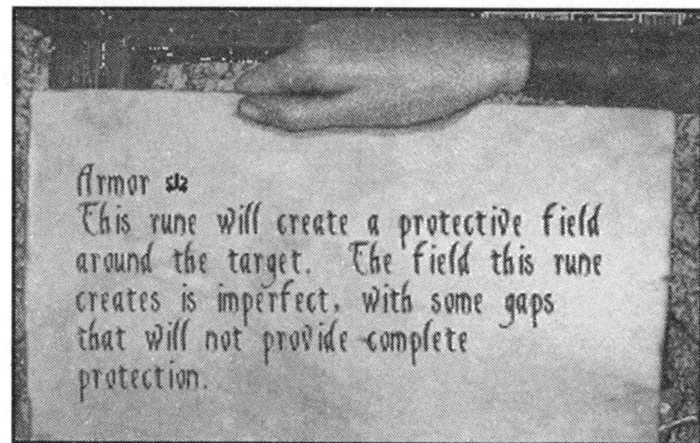

Armor Rune Scroll

You've done all you can do on this upper level. Your passage to other areas of the Dragon Feeding Grounds is blocked by the sprawling body of Vermatrix Goldenhide. You must find the other half of the dragon key, then get it reforged.

Go all the way back to the stairway at 26 and return to the Lower Level of the Dragon Feeding Grounds. Go through the door at 23 and turn left. Go 2S, 3E, 2S, E, turn right and follow the passage south.

49. Cave-In

Bash through the ***cave-in***. From the debris, go S, E, S, 4E, N, 3E, then head south.

50. Hurling Spores

Hack up the ***exploding fungus***, then turn the corner just to the south. From here, you can work your way back to the door with the Throg glyph at 7—it's in the southeast corner of the level—and enter the room.

Note Remember: Those red feathers you got from the Throg Shaman back at 31 (Upper Level) protect you from the glyph's deadly magick damage.

51. Devil in the Headdress

Another ***Throg Shaman*** waits just around the corner. When he expires, he drops his

useless ***broken runecaster***, some red ***feathers*** from his headdress, a ***rune scroll***, and, as your journal puts it, "half of a very sturdy key"—the other half of the ***dragon key***.

Scare Rune Scroll

On the floor of the room you find a ***super heal root*** and more headdress ***feathers***. Exit into the corridor, then return to the square just south of 4. From there, go 2W, 3N, 3W, S, W, then turn right to face the north wall.

52. Disarming Button Number 1

Push in the ***button*** to disable an ***arrow trap*** that lies directly behind you.

Tip Be sure the button is *pushed in*—it is flush with the wall when the trap is disarmed.

53. Arrow Trigger

If you neglected to complete step 52, then stepping on this square triggers the arrow trap on the wall just ahead. The trap fires two pairs of ***arrows*** in rapid succession.

Turn *left* at the arrow trap.

54. Disarming Button Number 2

This ***button*** on the north wall also disarms the arrow trap at 21.

55. In the Barrel

Break open the ***barrel*** to get two ***super heal roots***. From the smashed barrel, go south a couple of steps.

56. Behind the Barrel

Find the three ***oil bombs*** stashed behind the ***barrels***. Smash the barrels, then continue around the corners to the crackling fire, and get ready for combat.

57. Want S'mores?

A ***Throg*** tending a ***campfire*** doesn't like your looks. Too bad. After he dies howling, take his ***guard key***. Don't walk through the fire, though. You'll suffer significant damage. Go back south to the wooden door.

58. Glyph, Shmyph

Yes, another ***Throg glyph*** hangs in that doorway. But if you have any Throg Shaman headdress feathers (and you should have *plenty* by now), you can pass through undamaged. Stop after you step through the doorway, then turn right to face the west wall.

59. Disarming Button Number 3

Push in the ***button*** on the west wall to disarm yet another ***arrow trap*** just around the corner. (Again, be sure the button is pushed *in*—that is, depressed into the wall.) Take a step south, then west.

60. Arrow Trigger

If you neglected to complete step 59, then stepping on this square triggers the arrow trap on the opposite wall directly behind you. The trap fires two pairs of ***arrows*** in rapid succession.

Again, take a step south, then west to the door.

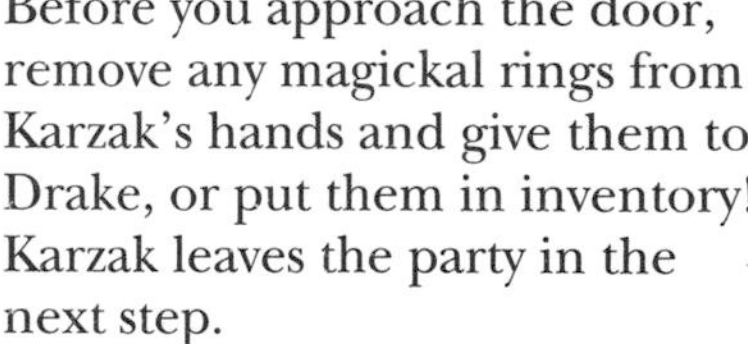

Tip Before you approach the door, remove any magickal rings from Karzak's hands and give them to Drake, or put them in inventory! Karzak leaves the party in the next step.

61. Passage to the Dwarven Fortress

These stairs lead down to Level 7, the Dwarven Fortress. If Karzak is still in your party when you step into this square, he takes this opportunity to leave.

Karzak: These are the stairs to our clanhall. I will go ahead and announce us.
Drake: Alright. Should we follow you?
Karzak: Wait before you enter. I must prepare the guards for your arrival. Since the Throggish incursion, the hall has been on high alert. Farli, why don't you stay with Drake?
Farli: Aye.
Dombur: See if those secret project supplies have finally arrived, would you?
Karzak: They've been gathering dust since you disappeared.
Dombur: Oh, dust should help, yes.
Drake: 'Til we meet again, Karzak.
Karzak: Aye. 'Til then.

Adios, Karzak. Prepare those guards for our arrival. We're right behind you.

Karzak leaves your party through the doorway. Although you possess both halves of the dragon key, you still must forge the halves together. To do this, follow Karzak into the Dwarven Fortress.

Go to Level 7: The Dwarven Fortress, complete the walkthrough for that level, then return here!

Welcome back to the Dragon Feeding Grounds. I trust your foray into the Dwarven Fortress was fruitful. If you followed the walkthrough for Level 7, you now have the ***forged dragon key*** (your journal calls it "a very sturdy key").

Unlock the dragon's leg irons at 32 and 37, then go to the dragon's head at 42. The dragon awakens and asks, "Ahhh, why do I awaken?"

If the DAL is 1 or 2:
Drake: We have the key!
Dragon: Excellent! Please don't stand there. Unlock my chains, and be sure to get all of the locks!

If the DAL is 3 or 4:
Dragon: Do you have the key?
Drake: Yes, yes, we have the key.
Dragon: Do not stand there, unlock me, unlock me now.
Drake: You promise not to roast me, if I do?
Dragon: Yes, yes. And I promise to roast you if you do not!
Drake: Ah!

Caution If you do not unlock the lock within 10 seconds, the dragon gets impatient: "Hurry, unlock me!" And if you do not unlock the lock within 10 *more* seconds, the DAL goes to 5.

Once you've unlocked all of the dragon's locks (at 43, 48, and 52), then:

Dragon: Thank you, human, I am in your debt.

Drake: You're welcome. I was happy to help.

Dragon: I must leave now. To fly the sky again is my greatest dream—a dream that you have helped to fulfill. We dragons always carry some treasure with us no matter where we go. That is yours to keep. I will never forget this, and my kind have long memories. You may consider yourself a dragon friend, and someday I will repay your kindness.

Drake: Good flying, Vermatrix.

At this point, Vermatrix leaves. After she lumbers away, step forward and turn left at the intersection. Go south a couple of steps, then enter the alcove on the right.

62. Treasure Cove

Much of the dragon's treasure is spread over the ground. Pick up two ***green gems***, two ***red gems***, a ***blue gem***, 18 ***coins***, and a ***heal potion***. Open the ***chest*** and remove another ***heal potion***, a ***blue gem***, two more ***coins***, and three ***rune scrolls***:

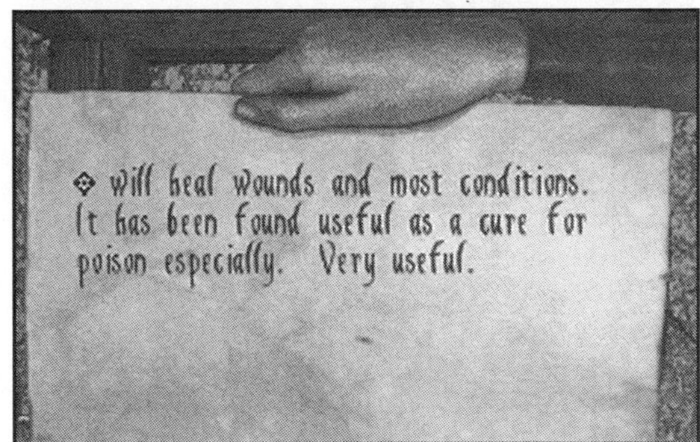

Dragon's Healing Rune Scroll

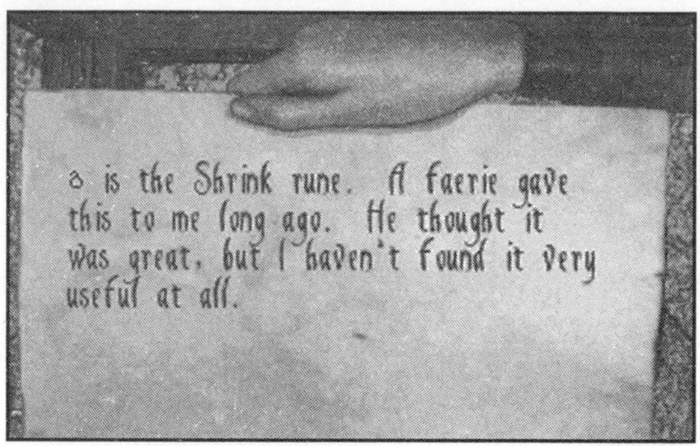

Dragon's Shrink Rune Scroll

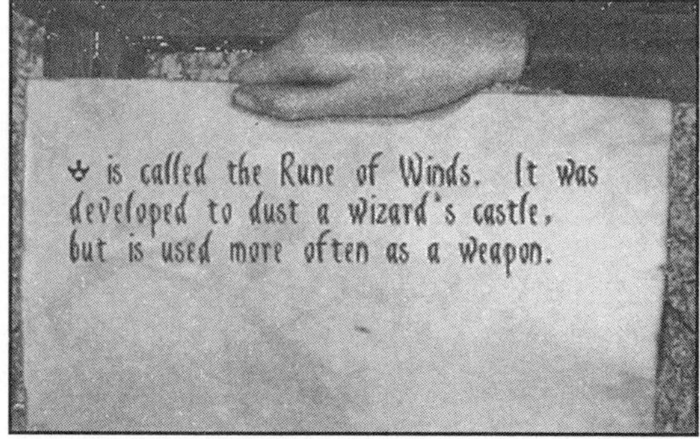

Dragon's Tornado Scroll

Exit the alcove and turn left, heading north.

63. Nice Tip

Don't miss that gold ***coin*** on your way up the passage. Continue north to the lock at 37, then turn left and follow the passage.

64 & 65. Spitters

Some ***exploding fungi*** litter the path south. Blow them up real good and continue.

66. Pit

Stop before you get to the ***pit*** at the end of the passage. It drops down to the lower level of the Feeding Grounds—not far from 61, the passage to the Dwarven Fortress! Mark this spot for later.

Tip If you're looking for a shortcut to 61—the passage to the Dwarven Fortress—hop in. But if you're following this walkthrough, you don't need to revisit your Dwarf friends just yet.

Pit Stop. Don't jump down that hole—unless you want a shortcut back to the Dwarven Fortress.

Go back to the dragon lock at 37, then turn left and follow the passage north. Don't miss the gold ***coin*** along the way. At the intersection at 34, turn left and proceed south.

67. Snack

Grab the ***super heal root*** in this alcove, then continue down the passage.

68. Throg Pessimist

When you approach this goofy ***Throg*** guard, he says, "Oh, by Throggi! Strangers to abuse me. Great Throggi, I exist only to be abused! Well, then. . . abuse me I say!" After you slay the whiner, he drops two ***coins***, a hunk of ***Throg food***, and a valuable ***rune scroll***. Open the scroll:

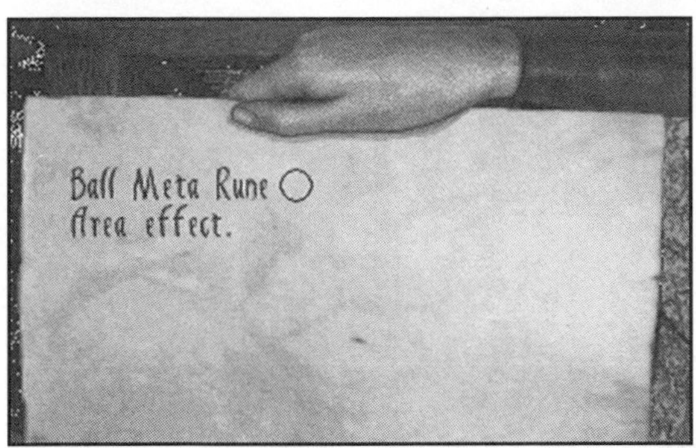

Ball Meta Rune Scroll

Before you leave, grab that ***super heal root*** in the northeast corner of the room.

Now go back up to 34, turn left (facing west), and follow the passage to the dragon lock at 32. (Again, keep your eye out for the ***coin*** on the floor just before the lock.) Turn left at the lock and head south down the passage.

69. Stairs to Lower Level

Behind this door is a stairway to the Lower Level. Open the door and go down the stairs.

70. Stairs to Upper Level

You emerge from the stairwell into a small, isolated section of the Lower Level. Go down the short passage.

71. Treasure

Three ***exploding fungi*** block your way to a ***chest*** in the corner. Flatten them, then open the chest and remove. . . another ***stoneshooter piece!*** You also get a ***super heal potion***, a ***strength gain potion***, an ***agility gain potion***, and another ***Potency Meta rune scroll.*** If you're following this walkthrough, we'll take the stoneshooter piece back to Dombur shortly, but first let's finish exploring these feeding grounds.

Go back to 70, climb the stairs, then step forward into the corridor. Turn right and go 3S, 5W, and turn left to face south.

72. Fungal Nuisance

Another ***exploding fungus*** spits at you here. Destroy it and continue working your way south.

73. Skuz the Friendly Sharga

This is ***Skuz***. (You gotta wonder what his parents were thinking.) Approach him, and he hails you:

Skuz: Hiyaz! Skuz happy to see friendly faces.

Drake: If you want a fight, we'll give it to you.

Skuz: No, no. Nice youz misunderstand. Skuz want outta dis place.

Drake: Well, I think you should find somebody else to travel with.

Skuz: You gotta take Skuz with youz! Skuz show you tings, Skuz will!

Drake: Oh, all right, if it will keep you quiet.

Skuz now joins the party. Take a step east, a step south, then turn left to face the door.

74. Passage to the Ice Caverns

Behind this door is a stairway leading down to Level 9: Caverns of the Ice Queen. Mark this for later—we'll be back. For now, continue south down the passage.

75. Tough Guy

A nasty ***Throg Shaman***, harboring a major grudge, waits for you here. When you approach, he says:

Throg Shaman: You think you are so tough. You kill my people and defile our temple. Yes, I've heard of your actions. You will pay for what you have done.

Drake: You are servants of Khull-khuum, but I can find it in my heart to let you go if you promise to leave us alone.

Throg Shaman: No, what you have done cannot be ignored.

Drake: Well, OK then.

The Throg Shaman fights to the death. After he succumbs to your superior strength and character, he drops a ***rune scroll***: The scroll contains the Duration Meta rune, which is already inscribed in your journal—that is, if you found the secret room in the Dwarven Fortress (at 24 on Map 7).

76. Throg Treasure Number 1

Open the ***chest*** and take the ***green mushroom*** and ***red mushrooms***, but leave the, uh, whatever it is. Continue down the passage. When you come to the split in the passage, take the right fork.

77. Mana Circle

Step into the lovely green ***Mana Circle*** and recharge. Turn around, retrace a few steps and take the first right turn.

78. Throg Treasure Number 2

Open the ***chest*** and remove four gold ***coins*** and the ***scroll***.

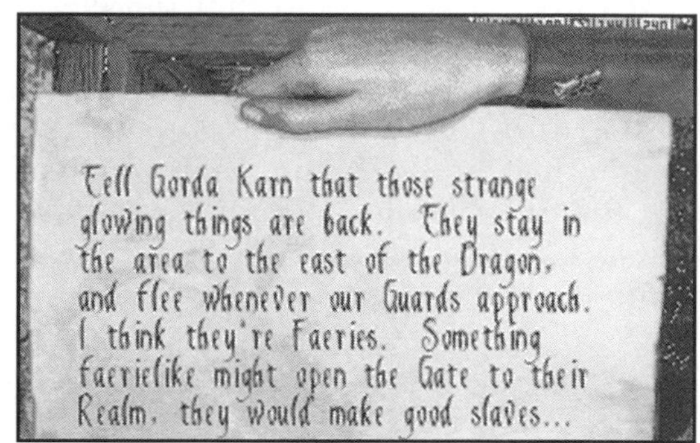

Return to the Dwarven Fortress and give Dombur the stoneshooter piece. The quickest route back is via the pit at 66. (Don't forget to cast the Featherfall rune on each member of the party before you jump.) You'll end up right around the corner from the entrance to the Fortress.

Note Skuz refuses to enter the Dwarven Fortress, but he'll wait patiently for you at the Fortress gate.

When you return to Dombur's quarters (at 5 on Map 7) with the third piece of the stoneshooter, he says:

Dombur: Well, what do you want?

Drake: It's me. I'm looking for your secret weapon.

Dombur: *Shhh!* Don't tell anybody about that, it's a secret. And it's in pieces, it's a bunch of secret pieces, I guess. Oh, I remember you. You're looking for it.

Dombur paces some more, then approaches to ask, "Do you have one of the pieces?" Give him the third piece of the stoneshooter, and he responds, "Ah, the final piece! Go away while I assemble my masterpiece. Return later and it will be ready for you."

Dombur stands at his worktable for about a minute, working on the stoneshooter. When he finishes the weapon, he continues his pacing. After a few passes back and forth, he approaches you again and says, "Ah, there you are. I have finished this up. I would have come looking for you, but something important. . . well, something. . . well. I entrust the stoneshooter, the ultimate weapon of destruction, into your hands."

Dombur then holds out the ***stoneshooter***. Take it from his outstretched hand.

Stoneshooter. Dombur calls this box of rocks "the ultimate weapon of destruction." Hmmm.

Next, Dombur suggests that you need instructions and holds out a ***scroll***. Again, take it from his outstretched hand.

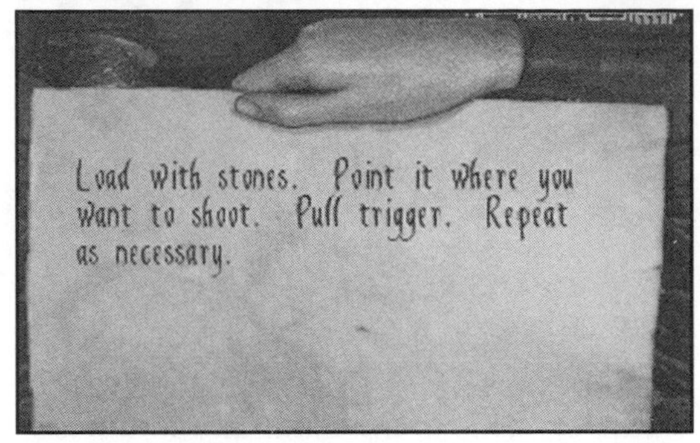

Stoneshooter Instructions. Not exactly rocket science, is it?

The conversation with Dombur concludes as follows:

Drake: Thanks.

Dombur: You know, Jake, there is something that bothers me about you. You're a little tall for a Dwarf, you know that?

Drake: Ah, yes, I, uh, had tall parents.

Dombur: Oh, that would explain it. Well, I'm a busy Dwarf and busy Dwarves. . . are busy, you know.

Drake: Yes, thank you, Dombur.

With the stoneshooter now in your arsenal, return all the way to the Upper Level of the Dragon Feeding Grounds. Go to the alcove where the Faerie Glows disappeared—area 41 on Map 6.2. Walk up to the east wall, then place five of the primroses (found at 46 on Map 6.2) on the ground.

Poof!

Go through the now-open passage into Level 8: The Faerie Realm.

Level 7

The Dwarven Fortress

The seventh level of Stonekeep includes just one map area—the Dwarven Fortress (Map 7). This is the clanhall of your companions Farli, Dombur, and Karzak. Dwarves are friendly allies of humans (particularly heroes like Drake), but there is a great evil roaming these Dwarven corridors. If you can destroy it, the clan will be most grateful.

Key to Map 7

1. Passage to Dragon Feeding Grounds
2. Fortress door
3. Thun Brightstone
4. Dombur's exit
5. Scrolls, potion
6. Library (scrolls)
7. Torin
8. Sardin (chisel)

8A. Forge, Seldin

9. Glorystone
10. Geldor (price scroll)
11. Armory tables (platemail, chainmail, helms, ax, firedagger, shields, potions)
12. Chest (coins)
13. Horn of fear, magick throwing axe
14. Meals
15. Barrels (roots, meal, stones)
16. Scroll
17. Karzak (rejoins party), chest (oil bombs)
18. Intersection
19. Fountain of healing
20. Dwarven picks, iron spike
21. Portcullis
22. Sarcophagus (zombie, ring, rune scroll)
23. Dwarf, illusory wall
24. Rune scrolls
25. Dwarf guardhouse
26. Chest (magick shield, rune scroll)
27. Hammers, swords, axes, spear, scroll

Map 7 The Dwarven Fortress

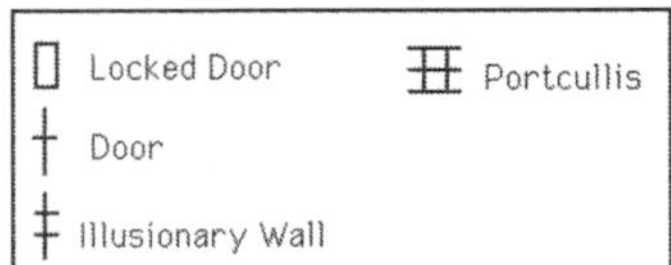

1. Passage to Dragon Feeding Grounds

To the north you'll find the stairs leading up to Level 6: The Dragon Feeding Grounds. Go south through the outer door, then step around the corner to the left.

Note Many Dwarf soldiers populate the fortress. It is possible (and maybe fun, if you're kind of twisted) to slay them. But the cost will be enormous—if you attack Torin the Elder (the Dwarf leader), or if you kill a Dwarf and another Dwarf finds his body, you instantly become an enemy of the clan.

This is bad, for several reasons. First, you lose valuable allies. There is no way to make amends with Dwarves once you've become their enemy—no self-respecting Dwarf would join your party now. Second, the Dwarves currently in your party will attack you.

2. Fortress Door

Dead ahead is the reinforced iron ***fortress door***. If you're an enemy of the clan (see the preceding note), the door is locked, and you'll need a Strength rating of seven stars to force it open.

Fortress Door. It opens easily enough the first time—but don't make yourself an enemy of the Dwarven clan on the other side, or the door will be locked in the future.

3. Guardians of the Gate

Step through the fortress door. A Dwarf, ***Thun Brightstone***, approaches to hail you:

Thun Brightstone: *Chalka!* Halt! Who goes there!

Drake: I am Drake, an adventurer. Karzak sent us.

Farli: Halt yourself, Thun, we've come to see the elder.

Thun Brightstone: Farli, I'd not thought you would've returned. If you want to see the elder, I'm not going to stop you. I'll take you to him, now.

Farli: I know the way, Thun Brightstone. You watch the gates.

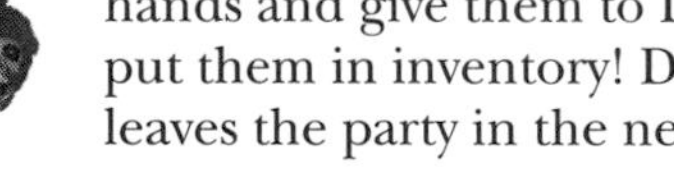

Tip Before you go any further, remove any magickal rings from Dombur's hands and give them to Drake, or put them in inventory! Dombur leaves the party in the next step.

Step forward, then follow good Farli's directions.

4. Dombur's Farewell

If Dombur is in the party, he leaves at this point:

Dombur: Ah! Yes, this *is* my workspace. Now where did those supplies go?
Drake: Farewell, Dombur.
Dombur: Oh, yes, yes. If you see my brother, send him to me, I have a new device he must see.
Farli: I'm right here.
Dombur: Oh, yes, well, stop by later would you, please.

Dombur then leaves the party and walks west. Follow him into his workroom—the first passage on the left, through the stone door.

5. Dombur's Workroom

Dombur marches randomly back and forth here, occasionally stopping and mumbling to himself:

"Now, what did I do with that. . . ?"
"If I. . . " (beat) "Yes, that would work!"
"Hmm, yes, hmm, hmm, no, no, that would be dangerous. Well, maybe, just a little."

The first time you enter this room, Dombur approaches you and speaks:

Dombur: Can I help you?
Drake: Dombur. . . it's me, Drake.
Dombur: Oh, yes, it's Drake. (beat) Jake who?
Drake: I saved you and your brother. . .
Dombur: (interrupting) Oh, never mind, what can I do for you? I'm busy, you know.
Drake: Yes, well, you mentioned some secret device.
Dombur: *Shhh!* It's my secret project. A new weapon to use against, well, against somebody. I almost had it developed. I just can't find the missing pieces. They must have been delivered incorrectly. I would not have misplaced them.
Drake: If I can find the pieces to this weapon, can I use it?
Dombur: Of course. What's the point of a weapon if it won't be used? But then, what good is a used weapon? Well, anyway, bring me the pieces and I will loan you the weapon.

After this conversation, Dombur resumes his thoughtful pacing. After a few passes back and forth, he stops again, muttering more lines to himself:

"Ahh, yes. . . "
"Now, *that* should've worked."
"The inner problem is resolved when the outer tincture, ahh. . . what was I talking about?"

After still more passes back and forth, Dombur finally walks up to you again and asks, "Do you have one of the pieces?" He holds out his hand.

Note If you don't give Dombur anything within 10 seconds, he says, "I don't have time for this," and walks away. If you give him anything but one of the three "pieces to a strange device," he says, "This has nothing to do with the secret project!" and resumes his pacing. At this point in our walkthrough, however, you should have two of the three stoneshooter pieces, found at 15 and 18 on Map 6.1, Dragon Feeding Grounds (Lower Level).

Give Dombur the first piece of the strange device. He responds, "Yes, this is part of the project." He'll walk away, pace and mumble some more, then return and ask again if you have one of the pieces. Give him the second piece; he says, "Yes, yes! This is another piece to the stoneshooter!" (Aha. Now you know that the "secret weapon" is a stoneshooter.) You don't have the third piece yet, so step forward into the room and ignore Dombur's pacing.

A nearby ***scrollcase*** holds two ***scrolls***. Take them and open them. They read:

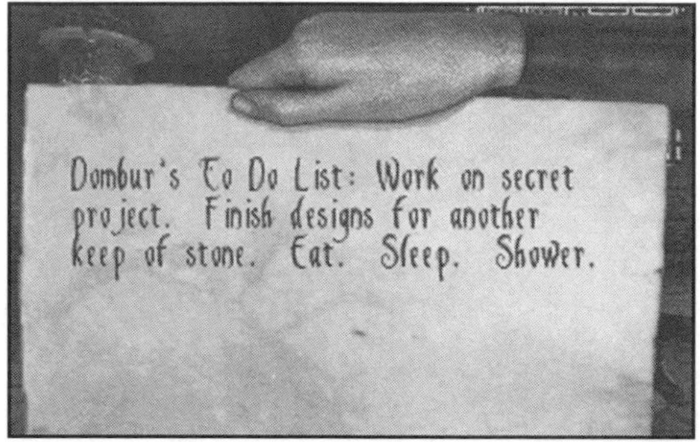

Dombur's "To Do" Scroll

Dombur's Language Rune Scroll

Some items sit on the ***worktable*** in the back corner. Take the ***heal potion*** and two ***stones***, but the blank ***scroll*** is worthless.

Exit to the corridor. Turn left and go west a couple of steps, then turn left again (as Farli suggests). Go down the hall and take the first right turn. (Farli will suggest you go straight, but ignore him for now.)

6. Orson the Librarian

Orson Stout-thinker is the official Dwarf librarian. He maintains a library full of interesting scrolls. The first time you meet Orson, he greets you warmly:

Orson: Greetings, I am Orson, librarian recorder of this clanhall. What can I do for you?

Drake: I'm looking for help.

Orson: Well, you've come to a good place. Wander these halls, and ask your questions. Feel free to peruse the scrolls in this humble library.

Examine the two ***scrollcases*** in the room. The three ***scrolls*** in the leftmost case contain the following historical information:

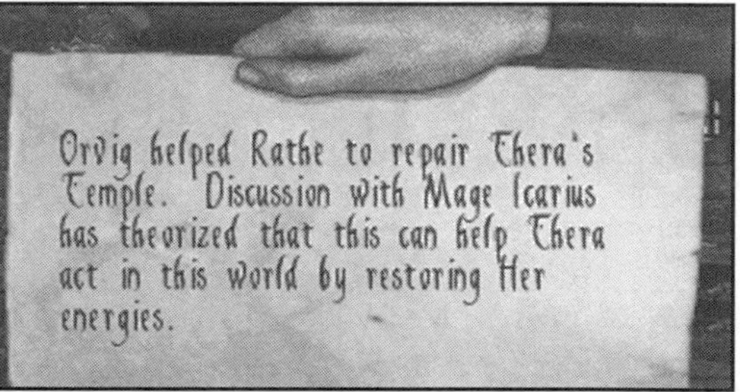

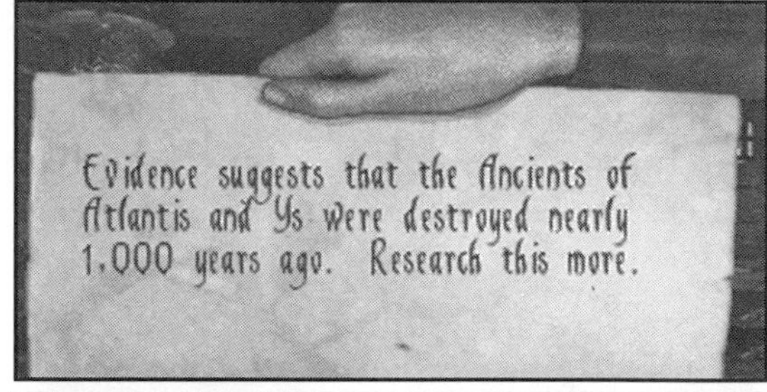

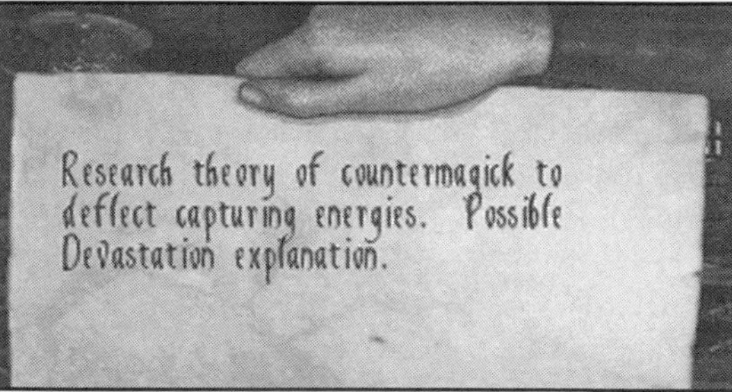

Here are the three ***scrolls*** in the rightmost scrollcase:

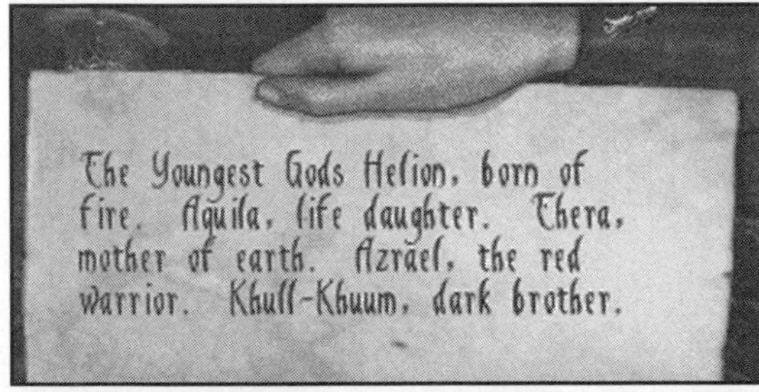

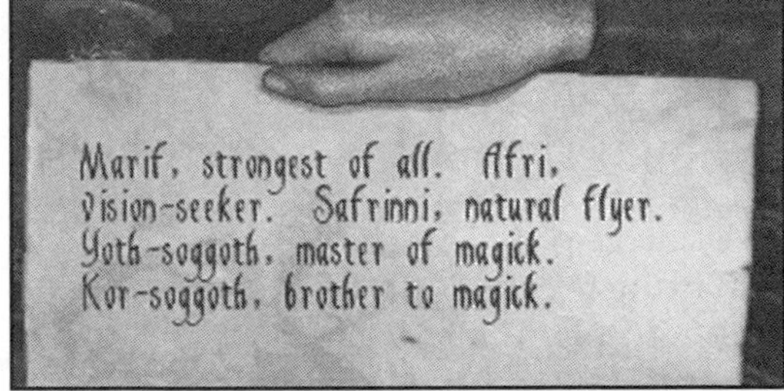

Marif, strongest of all. Afri, vision-seeker. Safrinni, natural flyer. Yoth-soggoth, master of magick. Kor-soggoth, brother to magick.

There is also another ***scroll*** on the floor, one that contains an important clue:

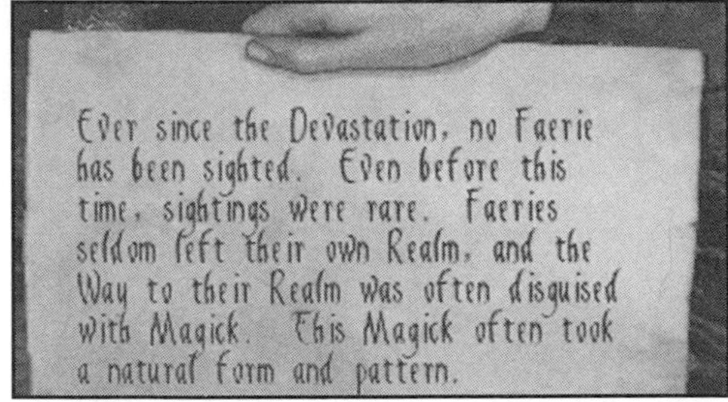

Exit the library, turn right at the corridor, and continue south to the next room. (Farli tells you when to turn right.)

Sounds like a heated conversation in there, doesn't it?

Tip

Before you enter this room, remove any magickal rings from Farli's hands and give them to Drake, or put them in inventory! Farli leaves the party in the next step.

7. Torin the Elder

The first time you enter this room, ***Torin the Elder***, leader of the Dwarf clan, is in the middle of a conversation with another Dwarf, ***Geldor Armorsmith***:

Geldor: We must take the battle *to* them, Torin.

Torin: No, Geldor, it isn't time. I cannot explain their recent actions, but we must remain calm. The clan needs us here.

Geldor: But if the Throgs attack us now, with all the disappearances, I don't know if we can hold the clanhall!

Torin: Lost Thera! I will have no more discussion about this. (beat) We have guests, Geldor, stand aside. (to you) Come closer.

(Move forward a square.)

Drake: I did not mean to interrupt.

Torin: Nay, they are old words, anyways. I am Torin, Elder of the Chak'ra clan. You must be Drake, I have heard of you. And Farli, you have returned at last.

Farli: Dombur needed. . .

Torin: Enough! Save it for later. Drake, what do you ask of me?

If you have talked to the dragon, Drake says the following:

Drake: The dragon Vermatrix has been chained. I want to free her. Can you help?

Torin: Free a dragon, are you daft?

Drake: She was chained by Throgs. . .

Torin: That is not enough reason.

Drake:. . . and she might be real friendly to those that help her.

Torin: Ahhh, and she would hate Throgs. Maybe I can help, or more likely, Sardin, our blacksmith, can. See him to the north, tell him I said to help you. Return when you have the time, I wish to speak with you some more.

If Farli is in the party, the scene continues:

Torin: Now, Farli, you disobeyed my direct command. You left the hall and went searching for your brother. What do you say to this?

Farli: I had to leave. I had to find Dombur. He would have done the same for me. . . sir.

Torin: Only if he remembered that you were gone, but that doesn't change the fact that you broke our laws. You are *ucktogoth.* Leave now.

Farli: But. . .

Torin & Geldor: (chanting) An *ucktogoth* cannot be heard or seen.

Farli: So be it. Goodbye, Drake. I must go.

Farli leaves the party.

Note that Torin asked you to return later. Exit into the corridor, turn left and go north. Take the second left turn, then follow the passage around the corner to the blacksmith.

Dwarf Guards. They look menacing, and they're everywhere. But don't attack Dwarves. You need allies in your quest.

8A. The Master Smith

Sardin Blackrock works the Dwarven forges as Master Smith of the hold. His greeting depends on whether or not you've seen Torin the Elder at 7 yet. In this case, you *have* seen Torin, so Drake opens the conversation:

Drake: Are you Sardin the blacksmith? Torin said you could help me.

Sardin: Aye. What can I do for you?

Drake: I promised to free a dragon. She is bound in magick chains and the Throgs broke the key into two pieces. What can I do?

Sardin: If you could bring me the pieces of the key, I might be able to fix it. But alas, my forge fire has died and I cannot light it.

Drake: Why not?

Sardin: It's a magick forge, and you can't just light those normally, you know. You need magick flint.

Drake: And?

Sardin: We ran out of magick flint, and I haven't been able to find any. It's pretty rare, you know.

Drake: OK, I'll get you your magick flint if you help me out.

Sardin: It's a deal. Take this magick chisel. You'll need it.

Take the ***chisel*** from Sardin. Now you need to retrieve a piece of magick flint for the smith. Here's how:

1. Head back through the fortress door to 1.
2. Take the stairs to the Lower Level of the Dragon Feeding Grounds. (You emerge at 61 on Map 6.1.)
3. Work your way north to the stairway at 25.

4. Take those stairs to the Upper Level of the Feeding Grounds. (You emerge at 26 on Map 6.2.)
5. Go to the magickal flint rock at 45.
6. Use the chisel on the rock. A piece of ***magick flint*** chips off.
7. Turn right and pick up the magick flint from the floor.
8. Now retrace your route all the way back to Sardin in the Dwarven Fortress.

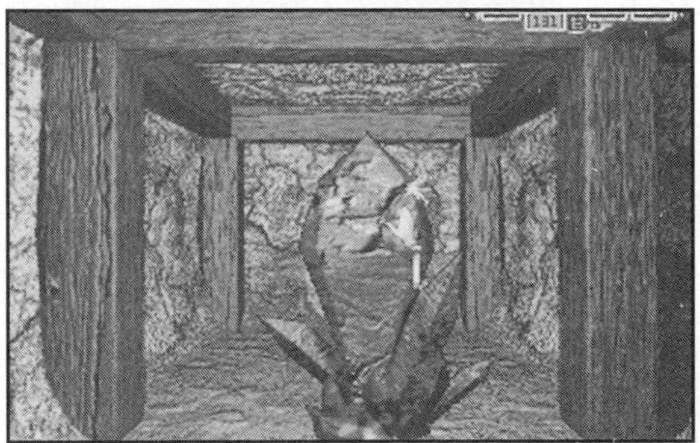

Chip Off the Old Block. Use the chisel Sardin gave you to chip off a piece of magick flint.

When you return, Sardin asks, "Do you have the flint?" He puts out his hand and waits for 10 seconds. If you give him the flint, he thanks you, goes back to light the forge, then returns to say:

Sardin: Thank you. A Dwarven clanhall needs a burning forge. I will be happy to help you.

Drake (if you have both pieces of the dragon key): I need a broken key fixed.

Sardin: Give me the pieces.

When Sardin reaches out, give him both pieces of the dragon key. He asks you to wait, goes back to the forge, fixes the key, then returns and offers it to you: "There you go. Completely fixed. Good luck to you." Take the key from his hand.

8B. The Forge

Don't go back by the ***forge!*** This only angers Sardin. Indeed, if you step past the first portcullis, he says, "Now stop right there! Can't let you go any further, see. Non-employees are not permitted on the shop floor. Step back behind the line." If you ignore him and continue, he becomes hostile and attacks.

Naturally, if you *attack* Sardin (with more then one blow), he becomes quite hostile and defends himself. Worse, Sardin's brother, Seldin, works the lit forge. If you're an enemy of the clanhall, or if you've made Sardin hostile, Seldin cries out, "You don't belong here!" If you've killed Sardin, Seldin attacks, sobbing, "You killed my brother! You'll pay for that!"

Note If you've made yourself an enemy of the clanhall by killing Dwarves, Sardin won't serve you. You can still re-light the forge yourself with the magick flint. However, it's not easy—you have to kill Sardin and Seldin, and you need a Strength rating of 6 to open the portcullis. After you light the forge, put both halves of the dragon key on it. Use a hammer on the forge, then take the forged key.

9. The Glorystone

This huge, scintillating ***stone*** hones the effectiveness of weapons. Hit it with any weapon. Each of the first three times you hit it, the glorystone raises your weapon skill for that particular weapon by 1 point.

Mine Eyes Have Seen the Glory. Take a few whacks at this scintillating stone with each of your favorite weapons.

Tip Whack away at the glorystone with each of the weapons you plan to use in the future.

Exit and go east to the next room.

10. Geldor the Armorer

Since you've already been to Torin's room (7), the door to Geldor's armory is unlocked and he waits for you inside. The first time you meet Geldor here, you engage in the following conversation:

Drake: You wanted to see me?

Geldor: Yes, I have heard of your travels. News travels quickly in the Underlands. I believe we may have similar goals.

Drake: (hesitant) I'm not sure if I understand what you're talking about.

Geldor: Ah, well, let me just say that I think the same about Throgs and their Shamans as you do. And anything you do regarding them is acceptable to me.

Drake: Ah, yes, I see now.

Geldor: Good. Please look around my little shop. If you see anything you like, pick it up and come talk to me about payment. Here is the price list. They are very reasonable.

Geldor holds out a price list scroll. Take it and look at it:

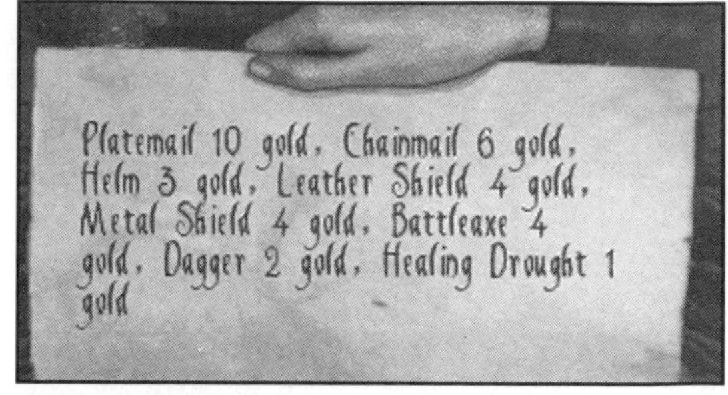
Platemail 10 gold, Chainmail 6 gold, Helm 3 gold, Leather Shield 4 gold, Metal Shield 4 gold, Battleaxe 4 gold, Dagger 2 gold, Healing Drought 1 gold

Geldor's Price List

Proceed into the armory.

11. Geldor's Wares

Combat equipment is displayed for sale on worktables in this room, including the following: ***Dwarven platemail***, two ***Dwarven helms***, some ***chainmail***, a ***battle-ax***, a ***firedagger***, a ***leather shield***, a ***small metal shield***, and two ***heal potions***.

How to Purchase Items:

Pick up the item(s) you want to buy, return to Geldor, and place the items on the table next to him. After he tallies the amount you owe, give him the money sack from your inventory. If you have enough money to cover the cost, Geldor automatically deducts the amount. Then he returns the money sack, saying: "Here is your change, my friend. Thank you for your purchase."

If you head for the door without paying, Geldor is polite at first, saying: "Excuse me, Drake, you haven't paid for that yet," or, "You weren't thinking of leaving without paying, were you?" But if you actually walk out of the room without paying, Geldor becomes hostile and attacks.

Tip If you give Geldor feathers from a Throg Shaman instead of the money sack, he says:

Geldor: You have slain a Throg Shaman, haven't you?

Drake: Yes.

Geldor: A Throg Shaman, maybe the Shaman you have killed, captured and tortured my family. Perhaps their inner souls will rest in peace now, no longer crying for vengeance. (beat) Please, help yourself to my goods. Take what you will, no charge.

Geldor will no longer charge you for any of his goods.

12. Geldor's Chest

Go north into Geldor's private chambers. Be a good adventurer and raid his ***chest***—you find three ***coins*** there. Exit the armory into the corridor.

Return now to Torin the Elder at 7. Remember, he wanted to talk further. Seems Torin has a small request:

Torin: Drake, we have a problem in the hall. I hope you can help us.

Drake: Tell me more.

Torin: This is a small hall, an outpost from the great Dwarven cities. We have been working these passages from the stone, but we have come across a great evil. There is a creature of the darkness roaming these corridors. We unleashed it, and it has been preying on us ever since.

Drake: What is it?

Torin: An undead warrior. One of great power. We have sent many of our warriors to their death in the corridors to the east. Find it. Kill it. I will reward you and we will be very grateful.

Drake: I'll check it out.

13. Horn of Plenty

Before you leave Torin's quarters, slip into his private chamber to the south. Some very good stuff lies on the table here—the ***horn of fear*** and a magick ***throwing axe***. Snatch these powerful weapons, then exit Torin's room into the corridor.

Note The horn of fear casts a powerful Scare spell. The horn has a ten percent chance of being destroyed each time you use it.

In the corridor, turn right, and take a step south. Go in the room to the left.

14. Like Mom Used to Make

Three ***home-cooked meals*** sit on a table here. Take them all—a home-cooked meal restores full vitality to whomever eats it. Go back to the corridor, turn left, and proceed down the hall.

15. Dwarf Storeroom

Break the four ***barrels*** here. In them, from right to left, you find:

- two ***heal roots***
- nothing
- one ***home-cooked meal***
- five ***stones***

After you gather your stores, continue east through the storeroom and around the corner. Enter the first room on the left.

16. Farli's Room

If you've seen Farli banished from the clan by Torin at 7, you find a ***scroll*** here on the floor, by the bed. It reads:

Drake, I cannot explain what has happened. I must leave for a while, to pay for what I have done. You would not understand, but please try.

—Farli Mallestone

Exit to the corridor, then go north to the next room.

17. Karzak's Room

Go face that Dwarf in the corner—by golly, it's your buddy ***Karzak Hardstone***. Step up to greet him.

Note

Of course, this reunion only occurs if you rescued Karzak from his cell back in the Sharga Mines, and he survived combat long enough to leave your party in the Dragon Feeding Grounds.

Drake: Karzak! How's it going?

Karzak: *Argh,* it is so boring around this place. There is much talk of battle with the Throgs, but nothing will come from it.

Drake: Well, Torin wants to know if you will journey with me again.

Karzak: Oh, for the glory of battle, yes!

Drake: Come on then, time is wasting.

Karzak now rejoins your party. Open the ***chest*** in the corner and grab the five ***oil bombs*** inside.

Now it's time to do a big favor for Torin and the clanhall. Exit to the corridor, then turn left and head north to the intersection. Turn right and follow the passage.

18. East/West Link

This intersection connects the east and west halves of the fortress. From here, go 2E, then head up the passage to the north.

19. Fountain of Healing

Ah, another beautiful, pink ***fountain of healing***. Drink up, fill your wineskin, then head back down to the corridor. Go E, 2S, 2E, S, E, then head south and follow the passage. (Say, did the music just get creepier?)

Pink Delight. Boy, that stuff tastes good. Don't forget to refill your wineskin.

20. Picks and Spike

Grab the two ***Dwarven picks*** and the ***iron spike*** in this alcove. Go back up to the main corridor, turn right, then follow the passage until you reach an intersection. There, turn right and follow the passage.

21. Easy Gate

When you step up to the ***portcullis***, it opens automatically. Go through, and continue down the alcove.

22. Burial Crypt

Get ready for a brutal battle, and click on the ***sarcophagus***. Out comes a gruesome ***zombie***. His attack is vicious and poisonous, so after you defeat him, pop a green mushroom into each afflicted party member.

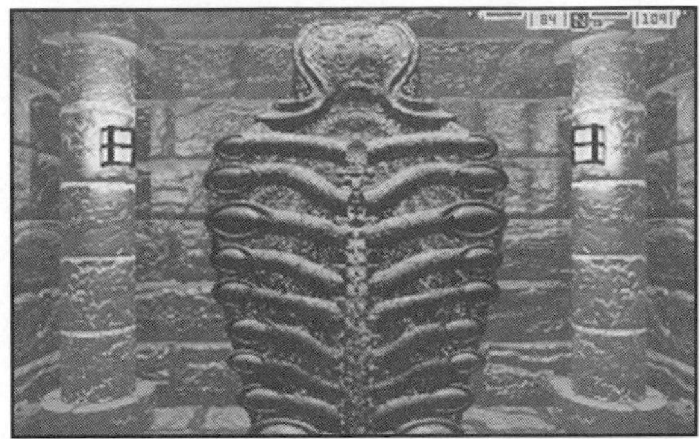

Knight of the Living Dead. This evil, poisonous creature is a brutal opponent. Cure yourself with a green mushroom after the battle.

Tip For this clash, use a good piercing weapon, such as the dagger of penetration.

Take the ***ring of poison resistance*** and the ***rune scroll*** from the sarcophagus. This ring enhances your poison resistance—put it on. The scroll contains the ***Power × 2 rune***, which you should already have inscribed in your journal.

Return to the intersection at 18 and go north.

23. Watch Your Back

The *Dwarf* facing the wall here seems to be working at a lock; hear the clanking? But he stands facing a blank wall. What's going on here?

Suspicious Activity. What's this guy fiddling with? And why is he so unfriendly?

Step up behind the Dwarf and find out:

Dwarf: (spins around) What do you want?
Drake: What are you doing here?
Dwarf: Nothing! Now go away!

If you wait a few more seconds, the Dwarf gets more emphatic: "I said leave me! *You* have no business here!" Don't go away, though. Let the guy stew a bit. Finally, the Dwarf says, "All right, have it your way then." He turns back around and continues with his clinking and clanking.

Now turn and go, but be ready. As you walk away, Karzak cries, "Drake! Watch out!" It's a cowardly ambush from behind! (Hey, isn't that a common Throg tactic?) Turn around quickly, because each sneaky blow to your backside in this encounter does five times the normal damage.

After you kill the traitorous Dwarf, he falls to the ground and turns into, yes, a Throg. Drake says, "He was a Throg in disguise. Some sort of illusion magick."

24. Meta-Treasure

Now walk through the south wall—it's illusory! There are five powerful ***Meta rune scrolls*** on the floor, some of which you've already inscribed in your journal:

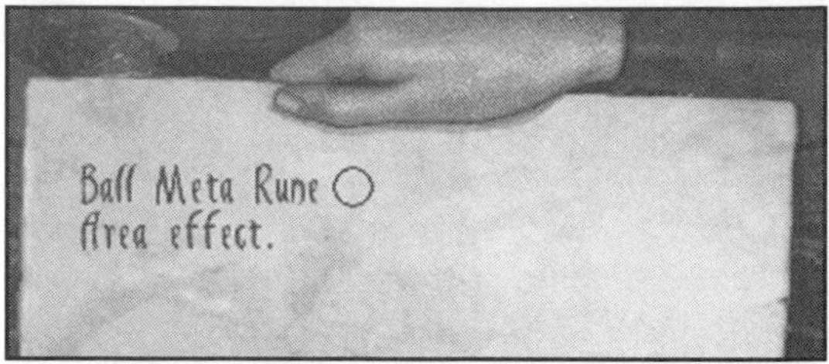

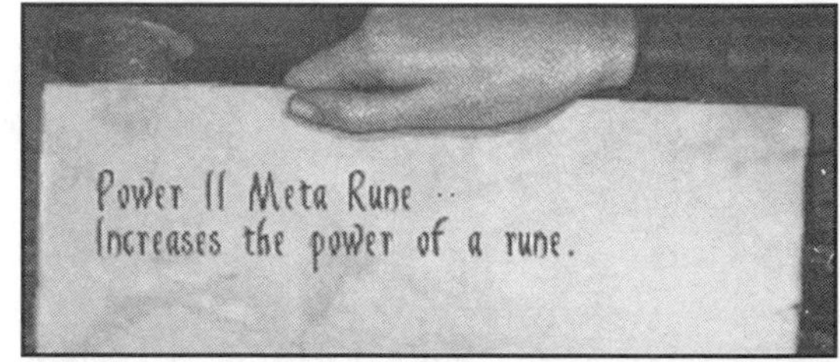

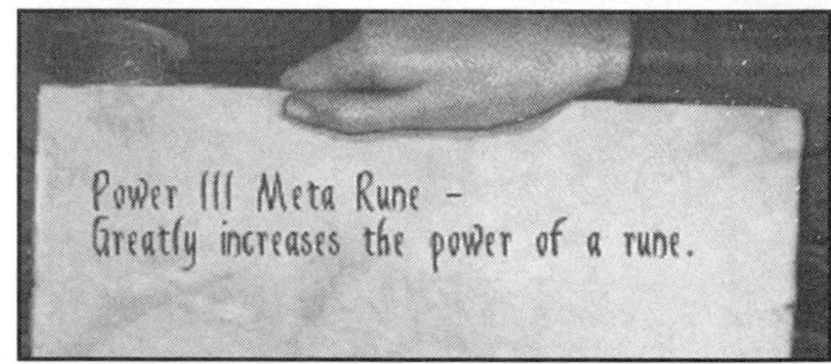

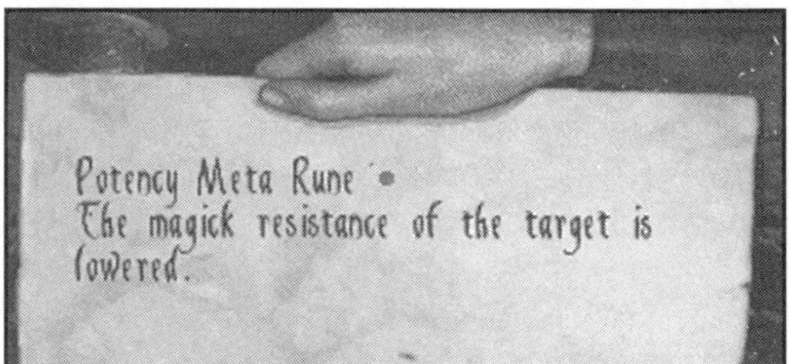

25. Guardhouse

Four ***Dwarf guards*** bunk in this room. You won't find anything worth taking in here, though. Return to Torin the Elder's room.

26. A Just Reward

When you revisit Torin the Elder after killing the zombie, the following conversation takes place:

Torin: Have you put that undead thing to rest?

Drake: Yes. It shall bother you no more.

Torin: I am very grateful. You have saved many of my people's lives. The gifts in the chest are yours.

Drake: I have a question. What is an *uck-togoth*?

Torin: It literally means 'the Forgotten.' If a Dwarf breaks a great law, then he is called *uck-togoth* and banished from our halls. The *uck-togoth* will never return.

Drake: (sad) Ah. Thank you for telling me.

Torin: It is hard, Drake, but we will all get over it.

Torin the Grateful. You saved his people from the undead. Now his chest is yours to loot.

Open the ***chest*** behind Torin and remove the ***magic shield*** and ***rune scroll***. Open the scroll to inscribe it in your journal:

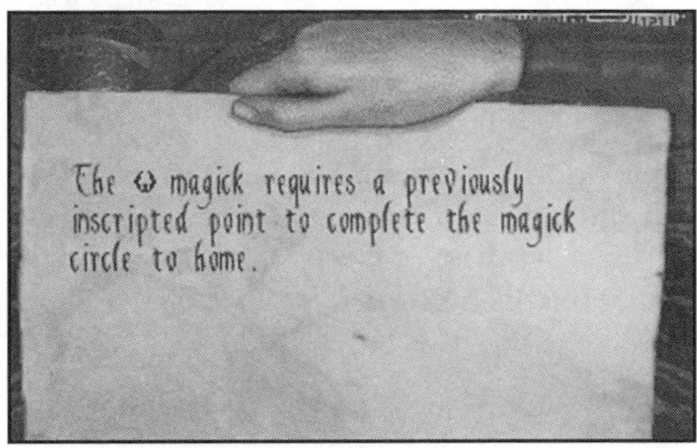

Homing Rune Scroll

Exit into the corridor and turn left. Go three steps north, then turn right and step forward to the door.

27. Geldor's Armory

The only way to enter this room is to kill Geldor and take his key. But there is nothing important here, so it's not worth angering the clanhall.

Exit and go back to the Lower Level of the Dragon Feeding Grounds. Work your way north to 25 (on Map 6.1), then take that stairway to the Upper Level of the Dragon Feeding Grounds.

Now return to the section following step 61 in Level 6: The Dragon Feeding Grounds, and complete the walkthrough for that level.

Level 8

Faerie Realm

The eighth level of *Stonekeep* includes a single map area—the Faerie Realm (Map 8). This level features very little combat, but lots of puzzle-solving and interaction with unusual characters. For more on the Faerie Realm, see the General Notes just after the maps in this section.

Key to Map 8

1. Passage to Dragon Feeding Grounds
2. Snort's welcome
3. Faerie Players' welcome
4. Faerie Players' performance
5. Sweetie (clover)—use daisy chain from 20
6. Flowers, berries, daisy chain
7. Flowers, moss
8. Spin square
9. Murph (rune scroll)
10. Faerie cake, fiddle
11. Binkle (Faerie pants)—use fiddle from 10
12. Decanter
13. Winkle (jester cap)—use drum from 36
14. Snort (brew)—use thyme, decanter, moss
15. Winkle (iron spike)—visit twice, then use book from 27
16. Iron spike, flowers, jester cap
17. Primroses
18. Surly (silver key)—use Faerie cake
19. Sweetie (Faerie cake)
20. Flowers, daisy chain
21. Decanters
22. Parchment
23. Crossroads
24. Mushrooms, book
25. Murph
26. Portcullis, Giggle, Binkle
27. Bone pile (book)
28. Lament/Sparkle (joins party)
29. Flowers, Faerie wasp
30. Flowers, Faerie wasp
31. Flowers, Faerie wasp
32. Moss
33. Charcoal stick, St. John's Wort
34. Toadstool alarm
35. Trolls
36. Flowers, drum
37. Flowers, berries
38. Heal root
39. Chuckle (jester cap)—use Snort's Brew from 14
40. Giggle (gold key)—use book from 24
41. Chuckle (portrait, Faerie shirt)—use charcoal stick, parchment
42. Outer Court gate—use gold and silver keys
43. Mana Hearth
44. Inner Court gate—use 5 primroses, circle twice
45. Iaenni (ring, pendant), Faerie cake
46. Trolls
47. Troll trap
48. Horseshoe medallion
49. Terrible Troll (Orb of Yoth-soggoth)
50. Decanter
51. Will-o'-the-wisp
52. Mushrooms
53. Elfwand, mushrooms
54. Hostile will-o'-the-wisp
55. Mushrooms
56. Rune scroll
57. Decanter, Troll trap

Map 8 Faerie Realm

Portcullis

Locked Door

General Notes

The Faerie Realm is a bit different from other Stonekeep levels. Before you explore, note some of its unique characteristics, listed below.

Talking to Faeries

You speak with several Faeries in their realm. The exact course of dialogue with each Faerie usually depends on the composition of your traveling party—Farli, Karzak, Dombur, and Skuz each have different responses. (In our walkthrough, Drake enters the realm with only Skuz and Karzak in the party.)

The Karzak Timer

Karzak despises the insipid cuteness of the Faerie Realm. If Karzak is in your party, Stonekeep starts a timer when you first enter Level 8. As the timer counts up, Karzak weakens, and utters a number of unhappy responses.

As soon as Karzak leaves the Faerie Realm, the weakening effect dissipates—but the timer does *not* reset, and it starts up again if Karzak returns to the realm. The counter reverses (restoring Karzak's combat skills) when he enters the dangerous Troll areas of the realm. Also note: The timer does not run while you talk to any Faeries.

Faerie Bashing

If you attack any Faerie, he/she transforms to "glow form" immediately, and flies off. If other Faeries are present during the attack, they fly off, too.

Flower Picking

The Faerie Realm is strewn with flowers—primrose, gladiola, foxglove, and so on. Pick freely. There's no penalty for denuding the realm of its flora, because some of the plants simply regenerate after a few minutes.

Troll Fighting

Trolls are invisible until you obtain a ***four-leaf clover***. Of course, if Trolls are invisible, combat is much tougher. Fortunately, there are five items of attire (all found in the realm) that give the wearer special protection from Troll attacks.

1. Passage to Dragon Feeding Grounds

You arrive here from the Dragon Feeding Grounds (41 on Map 6.2). Head south to the first right turn, scooping up ***flowers***—gladioli, foxglove, primrose—as you go.

2. Faerie Welcome

The first time you step into this square, a ***Faerie*** named Snort flies up in "glow" form. He says, "Hi, there! This is your body. (shakes) And this is your body in the Faerie Realm." Then Snort morphs into his male Faerie form, spins you 360 degrees, and adds: "Any questions?"

As a matter of fact, yes—but off he goes, before you can speak. Turn west and follow the passageway, scooping up more ***flowers*** along the way.

Tip Flowers line most of the passages in the Faerie Realm. Gather as many as you can. They will be useful later.

3. Meet the Faerie Players

The first time you step into this square, six ***Faeries*** in glow form approach you. All except one assume their human form. The leader, Chuckle, talks to you:

Chuckle: Welcome to the Realm of Faerie!

ALL: (various greetings, except Binkle)

Binkle: Go home.

Chuckle: Now then, I have a very important question for you. Do you have your Faerie Handbook yet?

Drake: Uh, no.

Chuckle: Good! 'Cause you don't need one! (laughter) Got you there! What you *do* need are performances from the Faerie Players! And that's us! I'm Chuckle, this is Giggle, that's Snort the Faerie . . .

Snort: That's my name, not a suggestion.

Chuckle: . . . and that's Winkle, Binkle, and, um, oh yes, Murph.

(Murph remains in glow form.)

Binkle: Don't make me angry, dog tick. You're not gonna like me when I'm angry.

Karzak (if present): I don't think much of you now.

Chuckle: Murph? Oh, MUR-urph!

Murph (de-glows): Sorry.

Chuckle: Yes, now then, the Faerie Players perform all over the Faerie Realm. So look for us around a Faerie corner from you.

Murph: Poo-head.

Giggle: If you haven't figured it out yet, we tack "Faerie" onto just about everything—Faerie-songs, Faerie-hats, Faerie creatures, Faerie Unseen Court—you'll get the idea.

The Faerie Players. A fun bunch of guys, these Faeries. Their story-songs are full of good info, though. Listen carefully.

Chuckle: Yes, and now we bid you adieu! By the way, did I mention compensation?

Giggle: A stipend, if you would.

Snort: The big payoff.

Winkle: (stuttering) Rec, rec, recompense!

Binkle: Cash and prizes.

Chuckle (after a pause): Mur-urph!

Murph: Sorry. Pay for play.

Giggle: That means you got to give us something, Spunky.

Chuckle: And now off to prepare our play! Away! Away!

Binkle: Let's just beat it. (They all flash into glow form and burst away.)

Karzak (if present): Can I just fall on my axe now?

What was that about a "Faerie Unseen Court"? Hmmm. Continue west.

4. If the Play's the Thing . . . ?

The Faerie Players pop up whenever you pause at one of these four squares. They offer amusing theatrical performances (or "story-songs") in exchange for items from your inventory—"pay for play," as Murph puts it.

You can buy certain story-songs with specific items—a primrose for "The Song of Wahooka," for example.

Entrances by the Faerie Players

There are three random entrance sequences. Each entrance opens with the Fairy Players swarming the area in glow form. Each gives you two chances to fork over payment:

Entrance Number 1

Chuckle: To arms, to arms!

Giggle: Two legs, two legs!

Snort: To be or not to be!

Binkle: That wasn't a question.

Winkle: To pay or not to pay!

All except Murph: Now *that's* a question!

Murph: Now *that's* a question!

Chuckle: Murph!

Murph: Sorry.

Chuckle morphs to male form, clears his throat, and holds out his hand for the payment.

Entrance Number 2:

Faeries fly in. Quiet music plays in the background, like the orchestra warming up at a real play. Then Chuckle says, "*Shh, shh, shh-shh-shh!* Quiet please. The play is about to begin. But first, a message from our patron. (beat) That's you, Bunky." Again, you get two chances to pay up before the Faeries exit.

Entrance Number 3:

Faeries fly in. In glow form, they come forward:

Chuckle: If the play is the thing, is the thing the play?

Murph: Well, I know I can play with . . .

All: MUR-urph!

Murph: Sorry.

Chuckle: The real answer, my friends, is on its way.

All except Murph: Not thing or play, what matters is pay!

Once again, you get two chances to pay or lose out on some high-class entertainment.

Here are the complete lyrics of all six story-songs performed by the inimitable Faerie Players. Each story can be repeated any time the players reappear—just offer the appropriate payment listed below each title:

"Why the Shadow King Is Like He Is"

Costs one foxglove.

Binkle
How come, Khull-khuum? How come?
Tell us why you turned into a nut,
Tell us why we don't just kick your butt,
How come, Khull-khuum? How come?
Chorus (including Murph)
Yeah, Khull-khuum, how come?
Binkle
How come, Khull-khuum? How come?
Long ago, you were real nice,
Now you have a heart of ice,
How come, Khull-khuum? How come?
Chorus (including Murph)
Yeah, Khull-khuum, how come?

Binkle
How come, Khull-khuum? How come?
Devastation gave your rule a rise,
But the world is not your booby prize,
How come, Khull-khuum? How come?
Chorus (including Murph)
Yeah, Khull-khuum, how come?
Binkle
How come, Khull-khuum? How come?
Are we safe until the end?
Remember times when you was our friend?
How come, Khull-khuum? How come?
Chuckle
Your common sense is now unknown.
Giggle
Your head's a roost but the birds have flown.
Snort
You have the brains of a backward stone.
Winkle
Your end will come and you will moan.
Murph
Your birthday gift has sure been blown.
Chorus
Yeah, Khull-khuum you scum!
How come, Khull-khuum. How come?

"I'd Rather Be a Dwarf"

Costs one gladioli.

If you have Dwarves in your party, Chuckle asks, "You sure about this?" If your gladioli offer is repeated or there are no Dwarves, Chuckle says, "We love this story, we do. Murph, get on up here. Murph. *Murph!*"

Chuckle
If you could be the king,
Wouldn't that be a dandy thing?
Murph
I'd rather be a dwarf.
Giggle
A hero great and tall,
Vanquish foes—one and all?
Murph
I'd rather be a dwarf.
Snort
"The wisest man in all the land,
Who holds all knowledge in his hand?"
Murph
I'd rather be a dwarf.
Binkle
A poet, artist, or a sage,
A singer or a mighty mage?
Murph
I'd rather be a dwarf.
Winkle
A tinker, tailor, soldier, thief,
A slug, a worm, an ugly leech?
Murph
I'd rather be a dwarf.
All
A pile of rocks, a lock of hair,
The lint beneath a rocking chair,
A broken twig, a hairy gnat,
The guano of a worm-sick bat!?
Chuckle
(loud whisper) Murph!
Murph
Oh—I'd rather be a dwarf.
(beat)
But I am pretty stupid . . . I guess I AM a dwarf!

"The Song of Wahooka"

Costs one primrose.

Chorus
(all chanting)
Wa-*HOO*-ka, Wa-*HOO*-ka, Wa-*HOO*-ka.
Winkle
Who is Wahooka, mysterious stranger?
Savior, conspirator, cause of danger?
Stronger than even the gods, say some . . .

Giggle
Others say he's just a bum!
Repeat chorus.
Winkle
Lost Faerie of Atlantis, may he be?
King of Goblins under the sea?
Part Throg Shaman, Avatar of Ys,
Saw the Devastation, if you please.
Repeat chorus.
Winkle
Greedy little long-lost child,
Loves his gems and magick, wild,
'Bah' is what he likes to say,
Tricks are what he likes to play.
Repeat chorus.
Winkle
Great Wahooka, a force Primal?
Making lines hard to rhyme-al.
When all is finally done and said . . .
All
(loudly)
He's really just a big Poo-head!

"Ice Wars"

Costs a rock.

Giggle
Cool as the frost on an icy witch,
Cruel as the mind of an evil . . .
Chuckle
Snitch?
Giggle
Cool as the tufts on a polar bear's nose,
Cruel as the chill when the cold wind blows . . .
That's cruel.
Cool as the minions by her side,
Cruel as the tanning of a baby seal's hide,
Cool as a swim in the icy flows,
The Ice Queen's as cruel as everyone knows . . .
And that's cruel.
Real cruel.
Cool under fire is what they have to be,
Cruelty to stop is important, you see,
Cool is the way they like their land,
So the Ice Shargas are a fighting band . . .
And that's cool!
Real cool!
It's down-right chilly, man. You dig?
(spoken)
The Ice Shargas are your friends.
Skuz
(if present in party)
Skuz always knew Skuz cool.
All Faeries
Be-skuz, be-skuz, be-skuz, be-*skuuuuzzz*,
Be-skuz of the pitiful things he duz.

The Gift

This one-time event costs one mushroom.

Chuckle: We're a bit much, aren't we? I mean, don't you just wanna squish us sometimes?

Karzak: All the time, actually.

Chuckle: Exactly! So we all decided that since you were such a good patron of our arts, we'd give you this . . .

Giggle: And then we can be patronizing!

Chuckle offers you a ***rune scroll.*** Open it and read it to inscribe it in your journal:

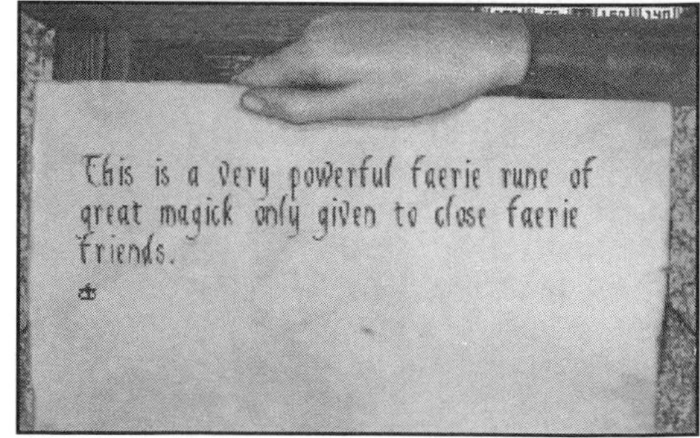

Duck Rune Scroll

The Curse of Lament

Costs one St. John's Wort.

Chuckle: It's time for a sad tale. And who better to tell it than a sad excuse. Snort?

Snort: Oh, and you're so great?

Chuckle: It's just an intro, Snort. Don't take it personally! It's not like I called you a Dwarf or anything.

Karzak: Just let me do one, Drake. Doesn't matter which one.

Chuckle: See? Dwarves take things personally!

Snort
The story of Lament is . . .
Chorus
True!
Snort
A cur-sed female faerie . . .
Chorus
Who . . .
Snort
Tells tales where evil Trolls can . . .
Chorus
View . . .
Snort
Must tell brave heroes stories . . .
Chorus
Two . . .
Snort
Before released from evil.
Chorus
Who?
Snort
The King of Shadows, he's a . . .
Chorus
Poo!
Snort
She sees the place where things go . . .
Chorus
Boo!
Snort
And knows what saves the likes of . . .
Chorus
You!
Snort
This tale is done, we thank you . . .
Chorus (except Murph)
Too!
Murph
(after a beat)
Too!

All: Murph!

Murph: Sorry.

Chuckle (if you've already met Lament): Of course, we knew you already knew this. But it's still a good story! And Snort is such a ham.

Troll Hint

Costs one skull.

Chuckle: A performance by Chuckle the Faerie and the Faerie Players. (Applause.) Thank you. Thank you. Company, are you ready?

All but Chuckle and Murph: Ready!

Murph: Ready!

Chuckle: You're late.

Murph: Sorry.

Chuckle: The performance is entitled "For Whom the Bells Troll."

Chuckle
For whom the bells Troll
All but Chuckle and Murph
They Troll for you!
Murph
They Troll for you!
Chuckle
You're late!

Murph: Sorry.

Chuckle: Wanna try it again?

All but Chuckle and Giggle: No!

All: (giggle and laugh)

Chuckle: Well, that concludes another performance. Shows twice nightly. You don't need reservations with us. If you're drinking, please don't drive. Don't forget to tip the waitresses, they had to pay to get in here too. Goodnight.

Snort: What you really need is a good hat! See ya!

Binkle: (like Quasimodo) The bells, the bells!

Giggle: Get it? It's a clue, baby. Pay attention. They-hate-the-bells. See ya! Good to know you.

5. Sweetie the Fairy

Continue west to that purple Faerie glow in the alcove. As you approach, it changes into a female form. Meet ***Sweetie***, the most insufferably cute Faerie in the realm:

Sweetie: Do you like my dress?

Skuz: Skuz thinks *you're* a cutie.

Sweetie: I'm not a cutie. I'm a Faerie!

Karzak: I think I'm going to be sick.

Sweetie: I'd look better if I had my daisy chain. I think Giggle hid it! He's a little poo-head! Would you find my daisy chain, please?

Karzak: (grumbles)

Skuz: Skuz keep eye out. Keep both eye out.

Sweetie: You're cute!

Yeesh. OK, now go 2S, 6W, S, then west into the alcove.

6. Berry, Berry Good to Me

Pluck all the ***flowers***, and don't miss the clump of ***rowanberries***. They may not look nourishing—and they're not—but they're kind of fun because they make you intoxicated. (For more on this condition, see step 14 below.)

Hidden under one flower is a ***daisy chain***. Could this be the one Sweetie's looking for? Step back into the corridor. Go around the corner and return to Sweetie at 4.

Sweetie is consumed by an almost pathological cuteness when you see her again. Don't dally. Give it to her—the daisy chain, that is. When you do, she says, "What, were you born in a cave? These are primroses!" The false daisy chain disappears and you get five primroses thrown in your face. Sweetie adds a last cryptic comment: "You know what they say—'Roses down and twice around!'"

Go back past the alcove at 6 and continue down the passage, picking flowers all the way, until you reach another alcove on your right.

7. Shut Up, Skuz

This alcove is full of ***flowers***. Tucked into the floral arrangement is clump of ***Brownie moss***. Take it. This prompts an inquiry by Skuz:

Skuz: Skuz have question. Why it Brownie moss if it green?

Drake: Because it was named after Brownies.

Skuz: Are Brownies brown?

Drake: Well, actually . . .

Skuz: Why not name Brownies greenies? Their moss green.

Drake: That's not . . . Hmmm. Something for you to think about, I guess.

Karzak: I have the perfect answer for his questions, Drake.

Skuz: That OK. Skuz have all answer he need, thank you!

Continue west a couple of steps.

8. Square Dance

Whenever you step into any of the four squares adjacent to 8, you suddenly spin around, then accelerate wildly down one of the four passages. Just keep running through 8 until the spell throws you down the north passage. (It should take only one attempt.) Go west down the corridor, grabbing that ***wild thyme*** on the way. Continue west until you see a Faerie glow shimmering just down the hall.

9. Murph and the Slow Rune

Approach the glow. It morphs into ***Murph***:

Murph: (slowly) They said . . .

Karzak: I'm just going to kill him. That's all. No one would notice. He wouldn't even scream until after he's dead.

Murph: (continues) . . . that I should . . . give you . . . this. (He gives you a ***rune scroll***.) They were laughing a lot. I don't . . . get it.

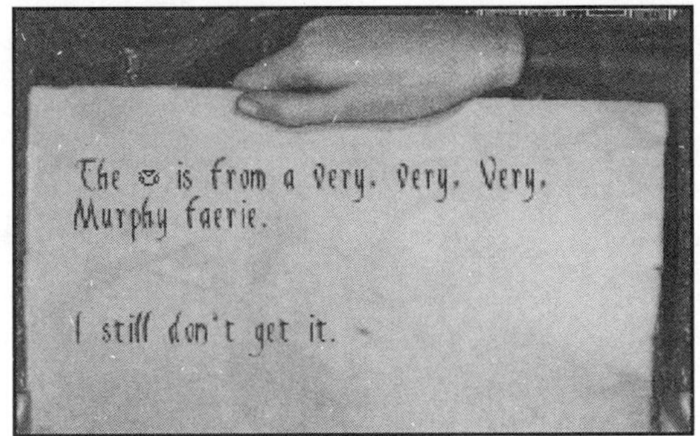

Slowness Rune Scroll

Murph changes back into glow form and flies away. Continue west down the passage.

10. Cake and Fiddle

In this alcove, clear out the flowers fast to find a ***fine Faerie cake*** and a ***fiddle***. (And for fun, say that sentence quickly a whole bunch of times.) Continue south down the corridor.

11. Binkle Wants His Fiddle

When you reach this square, another Faerie glow appears. ***Binkle*** approaches and says, "I'm looking for my fiddle. Hey, have you seen it? I tell you what, I'll drop my drawers to get my fiddle back. If you happen to go over into the Troll area to look, watch out for that nasty one in the west. Oooh, that's foul."

If you picked up the fiddle back at 10, Binkle suddenly notices it and howls, "*You've got my fiddle!* It's a love thing, *cha-ching!* I'll trade you for it."

Give him the fiddle and he keeps his promise to drop his drawers. Back up a step, grab the ***Faerie pants*** he left behind, and put them on Drake. Then take a step south.

12. Bottle for Brew

Grab that ***empty decanter*** on the ground. Move on, but keep picking flowers. (In particular, keep your eyes peeled for a ***wild thyme***.) Go W, 4S, 2E, S, E, then 2S and turn right into the alcove.

13. Winkle Wants His Drum

Approach the Faerie glow. It's ***Winkle***, and he's not too happy. He says, "I think that poo-head Giggle hid my drum. He's as bad about drums as Trolls are about bells." When Winkle disappears, exit into the corridor, go south, and enter the next room on the right.

14. How About a Little Snort?

Snort the Faerie waits for you here. When you approach, he says, "I'm Snort and welcome to my brewery! (sings) If you've got the thyme . . . and the moss and a bottle . . . get a snort here! Well? Don't just stand there!" Then he disappears.

You have all the ingredients for Snort's Brew so wait a few seconds until Snort reappears. When he sees you, he says, "Hand it over and stand back!" Give Snort the Brownie moss, the empty decanter, and some wild thyme.

Note An amusing tidbit: If you try to give Snort more than one moss, he cries out, "No moss, no moss!"

When Snort has all three items, he snorts, "One for you and one for me! Good stuff!" Then he drops a ***decanter with a red brew***, morphs to glow form, and zips away. Pick up the decanter, but *don't drink it!* You'll need it for a later trade. Instead, exit and go south to the next room.

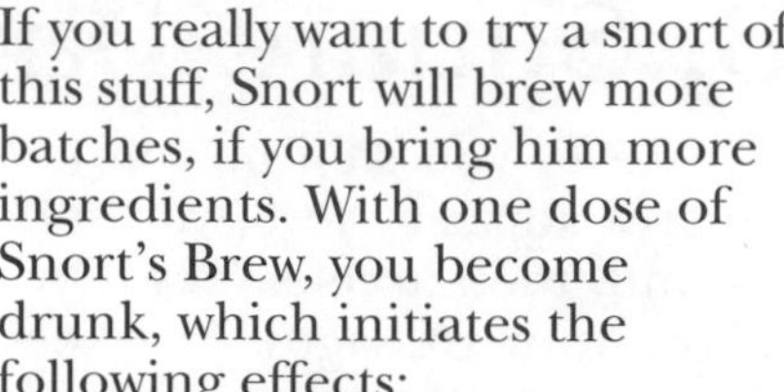

Note If you really want to try a snort of this stuff, Snort will brew more batches, if you bring him more ingredients. With one dose of Snort's Brew, you become drunk, which initiates the following effects:

1st drink: The drunken effect lasts three minutes, and is marked by the "damage-shake" and the spins—that is, you spin around to face random directions.

2nd drink: If you are already drunk and knock back a second snort, the drunken effect extends another five minutes, with more frequent shakes and spins.

3rd drink: Add seven more minutes to the drunken effect. Your vision is now affected.

4th drink: Add another 10 minutes. Drunken effects continue, and the screen blacks out occasionally.

If you attempt to take a fifth drink, Drake says, "Never again."

15. Winkle Seeks Last Tome, No Questions Asked

When you approach the purple Faerie glow, ***Winkle*** appears and stutters, "H-Hi. I'm Winkle. You'll like it here, even though it's not as nice as before He Who Casts Shadows sunk Lady Iaenni's beautiful realm below the earth. If I could only find the Last Tome of the Elves, maybe I could, you know, make a difference. I'd be ever so grateful if you found it." And off he goes.

Exit the room for a few seconds, then re-enter.

Winkle appears again. He says, "Hi. No luck finding the Last Tome of the Elves? Oh, well. I hope it's not with the Trolls! In case you go over there, here's something that might help." Winkle gives you an ***iron spike***, then says, "If you drive this in the ground, it will keep most Trolls at bay. See ya. Bye-bye."

Note The ***iron spike*** acts as a barrier—Trolls can't move past the spot where it is driven into the ground.

Exit Winkle's room and go south.

16. Cap With Bells

Step right through that imposing mushroom; right behind it, you'll find another ***iron spike***. Continue into the alcove. Pick bouquets of ***flowers*** until you find a ***jester's cap***. Put the cap on Drake—he's beginning to look pretty ridiculous, isn't he? Exit and go four steps north, then turn right. Take two steps east, then turn left to face the alcove to the north.

17. Primrose Patch

Snatch up all the ***primroses***, then take another step east. Turn right and go south into the room.

18. Man, That's One Surly Faerie

Approach the ***Faerie glow*** in the corner of this room. It turns into a female faerie and says:

Surly Faerie. Thank God they're not all cute. This one definitely takes the cake.

Surly: Oh, you *must* be kidding. I heard the "Chosen One" had shown up. That can't be *you.*

Drake: That remains to be seen, I guess.

Karzak: You know, I could almost *like* this one.

Surly: Well, I think the old songs are bunk anyway. But, no skin off my nose if you try. Tell you what, you bring me a Faerie cake and I'll give what you need to see the queen.

Drake: That's very generous of you.

Surly: Heh, not my idea.

Drake: I'm Drake, by the way. May I have your name?

Surly: Surly. One joke and you'll see where I got the name, OK?

Drake: Um, yes, um . . . ma'am?

Surly: Well, don't just stand there. You want to get on with this, or what? Hand it over!

Caution If you don't give her a Faerie cake within a couple of seconds, she gets angry and says, "What an idiot! How do you expect to get anywhere just standing around like that. When you're ready to give me the cake, come back." She then flies off and will not return for at least five minutes.

When you give Surly the cake, she says:

Surly: Don't that just take the cake? Hey, have I given you what you *need* yet?

Drake: Um, no actually.

Surly: Then you might consider laughing at my jokes, huh?

(Drake forces a laugh.)

Surly: I don't have real high hopes for ya, pal.

Surly then offers you a ***silver key*** . When you take it, she says, "This will help you see the queen," turns into a glow and exits. Exit to the corridor, turn right, and follow the passage.

19. Sweetie Cake

It's ***Sweetie*** again. When she sees you, she evanesces into her female form and says, "I heard you released my friend the dragon! Sweets for the sweet!" She offers you a ***fine Faerie cake*** (which, you may or may not know, is *way* better than a *regular* Faerie cake). Take it—it's edible, with a nice healing or poison cure quotient. Good for trading, too.

Note Obviously, if you haven't released or even *seen* the dragon back on Level 6, Sweetie will have a different response to your approach.

20. Flower Garden

Lots of flowers here. Bunches and bunches, of all variety, in every square here. But what's that in the corner? Looks like another ***daisy chain***.

Now go back east a few steps and take the passage heading north. When you get to 8, turn around and back into the square. You'll get thrown north again. Then follow the passage to the east, exploring alcoves and picking flowers as you go.

21. Ye Olde Brewholders

Take the ***decanter*** from the ground. Look carefully—there's another ***decanter*** hidden behind the stalk of that mushroomish thing in the alcove. Take it too, if you want. Continue down the corridor. After the passage turns south, you come to an intersection. Turn left and return to Sweetie.

Again, she goes berserk with happiness when she sees that you have a daisy chain. But is it *the* daisy chain this time? Give it to her and see.

Yes! Sweetie bubbles, "Oh, thank you so much! For a reward, would you like a kiss or a prize? Hold out your hand if it's the prize." She offers the ***four-leaf clover***. Grab it. (If you don't, she responds, "You want the kiss? *Yecck*, I'm a Faerie! Who'd wanna kiss a man?" Then she throws it at you.) Sweetie turns to glow, and flies off.

Note The four-leaf clover is magick. It allows you to see invisible Trolls. Is this a good thing? You bet your sweet daisy chain it is.

Go back south, then west. At the intersection, turn left and follow the passage.

22. "I Can't Read It"

Too bad, Drake. That ***piece of parchment*** behind the mushroom in the alcove looks interesting. Tuck it away in inventory for now and go east, then south down the passage to the intersection.

23. Crossroads

The first time you reach this intersection, turn left and follow the passage as it zigzags back north. At the next intersection, turn right and go to the end of the alcove.

24. Mushroom Farm

Time for some fungus plucking. Two ***green mushrooms*** and four ***spotted mushrooms*** dot the ground here. Grab that big red ***book***, too. (Could it be the Last Tome of the Elves?) Now work your way back to the intersection at 23 and head west down the passage. Take the first right turn.

25. Murph the Punching Bag

A ***Faerie glow*** approaches you in this alcove . . . Guess who?

Murph: Oh, I'm Murph. People call me Murph. But you knew that.

Karzak: (exasperated) *What do you want?*

Drake: Can we help you?

Murph: I am offering a one-time deal. I will train you . . .

Karzak: (screams in frustration)

Murph: (continues) . . . how to fight better. Go ahead. Try to hit me.

Karzak: *Now* he's talking!

Murph: I won't stay long. Practice while you can. I don't have to do this . . . again.

Go ahead. Pick a weapon that needs a boost in skill rating. Bash away at the glow. Even if you hit Murph (which is difficult), you can't hurt him.

Murph: I may talk slow, but I move . . .

Karzak: *Get on with it!*

Murph (finally finishes) . . . fast.

Resume combat with a second weapon that needs skill enhancement. After a few more seconds, Murph says, "Wheee. Yippee. I hope you enjoyed that as much as I . . . did. I'm done! See ya." After he zips away, see what he's done for you. When your journal flashes up in the corner, open it and check your combat stats—you've improved your skills with the two weapons you used!

Exit the room, turn right, and follow the corridor around the corner. Take the first left turn and follow the passage to the portcullis.

26. Troll Bridge

The first time you arrive here, ***Giggle*** and ***Binkle*** stand guard in front of a ***portcullis***. When you turn the corner and approach them, they begin a goofy dialogue:

Fool's Gate. Welcome to Troll Country. Would you trust your portcullis to these guys?

Giggle (pointing at Binkle): Troll Bridge. Pay Troll.

Binkle: I am not a Troll! *I am a Faerie being*—all right?

Giggle: Yeah . . . *now!*

Binkle: Hey, scum buzzard. You making fun of me, or what? Don't make me angry! You gonna pay!

Giggle: (giggles) Don't make me laugh, baby.

Binkle: Laugh, why I oughtta grab your neck—!

Drake: Excuse me. What's the Troll . . . uh, toll?

Binkle: Beat it! I'm trying to decapitate this munchkin, alright? Get outta here. Go on through. Here's a token. Go.

The portcullis raises with a squeak.

Giggle: You were supposed to take care of that squeak, big fella.

Binkle: Me? What are ya doing? Sniffing paint? *You* were supposed to take care of that!

Giggle: Was not.

Binkle: Was too.

Giggle: Was not.

Binkle: Was too.

After the Faeries disappear, go through the gate. Signs of danger are everywhere. Bones litter the floor. The music changes. Karzak's "weakness timer" reverses, and he beams with happiness at the prospect of Dwarf-ly combat. Skuz gulps. Yes, my friend, you are now in Troll Country.

Let's get right to it, shall we? Turn right at the intersection and follow the passage west.

27. Book Mark

Bash at that pile of bones to get another red ***book***. Maybe *this* is the Last Tome of the Elves. Continue down the corridor.

28. Lament/Sparkle

The first time you approach this area, a female ***Faerie*** appears at the end of the passage. Meet Lament, and listen to her sad story:

Lament: My name is Lament. I am cursed to tell two tragic tales of turmoil, then I may travel. If you would like to listen to my ever-so-sad lament, please linger. Else leave.

The undead land through an ancient gate,
Spirits walk that place.
A realm created through bitter hate,
Behind an empty face.
The spirits seek their final rest,
Magick is the key.
Beware of what your senses test,
Your eyes can never see.
The kiss of a bow or touch of a blade,
Will harm these spirits none.
Believe your soul and you shall live
Until your task is done.

Lament: (continues) You know, I'm tired of this curse. One story's enough! And this name? Uh-uh, no way, gotta go! I think I should have a *pretty* name, don't

you? What do you think about Kiss the Faerie? No, you're right. People might get ideas—like Dwarves. *Ick!*

Karzak: Ick is right, lady!

Lament: You're just a poo-head. I got it! Beamie is perfect. No, wait, it's not. How about Cutie? No. Blinkie? Maybe not.

Karzak: How about Leaving?

Lament: How about, You're a poo-head? (quickly) Perfect! It's—no, that's no good at all. I got it! I'm Sparkle! You like my name? I think it's a good one. Can I come with you? Can I? Can I, can I, can I, can I, can I, can I? *Pleeeeease?*"

Drake: Of course you may journey with us.

Note If your party is full, Sparkle cannot join, and the conversation ends like this:

Drake: I'm afraid there are too many of us as there is, Sparkle. Besides, I would not wish to see you come to harm.

Sparkle: Well, I didn't want to play with you anyway! (She starts crying and flies off down the tunnel.)

Sparkle reappears whenever you return to 28 and begs to join your party.

Retrace your steps back to 27. Continue east, then take, not the first, but the *second* right turn. Get ready for some good old-fashioned combat.

29. Deadly Beauty

See the gorgeous purple insect hovering over the flower patch ahead? That's a ***Faerie wasp***—its sting is bad enough, but it can also hurl Firebolt spells at you from a distance.

Tip The Faerie wasp carries nothing of value. My advice: Simply run past it. Your party may suffer a sting or two, but the wasp won't pursue.

The next three locations are bonus steps for warrior-types who want to fight every fight and gather every item. None of them are necessary to complete the level, so if your vitality meter isn't high, skip ahead to 33.

30, 31. Two Bees, Or Not Two Bees?

No, they're two Faerie wasps, one in each location. Each hovers over an assortment of flowers.

32. More Moss to Snort

After battling past deadly wasps, nothing looks better to a conquering hero than a nice slimy hunk of ***Brownie moss***. Well, I guess it is an ingredient of Snort's Brew. Next time you see Snort, he can whip up another batch.

Now go back south past 29. Continue south down the passage.

33. Troll and Troll, Inc.

Two tough ***Trolls*** roam this area. Be prepared! They could be anywhere along

this passage. (If you did not receive the four-leaf clover from Sweetie back at 5, then every Troll in the realm will remain invisible.) If you manage to dispatch the duo, continue down the corridor.

Trolls! Two of them, no less. Put down your iron spikes to limit their teleportation tactics.

Tip Remember, Trolls like to engage you in face-to-face combat, then suddenly teleport behind you. To thwart this tactic, plant an iron spike in the ground. Trolls cannot cross the spike.

34. Drawing Stick

Pick all the flowers, including that yellow ***St. John's Wort***. Then grab the ***stick of charcoal***, turn around, and head west.

Tip St. John's Wort is a wonderful poison cure. It restores full health to anyone who eats it.

35. Don't Be Alarmed!

See that ***toadstool alarm*** up ahead? Nail it from a distance, before it can send up its irritating shriek . . . and alert Trolls to your presence.

36. Winkle's Drum

Pick up the ***Faerie drum*** lying in the flower patch. No doubt it's Winkle's drum, and you want to return it to him ASAP. We've gone far enough east for now. If you make a tactical retreat here, you can avoid a lot of damage from the other deadly Trolls in the area.

Drum Up Business. What's Winkle's drum doing down here in Troll Country? Take it back where it belongs.

Retrace your steps east, then all the way back to the Troll Bridge at 26. Follow the passage to the intersection, then turn left and continue.

37. Petal Bonanza

If you're low on flowers, you came to the right place. ***Gladiola***, ***foxglove***, ***primrose***—a veritable floral explosion. Throw in a few ***rowanberries***, too.

38. Regenerating Health

Just up the corridor you'll come to another alcove full of flowers. In their midst, you'll find a ***heal root***. This is a

special spot, though—it regenerates a new root every few minutes.

Continue up the corridor to the next room on the right.

39. Chuckle the Clown

The first time you step in this square, Chuckle the Faerie appears and says, "Hello, I'm Chuckle. You know, being the head of the Faerie Players is thirsty work. How about I bribe you to find me some refreshment? Bring me some of Snort's Brew, and I'll give you something to help against Trolls!" Then, if you already have some of Snort's Brew (as in this walkthrough, for example), Chuckle says, "Wait! You *have* some!"

Give him the decanter of red brew. Chuckle takes it, drinks one dose, then says, in pure TV evangelist style, "Yee-ahss! *Thank* ya!" He gives you another ***jester's cap,*** leaves the empty decanter, and adds, "This will help, but, you know, you're really going to need a four-leaf clover just to *see* those Trolls! Gotta run, see ya!"

Exit to the corridor, turn right, and head north.

40. A Giggle a Minute

As you approach this square, ***Giggle*** flies up to you in glow form, then changes to male Faerie form. He says, "Hi. I'm Giggle. But you guys knew that. OK, hey, did something happen there? Funny things go on since the Shadow King did his thing. Hey! I rhymed! Now I love a good poem as much as the next Faerie. But I lost my poem book. O sadness. Hey, big idea! I know—how about you find it for me and I'll give you something you need to see the queen! (beat) And you'll *need* to see the queen."

Actually, you *have* the poem book—it's the first red book you got back at 24. When Giggle sees that you have his book, he stutters, "Gimme, gimme, gimme, gimme!" Give Giggle the poem book. After he accepts it, he says, "I take back nearly all the bad things I said behind your back. Here, you'll figure out where to stick this, buddy."

Giggle drops a ***gold key***, then morphs back into glow form. Then he adds, "Oh, yeah. Maybe it's Unseen because it needs some flowers," and flies off. What's he talking about? We'll find out shortly—but first, let's take the other book to Winkle at 15. Could *it* be the Last Tome of the Elves?

Of *course* it could.

When you approach, Winkle goes bonkers, saying, "Oh! You've *got* it! You have . . . the Last Tome of the Elves. Can I have it?" Give him the other red book in your inventory, the one you got from the bone pile at 27. He booms, "I have the book! Wait a second, I have something for you." Then, in his normal voice, he says, "There! Always practice safe spells!"

Hey, doesn't Winkle want his drum, too? He asked for it at 13, so let's go offer it to him there.

Winkle says, "You have my drum! Can I have it, please?" Give him the drum. "Thank you. Maybe Binkle and I can start the fiddle-and-drum corps again!" He glows away, leaving behind another ***jester's cap***. Put it on any party member.

Exit the room and work your way back to the flower garden at 20. Continue west to the corner, then turn north.

41. Chuckle Redux

If you gave Snort's Brew to Chuckle at 39, got the parchment at 22, and got the stick of charcoal at 33, then Chuckle appears here and says, "Well, I see you have both charcoal and parchment. How about letting me have a go?" Give him both items.

After a few seconds of furious scribbling noises, Chuckle offers you a ***portrait*** and says, "Not bad, eh? A great portrait of the queen, if I *do* say so—and I do. Maybe you should take it to the queen for *her* opinion, hmmm?" He goes to glow, then pops back and adds, "It's been a while since I've drawn. Thanks." He drops his ***Faerie shirt***, glows, then leaves, adding, "Roses down, twice around."

Put the shirt on Drake—he looks *totally* ridiculous now—and step north to the gate.

What a Joker. OK, so Drake looks like a goof. But those Faerie dud's will protect him from Troll attacks.

42. Court Gate

The ***portcullis*** is locked. Turn right to face the east wall. See that little ***slot*** in the center, just above the ground? It's a ***keyhole***. Use the gold key on it, then the silver key. The portcullis unlocks.

Go through the opening, turn right, and go around the corner to the alcove on the right.

43. The Mana Hearth

That odd, shrine-like statue is a ***Mana Hearth***. Simply touch it to recharge all of your runecasters. Continue around the corner, then turn right.

Mana Hearth. Warm your fingers at this hearth to give your runecasters a full charge of Mana.

44. Door to the Unseen Court

This ***door*** is locked. Remember that strange phrase that everyone seems to be repeating around here? *Roses down, twice around.* Put one primrose on the ground here, then go back around the 3-by-3 square twice. After your second circuit, go through the now-open door to the queen's throne.

45. Iaenni the Faerie Queen

Take the ***fine faerie cake*** in front of the pedestal, and step forward. The Good Lady ***Iaenni***, Queen of the Faeries, appears on her throne.

Note Take a look at your party's vitality meters. Every member of your party is fully healed every time you encounter the queen.

The first time you meet Iaenni, she says, "I am Iaenni, Queen of the Faerie. Please sit a while, and enjoy some refreshments, for you may rest safely in my court. But it is unsafe elsewhere. Beware the Trolls, for they are a corruption of everything Faerie and good. Without preparation, they can be deadly foes. Since they are still Faerie, even tainted, I cannot act against them directly."

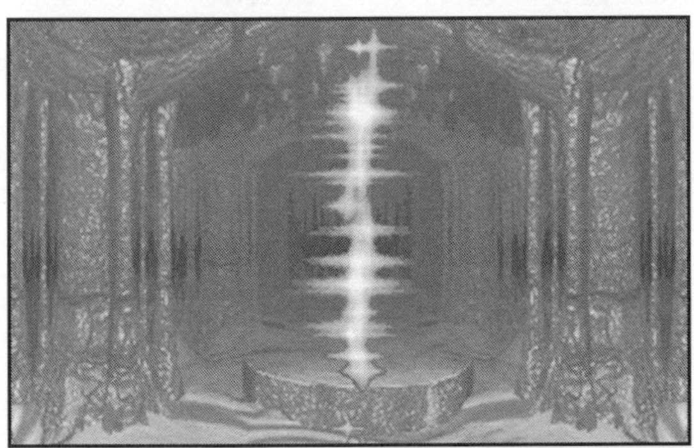

Iaenni, the Faerie Queen. Here she comes! A lovely hostess, Iaenni is a source of insight, charm, and magickal gifts. Be sure you listen to all four of her stories.

If Chuckle gave you the portrait of Iaenni back at 41, the queen says, "My Faeries say you have an offering to me. May I see it?" Give her the portrait. She says, "This is very beautiful, thank you. Please accept this gift in return." Iaenni gives you the ***Luckstone ring***. Put it on Drake. Now the queen tells the first of four stories.

Note You must listen to all four stories to receive a valuable object from the queen.

Iaenni's First Story: "Atlantis and Ys"

Iaenni: I have used my magick to watch your progress. You have traveled a great distance, but many tasks await you before your battle with Khull-khuum will be over. This started long ago, when the human world was divided into two great lands, Atlantis and Ys. The rulers of these realms despised and mistrusted each other, and there were many conflicts.

There might have been war and suffering among your kind, but there was balance as well. Then one day, a mysterious figure appeared before the rulers of Ys and offered magick potent enough to destroy their enemies. He did not lie, but he did not tell the truth. Ys cast the mighty ritual, and Atlantis used their most powerful countermagicks, but all was lost. Atlantis was destroyed, but as planned by Khull-khuum the backlash caused a cataclysm that nearly destroyed the world. This was the Devastation. All the races were affected, not just you young humans. In defending my children, my powers are taxed to this day.

I must rest for a while, return if you will hear more of your adversary.

Go back to the Troll Gate at 26. Pass through, turn left at the intersection, then follow the passage. Take the first right turn, heading south.

46. Trolls

Several ***Trolls*** wander this corridor. Drake fares better if he wears all the anti-Troll clothing (jester's hat, Faerie pants and shirt, Luckstone ring) you've gathered so far. Move on down the passage.

Note While Drake is now impervious to Trolls, the other party members remain susceptible to Troll damage. So don't get cocky; use good combat tactics when facing Trolls. The magickal Axe of Throwing is an excellent anti-Troll weapon.

47. Troll Trap

This square sits on the trigger for a bank of immobilizing ***magickal fog*** that confines you to this square for about 10 seconds. (Note that you can still spin, however.) If no Trolls attack, then this trap is only a minor nuisance. Be wary!

Tip You can use the Spoilspell rune on Drake to cancel this trap.

Continue down the passage to the first alcove on the right.

48. The Horseshoe Medallion

Grab that ***horseshoe medallion*** hidden amongst all the ***flowers***, then put it on Drake. By itself, this trinket gives its wearer a 20 percent resistance to Troll attacks. Combined with the other anti-Troll stuff, it provides 100 percent protection from Troll attacks! Wow. Continue down the passage.

49. The Terrible Troll

A particularly nasty ***Troll*** roams this corridor. This one is known as the Terrible Troll—the biggest, toughest Troll on the level. (Remember back at 11 when Binkle warned you about the "nasty one in the west"?) Don't underestimate him just because Drake is now almost Troll-proof. This monster can still teleport behind you, damage other party members, and run when wounded.

The big ugly guy carries the ***Orb of Yoth-soggoth***, the fourth of the nine receptacles of the gods that you must retrieve in *Stonekeep*.

Not So Terrible. This big fella just dropped the Orb of Yoth-soggoth.

Tip The Orb of Yoth-soggoth is a real treasure; it holds powerful magick. Once obtained, the orb automatically halves your Mana cost when you cast any rune. Better yet, you can click the orb on Drake in the mirror to immediately recharge all the runecasters in your inventory! Note, however, that this recharge power works only twice per map.

50. Empty Decanter

Grab the ***empty decanter*** in this square. Take a step south, then turn right.

51. Will-o'-the-Wisp

A floating, glowing, Faerie-like light approaches and hovers in front of your party. But it's blue, unlike Faeries, who are purple when in glow form. This glow is a ***will-o'-the-wisp***. It is a creature full of great curiosity, and inspects the party closely—*too* closely, at times. But it attacks only if you attack first.

Tip A blue will-o'-the-wisp is benign. Don't attack one unless it really bugs you. When attacked, 'wisps turn an angry red and fight back.

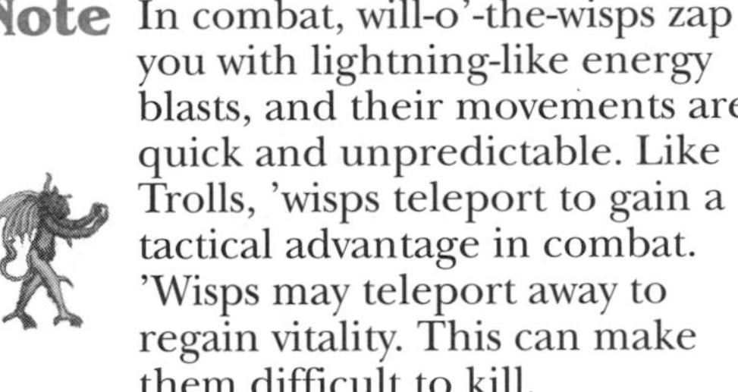

Note In combat, will-o'-the-wisps zap you with lightning-like energy blasts, and their movements are quick and unpredictable. Like Trolls, 'wisps teleport to gain a tactical advantage in combat. 'Wisps may teleport away to regain vitality. This can make them difficult to kill.

Now go west and get those mushrooms!

52. Mushroom Garden

Pluck the three ***green mushrooms*** and two ***spotted mushrooms*** from the damp floor. Continue west to the corner, then turn right into the 2-by-2 room.

53. Flower Power

Buried in all the lovely flora is a powerful ***elfwand***, a fully loaded runecaster with a Mana capacity of 60. Don't forget those ***red mushrooms*** in the southeast corner. Exit the room and take the first right turn, heading south. (Ignore the will-o'-the-wisps, if you can.)

54. Wicked Red Wisp

This ***will-o'-the-wisp*** is in a foul reddish mood, and attacks as soon as you draw near. Blast him and continue south down the corridor.

55. More Mushrooms

Pick the ***mushrooms*** here—two green, two spotted.

56. Rune Scroll

Check out the ***rune scroll*** here. Invisibility! So *that's* how they do it!

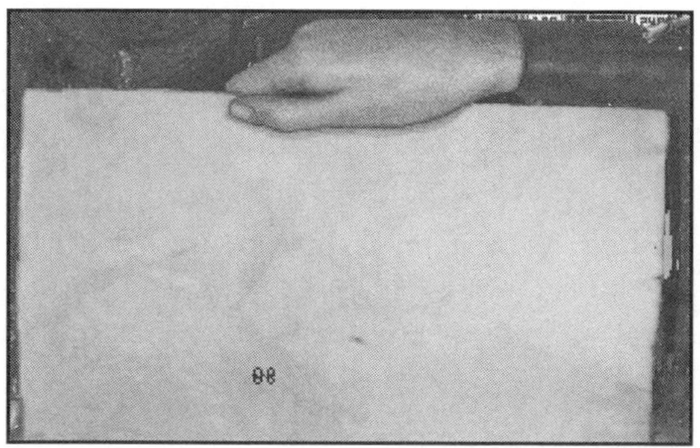

57. Troll Trap

Another ***empty decanter***—but beware! More ***magickal fog*** immobilizes you for 10 seconds. After the fog effects dissipate, continue east.

Now go back to the Faerie Queen at 45. She's rested and ready to tell more stories.

Iaenni's Second Story: "The Gods vs. The Shadow King"

When you approach Iaenni's throne, she reappears and says:

Iaenni: Tell me what you know of Khull-khuum's role in the Devastation.

Drake: I know little, my lady. Only that the gods were captured by the Shadow King and he rose to take power.

Iaenni: That much is true, though there is much more to be learned. Khull-khuum did not challenge the Immortals. He betrayed them and used the power from the deaths of their own followers to entrap them in the orbs you are carrying.

While the other weakened Immortals fought a hopeless battle against Khull-khuum during the moments of the Devastation, Thera damaged one of her own temples, a source of her magick power. She hid some of her powers away, and cast a spell that made it impossible for Khull-khuum to recover the trapped Immortals. This left her with a small measure of freedom. Since then, Thera has worked for the return of the orbs to her temple.

Now I must rest. I will return soon.

Iaenni fades away, but returns in 30 seconds.

Note

At this point you've explored the entire Faerie level, so you could just hang out and wait. On the other hand, you probably haven't seen all six Faerie Players story-songs yet. After the performance, return to Iaenni's throne for another story.

Iaenni's Third Story: "Why Wahooka Saved Drake"

Iaenni: There is another whom you should be aware of. Wahooka is not from this world, and he is shadowed from my magicks. I fear that he is something primal, perhaps more dangerous then Khull-khuum. Wahooka's involvement might be nothing more then a trick.

Drake: He did all of this as a prank? I find that hard to believe, Lady Iaenni.

Iaenni: For whatever purpose, only he could tell you for certain. I believe there is more to him then he wants you to see. If you succeed in your quest, then all we know will change . . . and he might want that.

Leave me for a while, but return.

Iaenni fades away again, but returns in 30 seconds. You must hear Iaenni's fourth story to receive the magick item she offers.

Iaenni's Fourth Story: "Enigma the Elf"

Iaenni: I am grateful that you have returned.

Drake: You are gratious to see us, my lady. Do you have another tale for us?

Iaenni: Yes, I have one final tale. It is the story of the last Elf, one who is dear to me.

The dark one was opposed by many, including the Faeries and Elves with our magicks. Khull-khuum was only annoyed, and while I used my powers to hide my people from his damning gaze, the Elves were not so fortunate. Every city and stronghold of the Elves was destroyed. The few Elves that survived were hunted to death by his followers.

Only one survived, for he was my lover and stood by my side while his people were ravaged. For hundreds of years afterwards, he contained his grief and misery. But his heart—and his love for me—was overcome with vengeance.

He left to destroy the dark one. He journeyed far, and I aided as well as I could, but he has been captured by the Ice Queen, a minion of the shadows. The keeper of my heart is but a living statue in her realm, trapped in ice. And I can do nothing.

As you seek to destroy Khull-khuum, seek my love and free him. He is a mighty warrior and knowledgeable in the ways of the dark one. Even if he chooses not to return to my side, I will be eternally grateful.

Drake: We shall try to find him, Lady Iaenni.

Iaenni: Then take this. It is my pendant, and I have placed what magick I could within it. Now, please go. I have used too much of my strength in this.

Iaenni disappears. Step back a square and pick up the ***magickal pendant*** that she leaves behind. Iaenni will not return.

Now you're ready to move on to the next level. Here's how:

1. **Go back to 1 (on Map 8).**
2. **Step through the portal to return to the Upper Level of the Dragon Feeding Grounds. You are now at 41 on Map 6.2.**
3. **Work your way over to 74 on Map 6.2.**
4. **Go through the door to reach Level 9, Ice Caverns.**

Level 9

Ice Caverns

Level 9 of *Stonekeep* includes just one map area—the Ice Caverns. Here, you battle the evil Ice Queen and her deadly coven of ice witches. You also face a greater, more pervasive enemy—the cold itself. These frigid tunnels sap your party's vitality, bit by bit, from the very moment you enter the Caverns.

Key to Map 9

1. Passage to Dragon Feeding Grounds
2. Ice Sharga
3. Ice Sharga
4. Ice Sharga healer
5. Ice Sharga advisor
6. Ice Sharga (rune scrolls)
7. Karzak's warning
8. Cave-in
9. Frozen Elf
10. Ice witch attack
11. Frozen Dwarf
12. Ice Sharga
13. Ice witch attack
14. Secret door
15. Chain-mail skirt, ice hammer, rune scroll
16. Parchment
17. Secret door
18. Skeleton (helm)
19. Rings, chain mail shirt
20. Coldfire
21. Ice witch attack
22. Strength pool
23. Weak walls (cave-in)
24. Secret door
25. Secret door
26. Secret door
27. Ice witch
28. Ice witch
29. Ice Queen (Helion's Orb)
30. Ice throne, scroll
31. Passage to Gate of the Ancients

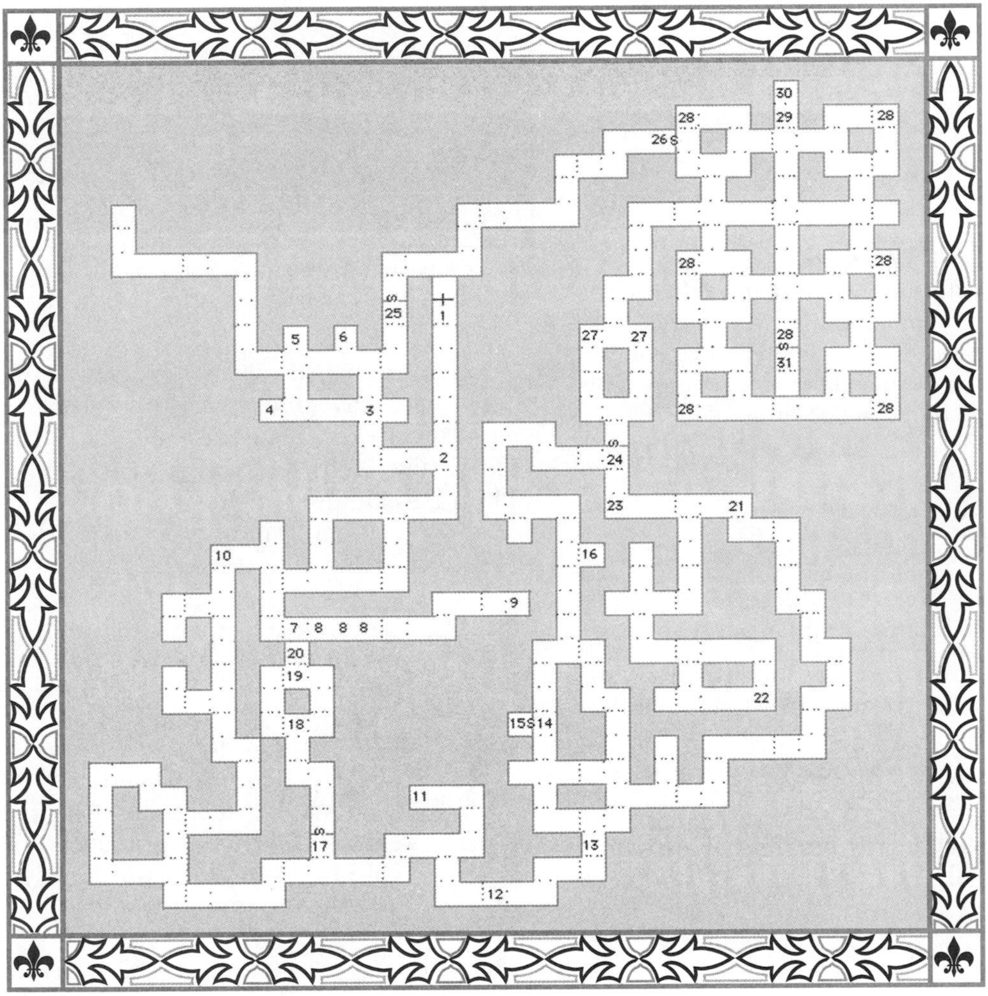

Map 9 Ice Cavern

$ Secret Door

+ Door

1. Passage to Dragon Feeding Grounds

You arrive here from 74 on Map 6.2, Dragon Feeding Grounds, Upper Level. Head south.

Note  This is *intense* cold. Unless protected by warming spells, each member of your party suffers 1 to 2 points of damage every 30 seconds. This damage begins the moment you enter the caverns.

2. Ice Sharga

Don't attack the ***Ice Sharga***! Approach him peacefully, and he speaks to you:

Sarkan: Are you the Ones? Come you have to save us from her evil? Have you?
Drake: Yes.
Sarkan: Then see our king, you must! Lead you there, Sarkan will. Come, now!

Follow Sarkan. He leads you west to the next turn. Continue past him, heading north.

3. King of the Ice Shargas

Another ***Ice Sharga*** waits for you here. This is Kandoc, king of the Ice Shargas on this level.

When you approach him, he says, "Kandoc's people not like Shargas. They live in tunnels with others in peace. Tunnels were Kandoc's realm until the Ice Queen's coven invaded this area. Much power she has, to kill Kandoc's

Talk to Kandoc, You Must. Ice Shargas they be. Odd diction have they. Friend to you they is.

people and steal their homes. Now, only these small caverns remain of Kandoc's realm. Kandoc's people flee; only his guards stay. Help Kandoc! A weapon you will find, to kill the Ice Queen, and Kandoc will show you secret. Kandoc's warriors will tell you what they can. Go now."

Note  Kandoc is a forgiving fellow. If you mistakenly attacked Sarkan back at 2, Sarkan runs to hide behind Kandoc. When you approach Kandoc at 3, he says, "Nasty, you are! Attacked Kandoc's guard you did, for no reason. Did that one attack you? No! Little you know, but Kandoc will tell you, yes—you learn."

Kandoc suggests you consult his warriors for advice, so let's do just that. Turn west and take three steps toward the Sharga in the alcove, but *don't step up to him!* Read step 4 below first, then decide whether or not you require his "services" yet.

4. Sharga Healer

When you approach this ***Ice Sharga***, he says, "Healing you need? Healing you shall have." Then he bestows full vitality on your entire party.

The catch? He only offers this healing service once per hour. So, unless your vitality is low across the board, or one of your party members is on the verge of unconsciousness, skip the Healer for now.

Turn right and head due north.

5. Good Advice

When you approach this ***Ice Sharga*** advisor, he says, "Fire defeats the Ice Queen, though visions say more than fire. Say need fire that is different. Go, find *different* fire . . . and return."

OK, dude, whatever. Step back into the corridor, then go east two steps to the next alcove.

6. Gorza the Giver

Gorza the ***Ice Sharga*** has good things for you, if you can bring him what he wants. When you first approach him, he says, "Help you, king says. Help you would Gorza, but cannot. Gorza lost rune scroll when she came. Find it, you do, and Gorza will help!" Then he holds out his hand.

You have nothing for him—yet. Back away, take a step east, then turn right and go back to 2. From there, go 2S, 5W, 3S, 2W, 2S, then take a step east.

7. Karzak's Warning

Years of working rock have given Karzak a keen eye for the structural integrity of underground passages. When you step into this square, he says, "Stop! This tunnel is dangerous. We need to be careful." Sure thing, guy. You go first.

Tip It's kind of fun to turn around here, face west, and walk backward down the tunnel.

8. Triple Cave-In

OK, so Karzak was right. Three times over, in fact. As you walk east, three sections of ceiling collapse into ***cave-ins*** behind you. For now, keep going east to the end of the passage.

9. Elfsicle

Yep, that's a frozen Elf. No doubt it's ***Enigma***, the lost lover of Queen Iaenni. But there's nothing you can do now to thaw the fellow. Note his location. Turn around, go back, and hack your way through those cave-ins blocking the passage. At the corner, go 3N, then turn west.

Elf on Ice. Here's a real Enigma. How do you thaw someone who's magickally frozen? The surprise answer: with magick.

Get your weapon ready! Take two steps west, then swivel quickly to the left, facing south.

Tip Arm yourself with a runewand etched with the Firebolt rune or some other good offensive rune.

10. Ice Witch Coven

Those spiky floating entities down the corridor are ***ice witches***, and those painful things they're hurling at you are ***ice bolts***. Blast the witches with firebolts and watch them melt.

Icy Reception. Are you a good *witch or a* bad *witch? Who cares? Axe the little spikeballs. Or, better yet, blast them with firebolts.*

Follow the passage until you reach an intersection. Turn left, go 3S, turn left again, then follow the cavern east. After 14 steps, a short passage branches up to the north.

11. Dwarfsicle

You cannot thaw this ***frozen Dwarf*** with anything you have now. Note his location for later, exit the alcove, then take the first left turn, heading south. Follow the cavern around the corner.

12. Mad Sharga

The attack of the Ice Queen has driven this ***Ice Sharga*** completely insane. When you approach him, he babbles, "Ha-ha! Queen's servants, you are! Yes, he is, he is. Mad, Rek is? Yes, mad is Rek. Kill you all, Rek will! Ha ha ha! *Die!*" Rek rushes toward you—but be cool, it's not an attack. Rek merely starts pacing in a menacing, if somewhat goofy, manner.

Don't kill Rek!

Instead, use a Cure rune on him. This heals his insanity, and he says, "The Ice Queen did not want Rek's hammer to be found, so she cursed Rek and hid his hammer. Find it, you do, it is yours. It will be helpful."

Thanks for the info, Rek. Now let's get that Firebolt rune ready again. Follow the passage to the square just south of the intersection, then stop . . . and wait.

13. More Wicked Witches

After a few seconds, another coven of ***ice witches*** pops into view ahead. Fortunately, they hop into the intersection one at a time; you can pick them off easily with firebolts. Be patient—there are nine witches, and they attack in irregular intervals. Step into the intersection and turn left. Go 2W, 4N, then turn left to face the north wall.

Caution Careful! More ***ice witches*** lurk at the north end of the hall.

14. Secret Alcove

Hit the ***ice wall*** with any weapon. It shatters, revealing a ***secret room***. Keep hammering the debris until it clears, then examine the newly revealed alcove.

15. Ice Prizes

Punch the ***snow pile*** in the alcove. The first punch reveals a ***magickal chain-mail skirt***. The second punch uncovers the ***ice hammer*** Rek mentioned back at 9. Take both, then take the ***rune scroll*** and read it:

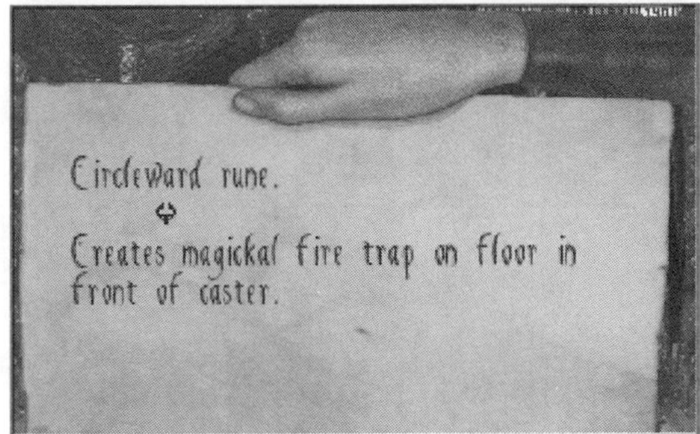

Circleward Rune Scroll.

Continue north up the passage. At the corner, take a step east, then go north four steps. Turn right to face the alcove.

16. Gorz's Scroll

Punch the snow pile in the alcove to reveal a ***piece of parchment***. This is Gorza's scroll.

Go back to Gorza at 6 and give him the piece of parchment. Delighted, the little fellow says, "Ah, found it you have! Thank you! More magick, you would like? Runes Gorza will give you, to help your quest!"

He hands you four ***rune scrolls***, one at a time. You already have two of the runes inscribed in your journal—the Ball Meta rune and the Armor rune. The other two are new:

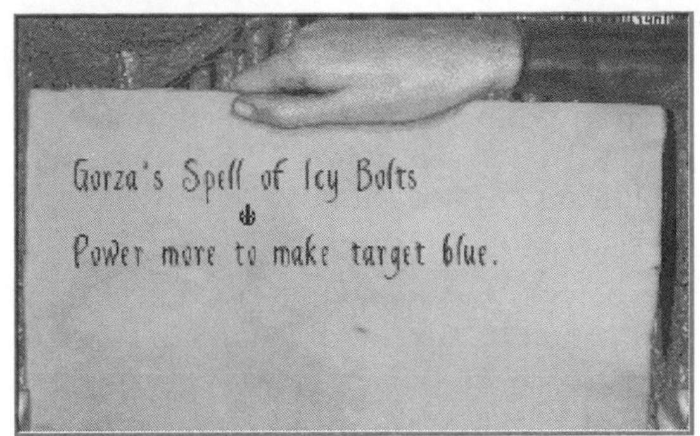

Icebolt Rune Scroll

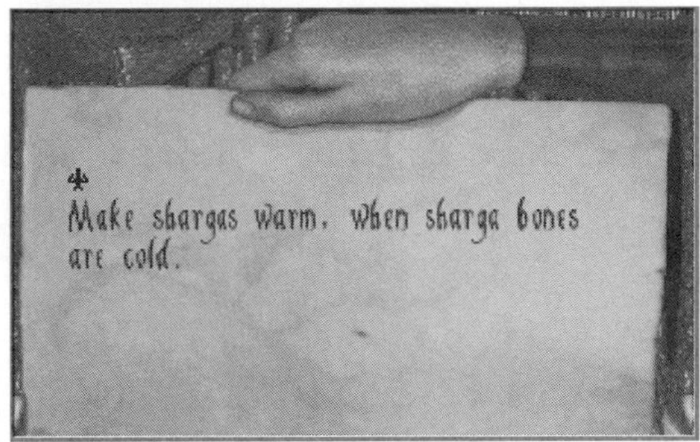

Warming Rune Scroll

Tip This might be a good time to go back to the Sharga Healer at 4.

Now you can thaw the Elf at 9 and the Dwarf at 11. For the sake of plot, I suggest you go back to the frozen Dwarf first. Cast the Warming rune to defrost the poor fellow. Nigel Hardstone steps forward and says:

Nigel: Karzak! It is good to see you, you old war Dwarf.

Karzak: Always good to see you, my clansbrother.

Drake: Glad we could be of service.

Nigel Hardstone: You have my life-debt, Sir Drake. In return, I will show you a secret. Come, follow me.

Follow Nigel west to the alcove.

17. Secret Door

Step up to the wall where Nigel waits. It is actually a ***secret door***. You'll hear the following conversation:

Nigel: I noticed this weak section of the ice before that Ice Witch got me. I must return to my family, but you might want to explore on. Good day to you, sir. *Haszrach cho'dai, Karzak-ovak.*

Karzak: *Ch'dai.* You live a long life, Nigel. May your sons and daughters pull your beard grey.

Nigel: (chuckling) May the gods return before that.

After Nigel leaves, bash open the weak wall with weapons or melt it with any fire spell. Follow the opened passage north.

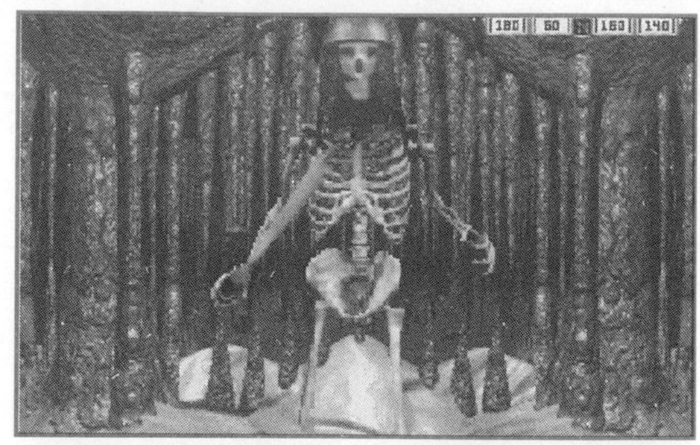

I Just Go to Pieces. *Wow. Wouldn't it be cool if you had this effect on everybody?*

18. The Guardian

Uh-oh. Looks like a ***skeleton*** warrior up ahead. Step forward to face it—and get a nice surprise. If you still have Iaenni's magick pendant (from 45 on Map 8), the skeleton recognizes it and says, "You have the markings of the master. You may pass." Then he crumbles into a harmless pile of bones!

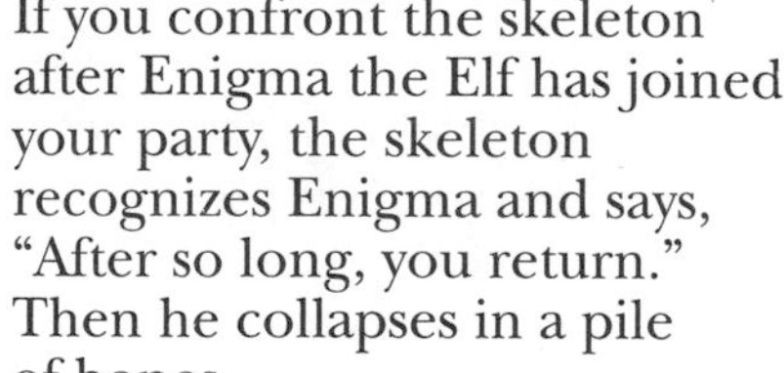

Note If you confront the skeleton after Enigma the Elf has joined your party, the skeleton recognizes Enigma and says, "After so long, you return." Then he collapses in a pile of bones.

Grab the skeleton's ***helm*** and step over the bony remains to follow the passage in either direction.

19. Mystic Armor

Grab the two ***Magick Armor Rings*** and the ***magickal chain-mail shirt*** from the ground. Turn to face the alcove to the north.

20. Coldfire

Is that campfire burning blue? Hey, it sure is. Grab it. You end up with a handful of ***Coldfire***, a small ball of ice-blue flame. This is a powerful magickal weapon, one that will be very important later. But it's a delicate item. If you put it down, or try to take it out of the Ice Caverns to another level, it melts!

Tip If the Coldfire melts, don't fret. A new one springs up in the campfire at 20.

Coldfire. Powerful, but delicate. Don't put it down or take it from the Ice Caverns.

Now go back to the frozen Enigma at 9. Cast a Warming rune spell on the Elf to thaw him. If you have Iaenni's pendant with you, Enigma sees it and speaks:

Note Be aware that the following conversation is much different if Karzak is not in your party. In this walkthrough, of course, he is with you.

Enigma: That token . . . where did you get it?

Drake: Why, the Good Lady Iaenni gave it to me.

Enigma: Then you and I have similar goals. I am Enigma, the last of my kind. Shall we join forces and defeat our enemies?

Karzak: (abruptly) It is time for me to leave.

Drake: What? Surely, we could use another sword.

Enigma: I will not be trouble, Sir Dwarf.

Karzak: (snaps) It doesn't matter, *Elf*, I shall not travel with you.

Drake: Karzak! This does not become you.

Enigma: Hmm. I will not intrude, then.

Karzak: No, no, that is not it. I am far from home, Drake. I am a warrior, with warrior's dreams. But we are going where I should not go.

Drake: Ah.

Karzak: And, well, this Elf can serve you better then I. Oh, enough, I am going, it is a long journey back to the hall.

Enigma: Well, at least let me save you that trip. I still have a favor or two with some elementals. (He casts a spell.) Done. Prepare yourself.

Drake: Ah! He's gone!

Sparkle: (excited) Ohhh, an earth elemental's vortex power. Neat!

Enigma: He is on his way home. I have said too much, let us go.

Drake: He is still a warrior.

Skuz: Hm, waz it?

Drake: Oh, nothing. Come, let us go.

Enigma now joins your party, equipped with his bow and Elven chainmail.

Enigmatic Ally. The Elven lord takes Karzak's place in your party. He is agile, good with a bow, and knowledgeable in the ways of magick.

Go back to 13. Step north into the intersection, go E, N, then turn right and follow the cavern. As you move up the long corridor, be ready for roving ***ice witches***!

21. Witch Bunch

When you turn this corner, another coven of ***ice witches*** attacks from the west. *Don't fire back!* The walls up ahead (at 23 on the map) are weak, and even slight damage will cause an impassable cave-in.

Avoid the witches for now; take two quick steps west, then turn right and head south down the passage.

22. Strength Pool

If you drink water from this ***strength pool***, Drake's Strength rating increases by one star. *Mmm-mmm, good.* (Too bad this works only once.) Now exit back to the corridor, turn left, and continue down the passage.

23. Weak Walls

Battle the waiting ***ice witches***. But remember, if you do more than 5 points of damage to the south or west walls here, this section of tunnel collapses in an impassable ***cave-in***.

Tip If you trigger the cave-in at 23, you have two options. You can work your way around to the other side of the cave-in by retracing your steps back to the corridor north of 13, then north past 16. Or, if you have the Coldfire, you can skip ahead to step 25 below and take the alternate route into the Ice Queen's lair.

24. Door to the Ice Queen's Lair

See that ***ice symbol*** on the right side of the north wall? That marks this section of wall as a ***secret door***. There is only one way to open the door: Strike the wall with the ice hammer you found at 15.

Breaking and Entering. *Here's one way to seek an audience with the Ice Queen. Hammer the wall next to the ice symbol. (See it on the right?)*

But wait! Before you brutishly hammer your way into the Ice Queen's lair, note that there is another way in.

25. Alternate Route Into Ice Queen's Lair

Remember the Coldfire you found at 20? If you take it back to Kandoc at 3, he says, "A weapon you have found? Yes! Yes! Coldfire kill Ice Queen! Done well, you have! Now, Kandoc will tell you secret. Passage, it is, to Ice Queen's realm. Go, now, and kill her!"

Kandoc then leads you through the now-open secret door at 25. Follow the passage to its end.

26. Wall Work

Bash at the east wall. Aha! It's another ***secret door***. Step through the debris into the Ice Queen's lair.

OK, back to our walkthrough. As you recall, we were standing at 24, breathlessly waiting, ice hammer in hand. Do it now. It only takes a single blow. Step through the breach. At the intersection, go left or right—you end up at the same place either way.

27. Ice Witch Sentries

A pair of ***ice witches*** guards the entrance to the lair at each of these locations. Blast them with firebolts and continue north up the cavern.

28. Ice Witch Minions

A single ***ice witch*** stands watch at each of these locations. (Count them—you'll find a total of seven guards.) Go to the center aisle of the lair, turn north, and head straight for the Ice Queen at 29.

29. Ice Queen

Here she is—the ***Ice Queen***, waiting in her ice lair in front of her ice throne wearing an ice aerobic outfit. When you approach her, she says:

Ice Queen: Well, if it isn't the hero. Feeling a little *cold*, are we?

Drake: (shivering) Warm enough, thanks.

Ice Queen: It'll get colder, hero. Trust me on that. The orbs you have are worth everything to the Shadow King. He'll grant me anything I desire when I take them from you.

Drake: Tough words, but you don't look that dangerous to me.

Ice Queen: (laughing) Oh, really? I hope you like my *frosty* sense of humor, then.

Cold-Blooded Queen. She's a wily, formidable opponent. If you can defeat her, Helion's Orb is yours for the taking.

Oops. Never get an Ice Queen mad. She's invulnerable to damage until you use the Coldfire on her. Then she resorts to maddening guerrilla tactics—attacking from behind or the flank, always moving. She is an extremely intelligent opponent, but she won't flee her lair.

Tip A few tips for combat with the Ice Queen: If you find your vitality running low during the battle, hustle up to the Ice Queen's throne at 30. Blast it with a firebolt or two—it melts! Drink the melted water to give your entire party a one-time-only vitality boost.

When you finally defeat the Ice Queen, she drops ***Helion's Orb***, the fifth of the nine receptacles that you seek in *Stonekeep*.

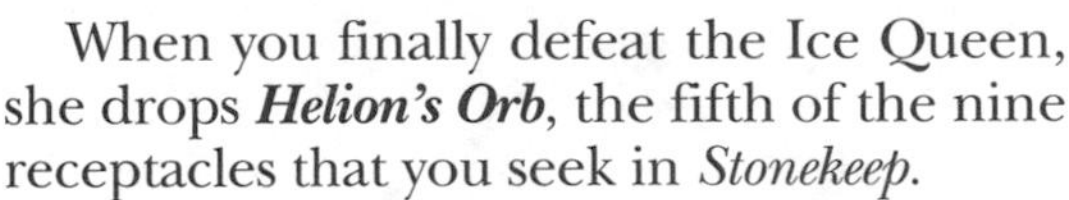

Note Helion's Orb is commonly known as the "orb of warmth." Once you have the orb, your party takes no more damage from the intense cold in the Ice Caverns or from ice-based spells and effects.

Ice Queen, Khull-Khuum wants you to invade the Faerie Realm! The Terrible Troll has informed Him that an Orb has been collected and is waiting for Him there.
The Prophecy will be turned.

30. The Ice Throne

This is where the Ice Queen parks her icy assets. Use a firebolt or warming rune on this throne—it melts into a ***pool of water***. If you drink from it, your entire party is fully healed. This works one time only. Pick up and read the ***scroll*** near the throne.

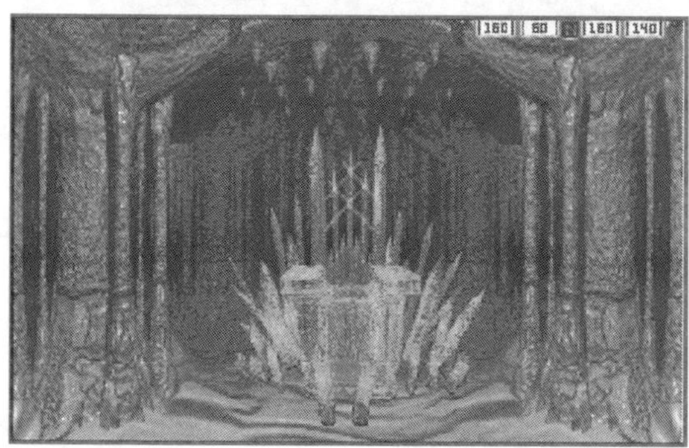

Ice Throne. Ever drink a chair? It's quite delicious. Of course, you have to melt it first.

31. Passage to the Gate of the Ancients

After you defeat the Ice Queen, this ***secret door*** opens. Go on through to Level 10: Gate of the Ancients.

Level 10

Gate of the Ancients

The tenth level of *Stonekeep* includes two map areas—the Gate of the Ancients (Map 10.1) and the Pits (Map 10.2). The good news is there are no beasts or fiends on this level. The bad news is that you face some very beastly, fiendish puzzles.

The Gate of the Ancients resembles a perverse version of "Chutes and Ladders"—12 pits and six ladders honeycomb the level. Only careful mapping can get you to the portal to Level 11—unless, of course, you cheat and use a *Stonekeep* strategy guide or something equally despicable.

Key to Maps 10.1 & 10.2

1. Passage to the Ice Caverns
2. Sign

3 A–B. Buttons

4. Handle (toggles 30 and 11)
5. Inactive clickplates
6. Carcass (arrows)
7. Campfire (rune scroll)
8. Clickplate—triggers fire trap
9. Unreadable signs
10. Carcass (stone), feathers, ring
11. Teleport to 12 (if handle at 4 is up)
12. Teleport from 11
13. Sign
14. Life Restore potion, rune scroll
15. Sign
16. Clickplate (activates 17)
17. Portcullis (use 16)
18. Potion, magick dagger
19. Illusory wall
20. Mana Circle
21. Potion
22. Buttons (open 23 and 24)
23. Button (vitality)
24. Button (health)
25. Button
26. Sign
27. Wolf key
28. Ring
29. Magick shield
30. Teleport to 31 (if handle at 4 is down)
31. Teleport from 30
32. Hammer, potion, helm, chain-mail shirt, chain-mail skirt
33. One-way door
34. Duck statue
35. Magick horn, magick quiver, potion, ring, scrolls, rune scrolls
36. Portculli
37. Button (deactivates 36)
38. Button (deactivates 41)
39. One-way doors (open from south only)
40. Locked door—use wolf key
41. Fire trap (deactivate at 38)
42. Campfire (eagle key)
43. Hammer, chain-mail shirt, chain-mail skirt, helm, scroll
44. Sign
45. Sign
46. Locked door (use eagle key)
47. Portcullis
48. Orb key, rune scroll, button (unlocks 27, 28, 29)
49. Clickplate (jump in pit A to activate), secret door
50. Mana Circle
51. Safrinni's Orb
52. Sign
53. Sign
54. Sign
55. Illusory wall
56. Inactive clickplate
57. Magick armor (helm, breastplate, leggings)
58. Locked door—use orb key
59. Gate, illusory door
60. Teleport deactivator (for 61), illusory wall
61. Teleport to Palace of Shadows
62. Mana Circle, silver runestaff, potions

Map 10.1 Gate of the Ancients

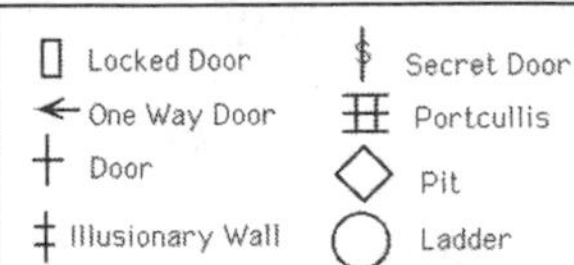

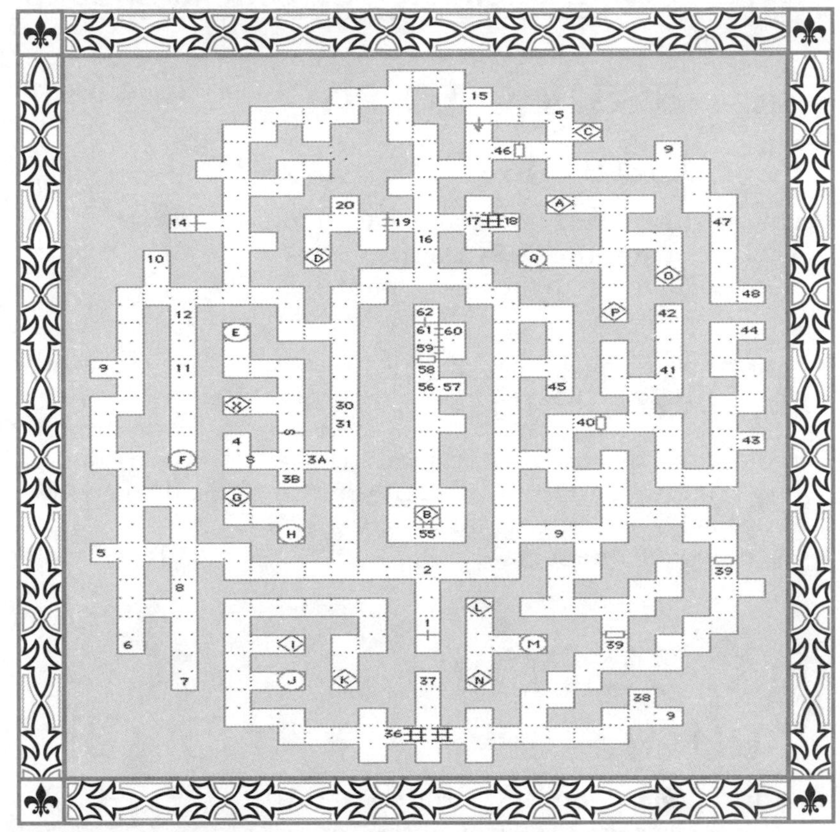

Map 10.2 The Pits

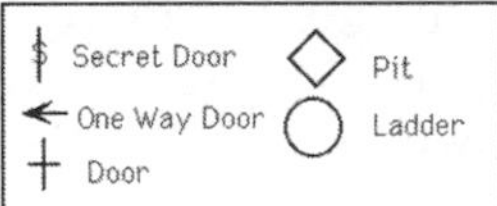

1. Passage to the Ice Caverns

This stairway leads down to the Gate of Ancients from the Ice Caverns (31 on Map 9). Go north to the intersection.

2. Wall Sign

Look at the ***sign*** on the north wall. Drake can barely read it, but manages to decipher, "The center is the key." Go 3W, 6N, then take one step west.

3A, 3B. Wall Buttons

Push the ***button*** on the north wall. This opens a ***secret door*** just around the corner to the north. Now go into that small alcove to the south. Push the ***button*** on the west wall. This opens a ***secret door*** just around the corner to the west. Exit the alcove and go west into the secret room.

4. Secret Room

Read the ***sign*** on the west wall. If you use a Language rune on Drake, he can read it. But if Enigma is in the party, save your Mana—the Elf can translate for you:

Enigma: It reads "Transfer Portal Selection Device."
Drake: Do you know what it does?
Enigma: No, but the ancients had many wondrous engines of magick.

Now go to the ***handle*** on the north wall. It's pushed up. Pull it down.

Note Do you wonder what you're doing with that wall handle? It toggles two teleports, at 11 and 30 on Map 10.1. Only *one* can be active at a time. If the lever is *up*, the teleport at 11 is active, and the one at 30 is inactive. When you pull the lever *down*, the teleports reverse—30 is active and 11 inactive.

Exit the secret room, go back east to the corridor, and turn right. Go 6S, 4W, N, then go west into the alcove.

Tip Don't go south down that first corridor! To see why, check step 8 below.

5. Clickplate to What?

When you step on this ***clickplate***—go ahead, don't be shy—nothing happens. You'll find a bunch of these plates strewn throughout the level. Some trigger things, some don't. (For an example of a trap-triggering plate, see 8.) You see, the ancients knew the value of paranoia as a weapon of confusion.

Step back into the corridor, then go due south.

"What Was That?" *Nothing—this time, anyway. But some clickplates trigger deadly traps.*

Note On both Map 10.1 and Map 10.2, I've placed a 5 at every inactive clickplate.

6. Vulture Tactics

It's never pleasant to poke through rotting ***carcasses***, but in this case, a couple of good punches yields two ***black slayer arrows***. Now return two steps north, go two east, and head south to the ***campfire***.

7. One Hot Rune

Gosh, what a cheerful little ***campfire***. Blast it to ashes with an ***icebolt*** (or use anything else that might put out a fire—potions, bucket of water, whatever). After you extinguish the fire, take the ***rune scroll***. Open it to read:

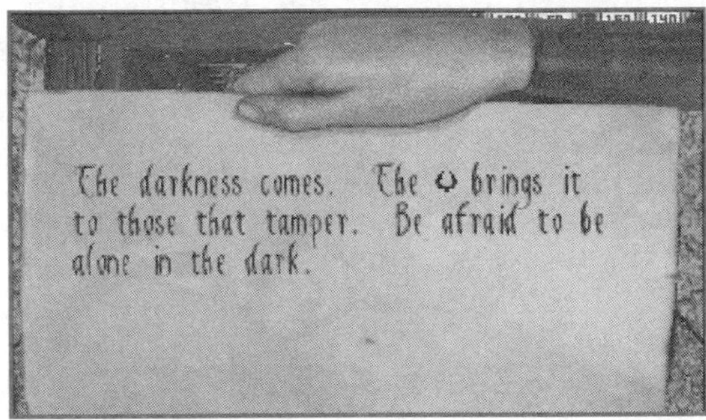

Scare Rune Scroll

Now turn to face north. Don't go straight north, though. (Why? See step 8 below.) Instead, turn left before you reach 8, go 2W, then follow the passage to the north.

8. Great Balls of Fire!

You trigger a deadly trap if you step on this ***clickplate***—a huge ***ball of fire***, roaring north up the passage from 7! If you make this mistake, simply turn sideways, facing east or west. It's best just to avoid it altogether, though.

Uh-oh. You stepped on the clickplate at 8, didn't you? Now look what's roaring down the hall.

9. The Sign That Can't Be Read

Don't waste any Mana on a Language rune here—this ***sign*** is unreadable. (Enigma can't translate the scrawl, either.)

Tip You find many unreadable signs on this level. (I've marked all unreadable signs with a '9' on maps 10.1 and 10.2.) When you look at a sign and Drake says, "I can't read it," or Enigma says, "I am sorry, Drake, it is impossible to read," don't waste Mana on Language runes.

If a sign *can* be read, Enigma will take a crack at it. Of course, his translation won't always be exact. Whenever Enigma makes an attempt to translate a sign, you might want to use the Language rune on Drake, then let him read it.

Step back into the corridor. Go 4N, take a step east, then turn north to face the alcove.

10. Stuff to Get

First, punch out that dead meat on the floor to find a ***stone***. Then grab the Throg Shaman ***feathers*** and that beautiful ***Ring of Poison Resistance*** from the back of the alcove. (You can ignore the ***broken runecaster***.) Step back into the corridor, take a step east, then head due south.

11. Teleport

If the handle in the secret room at 4 is up, this square is an active ***teleport***. When active, it zaps you back up the hall to 12, thus blocking your passage to the south.

Note The *only* way to get past this teleport is to deactivate it by pulling down the lever at 4.

12. Teleport Arrival

You arrive at this square if you step into the active teleport at 11.

Climb down ladder F. You are now in the Pits (see Map 10.2). Go 3S, 2W, go south to the wall, then turn left.

13. Warning

Step up to the ***sign*** on the east wall. If the Language rune is not active, Enigma says:

Enigma: It says the traps are set.

Skuz: Hey, Elfie, tell Skuz someding Skuz don't know! (beat) OK, OK, don't look at Skuz dat way.

When you turn away from the sign and take a step to leave, maniacal laughter fills the cavern. OK, we're all scared now. Retrace your steps back to ladder F. Climb back up, then go north to the end of the corridor. Turn right, go 2E, 4N, then turn left and open the ***door***.

14. One Cold Scroll

In the room, you find the ***life restore potion*** (called "bubbling blue potion" in your journal); when quaffed, this lovely drink adds one star to your lowest rated stat. (Health, Strength, or Agility). Now pick up the ***rune scroll***. (You may have to do this from outside the room.) When you do this, Drake reacts:

Drake: Aaaah! This scroll is intensely cold. There's some sort of magick running through it.

Enigma: I have heard of such magicks. They were common before the Devastation.

Open the scroll and read it:

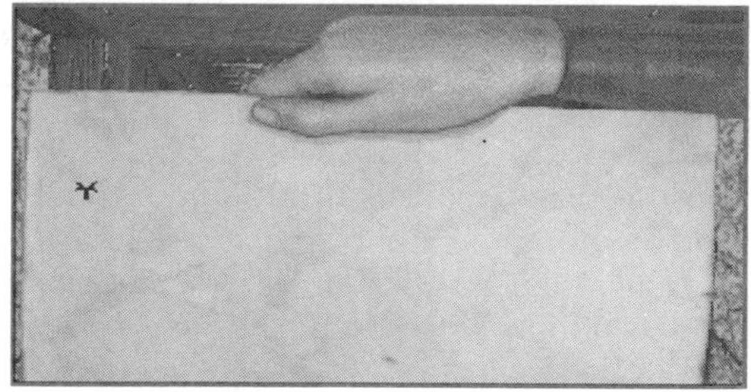

Vampyre Rune Scroll

Step back into the corridor, turn north, and follow the passage. When you reach the intersection, go left.

15. Cryptic Clue

Look at the ***sign***. If Enigma is with you (and the Language rune is not active), the Elf slowly reads it: "There is great magick . . . in the center . . . for those patient." Retrace your path back to the corridor and follow it south to the ***clickplate***.

16. Portcullis Trigger

Stepping on this ***clickplate*** activates the ***portcullis*** just around the corner at 17. Unfortunately, this doesn't simply open the portcullis. Instead, the gate opens and closes repeatedly until you step on the clickplate again.

Note This clickplate doesn't work if you happen to be carrying Safrinni's Orb (also known as the Orb of Levitation) with you, or if you're under the lightening influence of the Featherfall rune.

Go back north a step and turn east, toward the portcullis.

17. Cutting Portcullis

Those spears are razor sharp. Run through the ***portcullis*** just as the last spears disappear—and good luck. If you get caught, one of your party members takes up to 130 points of damage.

Cutting Portcullis. Time your jump right, or a party member will get filleted.

18. Worth the Risk

Grab the ***life restore potion*** and ***Dagger of Penetration***, two worthy prizes. Then run back through the portcullis. Continue west directly into the wall.

19. Phantom Wall

It's an ***illusory wall***. On the other side, turn into the alcove on the right.

20. Mana Circle

Yes, it's a ***Mana Circle***. Step in for a full recharge of all runecasters in your possession. Now continue down the passage to the pit (marked D on Map 10.1), cast a Featherfall rune on your entire party, and jump in.

21. Back In the Pits

You are now back in the Pits (see Map 10.2). If you didn't use the Featherfall rune,

your party (except Sparkle, who floats) suffered some damage in the fall. It's nice that somebody thoughtfully left a ***super heal potion*** to soothe the pain.

Now take the following steps:

- From the bottom of pit D, follow the passage around to ladder Q.
- Climb up ladder Q (see Map 10.1).
- From the top of ladder Q, go three steps east, then head south to pit P.
- Jump in pit P.
- From the bottom of pit P (see Map 10.2), go 4W, N, 3W, then take one step south.

22. Pair of Wall Buttons

Push the ***button*** on the east wall. A door to a secret room (see 23) opens to the northwest. Don't leave yet! Turn around and push the button on the west wall. This time, the door to a secret room (see 24) opens to the southeast.

23. Vitality Button

Push the ***button*** on the west wall in this alcove to activate a magickal spell that fully restores the vitality of each party member. This works every time you push the button.

24. Health Button

Push the ***button*** on the east wall to activate a magickal spell that fully restores the health—counteracts poison, etc.—of each party member. This works every time you push the button.

Exit this room and take the following steps:

- Go west to ladder E and climb up.
- Follow the corridor around to pit X and jump in.
- From the bottom of pit X, take one step east.

25. Another Secret

Push the ***button*** on the south wall to open a ***secret passage*** behind you on the north wall. *Important: Don't follow the new passage yet!* Instead, take a step east and face the north wall.

Caution If you follow the new passage north here, you'll step through a one-way door and cut yourself off from steps 26–29. To complete them, you'd have to climb back up ladder E, then jump back down pit X.

26. Good Advice From the Ancients

Look at the ***sign*** on the north wall. If you haven't used the Language rune on Drake, Enigma reads the sign: "Those who are greedy will close all doors." Continue east. You find three ***doors***—one each to the east, north, and south.

Caution *Go to the east room first!* When you visit the north and south rooms and take the items in both, all three doors lock. (Remember: "Greed closes all doors.") It is possible to unlock them again, but it's a tedious, time-consuming process. (You would need to press a wall button at 48.)

27. Wolf Key

Enter this room first, then grab the ***wolf key*** from the floor. Exit and go to the north room.

28. Ring of Poison Resistance

Look carefully on the floor to find the ***Ring of Poison Resistance***. Exit and go to the south room.

29. Magick Shield

Take the ***magick shield*** and exit. (The three doors lock now, but that's OK, you won't be back.) Now go back to the secret passage you opened back at 25.

Follow the passage north to the wall. Turn around and look behind you. The passage is sealed shut! You just stepped through a one-way door. That's all right, though. Just turn left and take the following steps:

- Climb ladder E.
- Go down to the wall handle at 4.
- Push the handle *up*. (This deactivates the teleport at 30—for more, see step 30 below.)
- Work your way north to pit D and jump in.
- Go to ladder Q and climb up.
- From the top of ladder Q, go 3E, N, then turn right and follow the short passage to pit O.
- Jump into pit O.
- From the bottom of pit O, work your way along the passage to the alcove at 32.

30. Teleport

If the handle in the secret room at 4 is down, this square is an active ***teleport***. When active, it zaps you back one square south, to 31—thus blocking your passage to the north.

31. Teleport Arrival

You arrive in this square if you step in the active teleport at 30.

32. Remains of the Day

Hey, this guy made it pretty far. Give him a hand, then take his stuff—the ***warhammer***, ***helm***, ***chain-mail shirt***, ***chain-mail skirt***, and, best of all, the ***heal potion***. Step back into the corridor and go 2S, 5W, then head south to the door.

33. One-way Ticket

Are you sure you want to go through here? You'd better be, because this is a ***one-way door***. On the other side, take the following steps:

- Climb up ladder M. (You're back on Map 10.1 again.)
- From the top of ladder M, go forward to the wall, turn left, and go south to pit N.
- Jump into pit N.
- From the bottom of pit N, follow the corridor to 34, the first alcove on the right.

34. If It Quacks Like a Duck . . .

Yes, that's a ***statue of a duck***. Only an entity with a totally Faerie sense of humor would put such a thing here. Check your Faerie runes. One of them sort of looks like a duck, doesn't it? (It's the rune you got from the Faerie Players back on Level 8; if you missed it, see the story entitled "The Gift" under step 4 back in that section.) Use the Duck rune on the duck statue to open a secret passage.

Speak Its Language. How? Use the "Duck rune" on the duck. (Here, it's the rune inscribed at the very bottom of the elfwand.)

35. Not Just Duck Soup

Scoop up the duck's numerous gifts—a magickal ***Horn of Fear***, a ***magickal quiver*** for your black slayer arrows, a ***life restore potion***, a ***Ring of Ducking***, two ***rune scrolls***, and two message ***scrolls***. (You have the Languages rune already, so I didn't include it in the following screen shots.)

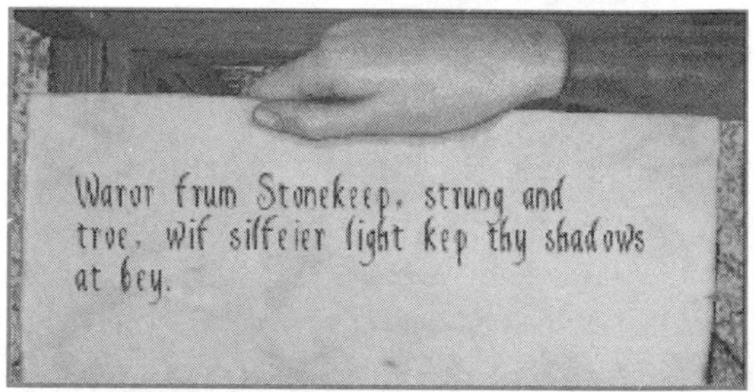

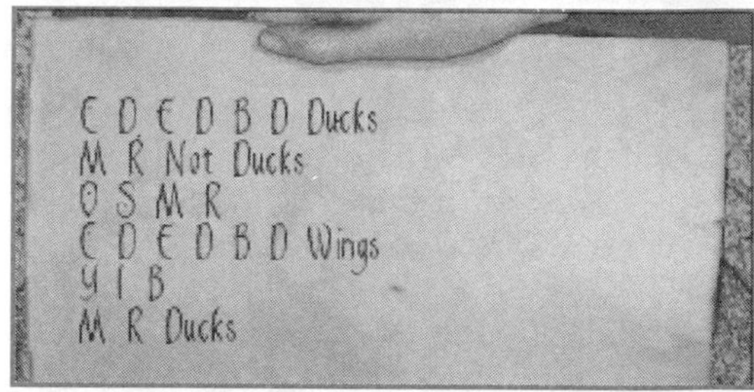

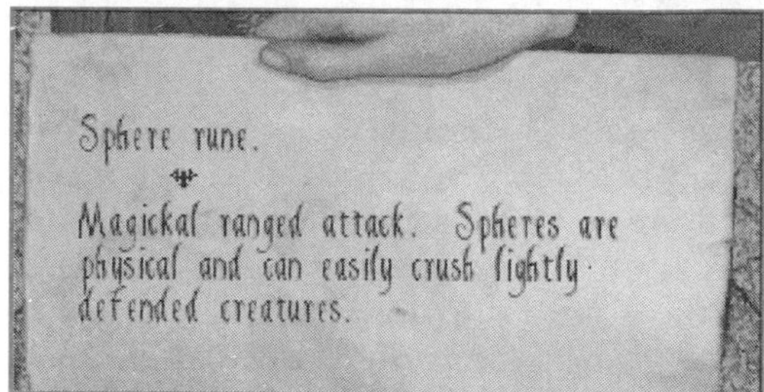

Sphere Rune Scroll

Exit the duck's room, turn right, and follow the passage to ladder J. From the top of ladder J, go W, 2S, 2E, S, then go straight ahead to the moving portcullis gate.

36. Hell's Gates

Step through the first moving ***portcullis*** and turn left. Go north to the end of the short passage.

37. Nullify Portculli

Push the ***button*** on the north wall. This permanently retracts the two moving portculli. Go back south to the corridor and continue east.

38. Lone Button

Push the ***button*** on the north wall in the small alcove at the end of the corridor. You just disabled an ugly trap far, far away (at 41). Now return west down the passage and take the first right turn.

39. One-way Doors

Both of these ***doors*** numbered 39 can be opened only from the south. Fortunately, that's the side you happen to be on. You can go through either of these doors, but for the sake of the walkthrough, let's take the closest one.

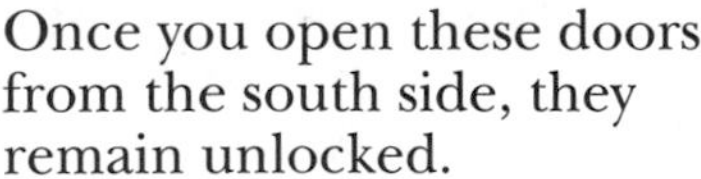

Note Once you open these doors from the south side, they remain unlocked.

From the other side of the door, go N, 2W, 2N, E, 2N, E, 3N, 2W, 3N, then east to the locked door.

40. The Wolf Door

Unlock this ***door*** with the wolf key you got at 27. From the other side of the door, go two steps east, north to the wall, then turn right and follow the passage.

41. Trap

Here's another ball-of-fire ***trap***. Step in this square and a fiery blast shoots down from 42—unless you deactivated it by pushing the button at 38. If the fire hits your party, it does 30–40 points of damage to each member.

42. Eagle Key

Gosh, another cheerful little ***campfire***. Extinguish the fire with an ***icebolt*** (or anything else that might put out a fire—a potion or a bucket of water, for example.) Then take the ***eagle key***.

Go back south to the corridor and turn left. Follow the passage to the first alcove on the right.

43. Another One Bites the Dust

Plunder the remains of this adventurer for items you might need. You find a ***standard hammer***, a ***chain-mail shirt***, a ***chain-mail skirt***, a ***Dwarven helm***, and a ***scroll*** with a chilling warning:

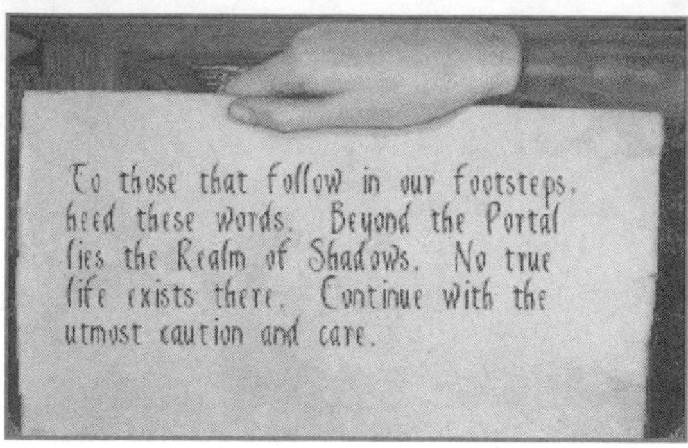

Follow the passage north to the end.

44. Another Center Sign

If Drake is under the influence of the Language rune, he reads this ***sign*** on the east wall: "Not all is as it seems in the center." If not, Enigma translates the message as this: "The center is hidden."

Now go back through the wolf door at 40. From the west side of the door, go W, 2S, 2W, 5N, 2E, then turn right to face the sign.

45. Another Sign

If Drake is under the influence of the Language rune, he reads this ***sign*** on the south wall: "Beware the guardian at the gate." If not, Enigma translates the message as this: "There stands a guardian at the gate. Beware him."

Now turn around and go 4N, 2W, N, W, N, 2W, 6N, then turn right and follow the short passage to the locked door.

46. The Eagle Door

Unlock this ***door*** with the eagle key you got at 42. Go through the door to the wall, turn right, and follow the passage.

47. Moving Portcullis

Another one. By now, you know that a moving ***portcullis*** is pretty easy to get past. Time it right, or somebody in your party suffers up to 130 points of damage. Continue to the end of the passage.

48. Orb Key

Grab the ***orb key*** (called "a very sturdy key" in your journal) and the ***rune scroll.*** Open the scroll and read it:

Stoptrack Rune Scroll

There's also a ***button*** on the east wall. Push this to unlock the doors to rooms 27, 28, and 29 (if your greed triggered their locks before you got what you needed).

Now go back through the eagle door at 46 and take the following steps:

- Go back through the illusory door at 19.

- Go to pit D and jump in.
- From the bottom of pit D, work your way back to ladder Q and climb up.
- From the top of ladder Q, go 2E, 3N, then west to pit A.
- You must jump into pit A without the Featherfall rune active! If it is active, cast the Spoilspell rune to remove it.

Safrinni's Orb. Yeah, it's floating. So would you, if you happened to be the Orb of Levitation.

49. Clickplate Landing

The bottom of pit A is a ***clickplate***. When you land on it, it hurts, but a ***secret door*** opens to the north. Go north into the room. Once you enter this room, the wall seals shut behind you.

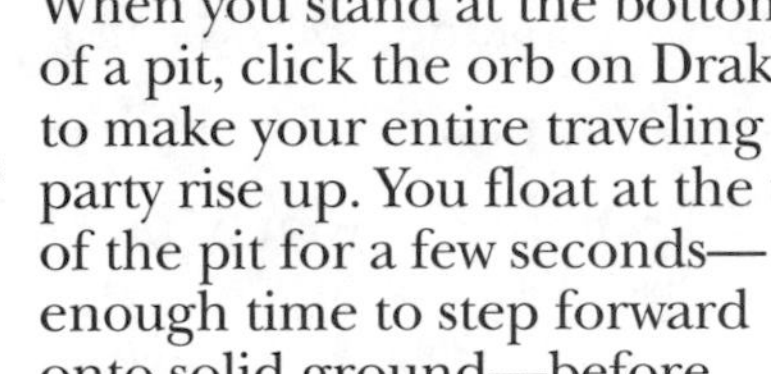

Note This is the Orb of Levitation. When you stand at the bottom of a pit, click the orb on Drake to make your entire traveling party rise up. You float at the top of the pit for a few seconds—enough time to step forward onto solid ground—before levitating gently back down.

50. Mana Circle

Ah, another ***Mana Circle*** lies inscribed in that first alcove on the left. Recharge, heal your party, recharge again, then continue north into the room.

51. Orb of Levitation

Go directly to the corner and snatch ***Safrinni's Orb***, known as the Orb of Levitation. This is the sixth of the nine receptacles of the gods that you need to successfully complete *Stonekeep*. Now check out the room's two ***signs***.

52. Shadow Clue

Look at the ***sign*** on the north wall. If Drake is under the influence of the Language rune, he can read it: "In the realm of shadows, the weapon is hidden." If not, Enigma translates it: "In the shadow realm, there lies a weapon."

53. Scourge Warning

Now look at the ***sign*** on the east wall. If Drake is under the influence of the Language rune, he can read it: "The Scourge has been banished to the shadows." If not, Enigma translates it:

"The punishment is banished in the shadows."

Now go back to 51, where you got the orb, and take the following steps:

- Turn to face the west wall.
- Click Safrinni's Orb on Drake. The party levitates to the top of the pit.
- When you reach the top, quickly step forward.
- Turn right and follow the passage. (A one-way wall closes behind you.)
- Go to pit D and jump in. (It won't hurt this time!)
- Go to ladder Q and climb up.
- Go to pit O and jump in.
- From the bottom of pit O, follow the corridor to the sign at 54.

54. The Final Sign

Here's one ***sign*** Enigma can't read, though he tries. With the Language rune, Drake reads it: "Do not pass this way unless you have the means to rise above your station." Of course, this refers to the Orb of Levitation, which you do have—or *should* have—at this point.

So continue west to the bottom of pit B. Face south, then use Safrinni's Orb on Drake.

55. Illusory Wall

When you reach the top of the pit, step forward quickly, right through the ***illusory wall***. Follow the corridor around and up to the north.

56. Clickplate of the Ancients

Step on the ***clickplate***—don't worry, it doesn't activate anything—then turn right to face the alcove.

57. Armor Treasure of the Ancients

Wow! Beautiful stuff. Grab that complete suit of magickal, ancient plate mail—***helm***, ***breastplate***, and ***leggings***. Now go north to the locked door.

58. The Orb Door of the Ancients

Unlock this ***door*** with the orb key you got at 48. Take one step to get through the door—but stop right on the other side.

59. Gate of the Ancients

Don't step forward through the imposing ***gate*** yet. Instead, turn right to face east . . . then step through the ***illusory wall***. After you pass through, take a step north.

Gate of the Ancients. Don't step through this portal until you make the rounds, so to speak.

62. Mana Monster

On the floor, on the edge of a ***Mana Circle***, you find a true treasure—the ***silver runestaff***, with a Mana charge of 120! Grab the three ***super heal potions***, too. Then step back onto 61 and retrace your short route through the illusory doors to return to 59.

Finally, step through the gate into the Palace of Shadows . . . and watch one of the coolest 3-D animation sequences you'll ever see on a home computer.

60. Teleport Deactivator of the You-Know-Who

This square disables the teleport at 61 so that you can step there without getting zapped to Level 11: Palace of Shadows yet. Turn left to face west . . . and step through another ***illusory wall***!

61. Teleport to Palace of Shadows

This square zaps you to Level 11 if you step into it through the Gate of the Ancients (from 59). If you stepped onto 60 first, *then* here, this teleport is disabled. Turn north and open the door.

Level 11

Palace of Shadows

The eleventh level of *Stonekeep* includes one map area—the Palace of Shadows (Map 11). The Palace's unique design makes the step-by-step walkthrough for this level unique, too.

Here's the general layout:

Look at the map—the east and west halves are mirror images of each other (with a few tiny exceptions). This symmetry is reflected in the creatures you meet and the items you find. In most cases, creatures or objects in the western half of the Palace have a twin (or "shadow variant") located in a corresponding position on the east side of the Palace.

Creatures in the west are more corporeal than their eastern counterparts. For example, a defeated skeleton clatters into a pile of bones, while a vanquished shadow-skeleton simply vanishes into thin air.

Two old friends join your party here in the Palace—well, *one's* a friend, the other's just old. Be prepared for a brief but painful encounter with your dark nemesis, the Shadowking. You also tangle with one of his deadliest lieutenants.

Key to Map 11

1. Start
2. One-way passage
3A–B. Thera's warning
4. Illusory wall, potions
5. Illusory wall, potions
6A–B. Wall triggers (closes 7)
7A–B. Sliding walls (closed by 6)
8A. Floating skulls
8B. Shadow-skulls
9. Yin symbol
10A–B. Connected teleports
11. Yang symbol
12A–B. Shadowking (one time only)
13A–B. Buttons
14. Marif's Orb
15. Farli returns
16A–B. Buttons
17. Dark mirror (shard)
18A. Skeleton, small skeleton
18B. Shadow-skeleton, small shadow-skeleton
19A. Skeletons
19B. Shadow-skeletons
20A–B. Wahooka (joins party)
21A–B. Chest (potions)
22A–B. One-way doors
23A. Skeletons
23B. Shadow-skeletons
24A–B. Chest (potions)
25A. Floating skulls
25B. Shadow-skulls
26. Shadow weapon (top), sign
27A–B. Connected teleports
28. Shadow weapon (base), sign
29A. Skeletons
29B. Shadow-skeletons
30A. Floating skulls
30B. Shadow-skulls
31A–B. Chest (potions)
32A. Small skeletons
32B. Small shadow-skeletons
33. Wall trigger
34. Teleport to 35, 38
35. Skeleton, half-orb (restores vitality)
36. Floating skulls
37. Wall trigger
38. Skeleton, sign
39. Floating skulls
40. Wall trigger
41. Teleport to 42, 45
42. Shadow-skeleton, half-orb (restores Mana)
43. Shadow-skulls
44. Wall trigger
45. Shadow-skeleton, sign
46. Shadow-skulls
47A. Skeletons
47B. Shadow-skeletons
48A. Skeletons
48B. Shadow-skeletons
49A. Teleport to 50A
49B. Teleport to 50B

50A–B. Purgatory
51A. Rune scroll
51B. Scroll
52. Scourge!
53A–B. Buttons, secret doors
54A–B. Poison traps
55A–B. Chests (potions)
56. Button (opens 57)
57. Teleport to Level 10: The Pits
58. Teleport to 59
59. Teleport to 58
60. Button (opens 61)
61. Teleport to Level 5: Temple of Throggi (Super Secret Room)
62. Passage to Tower of the Shadowking
63A–B. Buttons
64A–B. Buttons

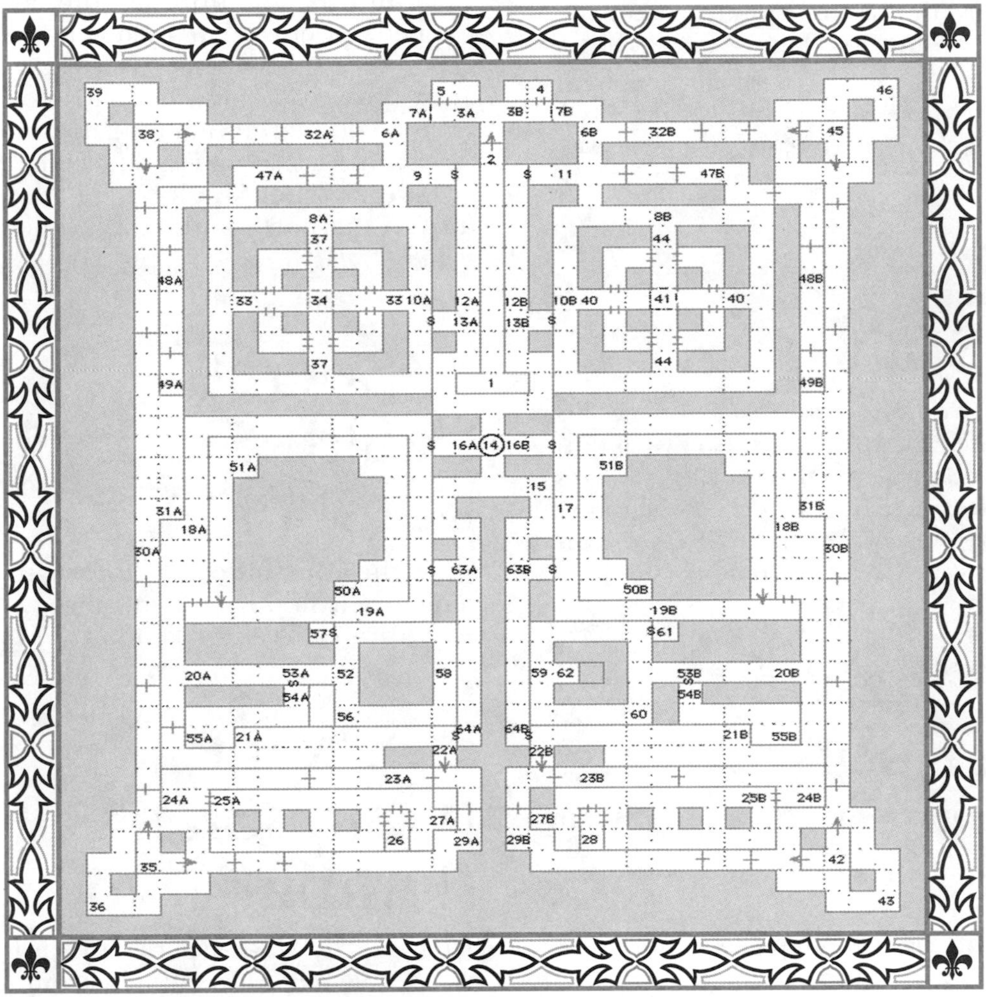

Map 11 Palace of Shadows

Note Again, the east and west sides of the Palace mirror each other. In this walkthrough, we primarily work the western half of the Palace. Many of the events on the west side are tagged with an 'A'—6A, 7A, 8A, and so on—with corresponding events on the east side numbered the same, but tagged with a 'B.'

At times it is necessary to teleport from west to east and back. Of course, hardcore gamers will want to explore every nook and cranny of *both* sides.

1. Start

You arrive here after a *wild* journey from the Gate of the Ancients. Go north to the intersection. After the fourth step or so, magickal walls begin to close behind you at every step. The final wall closes when you cross the threshhold at 2.

2. One-Way Corridor

Once you step north through this square, your passage back down the entrance corridor is forever blocked. Feeling trapped? Go to the north wall, then turn right and take one step east to 3B.

Tip There's a secret treat on the east side that you must grab now, because you lose access to it later (see 6).

3A & 3B. Thera's Warning

Thera's ghostly voice calls out when you step into either of these squares. She says: "Drake! Drake, listen to me. I have little time before he notices and all my trapped power is being used to create this vision. Heed this warning, my champion: Trust those you know, but all is not as it seems. This place is but a shadow of what is real. And a shadow is a reflection."

Take another single step east, then turn to the north and walk through the ***illusory wall***.

4. Secret Health Stash Number One

Grab the four blue ***heal potions*** in this room, then step back south through the wall. Turn right and take four steps west.

5. Secret Health Stash Number Two

Turn right, walk north through yet another ***illusory wall***, and pilfer four more ***heal potions***. Step back south through the wall. Head west to the corner, then take a step south to 6A and prepare for combat.

6A, 6B. Wallstop Square

Did you just hear a grinding sound? Two things happen when you step into this square. First, you trigger a mechanism that closes the ***sliding walls*** back around the corner at *both* 7A and 7B. Second, you trigger an attack by a ***floating skull*** or two from down the corridor to the south.

Note

These attacking skulls are members of a skull squad (see 8A) patrolling a corridor to the south.

If you linger here, more skull squad members join the attack. But if you hustle two steps south, then duck east into alcove 9, you can avoid the fight for now.

7A, 7B. Sliding Walls

Both of these ***walls*** slide shut permanently when you step into either 6A or 6B.

8A. Skull Patrol

Six ***floating skulls*** patrol this area, traveling in a clockwise direction. These skulls are nasty, persistent enemies who do not retreat. They attack with deadly energybolts that drain vitality *and* inflict weakness.

Tip Magick works fine for long-range attacks. But if a floating skull gets in close, use a magickal weapon. Two or three good hits with a Dagger of Penetration or magick throwing ax destroys these pesky skulls. When you kill a floating skull, it leaves its hollow shell behind.

Worse Than Skinheads. Yeah, they're skullheads, man, and they want to deprive you of your civil rights. Use magickal weapons against these nasty bigots.

8B. Shadow-Skull Patrol

Six ***shadow-skulls*** patrol this area, moving in a counterclockwise direction. These guards have some resistance against spells. When you destroy a shadow-skull, it leaves nothing behind.

9. Yin

The ***mystic symbol*** on the wall here can be combined with the ***mystic symbol*** at 11. If you combine them here at 9, a mechanism opens the secret door directly to the east. But in *our* walkthrough, we'll combine them at 11, so grab the yin symbol and take it with you.

Take one step west back into the corridor and go 2S, E, 4S, then turn left to face the east wall.

10A & 10B. Dark Mirror Teleports

The ***dark mirror*** hanging on the wall at 10A is a teleport. It is connected to another ***dark mirror*** at 10B. You can use the mirrors to travel back and forth between these two locations.

Caution When you pass through a dark mirror, all party members lose two stars of Strength. (Don't worry—no character's Strength rating can drop *below* one star.) Members regain the lost Strength at the rate of one star per minute. You can feed a green mushroom to party members to restore the lost Strength.

Mirror, Mirror On the Wall. Who's the darkest of them all? Hop in and find out.

Now step into the mirror at 10A to arrive at 10B. Go north up the corridor to 11.

11. Yang

Put the yin symbol from 9 on the ***yang symbol*** here. Turn left and go through the secret doorway to the west. At the wall, turn left again and head south to 12B.

Yin and Yang. Some things just belong together.

12A & 12B. A Little Taste of Shadow Magick

Be sure your vitality meter is high the first time you step into 12B (or 12A, if you go there first). When you step in the square, the ***Shadowking*** himself clanks around the corner and roars, "Mortal fools! You dare think you can free my little family? Begone!" With that, he slams you down the hallway with a mighty spell.

God, I Hate This Guy. Fortunately, this is the only time you meet him on this level.

You'll suffer serious damage—about 60–80 points of it, in fact—but you have no choice. You must face the Shadowking here to get a crucial item that lies just a little further down the hall.

Note This is a one-time-only event! In this walkthrough, the Shadowking gives you the big push at 12B. It won't happen again, not even at 12A.

13A & 13B. Secret Door Buttons

At 13A, a ***button*** on the east wall opens a ***secret door*** to the west. At 13B, a ***button*** on the west wall opens a ***secret door*** to the east.

In this walkthrough, push the button at 13B, but don't go through the newly opened door yet. Instead, continue south to 14.

14. Marif's Orb

Boy, that's a *really* big orb. It happens to be ***Marif's Orb***, but somebody blew it up real good. Shrink it with your favorite Faerie Shrink rune.

After you grab the shrunken orb and put it in inventory, Drake shudders and gasps:

Drake: (gasping) I can feel the power in this orb. Strength is running up my arms. I have been given the strength of Marif himself.

Sparkle: Are you in danger?

Drake: Nay, friend. The feeling is good. The strength is righteous.

Enigma: Your aura glows stronger.

Drake: We must proceed with caution now. I feel this is a critical time. We must go quickly to Thera's Temple and free the orbs. Khull-khuum must have planned for this to happen, and I do not think he would be so forgiving of our intrusion after this point.

Check your stats. You've just picked up two stars of Strength. Go due south until you hear a familiar voice.

Big Orb, Little Orb. You're a hero, but come on, nobody could pick up an orb that big. Shrink it with a Faerie rune first.

15. Welcome Back, Farli

Yes, it's the good-hearted Dwarf, your buddy, ***Farli Mallestone***. He sees you first, and calls out: "Drake! Over here!" Go greet him:

Drake: (happy) Farli! I thought you were *uck-togoth*, banished from your people.

Farli: I was. I travelled to Chak'higoth, the Dwarven capital, and made my peace with the elders as is our tradition. They absolved me, and I was no longer an *uck-togoth*, but Farli Mallestone once again.

Drake: Then what brings you here?

Farli: Couldn't let a friend down, and besides, this time I got permission.

Sparkle: Hmm?

Farli (continues): I spoke with the Queen Iaenni. You are summoned to her side.

Sparkle: Really?

Drake: Truly this is great news.

Sparkle: I don't wanna go. You need me!

Drake: Don't worry, Farli is here. He can help us. Correct?

Farli: Aye, that is my duty.

Sparkle: I can't wait to see my friends again. That is, my *other* friends, Drake.

Drake: I understand. Return home in Thera's safety.

Sparkle: I'll see you again . . . someday!

In *Stonekeep II,* perhaps? Farli joins the party, while Sparkle teleports away.

Drake: Good to have you back.

Farli: There's a job to finish. And I'm good at finishing what I start.

Enigma: (coughs)

Drake: Right. Farli, this is Enigma. An honorable . . .

Farli (interrupting): Elf. I can see.

Enigma: Drake has spoken favorably of you, Dwarf.

Drake: And I speak favorably of Enigma. He has earned my trust, like you have.

Farli: Drake's trust is enough for me. Well met, Enigma.

Enigma: Well meet, Farli. I wish it were a different place.

Drake: Agreed to all. Let us journey on, shall we?

Upgrade Farli's armor and weapons. Return to 14, turn right, and take a step east to 16B.

16A & 16B. Secret Door Buttons

At 16A, you can push a ***button*** on the north wall to open a ***secret door*** to the west. At 16B, you can push a ***button*** on the north wall to open a ***secret door*** to the east.

In this walkthrough, push the button at 16B first, then go east through the newly opened door. Go south three steps, then get a weapon ready.

17. The Darkest Mirror

Quickly now, turn right and break the ***dark mirror*** on the west wall. If you dally, Drake's dark reflection blasts your party with firebolts. After you break the mirror, grab a ***shard*** of its dark mirrored glass.

Drake and Anti-Drake. *That guy on the other side of the mirror is in a foul mood. Break the mirror quickly.*

Now go back through the secret door to 16A, push the button on the north wall, then go west through the newly revealed door. Turn right and follow the passage around to 18A.

18A. Skeleton Patrol

One ***skeleton*** and one ***lesser skeleton*** patrol this corridor. Crush them into piles of bones. They leave behind the usual ***broadsword***, Far Eastern ***helm***, and ***skull***.

Important: Snatch up one of these items immediately after smashing each skeleton! (See the following note.) Continue south to the next left turn at 20A.

Note Skeleton bone fragments begin to creep back together after you shatter them the first time. If you do not take the skull, helm, or sword, the skeleton re-forms itself—and you have to battle the creature a second time!

18B. Shadow-Skeleton Patrol

On the shadow (east) side of the Palace, shadow beings walk the halls—here, one regular-size ***shadow-skeleton***, and one ***lesser shadow-skeleton***. Unlike regular skeletons, these guys rise up from ground to attack, and they leave *nothing* behind after you banish them from the material plane (*i.e.*, destroy them).

Tip Shadow-skeletons have a high magick resistance and can poison your party members. The poison saps vitality points until you cure the afflicted character.

19A & 19B. More Skeletal Patrols

You can avoid these locations in this walkthrough. At 19A, two regular ***skeletons*** patrol the area. At 19B, two ***shadow-skeletons*** lay in wait for you.

20A & 20B. Party Time for Wahooka

The first time you step into one of these squares, the voice of ***Wahooka*** calls out:

Wahooka (off-screen): Greetings, again. Have a moment?

Drake: What do you want, goblin?

Wahooka (off-screen): Bah! About time we spoke again.

Drake: Then appear and we can do so. (Wahooka appears in the mystic mirror with your party.) What are you doing?!

Wahooka: It is time for us to join forces, Drake.

Drake: Hmm.

Wahooka: As you may guess, it was I who saved you that dark day so long ago.

Drake: You? Why?

Wahooka: Bah, don't be such a fool. We can profit together.

Drake: And since neither of us trusts the other, we can venture without trouble. I don't think so.

Wahooka: I don't say this is an easy thing to do. But I have no reason to harm you. I *helped* you long ago.

Drake: Maybe.

Wahooka: And I help now. Khull-khuum must be stopped. I know this.

Enigma: But why you?

Wahooka: There are riches ahead, I can smell them.

Drake: I'm sure you can. Very well, join us.

Wahooka: Oh, I already have. I already have.

Don't go any further east from 20A! If you do, you run into Scourge, an opponent you cannot defeat yet. (See 52 later in this section.)

Note If you don't have Marif's Orb, you can't go down the corridor past 20A, even if you want to—a magickal ***barrier*** stops you. In this walkthrough, you *do* have the orb. But know that if you try to move through the barrier without it, you will be repulsed.

Instead, take a step back west into the corridor. Go south through the skull doors, then follow the passage around the corner to 21A.

21A & 21B. Better Than Gold

Open the ***chest*** and grab the ***heal potion*** and the ***super heal potion***. From 21A, head due east to the wall, turn right, and go through the ***one-way door***.

22A & 22B. One-Way Door

Did I mention this was a ***one-way door***? Once you step through 22A, turn right. Prepare for battle and step through the skull doors.

23A & 23B. Bony Twins

Two ***skeletons*** patrol at 23A, while two ***shadow-skeletons*** patrol at 23B. After winning the fight at 23A, continue west through the skull doors, then around the corner to 24A.

24A & 24B. Another Stash of Treats

Open the ***chest*** and grab one ***super heal potion***, one ***heal potion***, and one ***poison cure potion***. Turn to face the opposite wall (opposite east wall), then step through it—it's an ***illusory wall***.

25A & 25B. Skull Attack!

Did I mention that you should prepare for deadly combat? Oops. The minute you step forward from the illusory door, a swarm of angry ***floating skulls*** drops on you. (Of course, the swarm is made up of spooky ***shadow-skulls*** at 25B.) Use a magickal weapon to fend them off—there are seven skulls in each area—then proceed to 26.

26. Shadow Weapon, Part One

Step through any of the three ***illusory doors*** leading into this secret room. On the floor lies the ***shadow weapon***—well, *part* of it, anyway. (Your journal ominously calls it "a piece of Shadow itself.")

When you pick it up, your party makes the following comments:

Farli: There is a mighty weapon in the making.

Wahooka: Bah! It is worthless . . . without its mate, that is. Do you want to trade it?

Enigma: An ancient relic. Use caution.

Tip You'll find the other piece of the shadow weapon maker at 28.

Before you leave, use the Language rune on Drake and read the ***sign*** on the north wall: "Light and darkness, formed together, form my strength, form my shape." Exit this secret room through the east illusory wall, then continue east to the dark mirror at 27A.

27A & 27B. Dark Mirror Portals

You can teleport freely back and forth between these ***dark mirrors***. But remember, when you pass through a dark mirror, your party members lose two stars of Strength, regaining it at the rate of one star per minute.

In this walkthrough, step into the dark mirror at 27A. The mirror teleports your party to 27B. Remember that a swarm of ***shadow-skulls*** (see 25B) awaits your arrival!

Tip If you want, you can avoid the shadow-skulls by hustling straight east through the illusory wall into 28. If you choose to battle the skulls, remember that chest full of Heal potions at 24B.

28. Shadow Weapon, Part Two

Enter this secret room via any of its three ***illusory doors***. Here lies the unmoveable base of the ***shadow weapon***. When you enter, the following conversation takes place:

Drake: I wonder what will happen when we bring both pieces together.

Enigma: Proceed with care.

Wahooka: Bah! Put it together. It must be *very* magickal.

Farli: I agree with the Elf. Hmmm. But I am myself curious.

Shadow Maker. Slide Tab A into Slot B, and there you have it—your choice of the five deadliest weapons this side of the Potomac.

Place the top piece (found at 26) onto the base. The top morphs from weapon to weapon—***shadow-sword***, ***shadow-hammer***, ***shadow-dagger***, ***shadow-ax***, ***shadow-spear***—every few seconds until you grab one. When you grab a weapon, it stays in that form until you place it back on the base again.

Tip Shadow weapons are magickal . . . and *very*, *very* powerful. Choose the type of weapon for which Drake has the highest skill rating.

If Drake is under the influence of the Language rune, he can read the ***sign*** on the north wall: "I am of darkness and light, and together with my twin form the weapon of twilight, the weapon of shadow. Fear me, fear my powers, shaped as shape can be."

Now take the following steps:

- Exit through the illusory wall to the west.
- Go back into the dark mirror at 27B to teleport back to 27A.
- Exit the room through the illusory door in the northwest corner, then work your way back to 23A.
- Go through the skull doors to the east.
- Continue through the skull doors to the south.

29A & 29B. Bony Triplets

Three ***skeletons*** patrol the corridor at 29A, while three ***shadow-skeletons*** patrol at 29B. Smash them to pieces with your chosen shadow weapon. (Remember to grab the remains of skeletons before they can resurrect.)

Continue west through two sets of doors. Go W, 2N, 2W, then head due north through the doors.

30A & 30B. Skull Squadron

Six ***floating skulls*** patrol the area north of 30A; six ***shadow-skulls*** patrol the area north of 30B.

31A & 31B. Reward

Open the ***chest*** to get two ***super heal potions***. From 31A, continue north through the next two sets of skull doors. After you step through the second door, go N, 2E, 2N, then head east through two more sets of doors.

32A & 32B. Mini-skeletons

Two ***lesser skeletons*** guard the passage at 32A, and two ***lesser shadow-skeletons*** are posted at 32B. Destroy the little fellows at 32A, continue east to 6A, then south to 10A. Turn away from the dark mirror, facing west.

Now take a step forward.

33. Wall Trigger

When you step in this square, a mechanism closes the conditional walls to the east and west of square 34. The mechanism also *opens* conditional walls to the north and south of square 34.

How do you get to 34? Try this:

- From 33, take a step toward 34, then turn north or south (it doesn't matter).
- Step through the illusory wall.
- Follow the passage to the next illusory wall, and step through that one, too.
- Get a good skeleton-bashing weapon ready, then go to 34.

34. Teleport to 35

If you step into this ***teleport*** from the north or south, you get zapped to 35. If you step into 34 from the east or west, you teleport to 38. In this walkthrough, you go to 35 first.

35. Teleport Arrival from 34

A ***skeleton*** awaits your arrival. End his wait, then touch that glowing green ***half-orb*** on the wall. It's a healing orb, and it will restore full vitality to Drake and any Dwarf in the party—in this case, Farli. (The half-orb won't heal Enigma, Sparkle, or Wahooka.)

Healing Orb. Touch this for a full vitality boost for Drake and Farli.

Two one-way doors are provided for your convenient exit. Use the north door.

36. Lurking Skulls

Some ***floating skulls*** lurk around the corner. Battle one, battle all—whatever you want. Head north up the long corridor and return all the way to 8A. Then take a step south.

37. Wall Trigger

The ***wall*** closed up ahead, didn't it? When you step into 37, a mechanism closes the conditional walls to the north and south of square 34. The mechanism also opens conditional walls to the east and west of square 34.

- From 37, take a step toward 34, then turn east or west (it doesn't matter).
- Step through the illusory wall.
- Follow the passage to the next illusory wall, and step through that one, too.
- Get a good skeleton-bashing weapon ready, then go to 34.
- When you step into 34 from the east or west, you get zapped to 38.

38. Teleport Arrival from 34

Another ***skeleton*** waits. Make bone meal of him, then use the Language rune on Drake and read the ***sign*** on the north wall. It says: "Where the reflection does not reflect, bind the shadow by destroying the magick."

Two one-way doors are provided for your convenient exit. Use the east door.

39. More Lurking Skulls

Be aware that more ***floating skulls*** lurk around the corner. Fight them, or not. Then take the following steps:

- Head east through the doors and return to the dark mirror at 10A.
- Step through the dark mirror to arrive at 10B.
- Take one step east to 40.

40. Wall Trigger

Of course, the east side of the Palace mirrors the west side, so it shouldn't surprise you to see that ***wall*** closed up ahead. A mechanism closes the conditional walls to the east and west of square 41, and opens conditional walls to the north and south of square 41.

Take the following steps (which, if you're following this walkthrough, might seem familiar by now):

- From 40, take a step toward 41, then turn north or south (it doesn't matter).
- Step through the illusory wall.
- Follow the passage to the next illusory wall, and step through that one, too.
- Get a good shadow-skeleton weapon ready, then go to 41.

41. Teleport to 42

If you step into this ***teleport*** from the north or south, you get zapped to 42. If you step into 41 from the east or west, you teleport to 45.

In this walkthrough, you go to 42 first.

42. Teleport Arrival from 41

A ***shadow-skeleton*** arises to greet you. Say hello with a nice shadow-axe, then click all of your depleted runecasters on the green ***half-orb*** on the south wall. It recharges each runecaster to full Mana capacity (except Throggish).

Two one-way doors offer exit. Use the north door.

43. Skulking Skulls

Some ***shadow-skulls*** lurk around the corner. Show them what's what. Or run like a chicken, I don't care. Head north up the long corridor.

Tip In this walkthrough, you haven't cleared this long corridor of its beasts yet—they hang out at 30B and 32B—so be prepared. The trip north offers plenty of combat fun. Don't forget to loot that chest of goodies at 31B.

Go all the way to 8B. Then take a step south.

44. Wall Trigger

Once again, the ***wall*** closes up ahead when you step in this square. A mechanism here closes the conditional walls to the north and south of square 41. The mechanism also opens conditional walls to the east and west of square 41.

- From 44, take a step toward 41, then turn east or west (it doesn't matter).
- Step through the illusory wall.
- Follow the passage to the next illusory wall, and step through that one, too.
- Get your shadow weapon ready (if you have one), then go to 41.
- When you step into 41 from the east or west, you get zapped to 45.

45. Teleport Arrival from 41

Another ***shadow-skeleton*** wants you to join him on the nether plane. Violently spurn his offer, then use the Language rune on Drake and read the ***sign*** on the north wall. It says: "I am he who traps without energy. None can escape my influence easily. I am at the center, yet I am everywhere. I am the giver of life, and I am the destroyer of all. My domain is my own, and none shall surpass me in my life."

Exit through the west door.

46. More Skulking Skulls

More ***shadow-skulls*** lurk around the corner. Take the following steps:

- Head west and return to the dark mirror at 10B.
- Step through the dark mirror to arrive at 10A.
- From 10A, go 4N, W, 2N, then turn left and go through two sets of skull doors.

47A–48A & 47B–48B. More Big Bones

Two pairs of regular ***skeletons*** guard the passage at 47A and 48A. On the shadow side of the Palace, of course, two pairs of ***shadow-skeletons*** patrol at 47B and 48B. Bash them all to smithereens with your shadow weapon and continue south. (What are smithereens, anyway?)

49A & 49B. Dark Mirrors to Purgatory

The ***dark mirrors*** at the end of the passage teleport your party to a most chilling location. The dark mirror at 49A leads to 50A, and the dark mirror at 49B leads to 50B.

50A & 50B. Repository of the Lost Souls

This is the Shadowking's collection of captured souls. Listen to their torments, then get the hell out of there (if you'll pardon the expression.) Follow the passage up north and around the corner.

51A & 51B. Scroll

Somebody tossed a ***scroll*** on the floor at these locations. In this walkthrough, you find the rune scroll at 51A:

Quickness Rune Scroll

In case you're curious, here's the one at 51B:

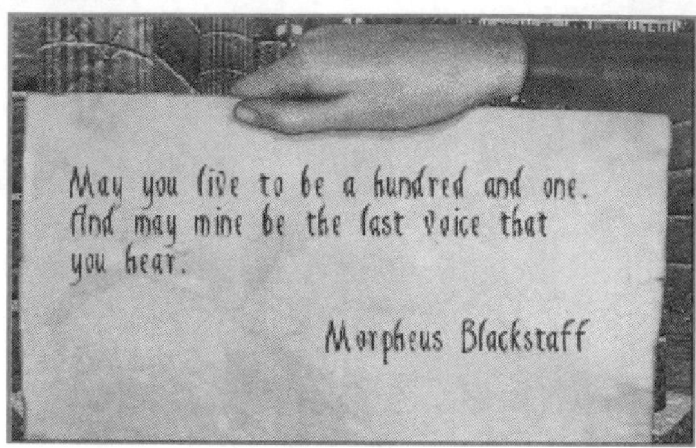
May you live to be a hundred and one. And may mine be the last voice that you hear.

Morpheus Blackstaff

Now take the following steps:

- Continue south down the corridor to the wall.
- When you reach the wall, a ***one-way passage*** closes behind you. (As if you'd really want to go back to purgatory.)
- *Don't go left*—remember the pair of skeleton guards (see 19A, 19B) to the east? Continue to avoid them by taking a step west, then north through the ***illusory wall.***
- Head around the corner to the south and return to 20A, the spot where Wahooka joined your party.
- From 20A, take a step east . . . and prepare for a brutal battle.

52. Scourge!

Welcome to the haunt of ***Scourge***, one of the Shadowking's most ruthless lieutenants. Scourge is actually three ***floating skulls***. The three skulls whirl around each other, making them hard-to-hit targets.

Scourge. The name pretty much says it all. Only a shadow weapon can harm him.

Each of Scourge's three skulls has a different type of attack:

- The ***first skull*** has the power to zap opponents and drain them of Strength—one star per blast.
- The ***second skull*** drains your party's vitality points—10 points per hit.
- The ***third skull*** drains your runecasters of Mana—2 points per blast, from *all* rune-items.

Scourge's skulls are immune to weapon damage except from a shadow weapon. Each skull has a magick resistance of 80 percent. Each skull regenerates one hit point everytime it zaps an opponent. The skulls must be destroyed one at a time.

If Scourge loses one head, he screams, "You shall pay for that! It has been a long time since anyone has caused Scourge such pain."

If Scourge loses a second head, he howls, "Pay, pay, you will pay!"

If Scourge's last head is destroyed, it moans, "Darkness! It is so dark! So dark. Khull-khuum, my lord, beware, darkness is falling."

After the battle, your party has the following discussion:

Drake: Thera's blood! That was tough!

Wahooka: Bah! You know not your own skill. And I was here. There was no chance of failure.

Farli: Wahooka, you were a coward in combat. Anybody could see that.

Wahooka: And any fool could say such rubbish! Bah! Let us move on. I do not think we have time to argue over the lack of Dwarvish intelligence. There is treasure to be found.

When the conversation is done, take two steps west from 52, then turn to face the north wall.

53A & 53B. Secret Button

Push the ***button*** on the north wall here to open a ***secret room*** directly behind you.

54A & 54B. Poison Gas Trap

When you step into this square, clouds of ***poisonous gas*** envelop the party. The gas poisons unprotected party members who breathe it for more than a few seconds. The poison is insidious—it saps the afflicted character of vitality points.

55A & 55B. More Health Snacks

Raid the two ***chests*** in the back of the room. Each one contains one ***heal potion*** and one ***life restore potion***. Exit the room to the corridor. Take two steps east, then two more south.

56. Secret Button

If you push the ***button*** on the west wall, a ***secret room*** opens to the north, at 57.

57. Teleport to the Pits (Level 10)

Do you want to go back to the Pits? I seriously doubt it. But if you do, step into the ***dark mirror*** in this secret room. You and your loyal party members lose three stars of Strength apiece (gained back at the rate of one star per minute) as you teleport to 53 on Map 10.2. In this walkthrough, skip the trip. Instead, go east to the wall then two steps south to the dark mirror on the left.

58. Dark Mirror Teleport to 59

Step into the ***dark mirror***. Your party teleports to 59 on the shadow (east) side of the Palace.

59. Dark Mirror Teleport to 58

This ***dark mirror*** teleport connects to 58 on the west side of the Palace. When you arrive here from 58, go 2S, 4E.

60. Secret Button

Push the ***button*** on the east wall. A ***secret room*** opens for squares to the north, at 61.

61. Teleport to the Temple of Throggi

Do you want to revisit Throggi's Temple? Yes you do! Jump into the ***dark mirror*** here. You lose five stars of Strength (gained back at the rate of one star every two minutes) and you end up in the secret room at 76 on Map 5.2, where a ***dark mirror*** now hangs on the wall—a portal back to the Palace of Shadows.

Look on the floor. Sure, Mana is good, but four juicy ***heal roots*** can really hit the spot after a long stretch of combat-heavy exploration. But man, that's only the beginning. This is a super-secret special square. Here's how it works:

1. Stand for at least 10 seconds in the square where you found the heal roots.
2. Turn left twice.
3. Turn right four times.

Now you and your entire party will be "poisoned" for 90 minutes. But don't get mad at me—this is a very, very *good* poison. It adds 3 points to your vitality every 15 seconds (up to the maximum amount allowed by each character's Health rating). Imagine that—a continuous healing potion!

Go back through the dark mirror to 61 on Map 11. After you arrive, go back to the dark mirror at 59, the turn to face the alcove to the east.

62. Passage to the Tower of the Shadowking

The first time you step into this square, the following conversation takes place:

Drake: There is something about this area. I do not know what, but it feels cold, even to the bottom of my soul.

Wahooka: Bah, you fool. Can't you see with more than just your eyes? (after a pause) Hurry, hurry, must I do everything for you?

Drake: I'm not sure what is happening here.

Wahooka (if you read the sign at 38): Bah! Remember the sign. The prophecy on the wall. Destroy the magick, it said. Well, do so.

Wahooka (if you did *not* read the sign at 38): Bah! There is strong magick at work here. You feel it, no? This magick is illusionary, it hides something from your sight.

To the Dark Tower. Screw your courage to the sticking post, as they say. The Dark One waits.

There are two ways to "destroy the magick"—with a Spoilspell rune or the dark mirror shard from 17. Use the Spoilspell on the wall, or use the shard on Drake to reveal a skull door. Open it. Gather up your courage. Climb the stairs into the Tower of the Shadowking.

You don't visit the following locations in this walkthrough.

63A & 63B. Secret Buttons

Push the button on the east wall at 63A to reveal a ***secret door*** directly to the west. Push the button on the west wall at 63B to reveal the ***secret door*** directly to the east.

64A & 64B. Secret Buttons

Push the button on the east wall at 64A to reveal a ***secret door*** directly to the west. Push the button on the west wall at 64B to reveal the ***secret door*** directly to the east.

Level 12

Tower of the Shadowking

Stonekeep's twelfth level includes five map areas—the four floors of the Tower of the Shadowking (Maps 12.1, 12.3, 12.4, and 12.5) and the basement of the Tower—the Lair of the Dark Dwarves (Map 12.2). By now you should be an experienced adventurer and hero, so I'll let the rest of this level speak for itself. Enjoy!

Key to Maps 12.1, 12.2, 12.3, 12.4, & 12.5

1. Gatekeeper
2. Wall panel (puzzle)
3. Floating spikers
4. Enigma's warning
5. Fire trap
6. Dead Dwarf, oil bombs, ax, handle (activates 5), metal bar
7. Secret door—need metal bar from 6
8. Stairs to Basement
9. Stairs to Main Floor
10. Button (opens secret door)
11. Mana Circle
12. Well
13. Dark Dwarf
14. Button (opens secret door)
15. Dark Dwarves, shrine
16. Dwarf (scroll), bone pile (root), rubble (Dagger of Penetration)
17. Scroll
18. Carcass (black slayer arrow)
19. Sign
20. Fire elementals
21. Potion
22. Floating spikers
23. Sign
24. Button (opens portcullis)
25. Floating spiker
26. King spiker
27. Silver ankh
28. Floating spiker
29. Fire elementals
30. Floating spiker, potion
31. Panel (rune inscription)
32. Floating skulls
33. Fire elementals

34A. Teleport to 34B (need silver cross)

34B. Teleport to 34A

34C. Half-orb

35. Central stairwell to top floor (see all maps)
36. Door trap—disarm at 2
37. Floating skull
38. Stairs to second floor
39. Stairs to first floor

40 A–B. Fire elementals

41. Fire elemental
42. Fire elemental
43. Teleport to 44
44. Teleport to 43, scroll
45. Fire elemental
46. Stopping point
47. Stopping point
48. Silver crescent
49. Energy source (shoots energybolts)
50. Stairs to third floor cell—use enhanced Spoilspell
51. Stairs to second floor
52. Scroll
53. Fire elementals
54. Teleport to 55 (need silver ankh)
55. Teleport to 54 (need silver ankh)
56. Fire elementals
57. Silver cross
58. Teleport to 59
59. Teleport to 58
60. Fire elemental
61. Teleport to 62 (need silver crescent)
62. Teleport to 61 (need silver crescent)
63. Silver circle

64. Fire elemental
65 A–B. Fire elementals
66. Button (opens secret door to 67)
67. Nothing! (open at 66)
68. Fire elementals
69. Teleport to 70 (need all four silver items)
70. Teleport to 69 (need all four silver items)
71. One-way door
72. Sunken pillar (use silver item)
73. Sunken pillar (use silver item)
74. Sunken pillar (use silver item)
75. One-way door
76. Shadowking (Thera's Orb, Kor-soggoth's Orb)
77. Sunken pillar (use silver item)
78. Gate to Thera's Temple

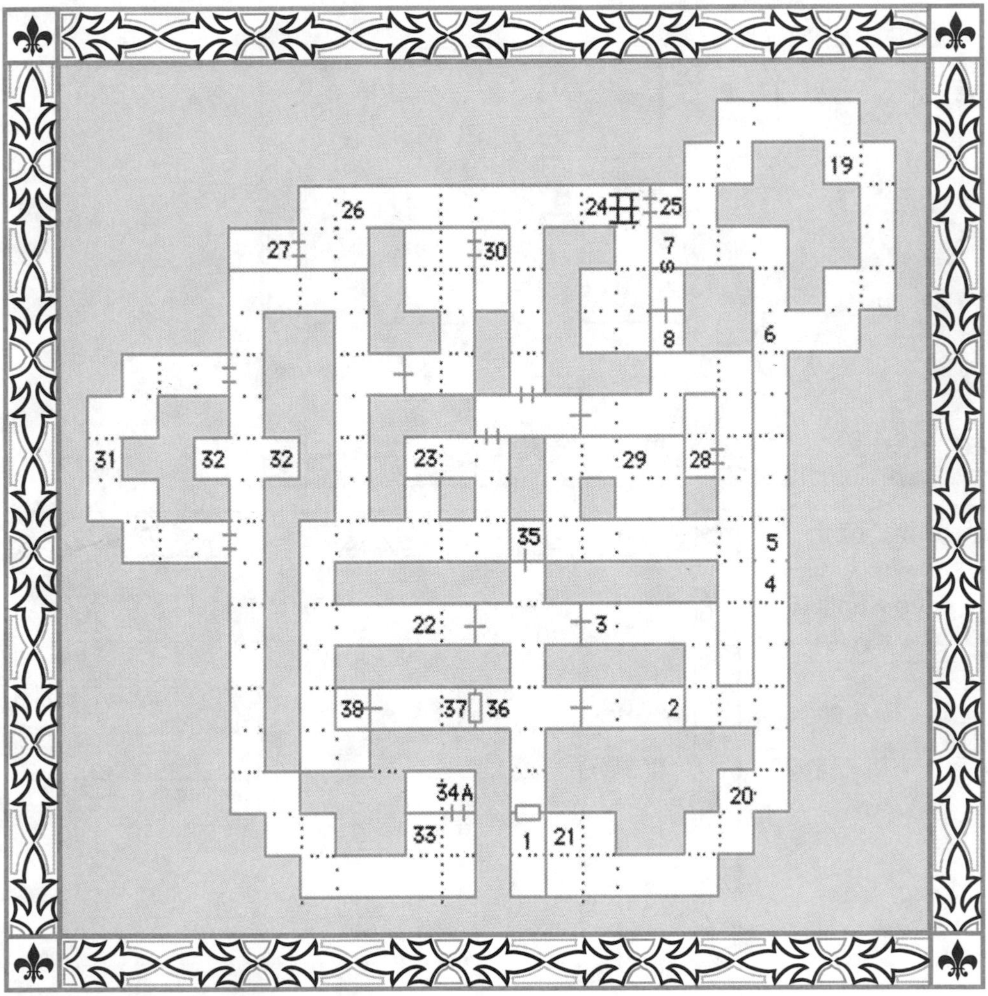

Map 12.1 Tower of the Shadowking (Main Floor)

Locked Door
Door
Illusionary Wall

Map 12.2 Lair of the Dark Dwarves (Basement)

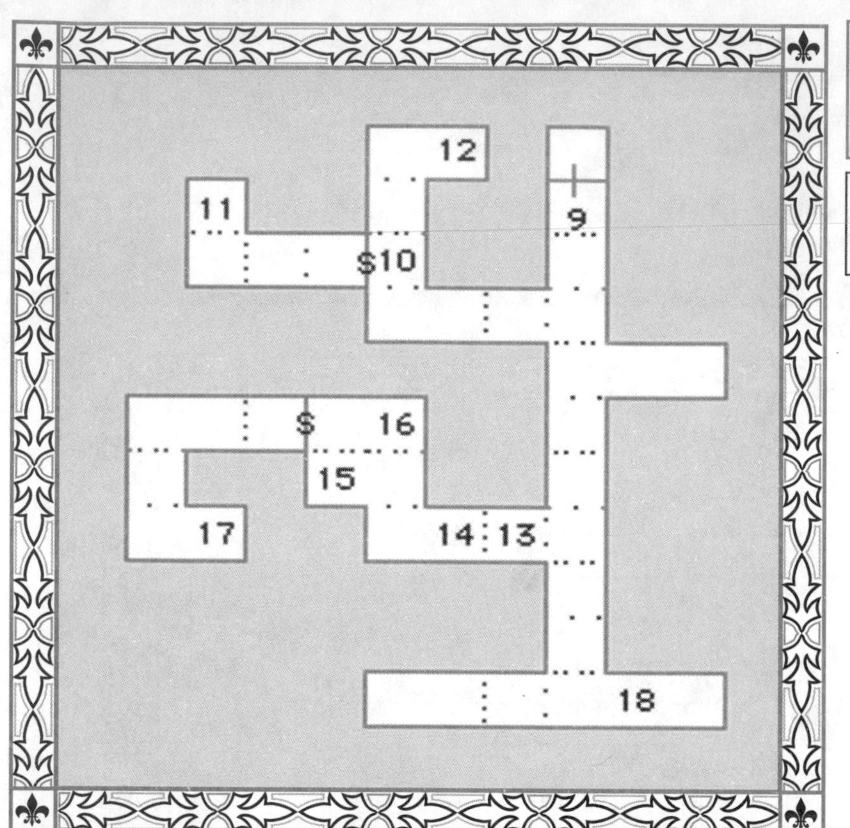

Map 12.3 Tower of the Shadowking (Second Floor)

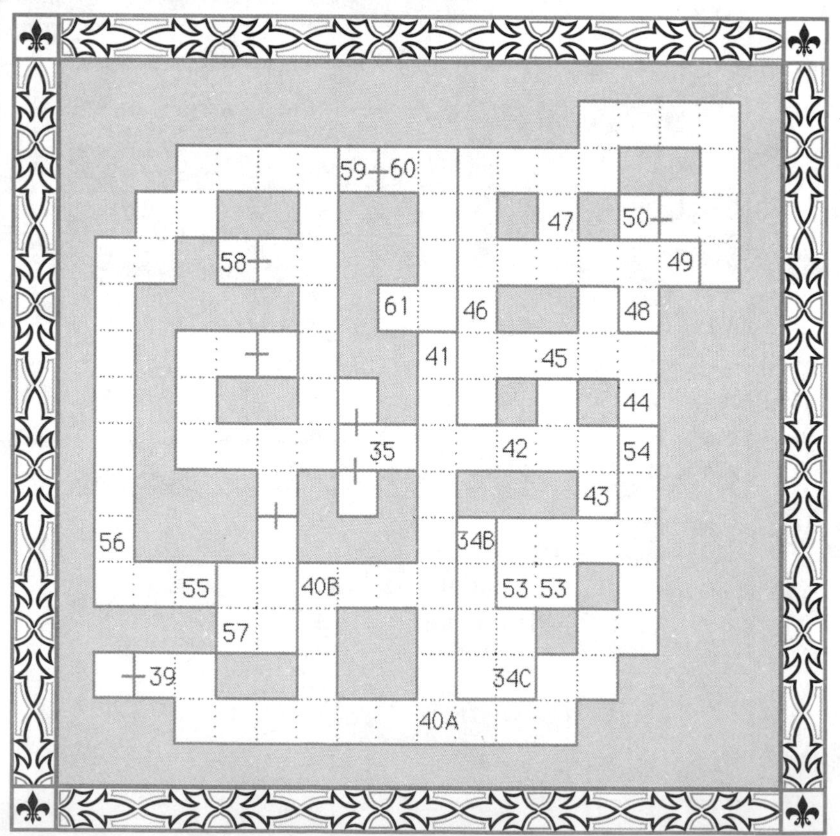

Map 12.4 Tower of the Shadowking (Third Floor)

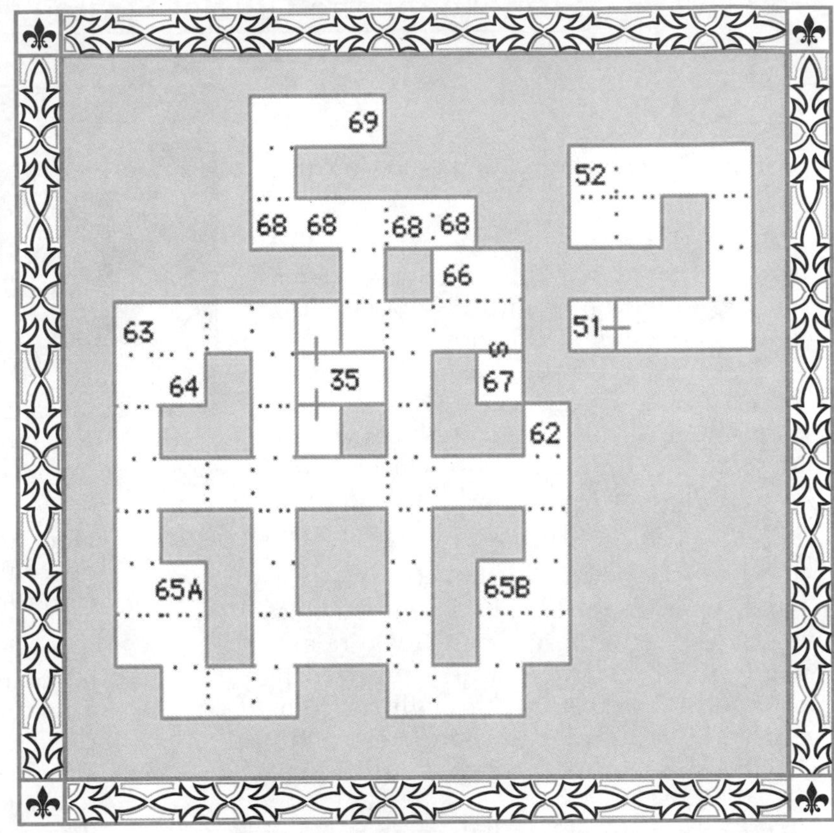

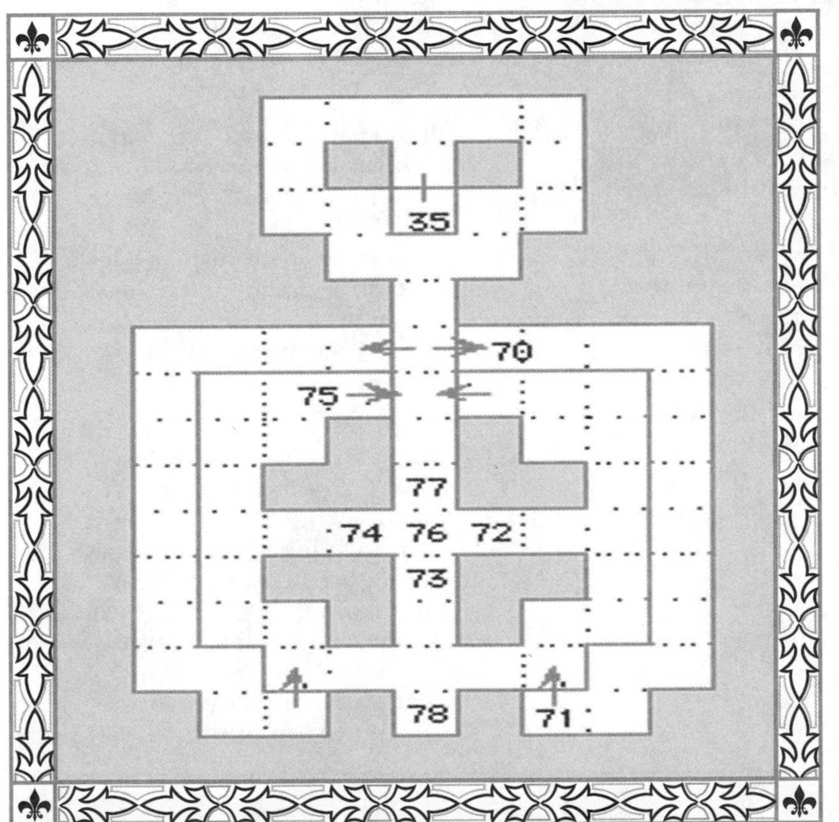

Map 12.5 Tower of the Shadowking (Top Floor)

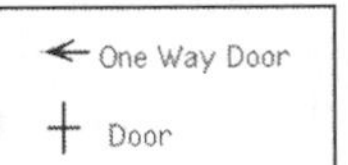

1. Start

The ***gatekeeper*** gargoyle appears on the door. He says:

Gargoyle: I am the gatekeeper of the Tower of Shadows. His Majesty welcomes all who would enter into his domain. Do you wish to enter the shadows?

Drake: What do you mean?

Gargoyle: (repeats) I am the gatekeeper of the Tower of Shadows. His Majesty welcomes all who would enter into his domain. Do you wish to enter the shadows?

Note the two ***buttons*** below the gatekeeper gargoyle. The green triangle is YES, the red square is NO. If you're not ready to enter the Tower, simply turn around and step south through the four entryposts. You will transport back to the Palace of Shadows through the doors at 60 on Map 11.

Of course, in this walkthrough you *are* ready to enter the Tower—you have all seven available orbs (Helion, Aquila, Azrael, Marif, Afri, Safrinni, Yoth-soggoth), and you are one buff adventurer. But the gatekeeper's question is a trick—who actually would *wish* to enter the shadows?

Push NO (the red square). The gatekeeper gargoyle says, "You have left your foolishness behind. Have you *need* to enter?"

Now push YES (the green triangle). The gatekeeper gargoyle says, "The time has come. The prophecy will be fulfilled and your fate written. As keeper of shadows, it's my fate to tell you that the silver light can keep the shadows at bay. Forgive me, Master!"

In case you didn't guess, this is a clue.

Gatekeeper Gargoyle. Nice guy, but somebody please give him a throat lozenge.

Note Here are the other possible outcomes in your encounter with the gatekeeper gargoyle:

- If you do not have all seven orbs found in the earlier levels, the gatekeeper says: "You are a fool to come here without that which his Majesty seeks. Go and do not return without all the orbs." Retrace your steps back through Stonekeep to find any missing orbs. (Hey, there's only a few thousand places to look.)
- If you have all seven orbs and push YES, the gatekeeper says, "Welcome, fool. You have served the Master well. Go quickly up the stairs. Do not turn from the main passage or you will be destroyed! He waits in his hall at the top of the Tower." The gatekeeper laughs maliciously, then fades, and the door opens.

This is a trick. If you take this route, you'll probably lose the game. You shouldn't face the Shadowking until you're ready to outwit him. It is very, very difficult (though not impossible) to go straight up to his hall and defeat him in combat. Also, Wahooka abandons the party before you reach the top of the Tower.

After the gatekeeper gargoyle disappears, go north to the first door on the right.

Caution Don't try the first door on the left yet! It's a trap, and will zap you with 10–20 points of electrical damage.

2. Puzzle Room

Enter the room and take a step east. Wahooka says, "Magick bars your way, magick is the key to the solution. (pause) Bah, the solution is simple. Can you not see it?" Turn right to face the south wall. Open the ***panel*** to reveal the strange ***puzzle***.

Tower Puzzle. No dark tower worth its salt would be without a hidden puzzle bearing indecipherable markings.

You can mess around with it if you want—it resets every time you close the panel. But the solution is—no, that's too easy, even for a strategy guide. Let's look around first, shall we? Maybe we can find some clues.

3. Floating Spikers

When you step through the door, a flight of ***floating spikers*** attacks from the east. Use a good piercing weapon on these odd exploding creatures, then follow the passage to the intersection. Turn left and head north.

Ugly Little Spikers, Aren't They? And deadly, too. Use a good piercing weapon, and leap back after each hit because they explode in your face.

4. Enigmatic Warning

When you reach this square, Enigma suddenly says, "Stop!" and fires an arrow up the corridor. (If Enigma is *not* in your party, Farli voices his concern about this area—see the next step.) Continue north.

5. Fire Trap

If Enigma is not in your party, your party suffers significant damage from a ***magickal fire trap*** when they step into this square. The trap is triggered by a traitorous Dwarf just up the hall. (See 6 below.)

6. Dwarf-On-a-Stick

A ***dead Dwarf*** lies in this square with Enigma's arrow in his back. The ***handle*** on the wall activates the fire trap back at 5. At first, Farli is upset with Enigma:

Farli: You have slain one of my brethren, dark one! For that, you will pay!

Drake: Why have you done this?

Farli: Speak, or your supposed quest for vengeance ends here!

Enigma: He was acting strangely. Look around first before you accuse me.

Now take a step closer to the Dwarf and wall handle. Upon closer examination, your party understands Enigma's action:

Farli: Hmmm, this lever connects to a trap mechanism to the south. How could you know this?

Enigma: My eyes see far more than you will ever know, Dwarf.

Farli: What is that supposed to mean?

Drake: Leave him be, Farli. Let us stop bickering and get on with this.

Search the dwarf body to find four ***oil bombs***, a ***Dwarven ax*** and a ***piece of metal*** that resembles a crowbar. (Oddly, it is given no name in your journal's inventory list.) Go north to the corner, then head west to the end of the hall.

7. Farli's Keen Dwarven Senses

When you step into this square, Farli says, "There is something odd about one of these walls. Hmm. There are hidden mechanisms of Dwarven construct, from the look of them." If you got the piece of metal at 6, he adds, "I could use this piece of metal to make it function"—then he does, revealing a ***secret door*** to the south.

Note

If Enigma is not in the party, and the Dwarf at 6 did not get an Elven arrow in the back, then he runs to the secret door, opens it . . . and leaves it open!

8. Stairs to the Lair of the Dark Dwarves

Go through this door and take the stairs down to the basement of the Tower of the Shadowking.

9. Stairs from Lair to Main Floor (Map 12.2)

Here's the bottom of the stairs that connect the Tower's main floor with the basement. From the bottom of the stairs, go 2S, 3W, N, then turn right to face the east wall.

10. Secret Button

Push the ***button*** on the wall to open the ***secret door*** directly behind you. Go through the door and follow the passage. Don't miss that ***black slayer arrow*** on the way.

11. Mana Circle

Recharge in the ***Mana Circle***, heal up your party, recharge again, then return to the corridor. Turn left and follow the passage to the end.

12. Dark Water

Well, well, ***well***. You still have your bucket, don't you? Fill it with water, then turn and follow the passage back around to the main corridor and head south past the bone piles to the busy Dwarf.

Tip

Move quietly down this hall. Don't smash bone piles. You can sneak up on the Dwarf this way.

13. Dark Dwarf

This hostile ***Dwarf*** picks over the remains of some dead thing or other. If you attack or step past him, he attacks—and grunts like a wild animal! As Farli says, "What evil magick!" There's only one way to dispel such powerful evil magick: Cast a potent Spoilspell × 3 at him—that is, a Spoilspell rune enhanced with both the Power × 3 and Potency meta runes.

Note

You can also fight all the possessed Dwarves, but isn't rehabilitation always more humane?

The dis-enchanted Dwarf retreats down the passage into the Dwarven lair. Follow him a couple of steps, then turn left to face the south wall.

14. Secret Button

Push the ***button*** on the south wall to open a ***secret room*** in the lair just around the corner. Take a step west.

15. Secret Shrine of the Dark Dwarves

An entire platoon of dark, hostile ***Dwarves*** encamps there. They attack as soon as you enter. Ignore them if you can and focus your weapon's attack on the ***shrine to Khull-khuum*** in the southwest corner of the room.

Tip

You need to lure the hostile Dwarves away from the shrine before you can break it. (They block your path to the shrine if you rush into the lair, forcing you to kill them all.) The best way is to retreat back to 13 and wait for the Dwarves to follow. When all three bad ones reach you, spin 180 degrees, back away from them quickly, then run to the shrine.

Attack the top of the shrine with a good weapon. When you knock off the top, it frees the Dwarves from the evil spell of the Shadowking, and they stop fighting.

Shrine of Khull-khuum. This thing has driven the Dwarves to darkness. Knock off its block to free them.

16. Pattern Scroll

When combat ends, go to the ***Dwarf*** standing in the northeast corner of the lair. He says:

Freed Dwarf: Thank you, Great Master. I have been in the thrall of magick for long time.

Farli: What did he say?

Freed Dwarf: The Evil One gave us food to kill. I made many traps. Don't touch the door!

Drake: Did he say there's a trap on the door?

Freed Dwarf: Yes! There button in wall across passage behind door. Push dem. This da pattern.

The cured Dwarf hands you a ***scroll.*** Take it and look at it:

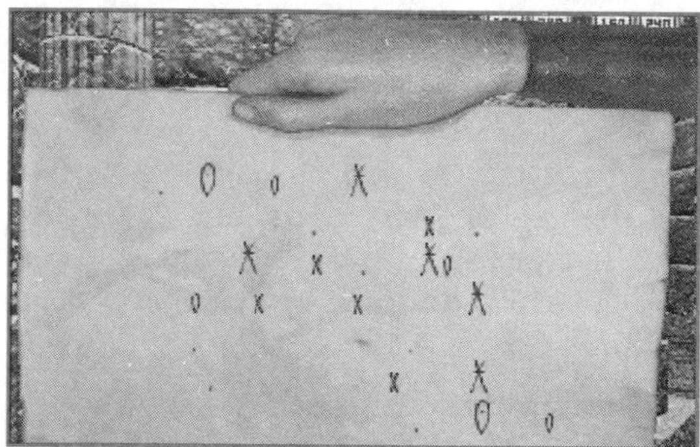

Puzzle Pattern Scroll

Be sure to either jot down the pattern or keep the scroll in your inventory. The pattern is the solution to the puzzle back on the first floor of the Tower (at 2 on Map 12.1).

Freed Dwarf: There more but I forgot.

Drake: Thank you. Do you need help getting out of here?

Freed Dwarf: I'm afraid Evil One come kill me. I hide from him now.

Drake: No! Come with us, we will protect you from his power.

Freed Dwarf: Ahhhhh! No no no no no no no! (runs away)

Punch out the ***bone pile*** to get a ***heal root***, and the ***rubble pile*** to get another ***Dagger of Penetration***.

17. Backup Scroll

If you follow the freed Dwarf down the secret passage, you come to another ***scroll*** with the same puzzle pattern—placed here just in case you missed the first one.

Note You'll notice that the end of the passage is the bottom of a pit. But you can't levitate up this pit.

Go back past 13 into the corridor and turn right. Go south to the intersection and turn left.

18. Meat Prize

Whack at the ***carcass*** in the hall to reveal another ***black slayer arrow***. Now go back to the Mana Circle at 11, recharge, cure your party, recharge again, then go back to 9 and climb the stairs.

You are now back on the first floor of the Tower (Map 12.1). From the doorway, take a step north, a step east, then turn left follow the passage to the north.

19. Dusty Sign

Look at the ***sign*** on the wall. Drake says, "It's covered with dust!" Enigma explains that it is the Dust of Zandi. Touching it

causes serious damage to Drake. Instead, use the bucket of water (or any potion) to wash off the dust, then read it. You don't need the Language rune—after a little prodding, Wahooka reads it: "And thus was balance restored in the end."

Continue around the passage until you return to the dead Dwarf at 6. Equip Drake with a runecaster in one hand, inscribe the Shield rune onto it, then enhance the Shield rune with the Power × 3 and Ball meta runes. Put a good cutting weapon in the other hand—for example, a shadow-ax or shadow-sword.

Go due south, following the passage until you hear something approach.

20. Fire Elementals

Those approaching creatures are ***fire elementals.*** Use the enhanced Shield rune on any member of the party. (The Ball meta rune spreads the powerful protective spell over the entire party.) This should make your party invulnerable to the deadly firebolts fired at you by the elementals. Cut the flaming freaks to pieces with your cutting weapon.

Don't Get Burned. Fire elementals will toast you pretty fast if you don't protect yourself with an enhanced Shield rune.

Continue down the corridor.

21. Bonus Potion

Grab the ***life restore potion*** in the corner.

Now go back to 2 and open the wall panel to reveal the puzzle. Remember the pattern scrolls from 16 and 17? Each had the same simple 4-by-4 pattern:

O	O	X	X
X	X	X	O
O	X	X	X
X	X	O	O

Enter the code by pressing the tiles of the puzzle—each 'O' indicates that you should press the corresponding tile on the puzzle. When you enter the correct pattern, you disable the electrical trap on the door directly across the hall at 36. As you can tell by the numbering, we won't go there just yet. Instead, exit the puzzle room, take two steps north, then turn left and go through the door.

22. More Spikers

Another gaggle of ***floating spikers*** attacks when you step through the door. Pierce them and continue west to the intersection. From there, go 2N, 5E, 2N, then west to the sign.

23. Another Dusty Sign

Wash the dust of Zandi from the ***sign*** with a potion or bucket of water. Wahooka reluctantly reads it: "In the beginning, there was darkness and light." Not real informative, but there you are.

Go two squares east, then step through the ***illusory wall*** to the north. Take one step east, then turn left and go north through another ***illusory wall.*** Continue north to the intersection, then turn right and go east to the portcullis.

Caution If you turn left and go west instead, you run into a large and very deadly floating spiker. Better to go east, where you can set up a trap for the killer creature.

24. Wall Button

Push the ***button*** on the north wall to open the ***portcullis***. Step quickly through it.

25. Hidden Spiker

Kill the sneaky, tough ***floating spiker*** that slips through the ***illusory wall*** to the east. You won't find anything in the rooms to the east or south. Turn west and move down the passage.

26. King Spiker Trap

Lurking down the hall is a huge, nearly invincible ***floating spiker***. You don't want to engage this fellow in combat—he can kill each member of your party with just a single powerful thrust. Instead, take the following steps:

- Run away! Run away! Hurry east through the portcullis at 24, then south into the room. (The spiker will follow.)
- Go down to the southeast corner of the room and face the spiker approaching from the north.
- When he reaches you, spin around to face south. (The spiker spins with you.)
- Back up to the wall, then turn right, hustle a step west to 24 and push the portcullis button on the north wall.

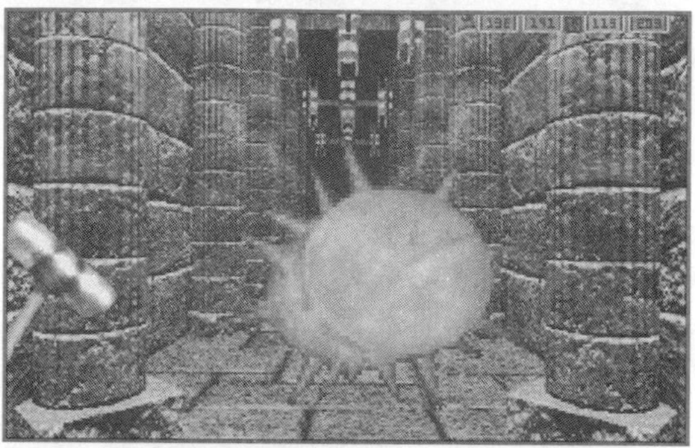

Long Live the King. Hammer him all you want—you just can't kill him without suffering big losses. So trap him instead.

The portcullis closes, trapping the big spiker behind it. Or not. If the beast gets out before the gate closes, you'll have to run west, then run back and repeat the process.

27. The Silver Ankh

Grab the ***silver ankh*** from the floor.

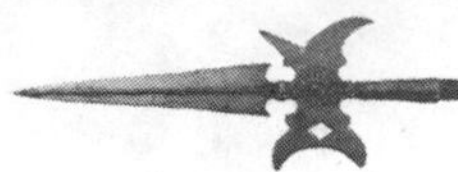

At this point, you have everything you need from this floor of the Tower. You can skip ahead to 36, if you want to. Most of you won't, I'll wager, so let's continue our exploration of the area.

28. Spiker Surprise

Another ***floating spiker*** pops through the ***illusory wall*** here in a surprise attack. Destroy it and continue exploring down the corridor.

29. Fiery Waste of Time

Two more ***fire elementals*** try to barbecue your party in this room. If you extinguish the pests, all you get is an experience boost—the room is empty.

30. Another Spiker Surprise

Another ***floating spiker*** waits to ambush you through the ***illusory wall*** here. This time, however, you find a reward in the hidden room—a ***life restore potion***.

31. Power Source

Open the ***hidden panel*** in the west wall to reveal a ***Power × 3 meta rune*** inscribed in the wall. If you don't have this powerful rune, it's inscribed in your journal. If you already have the rune, erase it now with a bucket of water or potion. This weakens the pair of skull guards patrolling the hallway outside (see 32).

32. Twin Hollow Heads

A pair of ***floating skulls*** loiter in these opposing alcoves. If you erased the rune at 31, they're much easier to defeat. Continue south down the corridor.

33. Elemental Squadron

Be sure the Shield rune is active on your party—a trio of ***fire elementals*** waits for you here. Chop them to sparks and step through the ***illusory wall*** to the north.

You can't follow steps 34 A–C yet, nor will we return to them later in this walkthrough. However, they do lead you to a valuable object that might be useful if you run low on Mana later.

34A. Teleport to 34B

See that flashing cross icon on the north wall? If you happen to have a silver cross, you can step through this wall and teleport to 34B on Map 12.3.

Cross Portal. If you have a silver cross, you can step through this wall and teleport to a Mana source.

34B. Teleport to 34A

This north wall is a ***teleport*** linked to 34A. When you arrive here, go south into the 2-by-2 room.

34C. Half-Orb

That gorgeous green glow on the east wall is another ***half-orb***. Touch each of your runecasters to this powerful source of magick for a complete Mana recharge.

35. Stairs to Second Floor

Forget it. Don't take these ***stairs*** unless you're ready to face an immortal god in combat. This enclosed central stairwell has three flights of stairs that lead directly to the Tower's top floor—the hall of the Shadowking.

36. Door Trap

If you try to open this door before solving the puzzle at 2, your party receives an ugly electrical jolt. Since you've solved that puzzle, the trap is disarmed and the door opens easily. Step into the room.

37. Stair Guardian

A ***floating skull*** guards this passage. Whack him out of the way, then step forward.

38. Stairs to Second Floor

Climb these stairs (rather than those at 35) to the next floor of the Tower.

39. Stairs to the First Floor

This stairway leads back down to the first floor. You're now on Map 12.3.

> **Tip** Be prepared to fight a lot of fire elementals on this floor. Keep your Shield rune (enhanced by the Power × 3 meta rune) active. Without it, elementals toast you quickly. Remember that cutting weapons, such as the shadow-ax or shadow-sword, work best against these fiery creatures.

Head east to the second left turn. (Skip the first one, unless you want an unnecessary fight.)

40A & 40B. Flame-Broiled Fun

Meet the first of many ***fire elementals*** on this level. (Your Shield rune *is* active, isn't it?) Put him out and head north. Another ***fire elemental*** lurks around that first turn to the left—if your Power × 3 Shield rune is up, you smash it easily. Continue north to the first right turn.

41. Another Flamer

You went too far north, didn't you? When you reach the end of this corridor, another ***fire elemental*** flames into existence. (You were supposed to take the first right turn, remember?)

42. Something Wick-Head This Way Comes

Yes, another ***fire elemental***. Strange beings, aren't they? Their personal life must be hell. But enough conjecture. Kill it. Head around that corner.

43. Teleport Connection to 44

Stepping into this ***teleport*** zaps you to 44. (That's why the scroll suddenly appears on the floor.) If you step into 44, you arrive back here.

44. Teleport Connection to 43

When you arrive at this teleport from 43, take a step back and grab the ***scroll*** on the floor. Read it—it's one of those inside jokes from the *Stonekeep* design team that means nothing to you but everything to them. (Humor the fellows, OK?)

Note Step into this square if you want to teleport back to 43.

Check your Power × 3 Shield rune protection, then head west and prepare for battle.

45. That Old Familiar Glow

This ***fire elemental*** wants to give you lessons in the ancient art of spontaneous combustion. Hack him to embers and proceed west to the wall. Turn right, but *take only one step north*—stop at 46!

46. Stop Here

See those ***energybolts*** slamming into the wall just ahead? An invisible energy source down the hall (see 49) fires these bolts at regular intervals. If one hits you, it can cause up to 100 points of damage—so let's avoid it, shall we?

That Wall Could Be You. Something's spitting deadly energybolts down the hall, so take a smart route east.

Wait until the next bolt explodes against the wall, then run straight north to the wall. Go two steps east, then take a single step south and stop.

47. Stop Here, 2

Wait here until you see another bolt fly past in the hall, then move quickly—one step south, two steps east—then duck into the alcove on the right.

48. The Silver Crescent

Wait until you hear another energybolt fly past, take a step back, grab the ***silver crescent*** from the ground, then step back forward into the alcove (to avoid getting blasted).

Get ready. Immediately after another bolt fires, rush out and retrace your route back up to 47.

49. Energybolt Cannon

An invisible ***energy source*** in the east wall fires energybolts down the hall toward the west. (See steps 46–48.)

You can skip 50–52 if you want; you gain no essential items or knowledge from those steps. Also, be aware that step 53 features only unnecessary combat. So if you're feeling impatient, skip ahead to 54.

50. Stairs to Third Floor (Limited Area)

From 47, take a step north, turn right and follow the passage around to the ***doors*** on the right. As your companions will tell you, these doors are locked by a powerful magick spell. To unlock them, zap the door with a potent, triple-strength Spoilspell—that is, a Spoilspell enhanced by the Potency and Power × 3 meta runes.

Open the doors and take the ***stairs*** up to the third floor (see Map 12.4).

51. Stairs to Second Floor

These stairs lead back down to the second floor. When you arrive here from 50, follow the short passage around to the 2-by-2 room.

52. Voice from Beyond

Lots of trapped folks met their fate here. Find the ***scroll*** amongst the bones, then read it:

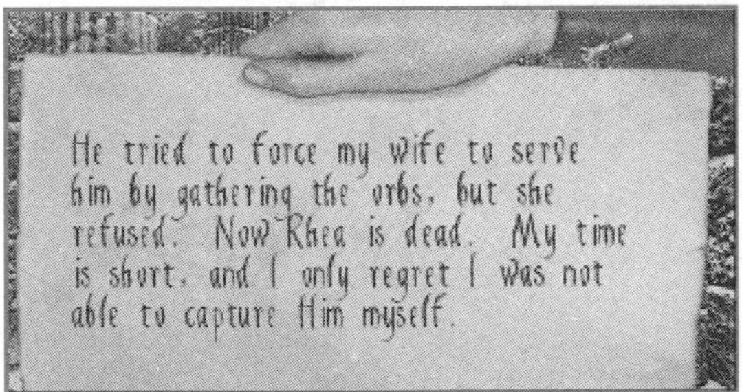

Take the stairs at 52 back down to 51. Return to the teleport at 44 and zap back to 43. Work your way back down south to 40, then head east and follow the passage.

53. Fire Fellows

Avoid this room unless you like fire fights. Two ***fire elementals*** are posted here, but you'll find nothing else of value.

54. Ankh Teleport to 55

Did you see the ankh icon flash on the north wall? This is the ***ankh teleport*** square, but of course you need a silver ankh to use it. Wait a minute . . . you *have* a silver ankh. OK, step through the wall and zap to the other ankh teleport square at 55.

55. Ankh Teleport to 54

This ***ankh teleport*** connects to 54. After you arrive, be sure your Power × 3 Shield rune is active, then follow the passage.

Note

You can step into 55 and return to 54 as long as you have the silver ankh.

56. Mini-Hell

Four ***fire elementals*** block your passage north. Ax them to charcoal, then continue around the passage past the first door on the right. Keep going south to the next door.

57. Silver Cross

Enter this room and grab the ***silver cross*** in the southwest corner. Exit and head north to the first doorway on the left (the one you passed on the way down).

58. Teleport Connection to 59

This is a ***teleport***. When you open the doors and step into the square, you zap to 59.

59. Teleport Connection to 58

Another ***teleport***. When you arrive here from 58, listen— something waits for you on the other side of the doors.

Note If you step on this teleport square, you zap to 58.

60. Fired Again

Destroy the ***fire elemental*** that waits in the hall. Proceed to the end of the corridor.

61. Crescent Teleport to 62

Face the south wall to see a crescent flash. This is a ***teleport*** to 62 (on Map 12.4) up on the third floor of the Tower. If you have the silver crescent (and, by golly, you *do*), step through the south wall.

62. Crescent Teleport to 61

You arrive on the third floor from 61. You're now on Map 12.4. Once again, check your Power × 3 Shield rune protection—many fire elementals roam the corridors.

Take one step south, head west to the wall, then north to the corner.

63. Silver Circle

Quickly, grab the ***silver circle*** in the corner, then spin around to face an enemy attack from the south.

64. Elemental Guardian

A ***fire elemental*** appears here when you step into an adjacent square. After you dispatch it, go 3E, 3S, 3E, 3N, E, then N.

You can avoid squares 65A and 65B—in fact, you can avoid the entire southern half of the third floor—unless you're keen for combat.

65A & 65B. Tough Elementals

One ***fire elemental*** is posted at each of these positions. The one at 65B is particularly tough. Remember your Shield rune protection before you wade into these brush fires.

66. Secret Button

Push the ***button*** on the west wall to open the secret room to the southeast.

67. Dirty Trick

Surprise! Nothing. An empty room. Back out and go due west to the corner, then head north into some heavy combat.

68. Final Fireline

Four ***fire elementals*** line this short hallway. Whack them to cinders, then follow the passage around the corner.

69. Silver Item Teleport

When you reach the end of the passage, icons of all four silver items flash on the east wall. This is a ***teleport***. If you have the silver crescent, silver circle, silver ankh, and silver cross, you can step into the east wall and zap to 70 at the top of the Tower (see Map 12.5)—the hall of the Shadowking himself.

Silver Portal. If you have all four silver items—ankh, cross, crescent, circle—you can step through this portal into the hall of Khull-khuum.

Note You cannot use the Teleport rune in the hall of the Shadowking. If you want to teleport away for any reason, you must first go down to a lower level of the Tower.

70. Silver Item Teleport to 69

You are now in the final map of *Stonekeep*, Map 12.5. If you have all four silver items, you can use this ***teleport*** to return to 69. When you arrive from 69, go 3E, then follow the corridor south to the end of the passage.

71. One-Way Door

Step through the north wall—it's a ***one-way door*** to the inner sanctum of Khull-khuum. (Don't worry, there are ways out.) From the other side, go N, E, 2N, then turn west. Take a step forward. Enigma says, "This room must be part of the ritual to capture the gods. This is where Khull-khuum caused the death of my race."

72. Silver Ritual: Pillar 1

Carefully now . . . take another step forward. See the four ***sunken pillars*** on the ground? See the square at the center? *Don't step into the center square!*

Stop Here! If you step over any sunken pillar into the center square, the Shadowking appears. That would be a bad thing.

Place any of the four silver items—ankh, cross, circle, crescent—on top of the sunken pillar. Watch the pillar rise up, then go 2E, 2S, W, S, 2W, and—again, *carefully*—take two steps north.

73. Silver Ritual: Pillar 2

Place one of your remaining silver items on top of the ***sunken pillar*** in this square. Watch the pillar rise, then go 2S, 2W, N, W, 2N, and take two careful steps east.

74. Silver Ritual: Pillar 3

Place one of your remaining silver items on top of the ***sunken pillar*** in this square. Watch the pillar rise, then go 2W, 3N, and turn east.

75. One-Way Door

Step through the east wall—it's a ***one-way door***. Turn left, then take a deep breath . . . and go south into the center square.

76. Encounter with Khull-Khuum

When you step into this square, the ***Shadowking*** himself appears with the two remaining orbs, ***Thera's Orb*** and ***Korsoggoth's Orb***, on either side of him. Then he launches into the following monologue:

> Shadowking: *Welcome. You have come to my tower. You can fulfill the prophecy and hand the orbs over to me. (laughs) Quickly now! Grasp the orbs of your own free will and your service to me will be complete. (beat) Do you think I do not know of your pathetic plans? Without all of the orbs you will not be able to pass the gate to her temple . . . but as soon as you have the orbs, you will be mine!*

Trapping the Shadowking. Place a silver item on three of the four pillars without stepping in the center square. Then step in and summon Khull-khuum for the final confrontation.

Pick up both orbs.

The Shadowking tries to cast a spell on Drake, but it has no effect, and Khull-khuum shouts, "What! What treachery is this? Kor-soggoth has granted you resistance to my spell. He will pay for that, but his pain will be nothing compared to yours if you do not give me the orbs! Hurry, I grow impatient. Give them to me now, or live in eternal darkness!"

Caution Don't give any orbs to the Shadowking, or you're dead meat! Don't strike at him, either—he goes directly into combat mode, and your finely crafted trap is wasted.

77. Final Step

OK, here we go. *Quickly* now, take the following steps:

- Back up one square.
- *Immediately* open your inventory.
- Place the last silver item on the last sunken pillar.
- Watch the show!

You did it, man. You beat the Shadowking. You can grab his black orb, or not. Doesn't matter. Go straight south.

Note There are actually three ways to defeat the Shadowking, but two of them are very, very difficult. The way outlined in this walkthrough—outwit and trap the Shadowking—is the easiest. However you can try to defeat him in combat. Of course, he is a *god*. He blasts you with ranged magickal attacks, magickally cancels all of *your* spells (armor, shield—*goodbye*). He teleports, casts blackness spells that blind you. He can take 1500 hit points. His armor is better than anything you've ever seen. If he lands only two or three direct hits, game over. Still want to give it a try?

The other possible winning strategy is only a little bit easier. Grab both orbs in your encounter at 76, then run like a bunny. If you have all nine of the orbs, but haven't completed the silver ritual, Thera's gate at 78 alternately opens and closes—open for five seconds, closed for 95 seconds. So if you time it right, you can slip through the gate before the Shadowking pulps you and your party. Unfortunately, you can't actually see if the gate is open or not, and it's very easy to get trapped by Khull-khuum if you hang out in the alcove at 78.

78. Gate to Thera's Temple

Approach the flashing silver icons on the south wall. Step through the wall. Your companions take leave, and you are transported to the sanctuary of Thera's Temple.

Free the Gods. Place each orb on a glowing pillar in the order of the planets as shown below—Helion, Aquila, Thera, Azrael, Marif, Afri, Safrinni, then finally (in either order) Yoth-soggoth and Kor-soggoth.

Endgame: Placing the Orbs

Place the orbs on the ***pillars*** in the order of the planets according to their distance from the sun, from closest to farthest. The glowing pillar marks the spot for each succeeding placement.

Tip If you don't know the order of the planets in the solar system, or can't figure out the correlation between the orbs in *Stonekeep* and the planets, here is the correct order: Helion (Mercury), Aquila (Venus), Thera (Earth), Azrael (Mars), Marif (Jupiter), Afri (Saturn), Safrinni (Uranus). The last two, Yoth-soggoth (Neptune) and Kor-soggoth (Pluto), can be placed in either order, because these two planets cross orbits and take turns being closer to the sun.

Congratulations! You've just beaten one killer game. And speaking of killer stuff, don't miss the chocolate-chip pumpkin muffin recipe in the final credits . . . or the final Faerie comments after the credits finish.

Appendix A
Monster Combat Stats

Stonekeep monsters come in all varieties and strengths. Some are vulnerable to fire, others are fireproof. Some are easily pierced, others must be crushed. Some drain your vitality with a single blow, others barely scratch you. Use this table to determine the overall attack strength of various monsters, and to learn their particular vulnerabilities.

Keep in mind that while all creatures in a particular category—all "Tough Shargas," for example—share the same stats, individual members of that category may exhibit some very distinct behavior and/or combat tactics. One Sharga runs, one flings rocks, another shouts, "Get him, boys!" and attacks with wild abandon. Still others won't attack at all, unless provoked. Some even throw down their weapons and grovel.

Note "Monster" is a generic term often used by game designers and roleplaying game enthusiasts to denote any creature that you encounter and/or fight during the course of your adventure. Some of the creatures listed (such as Faeries, for example) clearly are not "monsters" in the horror-movie sense of the word.

Definition of Table Categories

The table categories might be confusing, so let me define each one.

Max Hit Pts. Every time you strike a blow that penetrates a monster's armor (see Strong/Weak Armor on next page), *Stonekeep*'s combat system subtracts hit points from the monster's total. When the number reaches zero, the monster is dead.

Skill. This value determines the accuracy of the monster's attacks. The higher the value, the more frequently the monster hits you.

Damage Range. These values represent the minimum/maximum damage (in hit points) inflicted by each blow the monster lands on its target. Know that these values get plugged into complex damage equations that hurt your eyes and make your brain itch.

Dmg Distribution (Crush/Cut/Pierce). Whenever the monster lands a blow, the hit point damage is distributed in percentages among three different types of damage—Crush, Cut, and Pierce. A 50-50-00 value simply means that half the damage of the monster's blow crushed its target, the other half cut its target, and none pierced its target.

Mag Dmg Modifier (Mgk/Fire/Cold/Elec). Check this important stat whenever you meet a new type of monster. The Magick Damage Modifiers determine how the four different types of magick affect a monster. (The percentages are probably self-explanatory, but I've included a small table below anyway.) The higher the number, the more damage that type of magick inflicts on the monster. For example, a Tough Ant has a Fire modifier of 200, which means it suffers *twice* the normal damage from fire spells. That's a very good thing to know, isn't it?

Mgk refers to pure magickal attack spells, such as Vampyre or Energybolt. *Fire* refers to fire magick—Firebolt, Flame, Circleward. *Cold* means damage from Icebolt. *Elec* refers to electrical spells—Tornado, for example.

Magick Damage Modifiers

0 = no damage
50 = 1/2 damage
100 = normal damage
150 = 1 1/2x damage
200 = 2x damage

Damage Type. This simply indicates whether the monster inflicts Normal damage—i.e., Crush, Cut, and Pierce—or one of these four types of Magickal damage.

Strong/Weak Armor (Cut/Crush/Pierce). This may be the most important stat in the table. These numbers represent the monster's armor protection (measured in hit points) against each type of damage your weapons can inflict—Cut, Crush, and Pierce. Note that the monster's armor strength can differ *vastly* between damage types. A fire elemental's armor, for example, will stop 100 points of both crush damage and pierce damage, but only 15 points of cut damage.

Thus, these armor values help you determine which weapon to use against each type of monster. Against a fire elemental, use a good sword or ax, since both usually inflict severe cut damage. Once you determine which type of damage most hurts a particular type of monster, go to the Weapons Table in Appendix B to find a weapon that inflicts that type of damage.

Also note: Monsters have strong and weak armor areas, which you see reflected in the two sets of table values. In general, armor is weaker around the monster's face, legs, and arms.

Monster Combat Stats

Monster	Max Hit Pts	Skill	Damage Range	Dmg Distribution (Crush/Cut/Pierce)	Mag Dmg Modifier (Mgk/Fire/Cold/Elec)	Damage Type	Strong/Weak Armor (Cut/Crush/Pierce)	
Ant	14	1	1-6	40-60-00	100-200-50-100	Normal	2-1-1	1-0-0
Tough Ant	24	2	3-12	50-50-00	100-200-100-100	Normal	3-2-1	2-1-0
Fungi	25	6	10-40	100-00-00	00-50-50-50-50	Normal	8-30-10	8-30-10
Dwarf Elder	160	9	20-36	00-100-00	50-00-50-100	Normal	15-12-9	10-7-4
Dwarf Grak	200	6	25-35	00-00-100	100-100-100-100	Normal	15-12-9	10-7-4
Dwarf guard	100	7	15-28	00-100-00	50-00-50-100	Normal	12-9-6	10-7-4
Dwarf Seldin	120	8	35-50	100-00-00	50-00-50-100	Normal	15-12-9	10-7-4
Dwarf Torin	200	9	30-70	00-100-00	50-00-50-100	Normal	18-15-12	13-10-7
Ettin	300	5	10-50	100-00-00	100-100-100-100	Normal	4-2-1	1-1-1
Faerie, Female	100	1	0	100-00-00	100-100-100-100	Normal	1-1-1	1-1-1
Faerie, Glow	100	1	0	100-00-00	100-100-100-100	Normal	1-1-1	1-1-1
Faerie, Male	100	1	0	100-00-00	100-100-100-100	Normal	1-1-1	1-1-1
Faerie Queen	1000	1	0	100-00-00	100-100-100-100	Normal	1-1-1	1-1-1
Fire Elemental	75	10	30-60	00-100-00	100-00-50-50	Fire	15-100-100	15-100-100
Fire Elemental, Tough	100	12	40-80	00-100-00	50-00-50-00	Fire	30-100-100	30-100-100
Floating skull	60	7	30-40	100-00-00	100-50-50-100	Magickal	50-22-16	40-16-12
Floating skull, Scourge	120	8	30-40	00-00-100	50-00-00-50	Magickal	45-45-45	35-35-35
Floating skull, Shadow	60	7	30-40	00-00-100	200-100-00-100	Magickal	40-40-40	30-30-30
Floating spiker	60	9	25-85	00-00-100	00-00-00-200	Normal	32-37-20	27-30-18
Floating spiker, Giant	600	15	300-350	00-00-100	00-00-00-00	Normal	100-100-100	100-100-100
Floating spiker, Tough	95	11	50-100	00-00-100	00-00-00-200	Normal	35-40-22	30-35-20
Ice Queen	200	8	15-35	100-00-00	100-150-00-100	Cold	24-20-14	16-14-10
Ice Witch	50	6	20-45	00-00-100	100-150-00-100	Cold	18-15-12	12-10-8
Khull-Khuum, the Shadowking	1500	25	50-150	00-50-50	10-10-10-10	Magickal	55-50-50	45-40-40
Shaman (Throg)	150	5	15-30	100-00-00	100-100-100-100	Normal	13-15-10	10-12-9
Shaman, Leader	250	7	20-45	100-00-00	50-50-100-100	Normal	14-17-14	12-15-12
Shaman, Lesser	100	5	10-30	100-00-00	150-100-100-100	Normal	13-15-10	11-13-9
Shaman, Mad Hermit	300	8	5-50	100-00-00	50-50-100-100	Normal	15-16-10	10-12-9
Shaman, Tough	175	6	20-35	100-00-00	50-100-100-100	Normal	15-15-10	11-10-9
Sharga	40	3	4-10	00-100-00	100-200-100-100	Normal	5-6-2	1-2-1
Sharga, Big	250	4	25-50	50-50-00	100-25-100-100	Normal	18-16-10	14-12-10
Sharga, Ice	180	5	12-24	00-100-00	100-250-50-100	Normal	11-12-6	9-10-5
Sharga, Ice Leader	280	6	16-26	00-80-00	100-250-50-100	Normal	12-14-7	10-12-6
Sharga, Ice Shaman	200	5	18-24	00-100-00	50-200-50-100	Normal	15-16-9	12-14-7

Monster	Max Hit Pts	Skill	Damage Range	Dmg Distribution (Crush/Cut/Pierce)	Mag Dmg Modifier (Mgk/Fire/Cold/Elec)	Damage Type	Strong/Weak Armor (Cut/Crush/Pierce)	
Sharga, Leader	95	4	10-22	00-100-00	100-150-100-100	Normal	9-12-5	5-9-3
Sharga, Shaman	160	5	12-24	00-100-00	100-100-100-100	Normal	11-16-7	8-12-4
Sharga, Strong	85	4	8-22	00-100-00	100-200-100-100	Normal	9-12-5	7-10-4
Sharga, Tiny	20	1	0	00-100-00	250-250-250-250	Normal	3-4-1	2-3-0
Sharga, Tough	65	4	6-16	00-100-00	100-200-100-100	Normal	9-12-7	7-10-5
Sharga, Weak	25	2	3-8	00-100-00	100-250-100-100	Normal	4-5-1	1-2-0
Skeleton	250	8	25-60	00-100-00	50-50-00-00	Normal	30-22-60	30-22-60
Skeleton, Dead Adventurer	150	5	5-25	00-100-00	100-50-00-00	Normal	14-10-60	10-8-60
Skeleton, Lesser Shadow	130	8	25-60	00-00-100	50-50-00-00	Normal	18-36-50	18-36-50
Skeleton, Shadow	250	8	25-60	00-00-100	50-50-50-50	Normal	24-40-60	24-40-60
Slime	25	4	5-15	100-00-00	100-250-50-100	Normal	4-18-8	4-18-8
Slime, Tough	45	4	8-24	100-00-00	100-200-50-100	Normal	6-22-10	6-22-10
Snake	40	4	9-18	50-00-50	100-125-100-100	Normal	6-8-5	4-6-4
Snake, Guardian	95	5	13-25	50-00-50	100-150-100-100	Normal	10-13-8	8-10-6
Snake, Water	40	4	9-18	50-00-50	100-200-100-100	Normal	6-8-5	4-6-4
Tentacle Thing, Body	400	5	25-50	50-50-00	100-60-100-100	Normal	10-30-6	6-30-4
Tentacle Thing, Tentacle	150	6	20-40	100-00-00	100-100-100-100	Normal	6-30-4	6-30-4
Throg, Bodyguard	125	6	20-35	00-100-00	100-100-100-100	Normal	30-30-30	10-17-12
Throg, Tough	100	6	15-35	00-100-00	100-100-100-100	Normal	30-30-30	10-17-12
Throg, Guard	80	5	15-30	00-100-00	100-100-100-100	Normal	30-30-30	10-17-10
Throg, Leader	250	7	20-40	00-100-00	100-75-100-100	Normal	32-32-32	10-17-12
Throg, Weak Guard	40	3	10-20	00-100-00	100-100-100-100	Normal	30-30-30	10-17-10
Troll	280	8	25-45	00-100-00	100-00-100-100	Normal	16-16-18	6-12-12
Troll, Terrible	400	7	30-55	00-100-00	50-00-100-100	Normal	20-20-18	9-18-18
Troll, Weak	40	5	25-35	00-100-00	50-00-100-100	Normal	12-12-18	4-8-8
Wahooka	900	10	79-81	00-00-100	00-00-00-00	Electrical	5-5-5	5-5-5
Wasp	25	5	8-22	00-100-00	100-100-100-100	Normal	5-4-2	4-3-1
Wasp, Faerie	100	6	20-40	00-100-00	50-50-50-50	Fire, Magickal	12-8-6	8-6-2
Will-o'-the-Wisp	100	7	20-50	00-00-100	00-00-00-00	Electrical	20-20-15	00-00-00
Zombie, Ancient	600	8	18-32	00-00-100	25-100-25-25	Normal	15-40-12	12-30-10
Skeleton, Guardian	400	7	20-50	00-100-00	100-50-00-00	Normal	10-18-28	8-12-20
Toadstool	25	1	0	100-00-00	100-150-50-100	Normal	4-5-3	1-2-1
Evil Drake	140	6	20-20	00-00-100	50-50-50-50	Fire	15-15-15	15-15-15
Dark Dwarf	340	6	40-60	00-00-100	50-50-50-50	Fire	15-15-15	15-15-15

Appendix B
Weapon Stats

Stonekeep gives you a nice, grisly armory of weapons. Use this table to figure out which weapons best exploit each monster's vulnerabilities. Here's a quick definition of the table categories.

Weapon Reach. Just what it says—how far away from you the weapon can strike. A reach of 5-7 is short; 8-10 is medium; and 11 or higher is long.

Damage Range. These values represent the minimum/maximum damage (in hit points) inflicted by each blow you land on your target. As I mention elsewhere, these values get plugged into complex damage equations. If you see one of these equations, you may experience a cortical implosion.

Damage Type. The table classifies all but two of its weapons as Normal. The hit point damage of a "Normal" weapon receives a Strength Bonus—for every star of Strength rating, you get extra hit points added to the total damage points you inflict on your target. From one star to ten stars of Strength, the bonus damage per blow is 1, 3, 5, 8, 11, 15, 19, 23, 27, 32.

Dmg Distribution (Crush/Cut/Pierce). Whenever you land a blow with a particular weapon, the hit point damage is distributed in percentages amongst three different types of damage—Crush, Cut, and Pierce. A 50-50-00 value simply means that half the damage of the weapon's blow crushed its target, the other half cut its target, and none pierced its target.

Weapon Quality. The quality of the weapon you use affects the accuracy of the blow. (For more on this, see Hit Zone Radius under The *Stonekeep* Combat System in Part 2.)

Weapon Delay. This value represents the number of frames of delay between each swing of the weapon. In *Stonekeep*, there are approximately 12 frames of animation per second. So a Weapon Delay value of 12 means a one-second swing delay.

Weapon Weight. *Stonekeep* uses this value to calculate increases in your Strength and Agility ratings, as well as to determine the final Weapon Delay value and Hit Zone Radius (accuracy) of each strike. If Weapon Weight is greater than your Strength rating, you gain Strength points every time you land a blow with the weapon. If Weapon Weight is less than or equal to your Strength rating, then you gain Agility points with each strike.

Skill Used. This indicates which skill you use when attacking with the selected weapon. Your Skill rating in that category of weapon (see page 1 of Drake's journal) affects the accuracy of each blow.

Weapons Stats

Weapon	Weapon Reach	Damage Range	Damage Type	Dmg Distribution (Crush/Cut/Pierce)	Weapon Quality	Weapon Delay	Weapon Weight	Skill Used
Fist	5	1-4	Normal	100-00-00	Excellent	0	0	Brawl
Longsword	9	5-15	Normal	00-100-00	Normal	16	4	Sword
Broadsword	9	5-10	Normal	40-60-00	Normal	14	4	Sword
Dwarven sword	8	5-15	Normal	40-60-00	Good	14	4	Sword
Shadow sword	10	50-100	Normal	00-100-00	Excellent	15	1	Sword
Sharga sword	8	3-8	Normal	00-50-50	Bad	12	3	Sword
Ice sword	9	2-24	Normal	00-100-00	Poor	12	5	Sword
Throg sword	8	4-16	Normal	00-50-50	Poor	16	4	Sword
Stone sword	9	15-30	Normal	50-50-00	Poor	20	7	Sword
Hammer	7	6-14	Normal	100-00-00	Normal	26	5	Hammer
Stone hammer	7	12-38	Normal	100-00-00	Poor	38	12	Hammer
War hammer	7	10-28	Normal	100-00-00	Normal	30	8	Hammer
Ice hammer	7	6-18	Normal	100-00-00	Normal	28	10	Hammer
Shadow hammer	7	50-100	Normal	100-00-00	Excellent	18	1	Hammer
Battle axe	7	10-25	Normal	40-60-00	Normal	24	6	Axe
Dwarf axe	7	10-20	Normal	40-60-00	Good	26	8	Axe
Stone axe	7	15-30	Normal	40-60-00	Poor	32	10	Axe
Throwing axe	7	8-15	Normal	40-60-00	Normal	18	6	Axe
Axe of Throwing	-1	15-30	Normal	00-100-00	Excellent	44	4	Missile
Dwarf pick	7	6-16	Normal	00-00-100	Normal	38	10	Axe
Sharga pick	7	4-12	Normal	00-00-100	Bad	38	7	Axe
Shadow axe	7	50-100	Normal	50-50-00	Excellent	17	1	Axe
Dagger	6	1-4	Normal	00-00-100	Normal	6	2	Dagger
Throg dagger	6	3-14	Normal	00-00-100	Poor	9	3	Dagger
Shadow dagger	6	50-100	Normal	00-00-100	Excellent	15	1	Dagger
Fire dagger	5	3-6	Normal	00-00-100	Good	6	2	Dagger
Dagger of Penetration	6	15-35	Normal	00-00-100	Good	3	1	Dagger
Quarterstaff	10	4-10	Normal	100-00-00	Normal	12	4	Polearm
Spear	12	6-12	Normal	00-40-60	Normal	16	4	Polearm
Shadow spear	12	50-100	Normal	00-50-50	Excellent	15	1	Polearm
Short bow	-1	10-20	Normal	00-00-100	Normal	30	5	Missile
Stone	–	1-4	Normal	95-05-00	Normal	6	6	Missile
Stone bag	-1	1-8	Normal	100-00-00	Poor	28	2	Missile
Dart bag	-1	2-6	Normal	00-00-100	Normal	22	1	Missile
Stone shooter	-1	10-15	No	100-00-00	Normal	16	5	Missile
Sharga crossbow	-1	9-18	No	25-00-75	Poor	35	6	Missile
Shields	5	1-4	Normal	100-00-00	Excellent	0	0	Brawl

No Weapon Stats

Weapon	Weapon Reach	Damage Range	Damage Type	Dmg Distribution (Crush/Cut/Pierce)	Weapon Quality	Weapon Delay	Weapon Weight	Skill Used
No weapon	5	0	Normal	100-00-00	Normal	1	1	Brawl

Shields Stats

Weapon	Weapon Reach	Damage Range	Damage Type	Dmg Distribution (Crush/Cut/Pierce)	Weapon Quality	Weapon Delay	Weapon Weight	Skill Used
Small wooden shield	5	1-4	Normal	100-00-00	Excellent	0	0	Brawl
Small metal shield	5	1-4	Normal	100-00-00	Excellent	0	0	Brawl
Leather shield	4	1-4	Normal	100-00-00	Excellent	0	0	Brawl
Magical shield	5	1-4	Normal	100-00-00	Excellent	0	0	Brawl

Containers Stats

Weapon	Weapon Reach	Damage Range	Damage Type	Dmg Distribution (Crush/Cut/Pierce)	Weapon Quality	Weapon Delay	Weapon Weight	Skill Used
Crossbow bolt quiver	5	1-4	Normal	100-00-00	Excellent	0	0	Brawl
Quiver	5	1-4	Normal	100-00-00	Excellent	0	0	Brawl
Black arrow quiver	5	1-4	Normal	100-00-00	Excellent	0	0	Brawl
Dart bag	5	1-4	Normal	100-00-00	Excellent	0	0	Brawl

Appendix C
Armor Stats

Stonekeep wouldn't throw you to the wolves (or Throgs) without some protection. Armor reduces the amount of damage you sustain from an enemy's blow, and this table shows how much protection each piece of armor provides against the three types of damage—Crush, Cut, and Pierce.

In *Stonekeep*, armor protection is cumulative. If you wear a helmet, torso, and leg armor, you add the table values for each piece to determine your total armor protection against Crush, Cut, and Pierce damage. Also note (in the last column of the table) that some pieces of armor modify your Agility rating for purposes of combat.

Armor Stats

Armor Type	Crush	Cut	Pierce	Agility
Leather torso	1	2	1	0
Leather leggings	1	1	1	0
Chain mail chest armor	3	5	1	-1
Chain mail leg armor	2	3	1	0
Elven chain mail torso armor	7	9	5	0
Elven chain mail leg armor	4	5	3	0
Magikal chain torso armor	7	11	4	0
Magikal chain leg armor	5	8	3	0
Dwarven plate torso armor	8	10	10	-1
Dwarven plate leg armor	5	8	6	-1
Plate torso armor	7	10	7	-1
Plate legs armor	5	7	5	-1
Guardian plate torso armor	10	15	10	-1
Guardian plate leg armor	8	8	8	0
Faerie shirt torso armor	3	3	7	1
Faerie pants leg armor	3	7	3	1
Helmet armor	1	1	0	0
Dwarven helmet armor	2	2	1	0
Skeleton helmet armor	3	3	2	0
Guardian helmet armor	5	5	4	-1
Faerie cap helmet armor	2	2	2	1

Interplay™
BY GAMERS. FOR GAMERS.™
MACPLAY
CD-ROM
"Your Premier Macintosh Game Source."
FRP4